Things That Break Us

Things That Break Us

Lisa Felkins

For the broken people out there (a.k.a. everyone).
And to my mom,
whose death split me wide open.
Here's to uncovering,
the pearls of wisdom,
that can only be gleamed,
through deep pain.

PART ONE

NOW:

September, 2018

1

TESSA

I tug open my white coat, trying to ease the dread squeezing my throat. My wobbly life teeters on the brink of collapse. With shaky fingers, I clutch my chest, summoning any hidden courage. Coming up empty, I balk.

I've been avoiding this all day. But now, it's nearly ten p.m., and I have no choice but to open this CT scan.

In my seven years as a doctor, I've reviewed thousands of patient reports.

But *this* report is different.

Because *this* report belongs to my person.

My hero.

The sole bolt anchoring my mess-of-an-existence together.

The man whose opinion I value above all others, including my own.

My dad, Peter.

Two days ago, he called after dinner, his voice unusually shaky, his thoughts unfailingly pragmatic. "Tess, I just saw bright red blood in my urine. Something's wrong."

I gulped, scrubbing my kitchen countertops with renewed vigor. "I'm sure it'll be okay." Even as I said the words, I feared they were false.

But pretending things are fine is a skill I've expertly mastered—as instinctive to me as breathing. Seconds later, to ease both of our worries, I foolishly offered to order a CT scan of his abdomen and pelvis.

And now, the obligation lies with me to *actually* view the results.

I inhale sharply, lingering for one final second in this fragile space of blissfully naïve, unknowing hope.

Maybe it'll be okay?

Please, please let it be okay.

I double-click his report, my foot thudding against my office floor, sweaty fingers quaking on the mouse. As I scan the contents, my heart plunges past my ribs, burrowing into the hard ground below.

Words immediately pop out:

10 cm mass in the left kidney.

Probable metastasis in the right pelvic bone.

Suspicious lesion in the liver.

Final Report Impression: Probable metastatic renal cell carcinoma. Urgent follow-up recommended.

I swallow hard, my worst nightmare seemingly confirmed.

My dad has cancer?

No!

Shit!

No!

I force myself to review the images, gaping at the masses congealed within my dad's organs.

His bones.

His irreplaceable person.

This cannot be happening.

I need my dad to navigate life. The thought of a single day—no, even a single second—without him is my greatest fear. But I assumed I'd have decades still to solve this impossible problem. My dad's only sixty-eight and in perfect health. In his thirty years as a cardiologist, he's never taken one sick day.

A tear slides down my cheek as my mind races, doing what it does best: catastrophizing. The grim survival statistics for kidney cancer storm through my body, churning my insides into a hurricane.

My phone rings.

Maybe I'm dreaming.

Please, let me be dreaming.

I pinch my wrist. It hurts, but nothing changes.

Shit.

The phone rings again. My husband's name flashes on the screen.

In a daze, I answer. "Hello?"

"Hey." His voice is warm and familiar. "I was worried. You coming home soon?"

The sun has slipped away, leaving my center-city Philadelphia office cloaked in shadows, tinged with slivers of moonlight. I glance at my watch. My last patient and the office staff left hours ago; it's been even longer since I ate or peed. I try to speak but my brain is coated by a dense grey fog.

"Tess? You there?"

I clear my throat, instinctively recloaking my phony exterior. "Yeah, sorry. Everything's fine. I'm okay."

I'm neither fine nor okay.

"Tess"—he hesitates—"you sure?"

Even through the phone, I can feel his thoughtful eyes teeming with concern.

Why don't I just tell him the truth?

About this?

About everything?

What the hell is wrong with me?

"Yeah, see you soon. Sorry, I just lost track of time." Another lie spools off my tongue, past my lips, dribbling into the phone.

I'm drowning in an ocean of lies. My entire life is one pathetic performance, and I don't know how to stop. I want to. So badly. But that would mean admitting to my husband, my parents, my best friend—to everyone, actually—that I've made a lifetime of wrong choices. That I've built a life that looks good on paper, but on the inside, feels totally wrong. And I can't handle the consequences of setting off that horrific landmine.

"Okay, get home safe. Love you, bye," he says.

The line goes dead before I can respond. I sit in stunned silence, a burgeoning sense of panic encasing my lungs like shrink wrap.

My dad has cancer.

Holy shit.

My breath grows wheezy as the foundation supporting my family threatens to crack.

My dad has cancer.

Oh my god.

I have to tell him.

Now.

I could lose him.

No!

I pick up my phone and press his name, the top spot in my favorite contacts list.

As it dials, my mind—like it always does when I'm most vulnerable—drifts back to Botswana. To eleven years ago, when I was a medical student, in what feels like another lifetime. The memories swim through me. For a moment, I'm the twenty-five-year-old girl that I became there: authentic, truthful, brave, untethered, happy.

The phone rings.

I blink.

Reality snaps back.

That girl is long gone.

I'm the phony, broken liar once more.

I've spent the past decade trying to forget that time, that girl, that horribly wrong decision.

But I haven't.

And I can't.

I gulp down a mouthful of vomit, wishing desperately I could undo the past, alter the future, flee this moment. Transform into literally anyone else.

The phone rings a second time.

What am I going to say?

Hi, Dad, it's me. You have stage IV cancer and life as we know it is over.

Dad answers. "Hi, Tess, honey."

His voice is tired but steady.

He's always been the steady to my storm.

But now *he* is the storm.

And everything is about to fall apart.

THEN:

Eleven Years Ago

August, 2007

2

TESSA

The plane's wheels slam into the ground, jolting us into our arrival at Sir Seretse Khama International Airport in Gaborone, Botswana. It's here, as a fourth-year medical student that I'll start a two-month rotation in the city's main hospital. The pressure riding on this experience builds inside me, turning the butterflies in my stomach into black crows.

"I can't believe it! We're finally here!" my best friend, Liz Collins, exclaims from the seat next to me, her voice burbling with enthusiasm.

"I know, but that landing was so bumpy," I whimper. Despite the Ativan I took for our flight, my nerves are burning like wildfire. With quivering hands, I tug down my grey sweatshirt, now covered in a huge stain from the coffee I spilled during landing. "Ugh, I look like such a hot mess."

In truth, I *am* a hot mess, hiding two huge secrets from Liz and my parents—desperate to conceal my gruesome flaws from the people I love most.

"Tess, you need to work on being nicer to yourself," Liz chides, an orangey spray of sunlight reflecting off her strawberry-blonde hair. "It'll be good for you here in Botswana, away from Greg. Give you time to focus on yourself."

Greg.

The mere mention of his name causes my still-rumbling abdomen to do a flip-flop. I bite down on my lower lip, resisting a swell of unpleasant, too-fresh memories.

Greg: the disastrous three-year relationship I ended forty-eight hours ago.

Greg: part man, part monster, full-on terrible decision.

"You okay, Tess?" Liz asks, her eyebrows rumpling.

"Yeah. I'm fine," I lie.

Because, really, I live my life like an under-baked cookie, always seconds from crumbling apart. But, somehow, I've mastered the art of outwardly seeming fine.

Liz grabs her *Setswana for Beginners* book from the seat pocket and stuffs it into her backpack. "I'm so relieved you finally left him."

"Yeah, I'm grateful to be on a different continent from him," I manage, forcing a smile. "And clearly… I have a lot of work to do… on myself."

Frankly, I don't understand how I ever ended up in such a toxic relationship. I've always known that something inside me is irreversibly broken. But the dysfunction I endured to be with Greg was stunning by all accounts, even for me.

Why am I so fucked up?

That familiar sense of inner shame swallows me straight into the dark belly of a whale.

"If you want to talk about things, I'm here, Tess. You know that, right?" Liz gives my sleeve a gentle squeeze.

I nod, a stack of bricks settling on my shoulders—all that remains unspoken between Liz and me. We share an apartment together in Philadelphia, so Liz has overheard some of my arguments with Greg. But I've never admitted the full truth about our relationship to her or anyone—not even my therapist.

The aircraft doors swing open, giving me a welcome out from our conversation. We line up for Immigration. "So, how are you feeling since that phone call with your mom?" I ask, fumbling through my purse, searching for my passport, eager to shift the focus away from Greg.

Liz sighs, her green eyes darkening. "Well… my mom said some really mean things. Not that it was surprising, but still, it's disappointing. But I love Marley. If my mom doesn't like our relationship, that's her problem."

At JFK Airport, just before boarding, Liz had a blowout fight with her uber-conservative mom. For the past year, Liz, who's bisexual, has been dating Marley, an architect who makes her fantastically happy. But her mom has other plans, constantly begging to set Liz up with an array of "more suitable" bachelors. Eager to see Liz married. To a *man*.

"I'm sorry, Liz, that's so shitty. You and Marley are amazing together. You don't deserve to be treated like that."

Liz's lips twist into a frown. "My mom doesn't accept a lot of things about me. I'm just going to be me, and she can take it or leave it. Luckily, I have people in my life, like you, who accept me, no matter what."

We inch forward in line.

"You're so brave, staying true to yourself. I admire you so much," I whisper, envious of Liz's courage. Of her ability to listen to her own voice without needing parental approval. It's a skill I lack completely. Like, one hundred percent, I *entirely* do not possess.

Unlike Liz, I've fashioned my existence with the sole goal of making my dad proud, no matter the cost. Which is why I'm becoming a doctor, like him, even though I don't actually want to be one.

I'm struggling in medical school—emotionally, at least. Academically, I have the top grades in my class, and my professors say I have a natural talent for interacting with patients, putting them at ease. But the idea of being the sole intermediary between someone's life and death sends me into a quiet panic, like I'm being strapped into some medieval torture device. But I'm a perfectionist, through and through. I strive to do everything well, even things I don't like.

Which is why, to the outside world, I appear to be thriving.

But really, I'm drowning.

Dry drowning.

The water filling my lungs, robbing me of vital oxygen, is invisible to the rest of the world. But I gurgle on it, suffocating every day, all the same.

I'm the puzzle piece that doesn't fit against its neighbors—my other classmates—who are deeply passionate about medicine. Like Liz, who's genuinely enthralled by human crises and is applying to residency programs in Emergency Medicine. But me? I seem to lack passion for *any* type of medicine. Yet I keep jamming against my edges, hoping my internal configuration will finally shift.

Which is why, here in Botswana, at long last, I'm determined to fall in love with medicine.

Like Liz.

Like my dad.

I can learn to love it.

I'm going to make it my passion…

But what if I can't?

That stubbornly persistent voice of self-doubt sticks to my insides like maple syrup, no matter how fiercely I wish it away.

***

We finish with Immigration, pass through Customs, and step outside, the rich Gaborone air filling me with a renewed sense of hope. It's the tail end of winter, a balmy Thursday afternoon in early August.

To the left of the exit stands a stocky, middle-aged Black man with thick hair and dark brown eyes holding a sign bearing our names. *"Dumelang, bo mma,"* he says, greeting us in Setswana. "I'm Modise, the driver for the Botswana-UPenn Partnership. I'll be taking you to your flat."

"Hi, Modise. It's great to meet you. Thanks for picking us up," I say, giving him a smile.

"The pleasure is all mine." He pulls our luggage across the street as a red bird takes flight, soaring high into the cobalt sky. We follow him to a well-worn Toyota Camry.

"Is this your first time in Botswana?" he asks as he pulls the car onto a two-lane road flanked by browning brush and several large billboards.

"Yeah," Liz answers. "We're medical students from the University of Pennsylvania. We'll be training at Princess Victoria Hospital."

"Ah, yes, Princess Victoria is our main public hospital here in Gaborone," Modise says.

He pronounces Gaborone like *"Haborooonay."* He continues, "There is much sickness and suffering, largely from the HIV virus. The hospital is filled with children who've lost their parents, mothers who've lost their daughters, husbands who've lost their wives. There's been terrible loss, devastation of family structures. You'll unfortunately be quite busy."

"Well, we're honored to be here and enthusiastic to learn about Botswana," I say, leery about coming across as the over-privileged, naïve White American I probably am.

"Botswana is very beautiful, as you'll see," Modise says. "But the AIDS crisis has been extremely hard. Twenty-five percent of our adults are HIV positive."

"Wow, that's hard to even fathom," I admit, unable to wrap my head around this statistic.

"We're hopeful we can help, even in small ways," Liz adds as a stray cow wanders onto the roadway.

Modise slows the car for the cow, turning on the hazard lights. "What about you, Modise? Did you grow up in Gaborone?" I ask.

"No. I was raised in a village called Mochudi, about an hour away. I love my country and am most excited for you to experience it."

***

Forty minutes later, Modise parks in front of a two-story stucco building surrounded by a barbed fence. A sign outside reads *Timali Court*. The entrance is filled with blooming Madagascar periwinkles and honey mesquite flowers. Modise presses a clicker, and the black metal gates swing open to reveal the communal housing we'll share with our classmates.

"Princess Victoria Hospital is a five-minute walk down the road," he says, stepping out and gesturing to the left. My eyes follow along the loamy dirt path, my airway narrowing into a tiny straw.

What if I can't handle the hospital experience?

We follow Modise inside, where two of our classmates are waiting. There's Jeremy, with electric-red hair and a crooked smile, and Suzanne, who towers over everyone at six foot four. "It's great you guys are finally here," Jeremy enthuses.

Modise shows us to our bedroom, furnished with matching twin beds and cappuccino-brown carpeting. "Get settled in, because early tomorrow morning," he says, "I'll be driving you to Impodimo Lodge!"

Before our hospital rotation begins on Monday, we are traveling to Impodimo Lodge, an hour outside of Gaborone, across the South African border, for a two-night safari.

Modise says goodbye, and I start to unpack, surfing the worried waves of my overactive brain.

How am I going to recover from Greg?

How am I going to fall in love with medicine?

Why am I so freaking broken?

How do I stop being such a total mess… and finally… pull myself together?

"Tess? Hello? You're somewhere else, a million miles away?" Liz says, giving me a troubled glare.

I return a bashful shrug. "Sorry, just jetlagged."

"Okay," she says, gathering a change of clothes. "Anyway, I said I'm going to shower."

I nod, slumping against my bed, the cold pillow brushing the nape of my neck. Once she's gone, I grab my laptop and type a quick email to my parents, letting them know we've arrived safely. As I skim my inbox, my heart sputters at an email from Greg.

From: Greg.Winters1982@bmail.com
To: Tessa.Williams2@bmail.com

Date: Thursday, August 2, 2007

Subject: I love you

Tess, please, don't end things. I love you. I want to be with you forever. Whatever happened between us, we can figure it out. Don't give up on us. I'm not. I still want to marry you.

Love,
Greg

I snap my computer shut.

No, Greg can't hurt me.

Not here.

Not anymore.

Never again.

Somehow, during this experience, I'm going to transform—from this broken, pathetic mess into the strong, brave woman I've always wanted to be.

I can…

I will…

I must.

3

COREY

I roll my eyes and slam my safari Jeep to a screeching halt. The car rocks back and forth in the scorching plains. The noise from the engine grates on my nerves, a harsh intrusion in the wild.

Normally, I love every single thing about this place—the sound of lions rustling in grassland, elephants stomping through misty water, African black swifts chirping in acacia trees.

These are the sounds that calm me.

That pull me away from the thoughts I shouldn't have.

Thoughts of *her*.

Of everything I lost.

Everything stolen from me.

Everything that ruined me.

I turn around, facing the six giggling women, my guests for the day. Their high-pitched laughter dumps like toxic waste into the South African bush. They've traveled here from Los Angeles for one last hurrah, fresh college graduates about to face the real world. But, if their behavior in this vehicle is any indication, they're in for a huge fucking shock.

Not that I see a lot of value in the real world, anyway.

That's why I left it five years ago—after university—to come work here as a guide at Impodimo Lodge.

I love living in isolation.

The Madikwe Game Reserve is my idea of fucking paradise.

"Ladies," I say, hoping my South African accent hides my distaste, "please quiet down. The elephants don't care about gossip, not even Britney Spears shaving her head or Lindsay Loogahan going to rehab. Try to enjoy the beauty around you and save the chit-chat for later."

"It's Lindsay Lohan," the twenty-something brunette in the first row, middle seat, quickly corrects. Her name is Avery and she's designated herself the group spokesperson. She takes a fingernail and drags it against her shiny red lips, her eyes studying my biceps.

I tug down the sleeve of my khaki shirt, soaked with sweat from the blazing sun. "Sorry, Lindsay Lohan, but we need to be quiet to respect the animals. Our noise bothers them, and our job is to *not* bother them. Please, can't this wait until after the game ride?"

"If you insist, Corey, but I think you're wrong," Avery says, pointing to a baby elephant one hundred meters away. "That one seems especially interested in Britney's drama. Look how he's raising his trunk! He knows how unfairly the media's treating her!" She winks at me, scrunching her eyebrows into a tight furrow, her hand massaging into my shoulder blade.

Fuck.

Is she flirting with me?

Sometimes guests hit on me. Usually, the single ones. Occasionally, the married ones—but those situations tend to get hairy, especially if the spouse is a guest too.

By conventional standards, I guess I'm attractive. But I've never crossed that line with any guest—married, single, or otherwise. I'm a professional; this job is my life. Plus, Avery wouldn't be my type, if I had one.

Which I don't.

My favorite type of partner is the one that doesn't exist.

The one you never get too attached to, and thus, can never break you.

My favorite feeling is none: complete, internal numbness.

That's my superpower.

I follow Avery's finger to the young elephant, nuzzling its trunk against his attentive mum's belly. Unlike humans, these creatures never fail to amaze me.

"Ha, you're funny, Avery," I say, shooting her my biggest smile. Because Customer Service 101: the guest is always right.

She grins. "Corey, seriously, I get it. Living out here, you probably don't know a lot of important stuff! I mean, have you even heard that Brad Pitt and Jennifer Aniston split up? How tragic was that?"

"So tragic, devastatingly tragic. I'm still trying to get over it," I deadpan.

The truth is, I have no clue who Brad Pitt or Jennifer Aniston is.

I thrive on being unplugged. Out here, I don't have to deal with the phony bullshit of modern society. None of it matters. I only have to focus on the animals.

A look of relief swivels through Avery's eyes as she misses my sarcasm.

I glance at my watch. Another damn hour left in this ride.

Normally, I love my guests, love getting to meet new people from every walk of life, each corner of the world. Usually, the minutes of a game ride float by like an actual dream. But not today.

My walkie-talkie buzzes. It's Darian, my best friend and fellow guide. "Core, mate. I'm near the Tau Waterhole. Just spotted a pack of wild dogs chewing on the remains of two antelope. Spectacular! Get your ass over here, straight away."

"Incredible, mate. Nice going. Be right there!" I say. Wild dogs are a rarity on any day, but right now, they're a damn miracle.

My heart thumps from the thrill of it—the animals, the raw beauty of this place. Over the past five years, the magic has only intensified.

In my native language of Afrikaans, I add: "*Ek het 'n bier nodig,*" which technically translates to: *I need a beer*, but Darian knows it actually means: *I have a crazy guest.*

Darian cackles. "Got it. I'll have one waiting at the lodge."

"Awesome, mate. See you soon." I set the walkie-talkie down and start the engine. "You ladies ready to see some wild dogs?"

"Like some golden retrievers?" Avery asks, popping a bubble with her gum, tugging down her barely there miniskirt—totally typical safari attire.

Oh my fucking god.

"Exactly like that," I say, offering her a smirk as I drive off, away into my gorgeous home, the dreamlike bush.

4

TESSA

Modise parks the van in front of the circular entrance to Impodimo Lodge. I rush out, my excitement bubbling like a little kid arriving at Disney World. The air brims with succulent wildflowers and the sharp scent of turpentine grass.

Inside, the main lodge is grand, bright sunlight cascading down from the high-vaulted ceilings. "I'll check us in," Liz offers as the manager, Joe, hands us each a glass of sparkling water adorned by a lime wedge.

I nod my thanks, sipping the cool drink as I wander through the lodge. I step out onto a wooden deck that overlooks a large watering hole.

As I stare out at the scene below, my breath sticks against my throat, lodging there like silly putty.

Holy shit.

The cerulean sky is flecked by low-hanging marshmallow clouds. The green plains are littered with baobab trees. The murky brown water is crowded by elephants, seeking refuge from the midday heat. A few bathe in the mud. Most drink, standing in a straight line along the water's edge, slurping through curved grey trunks. The scene is entirely idyllic.

I'm mesmerized by these massive, playful creatures. I've never witnessed elephants in the wild before. Here, away from their zoo cages, they are strikingly free, entirely untamed, enthrallingly beautiful.

I suddenly remember the cage surrounding my existence. The familiar feeling returns—of being crushed beneath my dad's expectations.

I don't want to be a doctor.

But I have to be.

I'm trapped within the four walls of my life. I tug at my shirt, trying to ease that perpetual clamping around my neck.

"Oh my god! This view is beyond amazing!" Liz exclaims, startling me.

I turn to her, clinking our glasses. "Cheers! How freaking lucky are we?"

We both fall into appreciative silence, staring out, trying to absorb the scenery.

"Let's go get settled," Liz says finally, rolling her suitcase down the cobblestone path. "We're meeting for the game ride in an hour!"

***

The highlight of our cabin is the rear wall, a large glass pane overlooking the watering hole, where I spot three gazelle frolicking. Past the bedroom, a separate washroom leads to an outdoor shower.

"I'm going to clean up," I yell to Liz, grabbing my toiletry bag.

Outside, in the stone-enclosed shower, I step into the steam, staring at the birds circling in the sky, letting the water cascade over my tired body.

My muscles unclench under the spray, but the tightness in my chest lingers.

I scrub my arms, hard, as if the lavender soap can wash away my sorrows. I close my eyes, letting the water pour over me, trying to quiet the thoughts swirling.

Everything is going to be okay.

It's over with Greg.

I scrub harder.

I'm going to fall in love with medicine.

Here, all the broken pieces of my life are somehow going to fuse together into a functional person.

They have to.

I'm rubbing lemongrass shampoo into my hair when something warm grazes my shoulder. I look up at the shower ledge, startled to spot a baboon.

I scream.

He grins.

In a move that feels like something out of a nightmare, he holds his penis and sprays urine straight at my face. I scream louder, stumbling against the back of the shower. The baboon finishes peeing and scampers off.

Liz bursts through the shower door. "Tess! Are you okay? What's wrong?"

"Yeah, I'm okay. But... a baboon just peed on me!"

We both just stand there, stunned, before the absurdity of it hits us.

And then, neither of us can stop laughing.

***

At four p.m., we meet for the game ride outside the main lodge. Joe quickly divides us between two open-aired Jeeps. "Your guides, Corey and Darian, will be with you in just a moment," he says.

"Woo-hoo. Time to see the animals!" Liz cheers, taking the seat beside me, a giant camera strapped around her neck.

Jeremy sits on my other side. "Maybe you need a bigger camera, Liz? Not sure that one's gonna do the job."

"Ha, Tess, did you know Jeremy's changing career paths? He's becoming a comedian instead," Liz jests. "But seriously, I promised Marley I'd take tons of photos."

I start to smile, but my gaze is yanked to the man walking towards us, my eyes cementing to him like superglue. He's tall, with shaggy sand-colored hair topped by an Impodimo Lodge cap. The hue of his eyes matches the sapphire sky.

On his left bicep is a tattoo of a lion, and although I squint, I can't make out the writing below his sleeve. He's toned, save for the little pudge at the tail of his stomach, peeking out from beneath his jade-green shirt. And for some reason, the sight of his imperfect tummy makes my insides dissolve like the gooey core of a grilled cheese sandwich.

He stops just outside the Jeep, giving our group a teeny wave.

"I'm Corey Diallo, your safari guide for the weekend. It's great to meet you all. I'm excited to show you the Madikwe Game Reserve!" His voice is deep and husky, enriched by an over-the-top charming South African accent. I can't look away.

He begins shaking hands with each of us.

"I'm Corey, pleasure to meet you," he says, reaching me.

I hesitate, my fingers hovering for a moment before I offer him my hand. "Tessa Williams. Nice to meet you, too."

The second his hand touches mine, a spark jolts through me.

I pull my hand away quickly, the shock of his touch rippling through my torso, sweat forming on the back of my neck. I force a smile, trying to mask my panic, but the sensation lingers. A knot of something I don't want to name.

Corey climbs into the front seat. I force my gaze away from him—*anywhere* else—landing on the shotgun sitting in the front passenger's seat.

A lump springs up in my throat.

Why does he need a gun?

Is this dangerous?

My heart thuds, my focus dragging back to the slope of his shoulders, carved and steady in a way I suddenly envy.

"Oh, you spotted the gun?" he asks me, spinning his head around.

"We have to carry it in case of any incidents with the animals. Don't worry, I've never had to use it. I'll keep you nice and safe. I promise." He flashes a smile so toothy it blazes straight through me, turning my body into a raging forest fire.

I fumble for the stray piece of paper in my pocket and wave it uselessly at my face.

My cheeks burn, as if his words are meant only for me.

Ridiculous.

"Oh… okay… thanks," I manage.

Shit.

Get it together, Tess.

You sound like an idiot.

Corey seemingly doesn't notice my flusterment. Instead, he turns to the group, launching into a lively discussion of "The Big Five," the five large animals all safari-goers hope to spot: the lion, rhino, leopard, buffalo, and elephant. "Over the next two days, I'll do my best to show you them all!" His voice bubbles with enthusiasm for his work.

He swiftly lowers his sunglasses, hiding his blue beacons, the same ones I'm stumbling amidst.

"I may be dating a woman now, but wow, I can still appreciate he's dreamy," Liz whispers as the car pulls away from the lodge.

Yes, damn, he is.

"I mean… he's okay… but, ugh, how'd it get so hot out here?" I moan, still fanning myself, steering the conversation away from Corey.

After Greg—and that toxic, soul-sucking mess—it's pathetically obvious I know absolutely nothing about men. And honestly? That's fine. I'm not here for a hookup. My sole purpose for the next eight weeks is to fall in love with medicine.

To immerse myself in the hospital experience.

To figure out how to *un*-break myself.

The car jostles along the bumpy dirt path, forging deeper into the bush. The sun is sweltering, causing globules of sweat to pool beneath my bra. The velvety breeze helps cool me—as long as I keep my eyes off Corey. When I dare to look in his direction, a flashing heat envelops me.

Why is his ruggedness, his autonomy, so alluring? So enticing?

The answer is glaringly obvious.

His life is the polar opposite of mine. I'm trapped in a cage, and he's… just out here. Exotic, wild, untethered.

We make several stops as Corey expertly points out a tower of giraffes, an improbability of wildebeest, a dazzle of zebras, peppering us with numerous facts about the game reserve. With a scuffed hand, he grabs his walkie-talkie, receiving a message from the other group's guide. "Corey, mate! Found some lions, chowing down, two kilometers west of the Tau Waterhole."

"Fucking beautiful, Darian, thanks!" Corey says, his swift exuberance causing the corners of my mouth to tug up, too.

He accelerates, driving for ten minutes before parking in the middle of barren grassland.

"Shh." Corey quiets the chatter in the Jeep. "It's important to be silent so we don't disturb the animals. The slightest sounds can disrupt their natural order. Look to your left. There are two lion brothers, about seven and eight years old, respectively. They killed an impala a short time ago. Now they're feasting."

I follow Corey's pointer finger, spotting the lions a mere twenty feet away. Their bronze fur is nearly hidden by the thick sun-bleached grass. Their hungry faces are streaked with blood as they devour what remains of a poor impala. The dead animal lies on its side, swaths missing from its core, several ribs exposed, gleaming in the light. It's *so* primal.

Beside me, Liz and Jeremy marvel as Corey grabs his own fancy-looking camera, snapping image after image. He carefully reviews each photo before taking the next, shaking his head, seemingly awestruck. While he studies the scene, I study him, admiring his passion for his work. It's the very same passion I urgently need to cultivate as a doctor.

"Fucking incredible, eh?" he whispers to no one in particular.

"Yeah, it's amazing," I blurt, my voice squeaky and embarrassingly high-pitched, sounding like an insecure teenager once more.

Shit!

Get it together, Tess!

My eyes finally roar away from the roast of Corey's face and onto the view. It's spectacular and deserves my full attention.

As I watch the ravenous lions, I suddenly understand more in that one moment than I have in my previous twenty-five years combined.

I'm an expert at making everything in life so extremely complicated.

But maybe it doesn't need to be.

To these animals, life is stripped down to its essence.

The predators.

The prey.

Their only goal is to survive.

And yet, eventually, in the end, they all die.

Everything dies.

That's life—the full, achingly painful, miraculously beautiful circle of life.

Out here, none of the petty bullshit or hollow accolades of modern society matter.

But maybe they don't matter *anywhere*.

I close my eyes, forcing myself to take a mental picture. So I can remember this scene later, when invariably I'll get swept away by teeny problems that aren't important. Life has so few things which truly matter. But it's so easy to lose sight, to get carried away in minutiae and forget the bigger picture.

It's the story of my existence.

I do it without thinking.

Every.

Single.

Day.

When I open my eyes, one of the lion's whiskers is dripping fiery droplets of the impala's blood onto the soil. I stare as the red seeps into the muddy earth.

The circle of life.

Remember it, Tess.

Just freaking remember it, please.

And suddenly, I'm filled with one overpowering desire.

To escape my cage.

The expectations that bind me.

That suffocate me.

Like the animals out here, and seemingly Corey too, I long only to be *free.*

5

TESSA

"We'll have two vodka sodas, please. We're in Cabin Four," Liz tells the bartender in the main lodge, whose nametag reads *Gus*. He's an older man, bald, with wrinkled grooves coating his forehead. His grin is mellow, but there's a jaggedness to him, suggesting he's lived a lot of life.

Our group has just finished dinner, a wildebeest stew, served on the outdoor patio. Now, I'm relaxing on a beige leather couch as Liz grabs our drinks. Across the room, Corey and Darian are playing a heated game of pool.

Corey's right arm sails into the air as he celebrates his ball sinking into the back hole. A sliver of his tummy pokes out, and my pulse ticks up like I'm sprinting around the racetrack. His left hand slinks through his unshorn, buttery hair. Darian says something, which causes a giant smile to parse out from his full, freakishly perfect lips. Weightlessness and contentment seize me for the first time in as long as I can remember.

"Tess, you're totally staring at him," Liz giggles, returning with our vodka sodas, the leather sagging as she sits.

A burning heat storms my cheeks. I gulp my vodka. My head whirls, a mixture of jetlag and the magic of Impodimo Lodge, and if I'm being honest, my third—or maybe fourth?—drink. I accidentally lost count.

"Ugh, Liz. I should stop drinking and go to bed. But… maybe you're right. He's a *little* dreamy." In spite of myself, I'm wrenched to him like an unlike pole of a magnet.

"Or…" Liz says, arching a brow, "you could talk to him? He's cute, and you're single. Maybe, have some fun? Let him help you forget all about… what was that loser's name? Greg?"

I groan, slumping into the couch. "Liz, I love you, but I broke up with Greg three days ago. Three days! I need about twenty years to unpack the experience of our relationship. Besides, we're here for two nights. Then I'll never see him again. And for all we know, he's married. Plus, I'm sure he has zero desire to hook up with some random guest."

"All I'm saying is, not everything has to be part of some larger life plan. Sometimes, you could just live in the moment, have fun," Liz says, her tone light but pointed. "You don't always have to worry about how things look. Just do what feels good, to *you*."

This idea is so absurd I almost choke on my drink. A cheerful sarcasm soaks my words. "Hmm, that sounds nice… if only it wasn't the polar opposite of my entire life approach?" I force my gaze onto Liz, blocking Corey from even my peripheral view. "Anyway, have you heard from your mom yet?"

"No, nothing. Big surprise there." Liz takes a sip of her drink, the edges of her lips slanting down. "But this place is too amazing to talk about my mom."

"Fair enough. I'm sorry," I say, flinching at the idea of not having my dad's support. Ever since I was little, that feeling has been so unbearable I've done everything to avoid it. "Did Marley like your pictures?"

"Yeah, she loved them. They turned out great, thanks to my amazing new camera. Jeremy can suck it! I wish she was here, though. She's thinking of coming to travel at the end of our rotation."

"Wow, that's amazing! I'm so jealous you have a partner you actually enjoy traveling with." I let out a little sigh, recalling my disastrous vacation with Greg to Ireland last summer.

We fought every day of the trip, culminating in a colossal argument on the last night—over the color of a street sign, of all things. His face tinged red with rage, running off, leaving me alone on the streets of Cork at one in the morning. When I eventually made it back to our hostel, teary and furious, I resolved to leave him.

Finally.

But like a fool, by the time our plane landed in Philly, I changed my mind.

Again.

During the year that followed, our problems only escalated. Leading to that last terrible night.

"Tess, don't look now, but Mr. Safari Dreamboat is headed our way," Liz says, her voice tunneling through my memories, sucking up the past like a vacuum. A dusty residue of regret lingers behind.

Until I smell Corey.

His musk, a blend of burned wood, sweet vanilla bean and ripened grass, causes my nose hairs to shoot up. And suddenly, I'm no longer lost in a memory.

I'm here.

Fully.

Achingly present.

His voice is gruff, low, as he says, "Sorry to interrupt. Just wanted to check if you ladies enjoyed yourselves today? Mind if I sit?"

I can't formulate a single word, but Liz doesn't miss a beat. "Absolutely."

Corey takes the empty seat beside me, our thighs grazing. The spark is immediate—every nerve ending in my body firing simultaneously, like a twenty-one-gun salute.

Seriously, what is that?

Does he feel it, too?

Or maybe I'm crazy?

Crazy seems infinitely more likely. In my jetlagged haze, I'm losing my mind.

"Yes, we loved it!" Liz says, her energy filling the space I can't. "It was a great ride. So amazing, watching those lions eat that impala. I sent my girlfriend the pictures. She was blown away. Not to mention, ridiculously jealous."

"Yeah, I have to agree, that scene was pretty incredible," Corey says. "I'm glad you got to see it. Some game rides we don't see a whole lot. It's the luck of the draw, but today was a great one. Tomorrow, we'll start bright and early at six a.m. Sunrise, animals waking up—it'll be one-of-a-kind fucking awesome."

His eyes briefly hover over me, then flit away, the heat from his blue daggers still just as scorching despite the fact that the sun set hours ago.

"Wow, I can't wait," Liz says, glancing at her watch, offering a surprised look. "But six a.m. will be here so soon!" Before I know what's happening, she downs her drink and stands up. "Tess, I'm gonna head back to our room. I'm exhausted. You stay, finish your drink, take your time. Have a good night, you two!"

She covertly winks in my direction, leaving before I can form any words of protest.

What a manipulative bitch.

Suddenly, the couch feels too large, too empty. And Corey excruciatingly close.

I shift, sliding into Liz's vacant seat, somehow more self-conscious than when my tube-top slipped down at my eighth-grade dance, exposing my nipple to the entire school. I slurp my drink, trying to regain composure.

"Well, that was abrupt…" Corey offers, his words saturating the dead air clustered between us. "I guess she was really tired?"

The ceiling light beams down, causing his blue eyes to gleam.

"Yeah, she needs her beauty sleep, I guess?" I purse my lips, a trace of displeasure sneaking out over Liz's abrupt departure. "Anyway, how long have you worked here?" I aim for casual, but everything about me—my voice, my posture, even the death grip on my glass—is decidedly *un*-casual.

Corey takes a swig of beer. "For five years. I finished university, and my mum and pa wanted me to accept a job offer with a big bank in Pretoria, where they live. But Darian"—he gestures to his pool partner, who's talking to Jeremy—"was working here. We've been best pals since primary school. He invited me up one weekend, and that was it. I fell in love and never left. It's my dream job."

As he talks about Impodimo Lodge, the tension evaporates from his face.

I recognize *that* look—the one people wear when their work and passion are one and the same. I've seen it on my dad's face dozens of times when caring for his patients. And on Liz's face, too.

But on me?

Not once.

Not even in my white coat.

"So, what'd your parents think about that? Were they supportive?" I ask.

He arches a brow, like he's surprised I'm asking about his parents after a grand total of three minutes of conversation. But I can't help it—I'm always enthralled by stories of people who've managed to chart their own course in life.

"Well," he says, drawing out the word, "they weren't thrilled… but they had"—he hesitates—"other things going on. Mostly, they just wanted me to be happy." He takes another sip of his beer as I study, too closely, the way his upper lip puckers at the center. "Now, they love coming here for weekends."

"I can see why. There's something magical about this place. It's so isolated, so far removed from the day-to-day problems of modern life.

Watching those lions eat today, it just really hit home for me. Life is so simple, but we make it so complicated… at least *I* make it so complicated." The vodka swarms my brain, loosening my tongue.

Shit.

Why am I sharing my deepest thoughts with this total stranger?

"Yes, I couldn't say it better myself, actually." His gaze grabs mine, lapping me into an orbit where time briefly stops.

Gauchely, I guzzle my drink.

He continues, "I actually had a guest the other day who was still devastated about Brad Pitt and Jennifer Aniston's divorce. I'm so glad I don't have to worry about that nonsense. I don't even know who they are."

I mock gasp, clutching my chest. "Corey, you don't know who Jennifer Aniston is? Her rotating hairstyles were a significant focus of my teen years. Please, google her. Totally agree about most of the other societal nonsense, but not Jennifer. She *is* important."

His eyes narrow, then glint, unsure if I'm joking. "Ha, okay, Jennifer Aniston, got it. Adding it to my ASAP to-do list." His left eye devolves into a savage wink. "Anyway, what was your favorite animal today?"

I ponder his question, studying his firm jawline, the way the light vaults from his cheekbones like sunshine dancing off the water. "Hmm, well, it was definitely *not* the baboon who peed on me in the outdoor shower this afternoon."

The sound of his laughter is glorious, inflating me like a helium balloon. "A baboon peed on you in the shower? Why does that image make me smile?"

"I'm not sure, why does it? Are you a sadist?" I give him a savage wink right back.

He laughs again, tipping his beer to his lips, still smiling. "Only sometimes. Not today, though. So… what was your favorite animal, then?"

I rack my brain. "I'd have to say the elephants. They're massive but seem so gentle, so free. I think I fell in love with them out on the back deck. What about you?"

"For me, it's always a toss-up between the elephants and lions. The elephants... I agree, they're fucking extraordinary. I fall in love with them a little more every day, too. And the lions, well, it's fun watching them hunt. But, mostly, I love how each game ride is different. You never know what you're going to find. That's the fucking beauty of it all."

His fingers slide down the length of his beer bottle and I wonder what those fingers would feel like wrapped around my hip bones.

"You say the word *fuck* a lot," I say, oddly charmed by his free-spirited use of language. As if it's an indication of his very freeness.

The freedom I crave, too.

A blush sidles up his cheek. "I'm sorry, Tessa. I hope it doesn't offend you. My mum's always telling me I need to watch my language. I really try, but for some reason, I can't stop."

"No, I strangely like it. I curse a lot in my head but am too timid to say those words aloud to strangers."

"Well, feel free to say *fuck* as much as you want around me," he declares. His front teeth jut out into an explosive smile, making my chest crackle.

I chuckle, emboldened. "Okay, thanks. I *fucking* will."

Corey cackles, too, a hearty laugh so full and unrestrained it makes me feel a powerful sense of pride for being the one to cause it.

"So, what brings you to South Africa?" he asks. "Or should I say, *fucking* South Africa?"

The grin on my face creeps wider. "I go to medical school in Philadelphia. That's in Pennsylvania. In the United States." I pause, searching his face for recognition. Then, just to be safe, I tack on, "Of America."

"Yeah... I've heard of that place before." He smirks devilishly. "Only like... three or four... hundred times. Come on, I'm not that isolated out here, *Tessa*."

The sound of my name, wrapped around his delicious South African accent, makes my eardrums start to waltz.

"Okay, well, just checking—since you didn't know who Jennifer Aniston was. Anyway, there's twelve of us doing a two-month rotation at Princess Victoria Hospital in Gaborone. We start on Monday."

"So, a doctor, eh? That's awesome. I admire you. Such important work. Not like what I'm doing, just chasing animals all day."

"It's funny. I'm pretty jealous of your job, actually, and the passion you seem to have for it." My boozy-fueled words unveil my vulnerability.

Corey arches his eyebrows.

His blue beacons latch onto my face, and it momentarily feels like he's deconstructing every thought inside my mind.

Like, how sometimes, I wish I could have literally *any* other career besides doctor.

Like, how deeply terrified I am of never learning to love medicine.

"Why do you want to be a doctor?" he asks, finally.

The question lands hard. It takes effort—real, physical effort—to coax my gaze away from his, like I'm separating two ancient artifacts fused together a gazillion years ago. For one reckless second, I'm overcome by an overpowering urge to just tell him the truth. To share the dirty secret I've never told anyone.

I'm only doing it for my dad.

But the words stop short. I offer up my well-vetted line: "I just like helping people, I guess?" I shrug, effortlessly slipping back into the role of *The Girl Who Wants to Be a Doctor.*

"That's awesome," Corey says, apparently convinced by my acting. "My younger brother, Carl, is studying to be a doctor, too."

"Oh, yeah?" I gulp more vodka. "What type of doctor?"

"A radiologist. He's not much of a people person. He says he wants to stare at pictures all day and not interact with anyone."

"Ha, I get the appeal of that," I say with a grin. "Do you have other siblings?"

A flashing heaviness rips like a bolt of lightning behind his cobalt eyes. "Nope… just Carl. What about you?"

"Just me," I say, swirling the last remnants of my drink. "My mom famously hated being pregnant. I was her 'one and done,' as she says."

"Your mom's famous?" he asks.

"Ha, no, it's just an expression. My mom's amazing, and I love her dearly, but as a kid, I always wanted a sibling. I didn't know until years later, but she had her tubes tied the day I was born. She hated pregnancy *that* much."

I drain the last of my vodka, the glass suddenly feeling too light in my hand.

"Do you want kids?" he asks. "Or are you worried you'll hate pregnancy, too?"

I blink.

Now it's my turn to be surprised, the depth of his question catching me off guard. But, the alcohol and jetlag have already fogged—err, *erased*—the edges of reality.

"Yes, someday, when I'm ready, I definitely do." *In the far-off future, when I'm not a broken, lying shitshow.* "Do you?"

"No," he says, that heaviness reappearing, his eyelids tugging down like two window shades about to close. He stares at the ice cubes inside my empty glass. "Anyway… would you like another?"

Say no.

More vodka is a terrible idea.

"Hmm, Corey… are you supposed to buy guests drinks?"

The sound of his laugh is a low, husky hoot. "Officially, no, but the bartender, Gus, will cut me a pretty good deal, and I take pride in taking good care of my guests." His lips fuse into a blistering smile that eviscerates my decision-making.

"Sure, I'll have a vodka soda. Thanks."

Shit.

What am I doing?

As he walks away, I study the sloping cliff beneath his shirt, where his obliques and hips fuse together effortlessly.

He returns, handing me my drink, our fingers grazing, that sparky-blast reigniting.

He sits down on the couch, closer this time, his proximity causing a searing heat to flame from my belly into my chest.

"Here you go," he says, his voice silky. His own drink is brown, rumbling with ice and dripping in perspiration.

"What are you drinking?" I ask.

"Rum and Coke."

"Daring. Liquor then beer, you're in the clear, but beer then liquor, never been sicker."

He smiles. "Is that an American saying?"

"Yeah, every college freshman has to learn it. Some, like me, learn it the hard way."

He tilts his chin down, running his hand against his roughened five o'clock shadow. "Funny. I can teach you a few *Afrikaans* expressions."

"Oh yeah, like what?"

He takes a slow sip of rum. "How about: *Hallo, pragtige dame.*"

"And what does that mean?"

"Hello, beautiful lady." The sound is a hushed rasp that makes my cheeks sizzle.

Did he just call me beautiful?

In all my years with Greg, he barely ever said such things.

He made me feel ugly.

Especially on the inside.

"Wow, I like that saying," I whisper, the low hum of a bee buzzing in my throat.

I stare at his calloused finger: no ring.

Corey takes another drink, staying silent.

I can't stand it.

"So… are you single? Or do you have a wife hiding around here, somewhere?" I blurt, the vodka commandeering my bloodstream. And mouth.

He looks amused. "A wife? No. Definitely, no wife, Tessa."

Shit.

Why does it feel like magic every time he says my stupid name?

Around us, the lodge has grown quiet, now almost entirely empty. Behind the bar, Gus dries glassware.

"What about you?" Corey asks. "Have you got a boyfriend? Or a girlfriend?"

"I'm happy to know you're so open-minded," I say, laughing. "But no boyfriend or girlfriend. I'm single."

Barely.

For three days.

But I don't mention that.

Greg's cutting words suddenly barge in.

You fucking cunt.

You stupid whore.

I shove the memories back down, burying them in a dark corner, a place where they aren't razor sharp, where they can't slice me open.

"Are you okay?" Corey's voice is soft as he studies my face, like he somehow hears my echoing grief.

"Yep, totally fine," I lie, swallowing the mass blocking my throat. I force a smile. "So, where do you sleep, anyway? Do you live here?" I gulp more vodka.

"Yeah, just down the road, in the staff quarters. Not quite as luxurious as the guest quarters, I'm afraid." A tiny smile again sneaks out from his freakishly perfect lips.

And suddenly, I want to press my mouth to them. To explore every curve.

"It's amazing you get to live here, in this paradise," I utter.

Corey hesitates, like he's about to say something, but thinks better of it.

He drinks his rum as I watch Gus dry a wine goblet.

Finally, he mutters, "I can show you the staff quarters, if you'd like to see them?"

Yes!

I want to go, a surprising, unexpected amount.

But I'm leaving in two days.

I will never see him again.

And I've barely left—really, *escaped*—Greg.

He seems to sense my reluctance. "Of course, only if you want. No pressure. I'm just trying to be a good guide." He gives me a little wink, crinkling his nose and staring at me.

Beneath his steamy glare, pieces of my insides melt like polar icecaps, breaking off.

My thoughts race.

I could say no, return to my room, stay the safe, predictable, color-inside-the-lines person I usually am.

Or I could say yes—chase this wild yearn for freedom that's sprung alive suddenly, here, in this magical setting.

Liz's words come to me: *Do what feels good to you.*

It's been so long since I've made a decision out of desire, out of pure want, that I barely remember how.

The mental picture of the lions and impala flashes in my mind.

Only a few things in life truly matter.

And, puzzlingly, in this moment, saying yes feels like one of them.

"Actually, I'd *fucking* love to go." The words leave my mouth before the controlling, fiercely rational side of my brain can regain command.

"Awesome." He grins. "Let's go."

Nervous I might talk myself out of it, I down the last of my drink and stand. Corey's hand hovers at my lower back, a barely there touch, as he leads me outside.

6

COREY

I walk outside the lodge, Tessa in tow, the blustery breeze smacking me with cold, hard reality.

What the fuck am I doing?

Never once have I invited a guest back to my room. It's strictly against company policy. If Joe, my manager, finds out, I'm done.

Even worse, I'm violating my personal code of conduct: avoid all feelings.

Always.

Despite the bitter loneliness that sometimes creeps in, I've remained a stony rock inside for the past eleven years.

But fuck, she's beautiful.

And when I'm near her, it's like gravity shifts. There's this pull—an actual force field sucking me closer—like she's a planet, and I'm hopelessly stuck in her orbit.

Now, under the moonlight, specs of gold glitter and dance within her chocolate-brown eyes, momentarily thawing my frosty core.

And her sunny smile—with that heart-stopping dimple hollowing out her right cheek—really does me in. It makes me want to abandon my dumb rules. It makes me want to bury my face in her honey-streaked hair and forget the grief of the world, if only for tonight.

But the thing I'm most drawn to? That fragile hurt tucked deep inside her. It's the same type of pain I've spent the past decade shoving as far down as humanly possible.

In silence, Tessa follows me to the Jeep. I open the passenger door, helping her up. In addition to not cussing, my mum always harps about the importance of good manners, of treating women with respect. Call me old-fashioned, but chivalry matters to me. A lot.

"Are you okay to drive?" Tessa asks, her presence oddly familiar. It's more like I've known her for years, not hours. I'm eerily comfortable sitting beside her, a feeling that deeply fucking disturbs me.

"Yeah, I had one beer and one rum. Plus, we're only going about two minutes," I say.

She raises her eyebrows, seemingly unconvinced. My traitorous lips bloom into a wide smile.

We drive outside the main visitor gates. Tessa's skin radiates a lavender-lemony smell that makes it hard to focus on the pitch-black road. Hard to focus on anything.

I notice goosebumps dotting her arms. "Are you cold? I have a blanket in the back seat." Before she can answer, I idle the car along the deserted road and reach into the back, handing it to her.

"Thanks." She tugs the fleece against her bare shoulders, and suddenly, I'm fiercely jealous of the damn blanket. Of its enviable proximity to all the places I want to be.

"Listen closely," I say, forcing my attention back to the animals. "Hear anything?"

Tessa tilts her head, eyes starkly focused, like she's prepping for an exam, intent on acing it. "I hear rustling," she says. "What is it?"

"Hard to be sure in the dark, but it's probably one of the leopardesses. She has three new cubs and hunts at nighttime. I usually sit here, watching for her, on my way home."

Her lips part slightly, a soft "wow" slipping out. "Your commute is so much more exciting than mine." Her comment is lighthearted, but something serious lurks beneath it.

And for reasons I cannot begin to fathom, I want to methodically peel back each of her layers until I uncover her core. The truth behind her statement.

Tessa's gaze toggles over my gun, nestled between us, her sultry lower lip quivering. "You'll protect me, though, right, Corey? If any of the animals get too close?"

My name, slithering off her tongue, is a damn hard-on waiting to explode.

I nod, gripping the wheel tighter.

And, yes, I want to protect her.

But why?

What the fuck is happening?

After a decade of shutting everything out, it's egregiously, outrageously, horrendously unacceptable for feelings to inadvertently creep up on me like this.

But it's there—a sweeping, nonsensical desire to safeguard her.

A similar feeling to the one I had with Leona.

But I failed.

And now she's gone.

Fuck.

"Of course," I hear myself say, seemingly having lost all control over my damn mouth, my person around this woman.

Tessa gazes up, studying the stark blackness speckled with white dots. "In my apartment in Philly, I can't see any of the stars. The sky here…" She exhales. "It's so amazingly beautiful. Every minute I'm here, this whole place seems to get more magical."

"It is incredible," I agree.

There's a tussle from the leopardess nearby. I'm comforted by her low, familiar growl as she stalks, providing for her cubs. Next to me, Tessa's breathing grows slow and peaceful. My hand moves before I can stop it. My fingers brush against hers, tentative at first, then bolder, stroking her silky palm. The texture of her smooth skin spikes a tart chill down my neck.

For a moment, I allow myself to savor it.

To pretend it's okay to want this.

It's *not*.

I jerk my hand back, cold air rushing to fill the void. I'm suddenly desperate to shake off these unanticipated, unacceptable feelings. "Shall we keep going?"

She nods.

I start driving, placing my hands firmly against the steering wheel, far away from the alluring warmth of her touch. The Jeep bumps along the dirt path, the two minutes to the staff quarters stretching out, the silence punctuated only by the tattered hoot of an owl.

I park outside my cabin and quickly circle to open her door and help her down, glancing around in all directions for Joe.

"I'm guessing guests aren't supposed to be here?" Tessa asks. Her brow furrows into such a deep V that my heart does a flying long jump straight to the other side of the parking lot.

Fuck.

I feel like a complete idiot.

"No, not really. I'm hoping my boss doesn't spot us." I peek at my watch: 1:07 a.m. "But Joe goes to bed early. It should be fine."

"Is this something you do a lot?" Tessa asks, her voice barely audible, her forehead creased with lines of unease, like she's pondering becoming another notch in my belt.

The implication stabs me, even though it couldn't be further from the truth. "Bring a guest back here?" I shake my head. "No, it's not like that. Not at all. I'm really sorry if I gave you that impression. Actually…" I pause, the words lodging in my throat before I push them out. "I've never brought a guest here."

The truth feels like a spotlight.

Distressingly, extremely, superbly, over-exposing.

What the actual fuck am I saying?

Tessa processes my words, her forehead unclenching, her adorable dimple cratering back, puncturing a hole in my lungs. "Well, okay then, let's go inside. I mean, let's *fucking* go inside."

In spite of myself, I smile so big my cheeks nearly splinter apart.

I fumble with my key, opening the door, turning on the dim twenty-year-old lamp my mum insisted I bring from my childhood bedroom. *Something to make you comfortable*, she'd said.

The warm light pools around the room, not strong enough to chase away the shadows.

Tessa sits on my worn plaid couch, the soft glow cascading along her delicious curves. She looks like she entirely fits, somehow. I sink down, trying, but failing, to keep a safe distance from her.

"So, this is your place?" she asks, her warm breath tickling my neck.

"Yeah, in all its glory." I shift back from her, trying to regain some control. "Can I get you something? A drink?"

She laughs. "No, I've had all the vodka I can handle tonight."

My heart hammers with sudden concern. "You're not drunk, though, right? I don't want to force you to be here—"

She waves her hand, cutting me off. "Don't worry. I'm not drunk… or maybe, I am. But I can make good decisions. Well, maybe not *good* decisions, but I can definitely make decisions." Her fingers graze my chest, making my skin hiss. Her hands inch up my face, pulling me closer. "Anyway, trust me, Corey, I want to be here."

"Are you implying I'm a *bad* decision?" I ask.

She doesn't answer.

She just leans in, melting her curvy lips against the ledge of my mouth. Her breath is hot, like molten lava, diffusing with my favorite tastes—salt and sugar and alcohol. She nibbles on my upper lip, her arms looping around my neck.

The questions, the worries, the doubts, they vanish.

For a moment, there's only her mouth, her body.

Then, abruptly, she pulls away, her breath warm, uneven. "I'm sorry, Corey," she says, "this probably sounds crazy, but it's bothering me… I'm probably overthinking everything… big surprise… but I have to ask… do you have HIV? I hope that's not ridiculously rude. It's just… I'm a medical student here because of the HIV/AIDS epidemic… and it feels important to know…"

I'm surprised by her question—but also, in her squirmy discomfort, she looks cute. In her eyes, I watch a wild battle ensue between the carefree part of her brain, begging to let this go, and the practical part, stubbornly refusing to. I cross my arms, leaning back, a curious spectator wondering which part will win.

"No, Tessa, I don't have HIV," I answer softly.

"Okay, great… but have you tested recently?" Right now, her anxious side is definitely winning, and for some reason, this delights me. I want to laugh. Not at her, but how determined she is to do this right.

"Yes… not too long ago," I say. "But also, I don't really date much. Mostly, I spend my time with tourists and animals and Darian."

"I find it hard to believe you don't do a lot of dating"—she gestures her hands along my torso—"looking like you do. But thank you for answering, and sorry I'm such an uptight weirdo."

I simultaneously blush at her compliment and cringe at her self-deprecation. "Don't be so hard on yourself. You're not a weirdo. It's good to be safe. What about you? Do you have any diseases I should know about?"

She inches her face closer, a furious heat spiraling down to my toes.

"No, I'm clean. I tested right before I came," she says.

A few strands of her bronzed hair droop in front of her eyelid. I tuck them behind her ear, inhaling the lemony scent. "Okay, well, I'm glad we have all these formalities behind us."

"Don't you mean *fucking* formalities?" she whispers.

I laugh.

Her whiskey-colored eyes peer straight into mine, toppling my remaining willpower.

And then my mouth is roaming her neck, her fingers are racing up my chest, my hands are shoving into her citrusy hair.

And I'm lost.

In her.

In tonight.

In the moment.

7

TESSA

Four hours later, I huddle in the Jeep beneath the fleece blanket. A shivering Liz cuddles next to me, waiting for the sun to rise. My head throbs from the unwelcome after-effects of too much vodka and too little sleep. The morning air, tinged by a golden-reddish hue, helps jolt my alertness.

Behind the wheel, Corey stares straight ahead, vigilantly navigating the dusky plains. I want to climb into the front seat—*my* spot from last night—and rest my ear on his shoulder, drifting to sleep.

Somehow, when I'm out here in the wilderness with him, it feels like home.

It's the only place in the world I've ever felt so stunningly alive.

So released from myself.

And I don't want to leave.

"So, Tess, how was your night with Mr. Safari Dreamboat? You got back pretty late," Liz whispers, her mouth arching into a grin.

"It was good." I grit my teeth, swiftly nudging Liz in the ribs. "I'll tell you more in the room, quiet for now."

I lean back, shutting my eyes, lulled by the rumbling engine as we zoom through the bush.

Fifteen minutes later, Corey parks the Jeep in a wide field and climbs out. He opens the rear door, motioning for us to follow.

I rub my eyes and survey my surroundings, inhaling the daybreak smell, ripe with damp grass and sopping soil. My jaw tightens as I climb to the edge of the Jeep and stop. Corey waits with an outstretched hand. My body flirts with the idea of jumping into his arms, but my brain is screaming a different warning: to never leave this car. I can practically see the CNN headline: *American Tourist Mauled by Lion Outside Safari Jeep in South Africa.*

"Corey, is this safe? Won't an animal try to eat us? It seems like we're making ourselves painfully easy prey?" My voice is shrill. I sound like a helicopter parent, denying her child permission for a field trip to the aquarium.

His blue beacons scrutinize me, offering up a knowing grin. It's like, somehow, he already expects my nonstop anxiety and maybe even enjoys it.

"Ha, no. We scout the locations in advance. And we pick large, open spaces for a reason. It's safe, trust me. I do this every morning. Plus, I'll keep an eye out. I won't let anything happen to *you*." His emphasis on the word makes me shiver, goosebumps flinging like confetti along my arms.

"Corey's a professional, Tess. He knows what he's doing," Liz implores from behind. "Just try to enjoy the experience. Get out of your head, for once."

From Liz, it's an easy proclamation. Her mind doesn't trap her in endless loops of what-ifs and worst-case scenarios. I'm an expert at overthinking *everything*. I constantly miss out on the present, lost in the worries of my mind.

Liz gives me a tiny push. Reluctantly, I step down, taking Corey's hand. His coarse fingers snake around my cold wrist as that electric current blasts through me, nearly knocking me to the ground.

I stumble.

His right hand reaches for my waist while his left hand scoops the small of my back.

His sudden, overwhelming proximity siphons my lungs of all air, my head becoming a dizzyingly empty balloon.

"Easy, there, Tess," he says, his accent so deliriously sexy, I can't stand it.

I find my footing, mortified to see my classmates all staring at us. Their gazes aren't subtle, either. I quickly pull apart from Corey, instead huddling against Liz.

"I'm swooning, too, Tess. That chemistry between you guys is intense!" Liz mutters, squeezing my shoulder.

My cheeks burn hotter as I stand stiffly in the bronzed grass, tiny dewdrops leaking through my leggings, moistening my ankles.

A lion is not going to eat me.

All my classmates don't know that I made out with our safari guide last night.

Corey unfolds a small table, laying out pastries and supplies for coffee.

Coffee.

Yes.

Coffee might help me stop acting like a complete moron.

He goes around, attending to each guest, pouring steaming cups, offering croissants. By the time he gets to me, the others are lost in the beauty of our surroundings and breakfast.

"And what can I get you?" he asks. While he waits for my response, his sapphire eyes roam my face, starting at my forehead, working his way down past my nose, my lips, finally resting on my dimple. My usual defenses tumble away.

Under his gaze, I feel entirely naked.

And yet, oddly seen.

"Um…"

His curvy lips spread open, my stomach fluttering with a school of goldfish trying to escape.

Think brain.

Say words.

Any words will do.

"Coffee with three sweeteners and extra cream, please."

"So you want some sugar with a side of coffee?" he asks.

"I see that despite the lack of sleep, you're extra funny this morning. Extra *fucking* funny, I mean." I give him a three-quarters grin.

He leans in slightly. "Hmm, I wonder why I didn't sleep much?" The edge of his eye crinkles back into that diabolic wink.

He hands me the coffee, then goes to get his camera from the Jeep. I sip the hot liquid, letting it slip like tiny droplets of heaven down the back of my throat. It's rich, sweet and exactly what I need.

The sky stretches above us, a brilliant mélange of reds, oranges, and yellows. Darkness is giving way to light. In the savanna, life is rising, a new day unfurling.

Two hundred yards away, four giraffes graze on the tall, coppery grass. Their long necks bend to nibble, then perk back up, their ears flailing out, assessing their surroundings.

Corey lifts his camera, there's the soft click of the shutter, and I shake my head in awe.

Yes, tomorrow, I have to return to the real world.

To sort out my disastrous relationship with Greg.

My uncertain future as a doctor.

The gnawing guilt of being handed an undeserving amount of good fortune, and still I remain a complete and total mess.

But not today.

For now, this whole scene is a freaking dream. A shimmering pocket of time where nothing exists but this light, this air, this minute.

And Corey.

I close my eyes, letting the coffee warm me from the inside out.

I'm not ready to wake up yet.

***

Back in our room later that morning, I stare out the window, mesmerized by the watering hole. The elephants have returned. Seven of them strut together into the brown water. In the lead, a baby trots slowly. Behind, his mother pushes him, using her trunk to bathe him, coating his skin with mud. He squeals with glee as the water splatters his tattered belly.

I suddenly crave the comfort of my own mom, Claudia, who cares for me with a similar tenderness, delivering pure, unconditional love. My mom's praise has always come easily, free of obligation.

It's my dad's respect that's harder to earn.

That comes with heavy expectations.

Expectations I've never quite managed to fill.

With Liz still at the main lodge, I grab my laptop and log on to my email.

There's a new message from Greg.

From: Greg.Winters1982@bmail.com
To: Tessa.Williams2@bmail.com

Date: Saturday, August 4, 2007

Subject: Hello????

Tessa,

Please, say anything. I miss you so much.
Please, I love you more than life itself.

Please, I'm so sorry.

Just talk to me, I'm begging you. I swear to you it will never happen again.

I need you.

Greg

Staring at Greg's inadequate, too-late sentiments, a new kind of desperation wells up inside me—an ache to spill everything to my mom. Something about Impodimo Lodge has sparked this new possibility—of owning my shameful truth.

I open a message to her, the cursor daring me to speak.

> Help me, Mom. Somehow, I let everything in my life get so messed up. How do I fix it so that somehow, things inside will feel okay? I never told you, but my relationship with Greg was—

The door creaks open. Liz walks in, startling me away from my bone-chilling vulnerability.

"Hi, Tess, everything okay?" she asks, her gaze toggling between the computer and my humiliated face.

It must look like she just busted me watching porn.

"Yeah," I say quickly, my voice too high, too brittle. I delete the email, snapping the computer shut. "I was just emailing my parents a few pictures."

That teeny glimmer of truth evaporates.

Lying is still the only thing I know.

8

COREY

I step out of the piping-hot shower, wrap a towel around my waist, slap my cheeks hard enough to sting. I wipe away the steam, peering at my reflection in the bathroom mirror, disgusted by a new softness in my eyes.

Get yourself together, man.

I shake my head, tear my gaze away, and stride into the living room. My feet slow as I walk past the blue plaid couch, where last night my lips scoured Tessa's neck. I shove away the memories of her burrowing dimple, her lemony hair, her plush skin.

So what if kissing her felt good?

Really good?

I am a hardened rock.

I have to be.

In my bedroom, I avoid the ancient picture of Leona perched on my nightstand, too defenseless to see her cheery face. Instead, I tug on worn jeans, shaking the loose water from my hair.

I glance at the clock. I'm already ten minutes late for dinner with my guests.

Tessa's last dinner.

Why the hell should I care that Tessa's leaving tomorrow?

Guests come and go. This place is a revolving door of tourists. It keeps my job interesting, ensures no one sticks around long enough for me to get attached.

People leaving is usually a *great* thing.

So why does it feel like Tessa's looming departure is readying to detonate that years-ticking bomb?

The one I've buried so deep inside, it's never supposed to see the light of day?

Because its explosion might consume me alive.

I curl my fists, punching the air, furious with myself, with my moronic heart, for having the audacity to feel a single goddamn emotion.

I don't feel feelings.

I huff out a breath, grab my keys, and slam the cabin door behind me.

It's decided, I decide.

I'll allow myself one last evening in Tessa's admittedly pleasant company.

But absolutely nothing more.

Come morning, she'll leave, and I'll stay.

Here, in the majestic bush, my paradise.

Perfectly alone.

Completely fucking fine.

By this time tomorrow, it will be like none of this ever happened.

Tessa will be a distant memory, swept away with all the others.

Replaced again by glorious, all-encompassing numbness.

*

I slip her a note at dinner:

> *Tessa, meet me outside the lodge at 23:00. I want to show you something before you go. — C.*

***

At exactly eleven, I find Tessa leaning against the stone wall outside the main lodge. She's wearing a Philadelphia Eagles sweatshirt, her hands shoved into the pockets of black leggings, her damp hair curling at the ends. Unlike at dinner, her face is bare of all makeup and my chest twinges at how much I prefer her au naturel look.

Fuck.

"*Hallo, pragtige dame.* I'm glad you came." The words are out of my mouth before I can stop them. Even worse, they're true.

I swiftly pinch my wrist.

"Hi, Corey." Her russet eyes look tired but happy. "So, what'd you want to show me?"

She brushes closer, my pulse spiking like a circuit board about to trip. "It's a surprise. Come, get in."

I open her door and hand her the blanket, again jealous of the damn blanket.

The engine hums as we head into the blackened bush. I steer through the familiar, bumpy terrain.

The half-moon spreads its white glow, revealing a look of unease carved into Tessa's face.

"Everything okay?" I ask.

"Well, it's just… are we supposed to be out here? Alone? At night? Like this? Isn't it dangerous?" Her anxious side is back, and despite myself, I'm painfully charmed.

"It's safe. Don't be nervous. I know what I'm doing."

I'm considerably less confident than I sound.

Not about keeping her safe.

But what the hell am I doing?

What if word of this gets back to Joe?

I'm acting like a reckless imbecile, putting my job on the line for the second night in a row.

She studies me for a moment, then her shoulders relax.

"Okay, I believe you," she says.

Her smile resurfaces.

Her dimple indents.

My worries recede.

"You said you love the elephants," I say, guiding the Jeep towards our destination. "I want to show you a special one. With a little luck, she'll be where I'm expecting. It'll be worth it, trust me."

The night breeze blows Tessa's hair close to my nose. She rests her head against my shoulder, her warm breath pasting to my earlobe. Her hand grazes my thigh with striking intimacy.

Fuck.

No.

I will not like this.

I grip the steering wheel, keeping my eyes trained on the road.

Twenty minutes later, I idle the Jeep. "This is the Tau Waterhole. It's my favorite spot in the reserve. Actually, it's my favorite spot, period."

The mud-covered ground gives way to a large pool. Under the moonlight, ripples splay the water's surface.

"Wow," Tessa murmurs. "I see why. It's stunning."

I drive along the water's edge, dimming the headlights and popping my head out of the window to analyze the animal tracks congealed in the mud. I make a half-loop of the watering hole before shutting off the Jeep.

"Ahh, there she is!" I say, pointing to a herd of elephants clustered along the water's lip. The air is still except for the occasional elephant snort.

"Your tracking skills are impressive," Tessa says, a rosy glow coating her cheeks.

"Do you see the tallest one? That's the matriarch. Her name is Betty."

"Betty?" Tessa repeats, her eyebrows twisting. "That's a funny name for an elephant. How'd you know she'd be here?"

"Truthfully, I got a little lucky, but for the past few days, she's been here a lot. Betty's grieving her son. He died right by this watering hole four years ago. Bitten by a poisonous snake. Elephants have an amazing memory, an ability to feel feelings acutely. Betty returns to this place year after year. To grieve. To remember. How's that for fucking incredible?" My pitch grows high, tinged by adoration for these miraculous animals.

Tessa scrunches her nose, jutting out her heart-shaped jaw, studying Betty with precision.

I briefly consider my own grief.

Unlike Betty, I've learned it's easier to forget.

Remembering too much breaks you.

And inside, I'm already a mountain of crumbs.

"Everything about this setting, this place, is so spectacular," Tessa mumbles. "I really wish I didn't have to leave tomorrow. I just feel so strangely… at home here. Like myself. It probably sounds crazy, but I've never felt that way anywhere else…"

"I know what you mean. It doesn't sound crazy at all. The exact same thing happened to me five years ago. It's why I never left." To me, the wilderness shines clarity on life, illuminating all that truly matters in a way nothing else can.

"I'm dreading returning to the real world after the magical escape of this weekend," she says, her lower lip spiraling into a pouty frown, her shoulders sagging. For a moment, her inner layers crack open like an egg, bits of yolk seeping out, and I see her. Raw and scared.

Again, I'm overcome by an undeniable urge to make everything better for her.

To understand why she suffers.

But that's not my role.

I lighten the mood with the only thing I can think of. "I understand why you feel like that, but if you stayed here, you'd miss so much important information about Jennifer Aniston."

Tessa laughs, the sound teeming with heartiness, her outer façade regenerating strength. "That's true. Good point, Corey. I feel *so* much better about returning to my real life now."

"Phew," I say, wanting to ask so many questions—about her pain, her fears, the cracks she's hiding.

I stop myself.

Don't forget the fucking rules.

"I brought something," I say, needing another view besides her vulnerable, stunning face. I reach behind my seat, producing a bottle of Cabernet Sauvignon and two plastic cups.

"Okay, now this might be the best date I've ever had," Tessa says, smiling.

Me too.

Fuck.

Two guinea fowl scamper near the water's edge, their high-pitched squawks mimicking the fear rising inside my chest. I clench my fists, stowing my emotions. I open the wine and hand Tessa a generous pour, guzzling mine in two big sips, hoping the alcohol will curb this damn affection boiling within me.

I am a hardened rock.

"Are you okay?" Tessa asks. "Worried about your boss again?"

"Uh… yeah."

"Well, I appreciate you bringing me here," she whispers, scooting next to me, threading her arm around my neck. The smell of her lemony hair shoves a wave of desire through me.

"Of course, I knew you'd like it." I keep my voice even.

I'm fighting myself, every cell screaming to pull her closer, to lose myself in her, while my mind waves a thousand red flags.

Tessa sets her empty glass in the back seat, her hands cupping my face. Her eyes search mine for the briefest of moments. She leans over and kisses me, gently at first, a soft press of lips, but then her tongue starts probing my mouth. Tentative, then insistent. I've kissed my share of women, but something about her kiss is categorically different—better.

Fuck.

She climbs into my lap, straddling me. Her lips nuzzle my neck. I wrap my arms around her, trying to remember my stupid mantra about being a rock. I draw a blank.

Her hand slides down, reaching into my pants.

Fuck.

"Do you have a condom?" she whispers.

Suddenly, the pendulum swings hard, my head whipping back to reality. I want nothing more than to thrust inside her until dawn breaks, but there are two humungous problems:

1) My mum instilled in me an absolute need to treat women with respect. As she says: *Diallo men do not make love and leave.* I've had casual sex before, but not with a girl I actually liked, a girl who carried so much pain.

2) Which is the bigger fucking problem. I actually *like* her—and that is completely, utterly unacceptable. Not only because she's leaving tomorrow and lives on another continent, but because I can't get caught up in my feelings.

Never again.

Tessa starts to tug down my pants.

"Don't, Tess," I stammer, grabbing her wrists gently but firmly. "I don't have a condom, but even if I did, I still wouldn't think this is a good idea."

Her body recoils like it was just stung by a colony of wasps. "You don't want to have sex with me?"

It's clear no person has ever said such moronic words to her. For a minute, I'm positive I'm the dumbest man ever to roam Earth. "I do *want* to have sex with you. You're kind and funny and beautiful, but you're leaving tomorrow. Let's not make tonight about sex."

She stares at the elephants, her bottom lip agape.

"I'm sorry, Tessa… I didn't mean to insult you."

I reach for her hand, to soften the blow, but she shakes it away, her eyes wide like saucers, flickering with something I can't quite name.

She's silent for an uncomfortably long time.

"Tessa, please, say something."

Her jaw tightens before she finally speaks. "It's just… no one has rejected me… so intimately… I'm sorry, I feel like an idiot. Can you just drive me back to the lodge?"

"Of course I can take you back, but, Tessa"—I cup the bottom of her chin—"I'm definitely not *rejecting* you."

"How do you figure?" Her tone is frosty, her cheeks two sunken ships.

"In my eyes, I'm *respecting* you. You're leaving tomorrow, and I like you too much to have random sex. Can't we just finish our wine? Kiss a little? Enjoy the animals?"

A gust of wind whooshes through the Jeep, and she quivers.

I hand her the blanket as she stays quiet, her mind somewhere far away.

And again, I yearn to peel back her layers.

To figure out her past.

To understand her broken pieces.

Finally, she says, "Shit, well… maybe no guy has ever… *respected* me before?"

Her words hit like a punch. Her eyes pool with such sadness that sorrow floods my chest, too.

"Then those guys were fucking idiots and you deserved better."

She heaves out a sigh, scowling. "Actually, Corey, when you say it like that, it sounds shockingly accurate."

"I'm sorry, Tessa. You're awesome. You should know that."

She looks entirely unconvinced, but when I reach out my arms, she sinks into them, letting me hold her.

Comforting her feels treacherously good.

Fuck.

"So, Tess," I say, my lips brushing her hair, "tell me… what was Jennifer Aniston's best hairstyle?"

She presses deeper into me, her shoulders slackening.

"Well, Corey," she answers, her voice lighter now, "that's a hard question to answer…"

***

Nine hours later, in the main lodge, under Joe's watchful eye, I shake her hand goodbye, keeping my expression tight.

Wordlessly, she slips me a note.

I pocket it, avoiding her earnest, too-tempting eyes.

She climbs into the waiting van, disappearing from my sight.

She's gone.

I should feel relieved.

It makes zero fucking sense.

Because instead… it feels like a hippo is crumpled on top of my lungs.

I am a hardened rock.

I don't feel feelings.

How many times will I need to say it to make it true again?

9

TESSA

I'm lying in my bed at Timali Court, dreading the alarm, which will soon shriek. The room is quiet except for Liz's willowy breaths. I've been up for hours, nervous about my first day at the hospital and replaying Corey's words. The ones where he said he was *respecting* me by *rejecting* my advances. His statement was an earthquake, rumbling apart my self-image, the aftershocks still pinging now.

Is that how I ended up with Greg? I throw myself at any man who shows interest? Who makes me feel the slightest bit attractive or wanted?

I shut my eyes, and I'm back in Mr. Brown's eighth-grade science class.

***

My cheeks are chubby, my breasts are D-cups, my stomach is rotund. But until that moment, my figure has never defined me. It's barely even occurred to me.

Robby Marzone, the most popular boy in our grade, snickers, passing a note to his best friend, Charlie Coronado.

Mr. Brown lectures about mitosis as the folded paper falls to the ground. I reach down, retrieving it, the words jumping off the page.

Tessa Williams: she's stupid and she's fat but at least she's not flat.

This one sentence pulverizes my self-esteem, like a balloon drained with a quick stab of a blade.

I don't react. My face remains a calm mask.

I turn to Robby, handing him the note, smiling as if none the wiser. I don't share his words with anyone.

But the deep shame of them guts me.

Robby's words echo in my head over the next two years as I develop an eating disorder, shedding thirty pounds. An attempt to erase the girl he mocked.

They echo in my head three years later when he asks me to Junior Prom. I say yes, victorious to finally be worthy of him.

"You have the dopest body," he mumbles into my skinny, naked belly, taking my virginity. Every minute of my starvation is worth his momentary praise.

Over the years that follow, with the help of a nutritionist and therapist, I shed the eating disorder. But maybe, I realize now in the dim morning light, I've never healed my underlying disordered self-image.

I pull out my journal from the nightstand, flipping it open. The words come quickly as I jot them down:

Step #1 to figuring out my toxic relationship with Greg: MEN CAN NO LONGER DEFINE MY SELF-WORTH.

I underline it twice.

***

The alarm blares.

I push away thoughts of Robby Marzone, of awful Greg, even of sweet, mystifying Corey. There's no room for any of them today. Liz rumbles awake, yawning as she stretches, and we dress together in silence.

Outside our flat, Jeremy and Suzanne are chatting with Dr. Masego Sebopelo, our program director. The morning air sends a shiver along my spine as I shake Dr. Sebopelo's hand. He's in his late forties, Black, tall but portly, with a shiny bald head, bulbous nose and deep brown eyes.

"Tessa, pleased to meet you," he says.

"Likewise," I answer, my stomach looping into fifty-five nervous knots.

"I'm so excited for today!" Liz whispers, her eyes green and eager, making me wildly envious of her sweeping enthusiasm for all things medicine.

The rest of our classmates come out, and we start along the dirt road, beginning the trek to the hospital. As we walk, Dr. Sebopelo introduces himself. "I'm glad for the opportunity to teach you. We'll begin with some history about me. I grew up in Semolale, a small village in eastern Botswana. I was the oldest of four children, born to a single mom. In my village, there was no medical clinic or doctor. I spent my childhood attending school and helping care for our cattle.

"When I was nine, I got a badly infected cut on my hand. My grandfather took me by bicycle to the village of Bobonong. After a full day of travel, we reached the medical clinic. There, I was given antibiotics and introduced to the practice of medicine.

"For me, it was love at first sight. I *had* to be a doctor. When my grandfather died two years later, I decided to stay in school even though I was now the man of my family. My mother, who had little formal education herself, was supportive.

"I did well in school, and after two years at the University of Botswana, I won a scholarship to attend medical school in England. Since Botswana has no medical school, I had to train abroad. When I boarded the plane, I'd never flown, never left my country. I was terrified, but it was a wonderful experience living in London.

"After I completed my training, I worked in the UK for a time. But I came home ten years ago to help with the worsening HIV crisis. I've been working on the wards of Princess Victoria ever since."

I'm spellbound. His story is incredible, his passion for medicine inspiring.

We pause to cross a major intersection, cars whizzing past us during the busy rush hour in bursts of noise and exhaust. The group clusters, waiting for an opening.

"I'm sure you've heard the statistics," he continues. "But numbers alone can't convey the suffering HIV has brought. One in six children is now an orphan. The average life expectancy in Botswana has dropped from sixty-one years to just fifty years. But our government is very committed to offering free HIV testing and treatment."

The hospital comes into view, a sprawling single-story brick building. Trailers line the entire perimeter, which Dr. Sebopelo explains are the outpatient clinics. In the front, a small parking lot is occupied by two ambulances and a dozen cars.

"Princess Victoria is the country's largest public hospital," he says as we walk along the outdoor corridor lined with date palm trees. "It has five hundred beds and offers the most complete range of specialty services available in Botswana. But as you'll soon see, it functions quite differently from the Western hospitals you've trained in."

Although it's early, a flurry of patients and hospital workers diffuse in all directions, a mix of urgency and calm efficiency.

"The hospital consists of wards divided by gender and medical problem. For example, there's a female and male surgical ward, a female and male medical ward. Are you following?"

We nod in unison.

"We'll start with a tour," Dr. Sebopelo says, pushing through the double doors to our left, leading us into the male medical ward.

The air changes instantly, thick with antiseptic and something else—sweat, maybe, or the acrid edge of sickness. It's one long room divided into six bays. Each bay has twelve hospital beds, arranged one after the next. Small privacy curtains hang between the beds, although few are pulled shut.

The beds are full.

What catches my eye are the mattresses. Scattered across the floor, a desperate overflow. Each one holding a person. I scan the room, startled by the sheer number of patients, their cacophony of pained murmurs resounding in my ears like a gut-wrenching orchestra.

I spot one mattress by the ward entrance, where a twenty-something man withers beneath a blood-soaked sheet. He moans, his face scrunched in agony, his body curled into a tight ball. His eyes lock with mine as his arms stretch out, pleading for help.

I look around, observing the nurses rushing from one patient to the next. No one is available to help this man. My face feels cold and clammy.

There's so much sickness all around.

I'm so unqualified to be here.

Dr. Sebopelo lightly tugs my arm. "Come, Tessa. Let's finish orientation."

***

Two hours later, I'm assigned to the female medical ward. Dr. Sebopelo gives me four patients to examine. Timidly, I walk to the hospital bed of the first patient, feeling like a total fraud. My mind is screaming, *I don't belong here.*

In the bed lies a thirteen-year-old girl, deeply agitated. She thrashes her arms and legs, screaming. Her body is well-nourished, but her mind is delirious. A woman hovers over the bedside, stroking the girl's face, whispering in Setswana.

Unable to speak the language, I meagerly wave to the woman, retrieving the girl's medical chart from the foot of the bed. From the semi-legible handwriting, I piece together a history: three weeks ago, while on her family's farm, the girl was bitten by a mongoose. Two days ago, she presented with a grave fear of water, diagnosed with end-stage rabies.

"Have you had a chance to examine this patient?" Dr. Sebopelo asks, coming up behind me.

"Not yet," I say. "I was still reading her chart. But I've only learned about rabies from a textbook. I've never seen a case."

"Yes, it's very rare. As you probably know, once the symptoms start, there's no treatment. It will unfortunately be fatal, likely in a matter of days." Dr. Sebopelo talks in Setswana to the woman at the bedside. "This is her mother," he tells me, a cascade of tears seeping from the woman's bloodshot eyes. "She's asking us to help, but sadly, I explained again, there's nothing we can do."

The mother looks at me with such wild desperation that my chest blows to shreds.

Her daughter is going to die.

And there's nothing—nothing—we can do to stop it.

After we examine the girl together, Dr. Sebopelo excuses himself. Without him to translate, the language barrier between me and the mother inhibits further communication.

My stomach aches like it's being chewed up by a pack of wolves.

I feel so helpless.

I have no words, no solutions.

So, I do the only thing I can.

I clasp the mother's trembling hand and sit with her, wordlessly, as she comforts her dying daughter.

***

The next patient I see is a fifty-one-year-old woman with advanced HIV. She was admitted for probable pneumonia. *Probable* because the X-ray machine at Princess Victoria Hospital is broken. Her diagnosis rests on physical exam findings alone. The woman's been hospitalized for seven days, receiving the only oral antibiotic in stock at the hospital pharmacy. But she's not improving.

She is thin and pale, her long black braids tucked behind a bed cap. As she sleeps, her arthritic knuckles rest atop a beige blanket.

I place my stethoscope on the woman's chest, noting the lack of IV medications, oxygen cannula, or monitors to constantly assess her vitals. Just her and the bed. It's so different from an American hospital.

"Come here for a second, Tessa," Dr. Sebopelo says, "I want to show you something."

I glance at my sleeping patient before following him to the nearby bedside of a patient Jeremy's examining.

I return five minutes later to finish my exam, placing my stethoscope back over the woman's heart.

But there is only silence.

I study the woman's ribs.

Willing them to move.

The rise and fall has impossibly ceased.

I shake the woman's shoulders, but she remains motionless.

A whirlpool of panic twists through my body.

Shit! No!

There was no loud beeping from any machine to alert me of a problem. This woman was sick but *not* moments from death.

"Dr. Sebopelo, come here right away! She's not breathing," I call, my words slamming together.

The woman's mouth hangs open, her head tilted to the left. Her eyes are wide, her pupils glassy and fixed.

Dr. Sebopelo examines her, feeling for a pulse. "You are right. She has passed." His voice is low but steady.

The room feels like it tilts sideways, the air thickening, trapping my breath in my chest.

"Can't we do something? Anything?" I plead, my tone edging on hysterical. "We have to try!"

"Tessa," Dr. Sebopelo says. "There is no crash cart here, no code to call. With the resources available, there's nothing more we can do." He isn't done. "At this hospital, you will see patients die, and when it happens, it's very sad. But also, death is a part of life. Our job now is to give her dignity."

My training flashes through my mind—protocols for cardiac arrest, step-by-step drills for life-saving intervention. But none of that applies here.

In all my medical rotations, I've yet to see anyone die.

How is this possible?

This woman was alive one second, gone the next.

I've been in Princess Victoria Hospital for less than five hours, but already, I've witnessed the extreme fragility of life. With a higher level of medical care, maybe this patient could have survived.

A suffocating tightness squeezes my chest. I wince, bending over.

This is why a career in medicine feels so daunting.

I don't know how to accept the unfairness of life.

The fact that everyone dies sometime. And some die way too soon.

As a doctor, I'll be forced to navigate this intolerable truth day in, day out. But I can't. *I can't.*

The inevitable pain that comes with being a human is more than I can bear.

Stunned, I again survey the woman's slack face, the room starting to spin in blurry circles.

"Get some air, Tessa. I'll alert the nurses about this patient," Dr. Sebopelo says. "Take a moment to collect yourself."

Wordlessly, I nod, then push out into the corridor, where the sun swelters and voices chat. I sink to the ground, closing my eyes, trying to calm my breathing. But I see only her gaping mouth. Feel only the chilling finality of death.

I try to push the image away, but it festers. It blares—scorching like a branding iron—into my mind.

I'm supposed to be falling in love with medicine.

But I can't handle the pain of life.

I'm too weak.

Too broken.

And in that moment, my only desire is to run.

Far.

Far.

Away.

10

COREY

"You okay, bud?" Darian asks, hunched over his pool cue. "These past few days, you just seem… off?"

It's Thursday night, four days since Tessa left.

Not that I'm counting.

I'm definitely not.

Darian shoots. My eyes trail as his purple ball sails into the front hole. Around us, the main lodge bustles with guests sipping on after-dinner cocktails.

"Yeah, I'm fine," I say with an offhanded wave. "Just exhausted. Looking forward to having this weekend off. First time in four damn weeks."

I take a swig of beer, savoring the coolness as it slips past my tongue. It's my fourth, and the edges of reality are blissfully growing fuzzier.

I'm still trying to reclaim my revered numbness.

Normally, that doesn't require alcohol, but the past few days have been anything but fucking normal.

Somehow, I've become a messy bag of feelings.

And it's not just feelings about Tessa, although I've thought about her more than I care to admit.

It's everything.

Sadness, like yesterday, when a guest shared that her mother had just died.

Happiness, two days ago, when Darian's sister, Chloe, got engaged.

I'm not used to this—feeling *things*—good or bad.

It's unsettling, unsustainable, exhausting.

"Is it that girl?" Darian prods, his wide shoulders shrugged into a question.

"Who… Tessa?" I'm hoping to sound aloof, but a bonfire sparks in my belly just saying her name. "No… maybe… I don't know. My mind's a fucking mess, man." I shake my head, revolted by myself.

I take my shot and miss, the ball skimming the edge of the pocket, ricocheting away.

Fuck.

"If you like her, why don't you just contact her?" Darian asks. "Isn't she here for another two months?"

"Because, man… you know my rules."

Darian slides his fingers through his black hair. "Corey, has it ever occurred to you that your rules don't make a lot of sense? Don't you think Leona would want you to live again?"

Leona.

Her name drops like a stone, the ripples spreading.

"I loved Leona too," Darian continues, "but she wouldn't want this type of life for you."

Leona.

Leona.

Leona.

The sound stings, causing a messy scar to pulsate deep within my chest. For a second, the pain is so intense that I'm sure my heart is going to splinter apart.

Why the fuck would I ever want to feel again in a world so fucking cruel?

"It's not about Leona," I insist, my voice guttural, a lump of grief blocking my throat. "It's just… easier, better, necessary, not to get involved."

Darian nods, knowing better than to push.

I down my beer, trying to block out a flood of unwelcome images:

Leona's wispy blonde curls.

Her violet eyes.

The way her smile lit up a room.

How even total strangers were drawn to her.

She was the axis of my world.

And now she's gone.

Fucking gone.

While I'm lost in my head, Darian sinks his final ball. "I won, chump," he says, offering me a curved smile, shoving his pool cue into my chest.

***

An hour later, Darian drives us back to the staff quarters. The sky is black, bulky clouds blocking the moon. The Jeep's headlights slice through the darkness, landing on the leopardess, sauntering in the road, her orangey-brown spots twinkling beneath the beam.

Darian idles the car.

"What a fucking sight, mate," I mutter.

He nods.

I remember a similar moment with Tessa. Five days ago. It feels like an eternity has passed since then.

Time is fucking strange like that—how some moments stay fresh in your mind, even years later, and others feel like a lifetime ago, although they just happened.

"Incredible," Darian agrees.

We watch the leopardess disappear into the feathery grass, tail swaying before she vanishes.

Darian shifts the Jeep into gear and starts driving again.

A lion roars in the distance.

The cold wind whisks my hair.

I shut my eyes.

I'm suddenly jolted by the image of Leona's violet eyes, dulled from illness, gazing up at me from her hospital bed.

Before they closed.

Forever.

My body jerks forward.

I grab my shirt, the wounds of grief still so raw they're guzzling me up.

I've blocked this pain out for so long, but somehow, a valve inside me is open again, and I can't figure out how to jam it back closed.

Fuck.

Fuck.

Fuck.

Leona.

"Core, are you okay?" Darian asks, parking and eyeing me quizzically.

"Yep," I say, already pushing the Jeep door open. "I just need to get some sleep. See you in the morning."

My voice is terse as I flee to my cabin. Darian calls out, but I'm desperate to get away. To figure something out. To stop these excruciating, horrendous fucking feelings.

In my room, the first thing I see is *her.*

Leona's sweet face taunts me. I plop the photo facedown, not needing any more reminders that I couldn't save the girl I loved so fiercely.

I flop against the couch, my hands shaking, my mind racing, the room whirling a hundred kilometers per hour. I skipped dinner, and the four beers now dump my stomach inside out. I want to hurl or cry or both.

What the fuck is happening to me?

For years, I've lived as a shell—a hardened rock, impervious.

Now?

Now I'm a sopping pile of grief.

My sadness over Leona is overwhelming.

But strangely, in spite of the pain, or maybe, because of it, this is the most present—*alive*—I've been in eleven years.

I recall Darian's words: *Don't you think Leona would want you to live again?*

To live again.

What the hell would that even be like?

I remember Tessa's warm smile, the way her dimple deepened when she laughed, the ease I felt being with her.

To live *again.*

In my drunken haze, my desire to see her again momentarily outweighs my fear.

From my wallet, I unfold the paper she gave me.

> *Corey, thanks for an amazing weekend! I'm here until early October.*
> *Keep in touch! My email is Tessa.Williams2@bmail.com*

Grabbing my computer, I quickly type a message.

From: Coreytheranger@ImpodimoLodge.net
To: Tessa.Williams2@bmail.com

Date: Thursday, August 9, 2007

Subject: Hi

Hallo, pragtige dame,

Thinking of you and wanted to say hi. I'm off this weekend. Perhaps we could meet up?

Regards,
Corey

Before I can change my mind, I press Send, swallowing down a mouthful of bile.

Somehow, I'm not a hardened rock anymore.

So what the fuck happens to me now?

11

TESSA

I shut my bedroom door, letting the weight of my exhausted body sink into the mattress. It's Friday afternoon, and I've just gotten back from an overnight shift at Princess Victoria Hospital.

My first week there was depleting, ripe with profound human suffering, the pressure of it all about to rip my flimsy seams apart. I need my lifelong anchor to stabilize me, to remind me why I chose this path in the first place. I use Skype on my computer to dial my dad. It's six hours earlier in Philadelphia, and I'm hoping to catch him before he leaves for work.

He answers on the third ring. "Williams' residence. Who's calling?" His painfully formal greeting instantly makes me smile.

"Hi, Dad. It's me."

"Tess, sweetheart. Terrific to hear from you. How are things?"

I pause, taking a deep breath. "It's hard here, Dad. I'm pretty overwhelmed. The resources in the hospital are limited, and there is so much sickness. I saw two patients die this week. One from rabies and one from pneumonia… and I'm struggling. I know seeing people die is a part of medicine, but I hadn't had to do that yet…" I want to appear strong, but my voice buckles like a dandelion in the wind.

I'm too weak to handle it, I want to shout.

But I can't.

For years, my entire persona around my dad has been a carefully crafted performance. I'm terrified of pulling the curtains open. Petrified of disappointing him by unveiling that the girl he believes to be brave and driven is actually a pathetic, insecure phony.

"I'm sorry, sweetheart. I remember the first few patients I saw die, too. It really shook me. Reminds you of your own mortality. There are parts of medicine that are so hard, but there are great moments, too. They make those other moments worth it. You were made for this. You're going to be an extraordinary physician. You'll figure it out. Just give it more time."

That has long been my plan. Give it more time.

But how much more time will it take until I enjoy it?

What if the answer is never?

I gulp down hard, not wanting to consider this possibility.

"One sec, Tess, your mother's getting out of the shower. She'll want to talk to you, too." I hear him put the receiver down, his footsteps receding, as he goes to find Mom.

As I wait, my mind wanders, memories of my childhood unspooling in thick chunks.

Time rewinds until I'm living it again in high speed.

***

I'm six, sitting cross-legged in my bedroom, coloring, the day Dad comes home, a smile saddled to his face. He's been appointed the Chair of Cardiology, the youngest physician in department history. Without being asked, Mom resigns her position as a consultant at McKinsey to focus on raising me, allowing Dad to fulfill his dreams.

I'm seven, wide-eyed at the dinner table, scarfing down mac and cheese. Mom and Dad gaze lovingly at each other, munching on barbequed salmon, jersey corn, and Caprese salad. Dad sips a glass of wine, recounting a nightly story about his patients, this one about a fifty-year-old man with cardiac amyloidosis.

"How was his echocardiogram?" I ask.

Dad's eyes ignite with a fiery pride that I know such terminology. "You blow me away! Such a natural at medicine!"

His compliment coils a honeyed feeling that twirls through my body, sticking to my insides.

I'm nine, swimming my first meet. The stands are filled with cheering parents, including Mom. But not Dad. He's at the hospital, but I'm not upset. Heroism comes at a cost, and that cost is time with me. In my mind, I've already placed him on an untouchable pedestal, thousands of feet up in the sky.

I'm eleven and bring home my sixth-grade report card: straight A's. Mom hugs me, beaming. Dad looks it over, remarking, "Why aren't these A-pluses?" He's kidding, but he's not. He has exceptionally high standards for himself, and for me, too.

I resolve to do better.

To be perfect.

I'm thirteen, a chunky teen raging with hormones, slamming every door in the house, hurling insults at Mom. She's my outlet. Dad's gone, but I would never scream at him, anyway. I adore him. I retreat to my room, in a boiling fury, to keep writing my fictional stories. Writing is my chosen escape from the real world. In my imaginary worlds, I let myself get happily lost.

I'm fourteen, standing in front of the mirror, pinching pockets of fat that trail along my hips and belly. I'm disgusted by my body, which growls with hunger.

I vow to become thinner.

To be good enough for Robby Marzone.

Good enough for Dad.

Good enough for myself.

I'm sixteen, tagging along one Saturday morning while Dad rounds at the hospital. In his office, he hands me a spare white coat. I watch his eyes burst as I slip the jacket over my too-thin frame. I follow him along the hospital hallways, residents and fellows trailing us, in complete awe of him, hanging on his every word. This is the first moment I realize the power of his career. Of *him*. He's a hero to everyone in this place. I feel a stunning honor to be his daughter.

"Tess, one day, you're going to make a fantastic doctor, too," he tells me on the car ride home, a grin glued to his face.

I want to keep it there forever.

I'm twenty, a sophomore at Cornell, home for winter break. Timidly, I squeak out that I'm thinking of majoring in creative writing. A professor at school has taken a keen interest in my work, expressing I have real talent.

Mom squeezes me, elated.

But Dad is devastated. My choice crushes his long-held dream. "What about medicine, Tess? You're so good at it. Don't waste your talent. You can write anytime! You can't always be a doctor. You should go to medical school."

His scowl guts my insides, peppering them on the living room floor.

I stare at him, engulfed by that lifelong tug-of-war—a battle between his desires for me and my own dreams.

And I realize in that moment: there was never truly any choice.

I let the metaphorical rope slip from my hands, chafing my fingers, surrendering the war before the match has even begun. Deep in my heart, I've always known I would walk this path. For *him*.

"You're right, Dad. I'll major in biology instead."

"Excellent," he replies, his euphoria briefly washing away my doubts, my fate of becoming a doctor all but sealed.

***

Mom comes to the phone. "Hi, Tess. We miss you so much. How's everything there?" The tenderness in her words slice up my memories of the past. All that remains is my desire to be the perfect daughter for my hero.

"Hi, Mom… I was just telling Dad there have been some really hard parts. This week, I saw two patients die. The patients are a lot sicker than I was expecting. I guess I was naïve in my thinking."

"I'm sorry, sweetie. I can imagine that you're feeling overwhelmed. I wish I could hug you," Mom says.

"Thanks, Mom, you're the best." No matter how old I get, the comfort my mom provides never ages.

"How are things otherwise?" she asks.

"I really like Botswana. The sense of community here is so strong," I say. "We haven't had much free time, but we went out to two dinners in Gaborone. And the safari was beautiful, too. It was amazing to be in the wild with the animals, especially the elephants. You guys should come here sometime."

"Yes, we'd love to," Mom says. "Too bad I can never convince your father to take time off from work." Through the phone, I imagine the look Mom shoots Dad. "Have you heard from Greg at all?"

"A few emails, but we haven't talked. It's better this way," I say, a wave of shame washing over me.

Why did I fall in love with such a beast?

Corey's words blast into my brain.

Is it because I don't respect myself?

"It's good to be single," Dad replies. "You're young. You have your whole life ahead of you. Focus on your training."

"Okay, Dad," I respond meekly.

"You should appreciate what an amazing learning opportunity this is," he says. "Most medical students would kill to be in your shoes."

And I'd kill to be in anyone else's shoes.

I twist a strand of hair around my index finger, letting it unravel, mimicking how I feel inside. "Anyway, what's new at home?" I ask, suddenly desperate to talk about anything other than my own messy existence.

***

Fifteen minutes later, when we hang up, I still feel entirely unsure of myself but I'm grateful for my parents' love. I open my email, finding another one from Greg.

From: Greg.Winters1982@bmail.com
To: Tessa.Williams2@bmail.com

Date: Friday, August 10, 2007

Subject: ????

Tessa,

Please. You haven't responded in over a week. Are you ever going to speak to me again? I'm dying over here, wanting to hear from you. I'm sorry about everything. Please. I'll do anything. I'll go to counseling, do whatever you need to feel safe again. Just forgive me. Forgive me. I can't stand this. I love you. I hate myself. I'm sorry.

Greg

Disgusted, I close his email, about to shut the program, when I spot a message from Corey.

He wants to meet up?

Giddy elation snakes from my forehead to my toes, a sprawling grin coating my face.

My life is filled with a multitude of shoulds. You should go to medical school. You should stay thin. You should enjoy this experience. You should, you should, you should.

There is no space for my wants. That tug of freedom from Impodimo Lodge still lingers.

Here, continents away from my dad, in tiny slivers, my own voice is starting to break through.

I *want* to see Corey.

I push away all the shoulds and reach for my phone to text him.

12

COREY

I set down my fork, sliding out my chair, my plate of spaghetti carbonara wiped clean.

"Thanks for a great lunch," I say to my guests, who are still seated around the patio table. "Relax for a bit. I'll meet you at 16:00 for the game ride."

They nod their goodbyes, and I'm halfway to the main lounge when my phone vibrates. It's a text from an unknown number.

Tessa: Hi. It's Tessa. I got your email. I just
finished at the hospital until Monday. What'd you
have in mind?

Tessa?

Fuck.

I'd blocked out the memory of my drunken email—and yet, if the thrumming in my chest is any indication, my body wants to see her.

A lot.

Me: I hadn't really gotten very far in planning.
Give me a few minutes to come up with something.

I pace around the lodge, racking my brain for ideas. I have one, but it's over the top, fucking ridiculous, actually. It'd be appropriate if we'd been dating for months—or years—but we've only spent one single weekend together.

But… what would it mean… to live again?
Ahh… fuck it.

Me: Are u up for a weekend adventure? Not trying to be presumptuous, but I have to top our last date, which you did say was one of the best of your life.

Tessa: That's true :-) What are you thinking?

Me: I'll take care of the details, and yes, before you ask, it'll be safe. Just send me your birthday.

Tessa: Why do you need my birthday :-)??

Several minutes later, after I provide no further details…

Tessa: Okay. Fine :-) 2/14/1982

Me: You're a Valentine's baby? Somehow, that makes sense. And it's a surprise.

Tessa: Ha, what's that supposed to mean? And
always so mysterious, with the surprises.

Tessa: The fucking surprises, I mean :-)

Me: Pack an overnight bag and bring your
passport. Send me your address. I'll pick you
up at 8 tomorrow morning. I'll have you back by
Sunday night.

***

I park outside Tessa's flat at 7:47 a.m. I shift in my seat, fidgeting my keys, the noisy jangling matching my chaotic thoughts.

What the fuck am I doing?

It's a mistake to be here. I'm one hundred percent certain of that.

Being with Tessa will only end badly.

And yet, here I am, anyway, like a damn idiot.

A bag of fucking feelings out in the cruel world.

It's painfully distressing not being numb.

***

Sixteen minutes later, the door to Tessa's flat swings open. She's wearing a sundress, topped with a grey sweater and black ankle boots. The yellow dress clings to her petite frame, making her tanned legs glow, and instantly, I'm tempted to peel the damn dress right off her. She wears no makeup, but her nude lips shine, the morning sun weaving through her honey-streaked half-ponytail.

The metal gates part open, and I jump out of the car.

"*Hallo, pragtige dame*, it's good to see you again. You look beautiful." A fondness bubbles inside me, being back in her proximity.

"Hi, Corey, it's good to see you, too." Her voice is airy, her dimple out.

I pull her into a quick hug, my fingers brushing her lemony hair. That undercurrent draws me towards her, but I resist it, opening her door instead and throwing her bag in the trunk.

I climb into the car.

Tessa has barely buckled her seat belt before starting with a litany of questions. "So… are you going to tell me where we're going? I didn't know what to tell Liz. What if something happens to us? How would she know? How would word get back to my parents?" She stares at me, her pupils wide, her brow creased.

I smirk.

That worry again.

I fight the urge to stroke her rosy cheek. "Like I said, it's a surprise, but you'll see soon enough, and then you can message Liz so she knows where you are."

"Okay, fair enough." She slowly lowers her eyebrows—apparently appeased—for the moment. "I have a hard time not being in control."

I laugh a little, feigning surprise. "Really? I wouldn't have guessed. You're really good at playing it cool."

She swats my arm. "How'd you get to be so *fucking* funny?"

Her fingers on my arm feel outrageously good.

"So, how was your first week at the hospital?" I ask as we travel outside of Gaborone, traffic virtually non-existent this early on a Saturday morning.

"Ugh, pretty tough." Tessa sighs, her shoulders sinking like a water-logged ship. Again, I want to do something—anything—to lighten the load she carries. Tessa aimlessly picks at a cuticle on her thumb. "I'm not sure what I was expecting, but the patients are really sick. I saw two people die. I just feel helpless and useless. I'm having a hard time coping with death. Even though doctors are supposed to be good at handling death…"

"I'm not sure anyone's good at handling death," I say. "Maybe doctors just learn to hide their true feelings better than the rest of us?"

Tess chews on her lower lip, frowning. "Yeah, maybe that's what they do? I'm not sure how to master that skill, though."

"For what it's worth, I have no idea how to master that skill either. But I'm sorry… your week sounds brutal. You're so brave." Briefly, I glance away from the road into her russet eyes, soaked with worry.

"I'm not brave, trust me," Tessa insists, shaking her head. "I have no idea what I'm doing. Most of the time…" Her voice trails off, and suddenly she's lost in herself.

"Most of the time, what…?"

Her thigh jerks rhythmically, and I consider resting my hand on her leg to soothe her. She stays quiet, contemplating if she wants to finish the sentence. At first, it seems she does, but then she changes her mind. "Oh… you know what? Never mind. Let's talk about something happier. Tell me about your week. I'm still so insanely jealous of your job. I missed everything about Impodimo Lodge all week long."

She missed everything?

This notion causes my heart to dash out of the open car window.

"Even me?" I ask, wildly self-conscious.

"Yes, especially you," she mumbles, staring directly at me.

Fuck.

I open the window further, trying to dissipate the rising heat in the vehicle.

I finally give into my urge, reaching across the seat, entwining our hands, electricity barreling towards my heart.

Tessa doesn't look over. She uses her free hand to turn on the radio. "I need to learn the good stations here," she says, landing on Radio Botswana 2.

A contemporary DJ mash-up spills from the speakers.

She bobs her head a little, dancing in her seat.

"You're a cute dancer," I mumble, magnetized to her energy, her warmth.

Fuck.

What's gotten into me?

We drive along a two-lane road surrounded by brush. As we pass, a bell clangs, strung around the neck of a wandering cow. A flash of recognition crosses Tessa's face. "Wait… Corey, are we driving towards the airport?"

"Maybe," I admit, my heartbeat creeping up the back of my throat.

I'm suddenly terrified she'll think this whole trip is way too much.

What the fuck am I doing?

I'm without a compass, totally off course.

"Wow, okay," she mumbles, her forehead crinkling.

I'm such an idiot for planning this.

"I'm sorry, I didn't mean to overstep any bounds—" I start.

"No, it's not that. I just… I didn't bring my Ativan. I usually take it when I fly. I'm a terrible flier." Her lips tug upward. "I apologize in advance for whatever panicked behavior you're about to witness."

Why do I find her anxiety so damn appealing?

"Don't worry, Tess," I say. "I'll be there. I'll help you stay calm."

I squeeze her hand, her skin as silky soft as I remembered.

And in that moment, it's true.

It makes zero fucking sense.

But…

I want to protect her with everything I have.

Fuck.

13

TESSA

To me, everything about flying feels wrong—unnatural and dangerous. I live life by playing it safe, and nothing feels less safe than soaring thirty thousand feet above the ground in a giant metal vessel, aviated by a total stranger. Flying doesn't just rattle me, it triggers the generalized anxiety, which on a normal day, I hold precariously at bay.

"Hey, you okay?" Corey asks, seated beside me.

Our plane to Kasane shudders slightly, the engines humming louder, readying for departure.

Clenching my fists, nails biting into my palms, I'm trying to avoid ruminating on my mortality.

I am not moments from death.

I am not moments from death.

I am not moments from death.

His brawny arm scoops behind my shoulder. His grassy, vanilla musk settles into my nostrils, bringing a fleeting wave of comfort.

"Eh, not really," I admit. "I have a routine. I'm pretty superstitious when it comes to flying."

"Oh yeah?" His eyebrows pique with interest. In the row ahead, a baby starts to wail.

"Yeah," I mumble, my chin drooping. It feels incredibly vulnerable to reveal this part of myself, so soon, especially since Greg was always cruel about my fear of flying. He'd pretend to fall asleep during takeoff to avoid consoling me, leaving me alone to spiral deeper into fear.

Corey massages my neck. "Do you think Jennifer Aniston likes to fly?"

Despite myself, I smile. "You're so *fucking* funny."

"I try hard, just for you." His blue beacons peer at me, my overpowering anxiety briefly displaced by relief that he's next to me.

"So, are you going to tell me where we're going once we land in Kasane?" I ask.

"Not yet. You'll see soon enough." He gives me a dashing smirk that blasts like a rocket ship through my rumbling abdomen.

The plane hurdles down the runway, gathering speed, the thunder of the wheels matching the rhythm of my hammering heart. My hands shake as the cabin tilts and shifts, the weight of gravity pressing down harder than it should. I squeeze my eyes shut, slam my hands over my ears and start counting backwards from 214.

Because of my birthday, my mom always insists that 214 is my lucky number. I stumbled upon this odd counting routine once during a panicked takeoff, home from spring break in Miami. The plane didn't crash that time, so *obviously* it was because of my counting. So logically, I've counted on every flight since.

I'm at 176 when Corey says, "It's okay, Tess. We're off the ground. If you open your eyes, the view is pretty damn spectacular." His hand trails along my back, making a figure eight, causing my skin to prickle.

I shake my head, imagining the plane hurtling back towards the ground, my body splattering apart on impact. Despite years of cognitive restructuring therapy, I always fixate on the image of my dead body, split into a million broken shards, strewn against the earth.

My breath quickens.

Keep counting, Tess.

Keep counting.

Shit, I need my Ativan.

"Tess, it's okay. You're safe." Corey's voice breaks through, soft and gentle. "Keep breathing." His foot reassuringly brushes against my ankle.

Keep counting.

I'm at eighty-seven…

Sixty-five…

Thirty-four…

"I think we're at cruising altitude," Corey says.

Thirteen…

Zero.

I peel my eyes open to see the piercing blue sky zipping by the window.

Breathe, Tess, breathe.

I sit entirely still, muscles locked, letting air seep back into my shaky lungs.

"Thank you for helping me," I whisper finally.

He stares at me with such tenderness that it feels like a fuzzy blanket is being wrapped around my heart. There's no judgment, only patience, and it stirs a flicker of hope. His kindness says a lot about him. But I'm still scared to trust my instincts. They were so misguided with Greg.

"Of course," he says. "Want to hear about my game rides from this week?"

"Yeah, that sounds perfect, actually." My shoulders unclench as the plane glides through the air. I let my head settle against his chest. His stubbly chin tucks on top of my hair.

Keeping one arm looped around my shoulder, he tells me the story of tracking two lions on foot with Darian. In the safety of his embrace, I exhale. His voice is husky and comforting, lulling me into a trance-like state…

***

Corey gently shakes me. "Wake up, sleepy head, we're going to land."

I blink my eyes open. "Shit, did I fall asleep?" I lift my head, embarrassed to find his Pearl Jam shirt soaked from a puddle of my drool.

It's the only time in my life I've ever fallen asleep on an airplane without the aid of copious alcohol and/or pills.

"You slept for about an hour, but it's okay. You look pretty cute sleeping. I just didn't think my stories were *that* boring." His lips twist up into a grin as he pulls me back into his arms. My ear lands on the wet spot created by my slobber.

"They're not boring. I love them, I promise." I drape my arm across his chest, nuzzling closer, listening to his heartbeat.

Thump, thump, thump.

"Ladies and gentlemen," the pilot says over the loudspeaker, "we're going to circle for a few minutes. Wild boars are crowding the runway."

Corey and several other passengers laugh. But not me. Nothing about flying is funny to me. A current of anxiety rips through me. "Ugh. Circling makes me so scared."

"It's okay, Tess. It's not dangerous. It's perfectly safe." His tone isn't patronizing, like Greg, but disarmingly kind. He uses his free hand to cover my eyes, holding me close to his skin, creating a cocoon. "Want to hear about my craziest guest ever?"

"Yes," I whisper into his damp shirt.

We stay like that—him holding me, telling me stories—until the wheels touch down.

As soon as we land, I once again have a new lease of life.

That's the crazy thing about flying.

It terrifies the shit out of me.

But every time I survive a flight, I am—at least, for a few moments— fiercely grateful for even the most mundane parts of living.

***

Corey grabs our bags, then heads to retrieve the rental car. I wait for him in a seat by the airport exit. All around me, travelers whirl past in a dizzying scramble. That's one thing I've never understood. Why is it a universal practice, even in an airport, to live life at such a frenetic pace? What is everyone rushing to?

That familiar clamp around my throat returns—all the expectations and pressures still await. This weekend is merely a distraction. The real world's expecting me back.

Corey returns, his toothy grin out, shooting me a goofy expression. He waves the car keys in front of his face, his shirt clinging to his frame, accentuating his adorable tummy.

At the car, he loads our bags into the trunk, then holds my door open, hand resting on the handle. I note his impeccable manners. The gesture is small, but it knocks me sideways. Greg never did things like this—doors were more likely to be slammed in my face than opened for me.

Corey climbs into the driver's seat, his blond hair gumming to his forehead from the morning heat. He starts the car, giving me a sidelong glance as I buckle up.

"So, are you *finally* going to tell me where we're going?" I ask, curiosity dyeing my tone.

"Hmm, I don't know. Maybe I should make you wait…" His savage wink is back.

"Corey, please. You have to indulge my inner control freak a little." I curl my bottom lip into a fake frown.

"Okay, but only because your pout is really cute." He smiles. "We're going to the Chobe River Lodge. My friend Alice works there and helped arrange everything. We're heading on a sunset river cruise later today."

"Wow, that's amazing!" I squeal. "I'm so excited!" I can't remember the last time I felt so genuinely happy.

"Yeah, you'll love the Chobe River. It's home to thousands of elephants, and tomorrow, I thought we'd drive an hour or so east into Zambia so I can show you Victoria Falls. If you are up for it… that is." Corey squints.

He seems timid, that maybe I'll think it's too much for two people who barely know each other.

And maybe with someone else, that would be true.

But with him, somehow, it feels right.

"Corey, seriously, that sounds like an actual freaking dream. Seeing Victoria Falls is on my bucket list, but I didn't think I'd go there, especially not now. I can't believe you planned all this. I'm so touched." Emotion bleeds from my voice as I grab his hand. That sparky sensation follows, the air between us crackling.

Who is this magical man next to me?

"I want to ask you something," he says, his cheekbones indenting beneath a yellowy blaze of sunlight. "I booked one room for tonight, but I wasn't sure if you're comfortable with that. If not, I'm happy to add a second room to our reservation. I just want you to feel comfortable."

His words knock the air out of me—again—not because of what he's asking but because of the sheer consideration behind it. Another thing Greg never paid attention to—my comfort. It's hard not to compare them, the stark differences stacking up. But a small voice in the back of my mind whispers. *What if, somehow, underneath it all, Corey turns out to be just like Greg?*

Hoping to keep things light, half-jokingly, I say, "It's very considerate of you to ask. And I guess that depends… are you planning on rejecting my advances again tonight?"

Corey grimaces, his eyes crinkling. "Tess, I was seriously trying to be a good guy, following the manners my mum taught me. I didn't think you'd give me such a hard time about it… anyway, before you decide, I got you something else." He reaches into his back pocket, handing me a twice-folded piece of paper.

"I open it and see lab results. "What's this?"

"Keep reading."

I look more closely, words jutting out.

HIV 1,2 Screening Test: NONREACTIVE.

"Wait, you got an HIV test?" I ask, floored, my insides dissolving like a piece of chocolate abandoned under the scorching sun.

"Yeah, you seemed so worried. I want you to feel safe." The warmth in his voice sucks my breath away.

"Wow. Thank you, Corey," I murmur. "That's honestly the most thoughtful gift anyone's ever given me." I lean over and kiss his lips. "And to answer your question… I'd love to share a room with you."

14

COREY

Tessa grabs my hand as we stroll across the grassy field towards the motorboat docked outside our lodge. The afternoon sun hangs high, the air packed with thick humidity and no breeze. Tessa's skin shimmers beneath the heavy-duty sunscreen she insisted we both apply. "Corey, skin cancer is no laughing matter," she said up in our room, with a deadly serious expression, rubbing SPF 50 into every centimeter of her exposed skin.

I didn't have time yet to rip off her yellow dress, and it still slinks dangerously against her curves.

We're queuing to board when I spot Alice, a mass of curly red hair and sea-green eyes. I consider what, if anything, to tell Tessa about her.

This is my ex-girlfriend?

My friend with benefits?

A woman who wanted me to love her, but I couldn't?

Because I haven't been able to feel anything inside for years?

"Corey! Mate! It's good to see you. It's been too long." Alice ambushes me, holding me tightly, forcing me to drop Tessa's hand. The smell of her overpowering perfume charges up my nostrils.

I haven't seen Alice in over a year—not since she grew tired of my "emotional" distance and left to work at Chobe Lodge. We'd been guides together back then, at Impodimo Lodge, and our relationship was romantic, although lopsided. She said she was in love with me and wanted me to be her proper boyfriend, but I couldn't be that guy. Instead, it was mostly just sex between us and not the passionate kind. The lonely kind. The kind where even when I was inside her, I wished I was somewhere else.

"Hi, Alice! Thanks again for setting this up. This place is awesome." My words get buried in her giant curls as she keeps a firm hold of me, my awkwardness increasing as the seconds tick by.

I pat her back, hyper-aware of Tessa standing behind me.

Alice releases me, her eyes scanning Tessa's body like a cougar assessing its prey. "Oh. You must be Tessa. Corey told me a *lot* about you."

I cringe.

No, I didn't.

And what the hell?

I thought we were friends now?

I eye Phillip, the forty-something boat captain and Alice's new boyfriend, who is checking the engine logs, paying zero attention to our exchange.

"Oh, he did?" Tessa asks, eyebrows raised, sneaking a wondering glance at me.

Fuck.

I squeeze her palm in rhythmic pulsations, hoping to communicate… what exactly? Reassurance? An apology?

"Yes, but no need to worry," Alice replies with a laugh that falls superbly flat. "Only good things. It's just… so unusual to see Corey actually *interested* in a woman. When he said he was bringing you here, I almost fell out of my chair. But it's great. So great! I'm really, really happy for him. Extremely happy."

Fuck.

"Okay… well… great?" Tessa says, searching for words and seeming to settle on those.

"Anyway, I'll catch up with you more later, Core," Alice whispers in my ear, her lilac perfume pasting against my neck. Her fingernails skim my bicep, making my arm jerk back.

Another guest grabs Alice's attention as I hurriedly lead Tessa to two seats near the bow.

"So, she's your, um… friend?" Tessa asks once we're out of earshot from Alice.

Fuck.

"Yes."

It's the truth—but not the whole truth. I know she can sense that.

Tessa gazes at me, her eyes tunneling a blistering heat through my center, burning a hole into my stomach.

A bead of sweat trickles down my forehead. I wipe it away. "Is it hot out here, or is it just me?"

I squirm in my chair, using my hand to fan my face.

She keeps staring.

"Well, we briefly dated," I clarify. "But it didn't work out. She's dating the boat captain now." I point to Phillip, who's still studying the logs.

"What happened between you two?" Tessa's tone is curious, her dimple loose, her face relaxed.

Why do I wish she was more jealous?

Fuck.

"Well, nothing really. There just wasn't any spark." *Not like the damn insane one with you.* "Alice wanted a relationship, but I didn't. She said she was in love with me, but I didn't feel anything for her. So, she left to come work here, and that was it."

Tessa scowls a little. "You didn't feel *anything* for her?"

Maybe she's worried this reveals something sinister about my character, or lack thereof. It's not exactly a selling point to be a hardened, emotionless rock.

"No, not really," I admit, realizing this sounds crass—but it's also the truth.

"Okay, well… it doesn't seem like Alice is quite over things, so we should probably be sensitive about that around her." Tessa stretches her legs against the metal railing, her empathy surprising me. "And don't worry, Corey. I mean, I broke up with my boyfriend the day before I came here, so I don't have any room to talk."

Wait, what!

This news makes my stomach shove up through my throat. It's like I've just been socked in the gut. Apparently, *I* am the jealous type. In spite of myself, I want to know more about her damn boyfriend. She isn't mine, but I don't like the thought of her with someone else.

"Oh, you had a boyfriend?" I hope my voice is breezy. I pull my sunglasses down to hide the steam boiling off my eyes.

Tessa studies the undulating water. "Yeah, Greg. But let's not talk about him."

Greg?

Greg!

Before I can ask more, Alice's voice blares over the loudspeaker. "Everyone ready for a fantastic ride today? Let me start by telling you about the Chobe River…"

***

The boat drifts lazily along the riverbank, the air thick with the golden hues of the approaching sunset. Alice moves among the passengers, handing out cocktails, lingering over my hand too long while shooting Tessa a death stare. I pretend not to notice, reviewing my camera instead. I smile at an image of a crocodile sunbathing on the shoreline, its jaw splayed open, as a hippo breaches the water.

"Get any good ones?" Tessa asks, sipping her white wine. I look up at her, noticing that those golden specs in her eyes are frolicking madly beneath the fountain of light.

Damn, she's beautiful.

"Yeah, check this one out." I turn my camera to face her.

"You're really talented," she says, studying the image, reclining against her seat, her demeanor entirely relaxed. Around the animals, her spirit is lighter, that hurt part of her soul momentarily receding. I recognize the process intimately—because the same thing happens inside me, too.

"Thanks. It's just a hobby, but sometimes Joe indulges me and puts my pictures on the Impodimo Lodge website." I set the camera down, cupping my wine. "So, are you enjoying this?"

"Yeah, being in nature is just… amazing. And the elephants. I can't believe how many we've seen! I keep falling more and more in love with them." Her voice gushes with gusto but then softens. "Every time I'm out in the wilderness like this, the idea of my real life becomes harder and harder."

Her *real* life.

The one eleven thousand kilometers away, across an ocean, on another continent.

Fuck.

What the hell am I doing out here with her?

I gulp my wine.

Across the river, there's a tiny islet covered by brush and fractured tree limbs. The sun has started to drop, streaking the sky with violet, cherry and ginger. Birds cluster on the tree branches, their silhouettes black from the dimming light.

"See that one, there?" I ask, handing Tessa my binoculars, pointing to a bird with every patch of color along its body—blue wings, purple neck, green-and-white head, pink-and-red face, black eyes. "That's a lilac-breasted roller, but I call it the rainbow bird. It's supposed to bring good luck."

"Is there anything about animals you don't know?" Her voice tinges with awe as she peers through the binoculars. "Wow! My dad would love it here. Bird watching is his 'unofficial' hobby because he says he's too busy to have any actual hobbies."

I smile. "Well, maybe you can bring him back here sometime?"

Tessa crinkles her nose, seemingly wistful. "Yeah, maybe. If anyone can ever convince him to take a vacation."

"I take it he works a lot?" My gaze peels from Tessa to a herd of elephants in the distance, spraying water over their backs in the shallows.

"Yeah, basically, all the time. He's a cardiologist. He loves his work, though." She takes another sip of her wine. "Actually, the only person I've ever seen rival my dad's passion for his job is, well… *you*."

"Thanks, I think?" My gaze flickers back to her, my cheeks warming at what I hope is a compliment. "So… is your dad the reason you're becoming a doctor?"

It's an innocent question, but Tessa glowers at me with such intensity that the weight of her glare unveils a landmine buried inside.

Her body tenses as the color drains from her face. "Sort of… it's complicated." A small tear pools in her left eye as she clears her throat. "But it's too beautiful out here… to talk about why… I'm becoming a doctor…"

My desire to peel away her layers grows more intense.

What is she hiding?

But her desperation to avoid the topic makes me bite my tongue.

"Absolutely, let's enjoy the sunset," I say.

I finish my wine, the glass cool against my fingertips, and glance around. Alice is studying me; Tessa is studying the swirling water, completely lost in thought.

The last of the sun descends behind the horizon, surrendering to darkness.

The view is fucking incredible.

I consider shaking Tessa back to share it with me.

Instead, I snap a photo.

Of Tessa, her features muted by shadows.

Gazing out at the Chobe River.

Lost in herself.

As the sun slips away.

And somehow, it feels like the best shot I've taken all day.

15

TESSA

Corey fumbles with the key, trying unsuccessfully to open our hotel room door.

"Are you drunk?" I giggle, feigning surprise.

We've just finished dinner in the lodge, having overindulged in food (a little) and wine (a lot). And aside from one awkward encounter with Alice, the whole evening has been pretty darn perfect.

"Maybe," he admits, offering a wicked grin, the door finally opening. He swiftly pulls me inside, thrusting my body against it. The velocity of his actions surprises me.

And thrills me.

His weight pushes down on me, his lips trailing hot, hungry kisses up my neck. His hands grip my waist, his wrists enveloping my hip bones. There's a strange safety in being tucked beneath him.

"I'm so glad to finally be alone with you," he murmurs, his boozy breath landing on my collarbone. "I've wanted to peel this damn yellow dress off you all day long."

In his drunken state, his language is loose and uninhibited. His raw desire for me is a turn-on, driving me slightly mad. "I like hearing you talk like that," I say.

His lips move purposefully, climbing my jaw, parting my lips. His weight shifts, grinding hard against my pelvis, with just enough pressure to set every nerve alight. He picks me up, still kissing me, and carries me to the bed. There, he slips off my dress, dropping it onto the carpet.

"Thank god that thing is off," he rasps. "It was driving me fucking crazy."

I blush, lying there in just my underwear, as Corey steps back, his gaze roaming over me.

My arms twitch, wanting to cover myself. I suck in the loose skin covering my stomach. I haven't been able to exercise since coming to Botswana, and it's painfully obvious.

He's still not saying anything, and the silence amplifies every insecurity. I resist the urge to grab my discarded dress off the floor.

Slivers of light creep through the window, illuminating his face. "You're so *fucking* beautiful," he whispers.

I shiver, wishing for even one second of one day I could see my body the way he does.

He straddles me, the mattress dipping slightly, and lifts his shirt off, his toned chest and tummy pudge on full display. I resist an urge to bite into his belly.

He pushes my head against the pillow, kissing his way down my stomach, reaching my underwear. He slips them off, inching his head closer to the crease of my thighs. My body tenses like a bowstring as his head dips lower.

"Wait, Corey?" I tug at his shoulders, pulling his mouth back towards me.

The idea of him, down *there*, makes me squeamish. Greg hated giving oral sex, so it's been years since anyone went down on me. And in the past, I haven't enjoyed it, feeling entirely too self-conscious.

"Tess, please. I want to show you how much I respect you." It's part-snarl, part-command.

"Corey, don't. It's gross." I hope the darkness hides my embarrassment.

"It's not gross, Tess. I like it." He peers at me, begging for permission.

"You seriously want to?" I ask, wildly dubious.

"I do."

"Really?"

"Yes, Tess. Really."

"Are you sure?"

"Yes." He grits his teeth, his determination, somehow, *hot*.

I sigh, feeling vulnerable and a little excited. "Well… okay. Yes."

"Thank you." He winks, and then his face is between my thighs, his hands wrapped snuggly around my waist.

I try to quiet my mind, but as usual, my brain is busier than Times Square on New Year's Eve.

What if I taste disgusting?

Oh god.

My face scalds with humiliation, the thought threatening to yank me out of the moment entirely.

As if reading my thoughts, Corey murmurs against my skin, "You taste amazing."

He devours me like I'm his favorite chocolate cake.

My eyes drift shut as I struggle to free myself from my lifelong nemesis: my brain.

Tess, get out of your head!

Corey varies the pressure and intensity, and for the first time, I realize—it feels good.

Really good.

I squirm beneath him, trying to resist the growing pleasure. But his hands tug at my hips, pulling me back. My fingernails rake against his shoulders, grabbing on to steady myself. He pauses, lifts his head and shoots me a devilish smirk.

He likes this.

He likes doing this to me.

This thought is terrifying.

And electrifying.

A surge of confidence floods through me. Quieting the self-doubt. I finally abandon my worries, letting him take charge. He licks harder, with so much fury, that I start to break apart. To come undone. I'm a zipper, and he's furiously yanking me down. And then, as the tremors shoot through me, for one brief moment, my mind goes totally blank.

No fears.

No doubts.

Just this.

Just *him.*

16

COREY

Her muscular pulsations ripple beneath my tongue, her body responding in a way that sends a primal growl through mine. I can't remember the last time I wanted someone so badly. It takes all my willpower not to push myself into her right here.

Damn chivalry.

Instead, I pull away, dragging my head onto the pillow next to her. I slide an arm beneath the blanket, wrapping her into my chest, cradling her as her breath still comes unevenly.

"Corey, wow, that was intense." Her tone is throaty, her words raising my chest hairs.

Then she inches the covers up, burrowing like a gopher.

My smile flattens when she goes into hiding. "I'm confused, Tess. That's a bad thing?"

"No, it felt amazing… I just feel… super exposed. I'm sorry… I'm not used to something sexual… being all about me."

I can only see her crinkled forehead. "Tess…" I peel down the blanket, stroking her cheekbone, trying to erase whatever shame she's battling. "I liked making you feel like that. Don't be embarrassed. It's a turn-on."

"Are you sure?" She gazes at me with wide, disbelieving eyes.

How does someone this incredible not see herself for what she is?

"Yeah! It makes me happy, pleasing you." I cup her face, find her lips, kiss her slow, hoping she feels a fraction of what I'm trying to say.

She pulls back. "Okay, but now it's your turn."

Fuck.

Yes.

I want that, a dangerous amount—but her offer stirs something else inside me. Why does she feel she instantly owes me something?

And beyond that… I'm grievously worried about losing control of myself entirely if we have sex. I'm already so far outside of my comfort zone, I couldn't find my way back if I tried.

"Soon, Tess, but it's okay to have your needs met without giving me anything in return."

Something inside me—for no reason I understand—wants to challenge her thinking.

To show her that her own needs are something to prioritize.

Tessa's pupils triple in size. "What are you, Corey? The freaking Mother Teresa of sex? Doling out amazing orgasms and expecting nothing in return?" Her voice carries a hint of humor, but the vulnerability beneath it is impossible to miss.

A chuckle spills from my mouth. "No, believe me, I want you, but you shouldn't feel you owe me something. You don't."

She scrunches her nose and lets out a slow sigh. "Is this another one of your sexual lessons in self-respect?" After she says it, a pent-up smile escapes her lips, her dimple cratering back into its rightful home.

Her smile is contagious, spreading to my own face. "Yes, lesson number one was: Don't feel pressured to sleep with people when you first meet them. Lesson number two is: Enjoy your own damn orgasms without guilt."

She laughs, the heartiness easing that stitch in my chest. "And what will lesson number three be?"

"Hmm," I say, rolling her body on top of mine. "I'll have to think about that. I'm sure I'll come up with something…"

She shakes her head, her hair falling across her face. "You're quite the teacher, Corey. I don't even know what to say…"

I brush a stray strand with my thumb. "Something tells me you didn't get the memo of how awesome you are, how much you deserve."

Her breath catches, the light in her eyes faltering as pain swims through them, her inner scars shoving outwards. I see it—the hurt, the doubt, the things she won't say aloud.

"Yeah, maybe you're right," she mutters, regret coating like thick mud to her words.

She lifts her head, tracing her fingernails along my left bicep, her eyes suddenly fixating on my tattoo.

Fuck.

"It's a lioness," I blurt before she can ask, my breath welding like steel to my throat.

Her fingers hover over the ink, eyes narrowing as she studies the words printed beneath the picture. "*Happily Ever After?*" she reads. "What does that mean? I didn't peg you as a big believer in fairy-tale endings."

I've been dreading this question since the moment I took off my damn shirt. I'm an idiot for having something so personal permanently inked into my skin. She waits for my answer. I wince, acutely over-exposed, withering beneath the bright spotlight of her wondering eyes.

I like Tessa.

A lot.

But I can't talk about Leona.

Not now.

Not ever.

Deep inside, that wound, messy and poorly stitched, threatens to rip apart. My stomach flips from a wave of grief.

Suddenly, I'm drowning in a sea of feelings, yearning only to be that goddamn hardened rock again.

"Corey? Are you okay?"

How can I admit the answer is no?

That I'll never be okay again?

Time stops while I try to make any words leave my mouth, every explanation too raw, too real.

"Corey?" Her eyebrows arch wide, the corners of her mouth creasing with concern.

"Sorry… can I tell you the story of my tattoo another time?" Even I hear the shaky, pleading quality in my tone.

The pause feels endless before she nods, her voice barely above a whisper. "Yeah, of course."

Tessa lays her head on my chest, wrapping her arms around me like a shield against the storm. Pieces of her citrusy hair tuck under my chin, the smell unspooling a temporary calm.

I let my hand find her back, rubbing slow, steady circles.

We stay like this for a long time, the room quiet, except for the chirping of crickets and the lapping of water down by the shore.

It's not silence.

It's something better.

When I go to talk again, she's sound asleep.

17

TESSA

"Get off me, Greg!" I scream, bolting up in bed. "No! Greg! No!" My forehead is covered in a gooey layer of sweat. My pulse hammers.

"Tess? I'm right here. It's just a dream."

Corey, *not* Greg, stares at me sleepily, his voice punctuating my distress. The clock reads 3:37.

I'm safe.

I'm in Botswana.

At the Chobe River Lodge.

I look down. I'm naked, except for my bra.

Shit.

Did I fall asleep?

The last thing I remember is Corey rubbing my back.

He strokes my forehead, his touch unwinding my thumping heart. "Are you okay?" His arms wrap around me, tucking my quivering lips against his chest.

The way he comforts me in that moment reminds me of my mom. Of the mother elephant and her baby. That same tender care. It feels special.

"Just a bad dream, I guess. I'm okay," I mumble.

It's a half-truth, at best.

More accurately, a lie.

"Good," he whispers.

I stay perfectly still, allowing our breaths to sync. A few minutes later, he trembles, drifting back to sleep.

But for me, sleep won't come. My brain buzzes worriedly to the messiness I left behind.

To the path of destruction caused by Hurricane Greg.

To the wreckage still smoldering within.

***

I met Greg three months after starting med school while out with Liz at Dirty Franks, a dive bar hosting a two-dollar shot night. We were playing a game of "Photo Hunt" when Greg swooped in, spotting the winning difference at the crucial last second. Liz cheered as his dusky brown eyes settled on me. He was tall and lean, dressed in jeans and a collared shirt, with curly brown hair, black glasses and an infectious grin.

"Can I buy you a victory shot?" he shouted over the blaring music, my ears buzzing.

"Sure, vodka. Thanks."

Two hours of flirting, four shots, and eight dollars later, I went home with him.

The next morning, I slipped out of his bed, readying to do the walk of shame in my skimpy dress and heels. But he surprised me, dressing in a suit and tie, offering to walk me home. We strolled hand in hand through the leaf-strewn streets of West Philadelphia, Greg playing Maroon 5's "Sunday Morning" on his phone.

When we reached my door, his hand still loosely holding mine, he said, "Tessa, I'd like to bring myself back home to you every Sunday morning."

It was as close to swooning as I'd ever come. From that moment on, Greg was my boyfriend.

On the outside, he checked every box for the type of guy I was "supposed" to date: well-educated, charming, funny, kind. The first year sailed by, him working on his PhD in economics, me busy with med school.

But even early on, there were cracks. Subtle, almost imperceptible at first—little red flags waving in the periphery.

But I wasn't looking.

Or maybe, I didn't want to see.

***

Everything changed one snowy Saturday in January, fourteen months after we first met. Greg had gone to his roommate's bachelor party, promising to sleep over after. At four a.m., I paced my room, phone in hand, without any word from him.

An hour later, the door creaked open. He stumbled in, his speech garbled, his shirt ripped, lipstick marks painted along his neck. At the sight of him, fear and insecurity unleashed inside me. "Where have you been?" I demanded. "I was worried."

"I knew you'd be mad and give me a hard time. I don't even know why I came," he slurred, falling into the wall, his eyes flopping around like loose marbles.

He didn't sound sorry. Not even close.

"What'd you expect, showing up here like this?" I spat.

He spun around, transformed into a Hulk-like figure, his face swathed with rage, the vein in his neck bulging. He punched me squarely in the left eye. The pain was instant and searing, but the shock hit me harder. It was so unexpected, so out-of-the-blue.

Then, he stormed out.

I crumpled into a pile of tears, one thought burning into my brain: *Holy Shit, Greg just hit me!*

I blubbered a deep, desolate wail, needing a hug from my mom or Liz. Most fucked up of all, I wanted a hug from Greg. I wanted him to wrap his arms around me and pretend this hadn't happened. Pretend everything could go back to normal.

I dragged myself to the freezer, grabbed a bag of frozen peas, and bawled myself into restless, tear-soaked sleep.

***

Six hours later, I woke to a loud pounding on my door. "Tess, please, let me in." I hesitated, but the sound of his voice softened something in me. I opened the door.

Greg took in my black eye and despondent face, the evidence of his actions. Guilt splattered his eyes. "Oh my god. I thought that was a dream. Fuck. I can't believe it. Did I do that to you?"

I melted into his arms, the tears coming fast and ugly.

He cupped my chin, tipping my face towards his. "Tessa, look at me. I'm so sorry. I will never, ever touch you again. Nothing I say can ever make this right, but I'm begging you, forgive me."

I thought of my parents, of their loving marriage, and then I looked down at myself—so weak, so pathetic. How had they, unknowingly, produced such a failure?

I swallowed hard. "Where were you?" I asked. "And why'd you have lipstick marks on your neck?"

Greg's face twisted, a mix of embarrassment and self-loathing. "We went to a strip club. I got carried away. I'm so ashamed. I took it out on you because I was disgusted with myself."

His betrayal was a knife blowing deeper than his punch ever could.

"So you hit me because you cheated on me?" The air drained from my lungs, my legs collapsing.

I wasn't attractive enough for Robby Marzone in the eighth grade.

And apparently, I wasn't good enough for Greg, either.

"It was only a lap dance and some kissing. I swear. And it was only because I was drunk out of my mind. I love you, so much. I screwed up. I will literally do anything to make it up to you."

I couldn't listen anymore. I crawled under the covers, curling into a tight ball, violently sobbing, wanting to hide from him. From the world.

But when he slipped into bed and held me, I didn't push him away. His touch felt familiar, even comforting in some warped, desperate way. And hours later, when he started to make love to me, to ease the pain with a fury of mind-blowing passion, I didn't stop him.

I let him rewrite the narrative of the night.

And that was the precise moment I started to hate myself.

Hate myself for not walking away.

Hate myself for letting him stay.

Hate myself for believing, even for a second, that his love could make me whole.

***

I didn't forgive him, nor did I break up with him. For months, we existed in an in-between state, Greg on his absolute best behavior, me trying to convince myself it was a one-off event. An accident. A moment of drunken madness that would never happen again.

I lied about my black eye, telling my roommates I'd fainted in the bathroom and hit my head on the vanity. It sounded pathetic even to my own ears, but no one questioned me outright. At least, not at first.

Two weeks later, at the Phillies game, Liz confessed she didn't believe my story. "The fighting woke me up, Tess. I know what happened to your eye. I love you. I'm here for you."

My stomach dropped, the popcorn in my lap tasteless. I kept my eyes on the field, but my heart pounded loud enough to drown out the crack of the bat meeting the ball.

I knew Liz knew.

But still I couldn't admit the truth.

It was bad enough to attract a man who would hit me. But the shame of staying with him after he did ate me alive.

***

The next physical blow came five months later, following a night of heavy drinking at my cousin's wedding. As we walked into our hotel room, Greg was spitting fire, fuming that I'd been flirting with the bartender. "Do you know how that made me feel? Seeing you act like such a slut? Right in front of my face?"

His words hit me first.

His hands followed.

He shoved me against the wall, his knee bursting into my left thigh so hard that I toppled over. He kicked me again, harder this time, in the ribs.

"Don't touch me!" I screamed, dashing up and locking myself in the bathroom. Inside, I collapsed onto the cold tiles. Hours passed as I cried myself hoarse. I fell asleep in the bathtub, still in my bridesmaid dress, mascara streaked down my cheeks.

Morning came, and with it, the all-too-familiar script.

The over-the-top apologies.

The deflection of blame.

The it-will-never-happen-agains.

The desperate sex on the hotel floor.

But this time, he already knew I lacked the spine to leave. And I already knew he was a liar—and that he would do it again.

*****

Over time, bits and pieces of Greg's abusive childhood seeped out, fragmented confessions in quiet moments. I begged him to go to therapy. In the moment, he agreed but never actually went. I had a therapist, but I danced around the truth of our relationship like a carefully choreographed routine. Choosing Greg over my own well-being was so dishonorable I couldn't bear to own it, not even in therapy.

I broke up with him at least fifty times.

But it never stuck.

Sometimes, I followed through for two to three days. Greg would send various gifts to try to win me back—a dozen roses or lilies, tickets to Vegas for the weekend, handwritten poems about being his one true love. Eventually, he would show up at my door, begging and crying, his face splayed with such tenderness that I convinced myself the Hulk would never come back.

But eventually, he always did.

*****

Everything crumbled for the final time one night when we were house-sitting for my parents, watching my family dog, Fluffy. Greg, who'd just defended his PhD, was leaving in the morning for a month-long backpacking tour of Europe. When he came back, I was heading to Botswana. In my head, I knew this was my out. Greg probably realized it, too.

We were cuddling on my childhood bed, giggling about the pictures of Jonathan Taylor Thomas still taped to my wall, when suddenly Greg transformed. "So, are you going to fuck tons of random guys in Botswana?" he sneered. His jealousy often flared when he was drunk, but this was the first time completely sober.

No matter how many insults he slung, each new one stung like a splash of acid. "Greg, what are you talking about?"

"Is that why you want to go? Get far away from me, so you can do whatever your slutty brain wants?"

"Greg, no. I'm going for my training. Stop being ridiculous. And you're the one leaving for Europe for a month tomorrow. And you're the one who has *actually* cheated before." As soon as the words slipped out, I realized how foolish I was to provoke him.

But by then, his weight pinned me down, his hands squeezing my neck, his face gleaming burgundy. I gasped, wiggling beneath him, staring at the picture of Jonathan Taylor Thomas, wondering if it'd be the last thing I ever saw. If tomorrow, my parents would find me dead in the bed they'd tucked me goodnight in for years.

Fluffy barked loudly, jumping on the bed, getting in Greg's face. He kept barking until Greg recoiled, a look of madness springing in his eyes. "Look what you almost made me do, you stupid bitch!"

"Get out, Greg, before I call the police." My voice was raspy from his suffocation.

He grabbed his bag, bolting down the stairs, slamming the door so hard, the whole house shook. I stumbled into the kitchen, found my mom's sharpest knife, armed the alarm and double-locked the doors. I slept with the knife beside me, Fluffy hovering inches from my face.

***

From Europe, Greg emailed every day, always the same message:

I love you.

I'm so sorry.

It will never happen again.

You're the love of my life.

***

The day before my flight to Gaborone, we met at a coffee shop. It was the first time we'd come face to face in thirty-two days. "It's over, Greg. Our relationship is toxic. I hope you get help, but I'm done," I said before even taking my seat.

"You don't mean that, Tessa. I want to marry you. The ring is at my apartment. We're meant to be together."

I shuddered at the idea of being his wife. Of living this misery, day in and out. I'd spent years hoping to fix Greg. Believing if I loved him enough, he would get better.

But now, I had to choose myself.

I remained resolute. "It's over."

As I left the coffee shop, striding away from him for the last time, I didn't pause to look back.

18

COREY

I shake my head, trying to nudge my attention early the next morning. We're heading east towards Victoria Falls, the motorway dangerous, notorious for unexpected elephant and baboon crossings.

Concentrate on the damn road, man.

But I'm finding it impossible to focus. My mind keeps replaying Tessa's screams.

About Greg.

Fucking Greg.

"Hey, can we please talk about your dream?" I ask, slowing the car to round a sharp bend. "Why'd you think Greg was going to hurt you?"

The thought of someone hurting Tessa makes my damn blood boil.

Tessa looks at me, sorrowful bags drooping beneath her stunning eyes. "I'd rather not get into it." Her voice is curt, and although physically she's next to me, her brain is somewhere else, a million kilometers away.

"Tess, please. Whatever it is, you can tell me."

"Corey, trust me. You don't want to know. This weekend with you has been great. I don't want to ruin it. Please, drop it." Her tone is unyielding.

But I can't let it go. For some reason, I *need* to understand her pain. "Nothing you could say will ruin anything." My statement is earnest.

Tessa brushes it off. "It will change how you see me, Corey. Please, seriously, stop." Her voice is stern, her posture stiff.

Why am I pressing her so much?

I'm definitely concealing my own wounds.

Isn't Tessa allowed to do the same?

Plus, I'm not her boyfriend.

Ten days ago, we were total strangers—but there's an intimacy between us, and it's growing in spite of myself.

I don't know her, but I want to.

Why won't she let me?

"Tess," I say, taking my eyes off the road to meet hers. "I promise, just tell me. You can trust me. I want to help."

When I look back at the road, three elephants stand in front of our path. I slam on the brakes, reaching my arm out to brace Tessa. She gasps, lurching forward, her head flinging towards the dashboard.

"Fuck!" I grunt, my body surging with adrenaline as the car screeches to a halt. I heave for breath. "Are you okay?"

Wordlessly, Tessa nods. Lacking a care in the world, the elephants meander through. After they pass, I find a spot along the shoulder and pull over, switching on the hazard lights. Tessa starts sobbing, looking like a dam on the verge of rupture, trying to contain a seeping pain.

"Fuck, I'm sorry, Tess. I should've paid more attention to the road. I didn't mean to scare you." I reach over, unbuckling her seat belt, pulling her into my arms.

Tessa buries her head into my chest, my shirt growing wet from her tears. I can't tell if she's upset about my driving or her dream or something else, so I just hold her.

"Shh, it's okay, *pragtige dame*. I'll be more careful, I promise."

"How can you be so nice all the freaking time?" Tessa weeps.

What kind of a question is that?

"I don't understand. What do you mean?" I'm genuinely perplexed. Over the years, people have accused me of many flaws but never being *too* nice.

"You're just so freaking nice to me. And considerate. And care about how I feel. And want me to respect myself. Which, clearly, it's obvious to you, even after knowing me for like two weeks… I don't respect myself… which is so pathetic." The skin on her face mottles into a patchwork of red and white as she curls her hands into little fists, tapping against my ribs.

"Huh? Tess, help me understand. I'm really trying, but I'm not following this conversation. I just want you to know *I* respect *you*. Why is that a bad thing?" I'm at a loss. Tessa says nothing, just cries visceral sounds into my now-sopping shirt.

What the fuck?

Clearly, this wound she carries is deep.

I know about painful scars—the messy kind that don't heal nicely, if at all.

The kind you spend years building a fortress around, designed to keep everyone out.

Until one tiny stone comes loose, crumbling the whole damn structure.

Maybe, meeting Tessa was my stone?

Our silence stretches into minutes that feel like hours. Clearly, she's not ready to open up. I decide to let it go. If she wants, she can tell me later.

I'm reaching for the wheel when her tiny voice stops me.

"Greg was my boyfriend, the one I mentioned yesterday…" The words choke out so quietly I can barely hear. "We were together for three years. Things were good for a while, but then… they became horrible. It started one night, with a bad fight and a black eye. Then, it got worse. Physical abuse, verbal abuse. It was so dysfunctional. But I stayed. I kept thinking he would change. I'm an idiot for thinking that, but… I couldn't leave. Please don't hate me. No one hates me more than I hate myself. Corey, I'm so ashamed… I am… so pathetically damaged… a totally broken person…"

The expulsion of Tessa's pain is a dump truck crashing down on my lungs. It's suddenly hard to breathe in the cramped rental car.

Tessa's entire being deflates, gutted.

I study her, realizing she perceives herself as totally broken. But despite her scars—or maybe because of them?—I see someone beautifully whole.

"Wow, fuck, Tess. Thank you for sharing that with me. I'm so sorry that happened to you, but I don't think you are broken, and how could I hate you for what you went through? This Greg guy sounds like a monster. He didn't deserve you for one goddamn minute. Please, don't blame yourself. Whatever he did to you, it's not your fault. It's his. I wish you would realize how amazing you are." I wipe away the tears racing down her cheeks.

"You're so nice, so, of course you would say something like that." Tessa sighs, unable—or unwilling—to see herself as I do.

Man, how did her self-image get so fucked up?

"I'm not just saying that, *silly.*" I poke her chest, trying to lighten the mood, at least a little. "Did you ever stop to think, maybe it's true? How many partners do you think I've taken on last-minute trips to Victoria Falls?"

She offers up the world's smallest grin. "I don't know. Five?"

"Ha, funny. Zero, Tess. Only you. If Greg didn't appreciate how lucky he was to have you, he's the dumbest dude on the planet. There's no excuse for the terrible things he did to you. I'm deeply sorry you went through that, but nothing's your fault. Try to stop thinking so negatively about yourself. You aren't broken… I can't even explain it. Fuck, I don't understand it myself, but you're so special… you have no idea." The words gush out like an opened floodgate. In my desperation to make Tessa feel better, I've developed an explosive case of verbal diarrhea, sharing way too much of my budding affection for her. Way too soon.

What the fuck am I doing?

That familiar thought again.

Here we are, sitting on the side of some dangerous road near Zambia, having a heart-to-heart in this rental car.

This whole situation is beyond crazy.

It makes zero fucking sense to be with her.

She's an American.

She's leaving soon.

This thing between us—this intoxicating blur of chemistry and passion—will only end badly.

I'm more sure of that than ever.

But why can't I stop myself?

The other truth, glaringly clear, too.

I want to be with her now more than I fear what will happen after.

Somehow, she's opening me back up again, making me feel.

In her presence, light is seeping back into my deepest holes, where for eleven years, only darkness has existed.

Tessa seems to sense my vulnerability. "Seriously, I don't know how to process all the nice things you say about me. Thank you. Your view of me is much kinder than my own… I've never told anyone about the abuse that happened with Greg. Not Liz, or my parents, or even my therapist, so I guess you're pretty special to me, too. Like it or not."

Her demeanor shifts a little. She's more buoyant. It's as if discharging some of her pain has helped reduce the burden she carries.

"I like it," I murmur.

Way too fucking much.

I pull her towards me.

Kissing her forehead.

Her eyelids.

Her cheeks.

Her nose.

Her round, pouty lips.

Kissing her, until all her tears have dried away.

19

TESSA

The sound of the powerful water as it rushes from the Zambezi River, plummeting into the gorge below, is deafening. It's so loud, it nearly drowns out all my thoughts.

Nearly.

A lifetime of nonstop thinking can't be easily silenced.

We're standing by a tourist viewpoint for Victoria Falls, mist spraying from the cascading sheets, Corey's arm draped around my shoulder. "Pretty fucking incredible, eh?" he shouts, tugging me into him.

"Yeah," I mutter, droplets of water clinging to our skin and dampening my hair.

And the view is miraculous.

But even as I try to focus on the beauty before me, my mind incessantly replays the car ride. The moment I told Corey about Greg.

I was sure it would permanently repulse him, that knowing I'd stayed with an abusive monster who repeatedly hurt me would be a total deal-breaker. The words had spilled out of me like poison, the shame so thick, I could hardly look at him.

But Corey didn't turn away. Instead, a wall between us fell.

Because Corey, miraculously but fully, accepted me.

For the first time, someone *sees* me.

And not *Phony Tessa*, the false persona I cloak for the outside world. The perfectionist who's becoming a doctor to please her dad.

But *True Tessa*, my inner being, deeply insecure and fragile, towing a mountain of hurt and anxiety.

"What are you thinking, *pragtige dame*?" Corey asks, yanking his baseball hat against his forehead as the breeze picks up.

"I'm just so grateful for how kind you were when I told you about Greg. Thank you. It means so much that you were understanding about my past."

The air is cooler by the falls, and I shiver, staring at the gushing water ferociously splattering into the ravine below. It's cathartic, watching the earth so freely release its pain.

How can I let go of my pain, too?

His fingertips trace my back. "Of course, what'd you think I'd do?"

"Truthfully?" My voice snags at the monumental idea he could so easily accept my broken parts. "Run screaming."

His lower lip twists down. "Why? Because you've had pain in your life? Or because there are things you'd do differently if given the chance?" He shakes his head. "Everyone has scars, Tessa. Your scars make you interesting. They give you depth."

My forehead crimps, considering this. "Maybe… I guess I've only ever thought of my scars as a bad thing. And honestly? Since I'm on a truth streak here… I think I'm pretty terrible at being a human."

He laughs, a rich, wholesome laugh that soothes my aching wounds. "Honestly? Me, too, but I don't think most people are good at being humans. Life is basically a shitshow."

I grin at his candor. "Yes! Why is life such a *fucking* shitshow?"

"I don't know, but let's enjoy this view, okay? Try to forget our scars, stop reliving the past. Let's just be *here*, appreciate how fucking amazing

Mother Nature is." He gazes at me, his kindness warming my chest like hot chocolate on a snowy day.

"Sounds good," I say.

And for a few fleeting moments, I manage to stay out of my head, watching the waterfall, just being present.

He takes my hand, interlocking our fingers. And when he does, the world feels a little more hopeful. Less scary.

"Come, let's head this way," he says, leading us towards the Victoria Falls Bridge, the massive steel structure that spans the divide between Zambia and Zimbabwe.

A sign indicates that the bridge, built in 1905, towers one hundred and twenty meters above the gorge below. Large crowds of tourists hover around a hut that reads *Shearwater Bungee Jump*.

"What's that?" I ask, pointing to the crowd.

"Bungee jumping." He eyes me with a swashbuckling grin. "It's about a hundred-meter jump down."

I crinkle my forehead, trying to do the math. "What's that in feet? My American brain thinks in feet, not fancy meters."

"Hmm, okay, Ms. America," he says with a chuckle, "I think it's about… three hundred and fifty feet down."

"Wow. Fuck."

We watch as two jumpers dive off the ledge, plummeting from the bridge into the gorge below. Their screams cut through the roar of the falls. Their bungee cords quickly unravel until nothing's left. They dangle precariously by their ankles, swinging wildly over the water. Eventually, a crew hoists them back up to the bridge, where they emerge from their jump, faces lit with adrenaline-fueled triumph, to a round of fierce applause.

"Holy shit," I mumble, fear slanting my voice. "That looks insanely scary. Have you done it before?"

"No, I've thought about it once or twice but never done it."

Of course, I've never bungee jumped, either. It's dangerous. And my modus operandi is: *Don't do dangerous things.*

But as I stand there, a different thought bubbles up. What if my whole life approach has been wrong?

I remember the scene at Impodimo Lodge. Of the lions eating the impala. Of how little in life actually matters and how easily I get caught up in non-important bullshit.

What actually matters to me?

What do I want from my life?

Maybe, to figure it out, I need to get out of my own freaking head. To stop worrying and overthinking and just live.

Before I can reconsider, I say, "Let's do it."

Corey's bottom lip drops open, his eyebrows stitching together in disbelief. It's clear what he's thinking—the girl who was terrified of having coffee outside of his safari Jeep now wants to vault off a bridge? "You… uh… want to bungee jump? Tess, you sure? That doesn't seem like something you'd be up for."

"Yes, let's sign up. Right now. Before I change my mind." I quickly pull him towards the information desk.

***

Forty-five minutes later, I teeter on the small makeshift ledge jutting off the Victoria Falls Bridge. I'm next to Corey, both of us strapped into harnesses with ropes tightly fastened to our ankles. Ten minutes before, I reluctantly signed an indemnity waiver, making it clear if I die, it's no one's fault but my own.

I dare, foolishly, for a moment, to glance down. It's a shockingly far way to the bottom.

Shit.

My stomach wobbles like gelatin, my breakfast rushing back up into my mouth. Similarly to when I fly, I imagine my body splattering onto the rocks below, cracking into a million tiny shards.

Get out of your head, Tessa.

"Almost time, jumpers! Get ready," the bungee instructor calls.

"You okay, Tess?" Corey yells amid the buzzing crowd, seemingly more concerned for my well-being than his own. I peek at him, jealous of his loose shoulders and wide smile. Somehow, he looks like he's going for a quick jog, not preparing to jump off a freaking bridge.

"Yes… I think… I'm… all right." The words squeak out unconvincingly. But inside, I strangely feel the most okay I have in so long.

I glance at the ground again, that familiar voice of doubt creeping back.

What the heck am I doing?

I don't want to die.

It's not too late to back out.

I should definitely back out.

But before my head can talk me out of it, I commit to taking this plunge. To jump and trust the rope to catch me.

Maybe, in life, only by soaring off scary cliffs do we discover the beautiful truths. The ones unknowable within a caged existence.

Maybe, it's better to repeatedly shatter apart living bravely than remain intact by playing it safe.

"Okay, jumpers. Here we go," the instructor's voice booms.

Shit.

"Five,

Four,

Three,

Two,

One,

Go!"

I don't want to die.

Shit.

This was a huge mistake.

Shit.

Shit.

Shit.

My heart bangs, a vortex of panic churning in my core.

I close my eyes, slurping in a gigantic breath.

And then, I

J

U

M

P.

20

TESSA

"Tessa, you have a patient waiting." Dr. Sebopelo's sonorous voice rattles me three days later. I'm working in the maternal outpatient clinic, but in my mind, I'm still dangling by the rope, hanging upside down above the gorge, my body swaying forcefully, blown by the wind, the thrill of my unique aliveness spurting through my veins.

"I'm so proud of you, Tess. I can't believe you did that!" Corey called as we were hoisted back onto the bridge.

"No one's more stunned than me," I shouted back.

And for that one glorious moment, as my toes touched the land again, I was wholly free, entirely untamed.

Just like the elephants.

"Tessa? Here's the patient," Dr. Sebopelo says again, staring at me expectantly.

I blink.

My freedom is gone. That clamping sensation gnaws again at the base of my neck. "Sorry, Dr. Sebopelo. I'll come find you after I evaluate her."

He nods. "Very good. Thank you."

I face the young Black woman who's wearing a colorful red-and-green print dress, clutching a swollen abdomen. A scarf covers her hair as a look of trepidation knits within her auburn eyes. "*Dumela, mma*. This way, please." I motion, heading towards the exam area in the back of the trailer. As I walk, I grip my stethoscope, adrenaline rippling through me.

I'm such a phony.

I don't belong here.

I'm a novice actor debuting in a Broadway role.

The woman follows hurriedly, taking a seat on the exam table. "I'm pregnant and I'm bleeding and I'm scared. Please help," she blurts in perfect English. I'm struck by the clarity of her language. With most patients, I've adapted to obtaining a broken history with minimal shared dialect. Only occasionally is a nurse or other translator present to assist.

"It's okay. Of course I'll help you," I say, trying to still my own panicked thoughts.

What if I can't help her?

Inside, I'm a sheaf of nerves, but outside, I try to project calmness. The woman's legs tremor against the weathered green exam table.

"What's your name?" I ask.

"Evah." Her fingers encircle her bump in broad, shaky strokes.

"Hi, Evah, I'm Tessa Williams, one of the medical students here. How old are you?"

"Twenty-eight… and I'm six months pregnant. This morning, I was at my job. I work as a maid, and I found bright red blood in my underwear. I know blood isn't supposed to be there. I'm worried it's a bad sign." Evah's cheeks puff out, brimming with concern.

My pulse concomitantly shoots up. "Blood isn't always dangerous," I say, hoping it's the truth. "I know it's hard, but try not to worry, Evah. Are you in pain or having cramping?" I place my hands on Evah's stomach, palpating for uterine contractions.

"No. This is my third baby, but I've never had bleeding before. Is my baby okay?" Evah's pupils dilate as she scrutinizes my face, seemingly searching for clues about her baby's well-being.

I smile brightly, hoping she won't sense my fear. "We'll check on the baby soon, I promise, Evah. Just a few more questions. Do you have any medical problems?" My hands linger on her belly.

There are no contractions that I can detect, although I have admittedly minimal experience.

Evah nods. "Yes, I am infected with HIV."

I take a steadying breath, keeping my voice calm. Like I've been taught. "Have you been taking your antiviral medications every day?"

"Yes. I get them each month from the hospital pharmacy."

We quickly review a few other questions: Does Evah know her blood type? (O-positive, which poses no risk to the baby.) Was there any trauma? (No, none that she recalls.) Is the baby moving? (Yes, a few kicks an hour ago and hiccups this morning.)

"Okay, let's do an internal exam to check your cervix." I step out, giving Evah privacy to undress.

In the hallway, I vex.

In my short career, I've only performed eleven internal exams. From medical textbooks, I'd assumed that locating a cervix was a relatively straightforward task.

It's not.

On *real* women, cervixes frequently like to hide.

It'll be okay.

I'll find her cervix.

But what if I can't?

I re-enter the exam space, my legs two wobbly stilts. I carry a metal speculum and don gloves. Evah scoots to the edge of the exam table, letting her legs drape open. "This might feel a little cold and uncomfortable," I say, timidly inserting the speculum as Evah clutches her belly.

Please let me find her cervix.

Please let me find her cervix.

Blessedly, within thirty seconds, Evah's cervix materializes. There are droplets of dried blood coating the lip, but it's closed with no signs of active bleeding.

Thank you!

Thank you!

Momentarily satisfied with my skills, I remove the speculum. "All finished. Good news. Everything looks normal."

Evah sits up, a hopeful smile sprouting from her round lips. Next, I would ideally perform an ultrasound, but at Princess Victoria Hospital, no such machine is available. Instead, I have to settle for using the handheld Doppler. "Let's listen to your baby's heart so we can hear things are okay," I say with false confidence.

Please, let the baby be okay.

Please, let the baby be okay.

I spread petroleum jelly onto Evah's belly, the coldness making Evah wince. I move the Doppler around, starting at the upper left part of her abdomen, slowly making my way down. The silence in the room reverberates, piercing my eardrums like sharp pins. I continue to scan in small, deliberate increments.

Please, let there be a heartbeat.

Please, let there be a heartbeat.

Evah furrows her brow, heavy creases fissuring into her forehead as the seconds tick by. Dead silence emanates from the Doppler. My breath stalls.

Shit.

Shit.

Shit.

"Sometimes babies like to hide from us. This happens all the time. Don't worry, Evah," I lie, the dent from my dimple rippling into my cheek.

"Okay," Evah mumbles, heaving a hefty sigh, the wand temporarily displacing with her exhalation.

I reposition the Doppler.

And then, near the right lower quadrant of Evah's stomach, a magical sound bursts out.

Thump, thump, thump.

The most beautiful sound I've ever freaking heard.

I quickly count the beats, estimating the baby's heart rate. "Great strong heart! One hundred and forty beats per minute. Perfect!" A tear of relief tries to escape from my eye, but I blink it away.

"Thank you, Tessa." Evah's shoulders fall as the fear she was carrying is supplanted by gratitude.

I squeeze her hand, overcome with tenderness. "I'm going to get my Attending, Dr. Sebopelo. I'll be right back."

For now, much remains unknown, like why Evah bled or if it poses an ongoing risk to her or the baby. But such things can't be determined with the resources available. All I know for certain is that in *this* moment, Evah's baby is alive.

And what a beautiful miracle that is.

Here, inside Princess Victoria Hospital, where I've witnessed so much death and despair, this baby's heart steadily beats.

Thump, thump, thump.

A spectacular vibration of hope.

And for the first time, I feel optimistic that *maybe*, just maybe, there are parts of medicine I can learn to love.

21

TESSA

"What made us think hiking this trail in the afternoon heat was a good idea?" Liz laments, panting, her neon pink tank top laced with sweat from the fiery sun.

"We're almost at the top," I say, scooping my dampened hair into a high ponytail. "Plus, Modise promised the view will be worth it."

It's Sunday afternoon and we're nearing the summit of Kgale Hill, a small mountaintop on the outskirts of Gaborone. I'm loving the heavy burn in my thighs. Intense exercise—something I've done none of recently—remains my best coping mechanism for managing the demons in my head.

"After this, we're going straight to Bull & Bush! I need a heaping plate of ribs to eat back all the calories I'm burning," Liz says, referencing our favorite local restaurant, where we sometimes grab dinner and beers after a long day at the hospital.

"Yes, deal!" I agree, smiling.

Liz gurgles some water, continuing along the dirt path. A chain-link fence separates us from the dense brush. "Hopefully we don't run into any baboons like Jeremy did last weekend. I know how much the baboons love to pee on you, Tess."

I scrunch my eyes. "You're so funny."

"You love me," Liz says, pumping her arms, her grey sneakers browning from the dirt. "Anyway, how was clinic yesterday?"

"I was in the peds ward. It was tough. Three of the kids were orphans. Their parents died from AIDS, and now they're really sick with HIV, too… I'm having a hard time, feeling so helpless."

"Yeah, I was on peds Monday. It made me really sad, too," Liz says, taking another sip of water, spraying some on her forehead. "There is something about sick kids especially that breaks my heart."

"How do you deal with the sadness? So the sickness and death we see doesn't consume you?" This is the part of medicine I can't master. Every night, I lie awake, the misfortunes of my patients swarming my mind, cutting like a saw through my chest.

"It's hard, I'm still learning," Liz says. "But I try to remember, a lot of life is out of my control and if I want to help people, I have to be okay with the notion I can only do so much. I try to stay excited about the things I can do but let go of what's beyond my reach. Then, when I'm not at the hospital, I don't dwell on things."

"I wish I could be more like you. I dwell on everything," I say. "Sometimes… I worry… I'm too sensitive… too weak, to be a doctor…" I stare at the ground, avoiding Liz's probing eyes.

"Don't say that, Tess. You're going to be an awesome doctor."

But what if I'm not?

What if this isn't the right career for me?

I've been here for three weeks, but my self-doubt remains molded to me like a concrete shackle.

We fall into silence as a large divot in the ground requires careful navigation. I step over a pile of loose stones, the path leveling off. "Anyway… how's everything with Marley? And your mom?"

"Marley's good. She just booked her ticket to come the day our program ends. We're going to travel for two weeks. And my mom… is my mom. Last night, she sent me an email with three different 'bachelors' she wants to set me up with, her friends' sons. Each one had pictures and a one-page bio attached to the email."

"Wow, not cool. Not cool at all, Mrs. Collins… but that's great news about Marley!"

"Yeah, I miss Marley so much. I can't wait to see her." Liz's lips wrench up into an expansive grin. "Speaking of which… what's going on with Mr. Safari Dreamboat?"

My mouth cracks into a similarly wide smile. "Things are good. He's so different from the guys I've dated before. Not that we're dating, but we've been texting and talking a lot. We don't have a label or anything, but he's really nice to me… and considerate… and chivalrous. And he's taught me a lot about respecting myself more. He makes me think differently. I mean, somehow I jumped off the Victoria Falls Bridge!"

Beneath the sunlight, Liz's crooked top incisor glints white. "I know, I still can't believe *you* did that. Voluntarily!"

"Me neither. But something in me is different here. I can't explain it. I just feel more like myself."

In Botswana, I've become more wild and free, less contained and cautious.

I tell the truth more, fake being okay less.

"I'm really happy for you, Tess, but what's going to happen when you leave?"

My stomach drops. "I have no idea…"

We reach the apex of Kgale Hill, the cloudless sky bursting into full view. Below us, the metropolis of Gaborone collides with the sprawling green shrubbery and tan hills. "Wow, this country is so stunning," Liz mutters, collapsing on a large rock, gazing out.

"I know, I love it here. Everyone has been so welcoming. There's such a strong sense of unity. I don't want to go home."

Home.

The word brings a sinking heaviness to my lungs. It's a place without Corey. Where Greg lives seven blocks away. Where my dad's expectations will once again drown me. I take a slow sip of water, unsuccessfully trying to shove the worries from my mind.

Liz flexes her legs against the ground. "Have you heard from Greg?"

The heaviness around my lungs scrunches tighter. "Yes, he emails every day. He loves me. He wants me back. Blah, blah, blah. But I haven't responded. I'm grateful to be done with him."

Liz faces me, drops of sweat glistening off her forehead. "That's great, Tess. I'm really glad to hear that."

Tell Liz.

Corey accepted me.

Liz will be the same.

I open my mouth but no sounds come out.

"You know I'm here, right, Tess? If you want to talk more… about things… with Greg?"

Liz has said this same statement hundreds of times. But I've never had the courage to reveal that I loved Greg more than I respected myself.

I clear my throat. "Yes… Liz… actually…"

Just tell her!

Get out of your own fucking way, Tessa!

Liz stares keenly at me, with neither a smile nor frown, just a wholly neutral expression.

Three other hikers reach the summit, standing fifty feet away, snapping photos. I draw in a breath.

"You were right." It's barely a whimper.

"Right about what?" Liz asks, flummoxed.

"That day at the Phillies game. When you said my black eye was from Greg… you were right."

"Oh shit, Tess." Liz's lips diffuse into an exhaustive frown. "I'm so sorry to have been right about something so terrible. That's awful. He had no right to lay a hand on you. *Ever.*"

"Thanks, Liz. I'm really sorry I lied. I wanted to tell you the truth… so many times… but I was so ashamed. I'm still so ashamed… I'm sorry." Tears plunge from my eyes. "I know I have a lot of work to do on myself. I'm trying. When we get home, I'm going to tell my therapist the truth, too."

"Tess, I understand why you lied. You don't have to apologize. I just wish I could have helped you get away from him sooner." Liz ruffles in her fanny pack, handing me a tissue. She scoops her arm around my back. I rest my head on her shoulder.

And we stay like that as I tell Liz the entire gruesome truth.

An hour later, I sit incredulous at how lucky I am when Liz says, "Thanks for telling me everything. I'll be here for you however I can as you heal. I love you, no matter what."

22

COREY

I jerk awake, dread permeating every pore of my being. The sky outside is black, matching my sullen mood.

On my nightstand, the alarm clock displays the date in taunting red letters: *August 30.*

The anniversary of the worst fucking day of my life.

Eleven years ago today, I said goodbye to Leona.

I tug the duvet over my head, craving total darkness. A bottomless emptiness stirs in my stomach.

Somehow, despite all the time that's passed, her loss remains excruciating. That's the fucking horrible thing about grief. It doesn't lessen.

When she died, everyone said, "Time will help."

But that hasn't been true.

The waves of anguish come less often, but when the memories surge, their jagged edges remain so sharp, they instantly slice me apart.

***

"Are you sure you want to be alone tonight, bud?" Darian asks, fourteen hours later, his brown eyes swollen with sympathy. "I've been thinking of Leona today."

It's after dinner, and we've just arrived back at the staff quarters. "Thanks, man," I say. "That means a lot."

Darian nods, throwing his arms around me. Although we're like brothers, we rarely touch, but tonight, I grip Darian's shoulders tight, accepting his comfort.

At my door, I fumble with the key.

Finally, the lock gives way.

I enter, the door closing with a loud click.

The sound is a potent trigger of memory.

Time buckles.

Suddenly, I'm back, hearing the same click of the closing door as Leona's body was wheeled away.

I shake, recalling the stretcher draped in an abrasively crisp white linen, hiding the horrors that lay beneath it.

I stumble to my couch, sinking down.

My pounding temples drop into my hands.

That scar in my chest pulsates, its rickety closure gushing open, grief bubbling all over me.

I *want* the fucking tears to come.

I *need* the fucking tears to come.

They don't.

***

It's been years since I've cried for Leona.

In the beginning, I was a damn waterfall. But the sadness... it was too much, like being swallowed by a riptide with no chance of coming up for air.

The feelings were so overwhelmingly terrible that my brain did the only thing it could to protect me—it shut them all off.

At first, it felt like a choice, a survival mechanism.

But I couldn't figure out a way to *only* filter out the hard feelings. Which meant I had to stop feeling *all* my feelings. I muted every emotion—grief, joy, love—to a static hum.

To survive in a world where Leona was dead, I became completely numb.

Her loss was a grief so profound it sank me to the bottom of the ocean, making me resolve never to endure such pain again. Which is why I haven't let anyone inside. Not Alice or the handful of others that came before her. Not anyone.

But then, Tessa came along, and in some crazy fucking way, resuscitated my emotions. It happened so quickly, so unexpectedly. Somehow, she's the defibrillator that shocked my cold heart back to life, reawakening my feelings after a decade of hibernation.

How the fuck did it happen?

I still don't understand.

I reach into my pocket now, digging for my phone, dialing my mum.

"Hi, Core." She answers before it rings. "I'm glad you called, honey." Her tone is heavy; I billow with guilt for not being a more available son. Suddenly, I can't speak. No words can match the depth of my loss. "Core? You there? Core? Is this old phone acting up again?" She presses buttons haphazardly.

I grin in spite of this awful grief.

"I'm here, Mum."

Broken but here.

Ready to try living again…

I think?

Maybe?

"Oh, okay, good. How are you, honey?"

"It's August thirtieth, Mum. I'm terrible," I confess.

"I know, my boy. I can't believe it's been eleven years. Can you imagine what Leona would think of the world today?" She lets out a gargled snort—a mix of a wail and a chuckle—and it yanks at my calloused heart.

"I miss her so much, Mum." My voice cracks like a snapped twig. "I saw this lioness today on the game ride. It made me think of her."

"That's special, Core," she whispers.

Sometimes, when I'm out in the bush, I feel Leona. The moments are rare, but the wind will blow a certain way, or I'll see an animal running in the distance under a spray of sunlight. A flash comes over me, and for just a second, it feels like she's there. Just as quickly, she's gone. I live for those stunning, brief assurances that wherever she is, she's *okay*.

"I'm sorry if I've been distant," I say. "I'm starting to realize, I haven't coped very well… since Leona died. I love you, Mum. So fucking much."

"I love you too, but Corey, don't cuss."

"Sorry, Mum. Dammit."

"Corey—"

"I'm hopeless, Mum."

"One thing I know, Core, is you can't get through this unless you feel it." She sighs. "Remember, Corey, feelings aren't permanent. Don't be afraid to feel your feelings."

"That's good advice. I need to work on that. Thanks, Mum."

"Sweet boy, Leona would want you to be happy."

Ten minutes later, I hang up, realizing at last that outrunning my grief is a losing game. The pain will keep finding me, and I need to let it. Otherwise, I'll never emerge on the other side of this endless hell.

The valley of grief is so deep that I have been tumbling for years.

Even though I thought I was fine.

But I'm not fine.

I shut my eyes, a memory coming.

For the first time, I let it wash over me, not forcing it away, just sitting with it.

Leona is too weak to walk, so I'm pushing her. It's very sunny, and she says, "Wow! It's such a nice day, right?"

Even as she was dying, all she saw was beauty.

She deserved so much better than she got.

Fuck.

Fuck.

Fuck.

I grip my chest, my heart a swath of exposed nerve endings, the pain wicked. It feels like a machete is literally splicing my body into shards.

I want comfort.

I need comfort.

Tessa.

Before I can second guess myself, I text her.

```
Me: Hi, pragtige dame. Can I come see you now?
```

23

TESSA

I stare at the blank computer screen, the cursor blinking at me. For an hour now, I've been sitting here, trying to figure out what to write Greg. Not one single word has made it onto the page. But I want closure. I need it. To make sure Greg knows we're done.

Admitting the truth to Corey and Liz has helped me analyze things. To confront my patterns, my choices. In reality, since Robby Marzone called me fat in the eighth grade, I've craved approval from men, especially the *wrong* men. I need to learn to love myself. Respect myself. I have no idea how to do that, but the first step seems to be to draw a firm boundary with Greg.

Sighing, I resolve to type whatever comes to mind.

> *Dear Greg. I've been trying to write this email for days, hoping the words would magically come...*

My phone buzzes.

    Corey: Hi, pragtige dame. Can I come see you now?

I reply instantly.

```
    Me: Yes :-)
```

I shut my computer, a buzz of anticipation brewing in my chest. My email to Greg can wait.

***

An hour later, Corey arrives outside my flat.

But his eyes are beet red.

His magnificent lips are sculpted into a deep grimace.

His blond locks are wildly unkempt.

There's a heaviness permeating him that wasn't there before.

Or maybe I'm only noticing it now.

His visible sorrow makes my heart twinge. "Corey? What's going on?"

"I just really wanted…" He pauses, swallowing. "To see you." He pulls me against him, whimpering, his stubbly chin scratching my ear.

Being back in his embrace feels good. So good. And suddenly, I'm painfully aware that our time together is drawing to a close. In four weeks, I have to go home, and all of this will be over.

I pull back and study his blue irises, flecked with these intense black dots. "Are you sure you're okay?"

He nods yes.

But his eyes scream no.

What happened to him?

I take his hand, leading him inside. "This is my bedroom," I say with forced enthusiasm, gesticulating in a circular motion to my small but tidy room.

At the sight of my bed, his lips yank upward, revealing his four top teeth. "I'm honored to finally be inside here. Where's Liz?"

"She's working an overnight shift at the hospital," I say, closing the door.

A sinful twinkle breaks through his wounded eyes. "Oh… so that means… we're *alone*?" He slides next to me, his body heat soaring into my limbs, turning my legs into brittle sticks.

"Yep." My voice is subdued as his sturdy hands cinch my waist, pulling me closer.

We haven't had sex. Aside from that one magical night at Chobe River Lodge, we've barely done more than kiss. In the past, I've usually gotten to know a man *while* sleeping with him. Or sometimes, as with Greg, *after* sleeping with him. But Corey's lessons in self-respect have steered me into unchartered waters.

"I guess my horrible day just got a little better," he murmurs, pressing his lips to mine.

"Why was your day terrible? What's going on?" I trace along his curved jawline, affection bubbling for him like a hot spring inside my chest.

He winces, his body stiff, as he talks into my ear. "Tess… right now… I just want to get lost in you… and forget everything. Can you let me do that?" His tone is raspy. And sexy. I'm torn between my two desires: to emotionally dissect him *or* to let him rip my clothes off.

"Tell me what happened," I whisper, sucking on his neck. He sighs, his calloused fingers gripping my waist, not answering.

"Let me be here for you." I peck his left earlobe. "Like you were for me, at Victoria Falls."

He presses his chest against mine, shutting his eyes.

Through his shirt, his heart thunders.

"Corey?" I tousle his hair.

"I want to tell you… but…" He hesitates, squeezing my ribs tighter, like he's afraid I might disappear.

I grab his hand, leading him to my bed. "Sit, talk to me."

He sinks down, a cavernous pain painting his face, his expression reminding me of a suffering puppy.

Of how my dog Fluffy looked standing over my bed the night Greg assaulted me.

Corey's a wounded soul, lost at sea.

And I suddenly understand; I want to be his lighthouse.

"Corey." I toss my arms around him, his lungs heaving, pushing my body up and down.

His voice is so low I can barely hear his words. "I-I-I… lost someone very special on this day, years ago. Her name was Leona." The edges of his mouth collapse at the utterance of "*Leona*," tugging his whole face down.

My stomach concurrently collapses. "Oh, Corey, I'm so sorry." I cup his face, feeling protective, like a mother bear guarding her defenseless cub. "Will you tell me about her?"

"I-I-I… can't." He lets out another hefty sigh.

I want to know who Leona is. To ask what happened. How he lost her. But I just nod, pulling him down beside me on the pillow.

We're silent for a while as I cradle his head.

The clock reads 12:22 a.m.

He sucks in a slow breath, burrowing deeper into my skin like I'm his cozy den. "Your hair always smells so damn good. It calms me down."

I smile, flattered. "Bath and Body Works. Lemongrass shampoo. It's from home."

His sad eyes turn blank. "Bath and Body what?"

"It's an American store… but it's not important to know, not like knowing Jennifer Aniston."

His lips twist up slightly, the tips reaching his eyes. "Well, of course, nothing is as important as knowing who Jennifer Aniston is."

I chuckle from my sunken belly. "I'm glad I've at least taught you something."

He turns his head, his gaze trailing up my face, settling on my eyes.

He brushes his fingers along my cheek. "You have," he whispers.

I stop giggling, acutely aware of my own vulnerability. Of how much I like him. "Corey, you've taught me a lot, too, especially to be kinder to myself. I'm so thankful for that." My stare latches onto his blue beacons, their force pulling me under.

He peers straight at me. Breathing becomes difficult. "You're so beautiful, Tess. You have these little golden specs in your eyes that dance around under the light. They drive me fucking wild."

A shiver slithers down my spine. "It's hard to manage all your compliments. You make me feel so good about myself."

His hand rakes through my hair, brushing little tendrils away. "You deserve someone who makes you feel good. Every damn day."

I want that to be you, I nearly blurt.

But it can't be…

Because we live on different continents.

I try to ignore our ticking clock, pressing my lips to his, exploring his mouth like it's a new planet and I'm an esteemed astronaut.

He returns my kiss, softly at first, then building in intensity until he's gripping my shirt, pressing the length of his body against mine.

"I want you," he mumbles gruffly. "Now. *Please*." His hands slip beneath my flannel pajamas, cupping my breasts. His grassy vanilla musk shoots through my veins, making me feel like I've just downed an entire bottle of vodka.

"Oh," I tease. "So you *finally* want to have sex with me?"

"Tess, I should be so damn lucky." His voice is throaty and deadly serious. "I've wanted to since the second I laid eyes on you."

This confession makes lightning ripple between my thighs. "I like your sexy talk… I haven't heard it since Chobe Lodge." I lift his shirt over his head. "And I like this part of your tummy." I grab his lower stomach between my hands, dragging my lips from his chest towards his belly button.

"I like your dimple." He kisses it, sucking a piece of my cheek into his mouth. "No, actually I fucking *love* your dimple." He takes off my pajama top, unfastening my bra.

"I like your accent," I say, unbuttoning his pants.

"I like your goodness." He slips off my leggings and underwear, stopping to study me. His eyes soak me up like sourdough bread plunging into oil. "And your nakedness. Goddamn."

A little moan escapes his throat.

My vision clouds with flakes of glitter.

He entwines around me like ivy, the wall surrounding him earlier now crumbled.

He kisses me until my lips chafe.

I haven't had sex with anyone besides Greg in three years.

But there are no butterflies.

I feel safe—at home—with him.

"I *need* you. Now," he rasps again, grabbing his wallet from the floor and fumbling for a condom. I moan, too, my anticipation building as he puts it on.

He enters me slowly, thrusting harder and harder.

I abandon myself.

And happily drown.

In *him*.

24

TESSA

From: Tessa.Williams2@bmail.com
To: Greg.Winters1982@bmail.com

Date: Wednesday, September 5, 2007

Subject: Our relationship

Dear Greg,

I've been trying to write this email for days, hoping the words would magically come. But it seems clear they won't.

So here goes…

I've read all your emails but wasn't sure I could bring myself to write back. But I think we both need closure.

I don't want to provide you with any false hope. I want to make it clear, I have no intention of being with you ever again.

I've had space in Botswana to process how extremely unhealthy our relationship was. It was toxic in every sense of the word. Obviously, the physical and verbal abuse. But also the crazy depths we sunk to together.

Throughout our relationship, I tried to understand your inner pain. I wanted to know why you hurt so I could heal it. And the worse things got, the more desperate I became to fix you. To fix *us*.

There were so many fights. An unbearable amount of mental anguish. I would sit there, crying on my bedroom floor, *needing* you, feeling so alone. Inside, I was falling apart, but because of all the secrets in our relationship, no one knew how shattered I was. Except you. But, of course, you were falling apart, too.

I thought if I loved you enough, you'd get better. And things between us would be better, too. But I was so worried about fixing you, I forgot about fixing myself.

I wanted to live in a world where love was enough to heal anything. To heal *everything.*

But I realize now that was idealistic and so unrealistic. Love alone cannot heal things. Romantic love can't complete a broken person. True healing has to begin with self-love. And the deeper we got in our dysfunctional cycle, the further I came from loving— or respecting, or even liking—myself.

Greg, I understand now that only *you* can fix *you.* The sole person I can fix is *me.* I have a long way to go towards building a respectful, loving relationship with myself. But I'm working on it.

For your part, you need to address your anger. Deep inside, I know there's a lot of trauma and pain. I pray you *never* do to another partner the things you did to me.

Neither of us can change the past. The only thing now is to learn from it. To use this experience to shape us into better versions of ourselves.

I hope you can find your way to do that. But to heal, I need to be free of you. Stop contacting me. I hope, with time, you find inner peace.

Tessa

***

From: Tessa.Williams2@bmail.com
To: Claudia.Mama.Consultant@bmail.com

Date: Wednesday, September 5, 2007

Subject: My truth

Hi Mom,

I'm writing you this email because I'm too scared to say the words aloud. I've wanted to tell you the truth for so long. I hope you'll forgive me for keeping it from you.

I know you had suspicions, even if you never said so directly. My relationship with Greg was abusive—physically and verbally. I'm ashamed to have chosen a partner like him. I stayed because I kept hoping to fix him. It was as dumb as it sounds.

I want to tell you everything, and I will when I get home. But for now, I just need you to know.

I'm so sorry for choosing a relationship like that. I should have known better. But I'm safe now, and I'm working on healing myself.

Please don't tell Dad. I still need to work up the courage to tell him. I can't stand the thought of breaking his heart. He expects more from me and I failed him.

Thanks for being the best mom.

I love you so much,

Tessa

NOW:

Eleven Years Later

September, 2018

25

TESSA

I fidget with the stethoscope draped around my neck, trying unsuccessfully to swallow the massive lump stuck inside my throat. Seated to my left, my parents look equally distraught. Mom's French-manicured hand shudders as it rests atop Dad's black pants. Her other hand twists a tissue into a crumpled mess. Dad removes his glasses, wearily rubbing his eyes, each stroke seemingly adding five new wrinkles to his face.

It's been four days since I told him about his CT scan results.

In those four days, he's aged forty years.

We are seated together in Dr. Burkland's office on the fifth floor of the sparkling new hospital wing, built to house the Oncology division. The room is flashy and bright but a sense of unshakable dread permeates the space.

Only bad things happen here.

The sun blazes, its midday heat radiating through the room's glass panes. The Philadelphia weather is hot and muggy, providing no hint that summer's preparing to succumb to fall. Outside, city life bustles on. Taxicabs honk and pedestrians jostle, the frenetic pace of life unchanged. My world screeched to a halt four days ago. But for everyone else, it's business as usual.

I fan myself with my hand, beads of sweat puddled beneath my white coat. I ran here following a packed morning of patients. I work two blocks away as a primary care doctor in a demanding center-city practice, the idea of rushing hardly unique to today. All my workdays are breathless sprints towards the finish line—a frenzied jumble of too many patients and too little time.

Now, time stretches unbearably, thick and endless.

"You okay, Petey?" Mom whispers, her eyes red and swollen, reaching for Dad's hand.

"Yes. We'll get through this together." Dad grasps Mom's fingers, his grimace slackening from her touch. Despite the challenges they've endured, my parents' marriage remains fierce. They love each other, but perhaps more impressively, they still *like* each other.

Things in my own marriage are okay.

They're fine.

We're a good team, dependable, functional.

But there's never been *that* spark—that fiery passion that flames through your chest, curling your toes, seizing your breath.

***

A knock comes at the door, startling me. My lungs constrict like dried-up raisins.

Shit.

Here we go.

Dr. Burkland enters, brimming with confidence and kindness. She's forty-something, dressed in grey slacks and a form-accentuating white button-down shirt, her jet-black hair pulled into a high ponytail. She's widely regarded as one of the best urology oncologists in the country. I feel a pang of envy towards my colleague who seemingly loves her job.

"Claudia, Tessa, Peter. It's great to see you again, although I wish it wasn't under these circumstances." Her voice is heartfelt as she shakes our hands.

"Dr. Burkland, thank you for getting us an appointment so quickly," I say. Normally, the waitlist would be several weeks long, but Dr. Burkland squeezed Dad into her schedule immediately. The incredible privilege he possesses—accessing world-class medical care at the tip of his fingers—isn't lost on me.

"Kelly. Please still call me Kelly!" She smiles softly, typing her credentials into the hospital medical record. She looks at Dad with practiced compassion. "So, Peter… what's going on that brings you in today?"

It's a standard opening line, one I've asked thousands of new patients. But the idea of discussing *why* we are here makes my stomach smash to my feet.

As Dr. Burkland types, Dad describes his nagging back pain, his lingering fatigue. And then, six days ago, the unexpected blood in his urine.

Which led to the CT scan.

Which showed *the cancer.*

The word echoes in my head, a bell I can't unring.

I want to stay present, to actively listen, but if I do, that might make this real. And my dad, my hero, my glue, cannot have cancer.

No!

No!

No!

My phone buzzes.

Jake: Good luck at your dad's appointment. Love you.

I silence the message without replying, trying to focus on Dr. Burkland's questions. Absentmindedly, I twirl my wedding ring, a rose-gold band. My engagement ring—the two-carat, princess-cut solitaire Jake bought me, despite my requests for something understated—is at home. It's too flashy to be worn around my patients. Or really, most people.

Jake.

My husband, Jake.

Although we've been married for five years, the idea of having a husband still feels foreign, almost fake. The title of "wife" is another role I portray convincingly, similar to "doctor" and "well-adjusted human."

Dr. Burkland's lips move. I untangle words like "biopsy," "metastasis," and "chemotherapy." My gaze darts around the room, looking for somewhere, *anywhere*, else to devote my attention.

I examine the artwork adorning the wall, studying a picture of the ocean. A dramatic sunset paints the horizon, the colors fading from golden yellow to sapphire blue. On the water is a single boater. The text reads: *You can't stop the waves, but you can learn to surf.* It seems profound, but my brain is too overwrought to make sense of it.

Dr. Burkland speaks again, detailing the newer, immune-modulating treatments for kidney cancer. I want to know, but my mind can't process the information. Dad asks a question while I imagine sitting on Eagle Beach in Aruba, a Mudslide and my Kindle in my hands, the sand tickling my toes.

Yes, I want to be there, not here.

Anywhere but here.

"Dr. Burkland, can you give an idea about the prognosis?" Mom asks, her shoulders knotted together, plunging me back to reality.

Why, Mom?

Why would you ask that?

That's the number one question not to be asking!

The question I've been dreading since the moment I saw the CT scan.

"Well, we need to do some additional testing, but it appears Peter has advanced kidney cancer. Likely, our goal won't be to cure it but to keep it at bay. Peter, we want to keep you doing the things you love. Working and enjoying time with your family. That's our main priority. Quality of life."

I can't speak as Dr. Burkland's words congeal to my brain.

No cure.

Preserve quality of life.

Shit.

"So, how much time are we talking, Doc?" Dad's voice is barely a whisper. Behind his glasses, his brown eyes shrivel. This wonderful man—this life force whom I've always believed to be indestructible—looks scared to death.

"A few years ago, I would have said, maybe a year, but with some of the newer treatments, I think we're looking at significantly more time," Dr. Burkland says. "But let's not get ahead of ourselves. We need to take everything one step at a time… I know it's hard but try not to jump too far ahead."

A year.

A year?

A freaking year!

More if we're lucky?

How quickly the definition of "lucky" can change.

Dad asks something else, but panic detonates inside my body, the hysteria in my mind drowning out everything.

I'm going to lose my dad.

Oh my god.

I now take Lexapro to control my anxiety, to manage that nagging inner voice caused by perpetual discontentment. The medication, along with daily running, usually helps.

But not with this.

Nothing can help with this.

***

I glare at the clock: 2:24 a.m.

My body is exhausted but my mind is one trillion percent alert.

Dr. Burkland said to take things one step at a time, but in typical fashion, I'm already twenty-seven theoretical steps ahead.

How can I live without my dad?

How can I make his remaining time as meaningful as possible?

My legs are restless against the mint satin sheets.

Maybe I need to give him a grandchild.

He's been begging for one since he walked me down the aisle.

Jake's asleep next to me, his right arm slung above his head, his eyebrows undulating with each snore. Beneath the overhead fan, his auburn hair sways. I study his face: kind and tender and dependable.

I consider rustling him awake. To seek out his comfort.

But it won't help.

Because even right next to him, I'm impossibly alone.

He doesn't know me.

The real me.

I've only ever confided my true self to one man.

We shared the most magical connection… and then…

Poof.

He was *gone*.

THEN:

Eleven Years Ago

September, 2007

26

COREY

"Wow, this view is insane. *Fucking* insane, I mean. You've managed to outdo yourself again. Somehow," Tessa mutters, threading her arm around my waist. Her touch causes those familiar, zappy goosebumps to slink up my arms.

We're standing together on the balcony of our hotel room. We've just checked in to the Asara Wine Estates in Stellenbosch, South African wine country. The vineyard ahead is expansive, filled with rows of green and purple grapes. The sky above is a concentrated blue, speckled with woolly clouds. Mount Stellenbosch towers in the background. The air is ripe with wildflowers, fruit and Tessa's lemony hair.

I press my nose to her head, guzzling her scent, trying not to contemplate her looming departure.

She's going home.

In two damn weeks.

Fuck.

She burst into my life so unexpectedly—like gleaming sunshine—illuminating my darkest parts. Now, I can't imagine returning to blackness. To total numbness.

"Are you okay, Corey?" Her russet eyes pierce my thoughts, a raw, defenselessness frothing inside me.

I nod, but I'm not okay.

Because, in spite of the fact that she lives 12,000 kilometers away and is leaving me so damn soon, I'm moronically, idiotically and entirely in love with her.

The feeling terrifies the shit out of me—scarier than being stranded in the bone-dry savanna with three sips of water left.

"What time's the van driving us to lunch?" Tessa asks, the sun pecking her face with flashes of hot pink.

"The golden specs in your eyes are doing that thing right now," I tell her, brushing my thumb to her upper lip. "And we have to be downstairs in the lobby in an hour."

"An hour? Hmm. I wonder how we can pass the time…" She presses her mouth to mine, and then she grabs my hand, leading me inside.

***

Ninety minutes later, I take my seat across from her on the patio of the Moreson Winery. The table's center is marked by an assortment of white and orange lilies. The sun is tepid, threatening to unleash its heat, but for the moment, restrained. Tessa is wearing a red sleeveless shirt, her honey-brown locks still a little tangled from bed.

"I like your hair when it's messy," I tease, picking up my menu, skimming the fixed wine-paired lunch. "I hope you like this place. I came here with my brother, Carl, two years ago. We decided it was one of the top five lunches of our lives."

"The menu looks amazing and I'm starving," Tessa says, her dimple shooting out, my chest humming like a bird is stuck inside.

A lanky waiter with spiky red hair saunters over, toting a bottle of wine. "Greetings! I'm your server, Sebastian. I have your first glass, our decadent Chardonnay. I believe you'll find it the perfect blend of fruity and dry. It was produced on the vineyard four seasons ago." Tessa nods appreciatively as he pours us a glass. "I'll be back with your first course shortly."

I hold up my wineglass. "Cheers. To you, Tess."

"To *us*," she replies, clinking our glasses together.

Us.

What the hell are we?

We haven't discussed it, and I'm scared to ask, worried I'll learn that I'm merely a fling, almost entirely flung.

Only two more damn weeks.

Fuck.

I let the wine slide down my throat. "Hmm, that's good."

I always find the power of alcohol so seducing.

Sometimes, too seducing.

Tessa unfolds her napkin, draping it in her lap. "My dad's a huge proponent of proper dining etiquette," she offers before I can even ask.

"Oh yeah?" The topic of her father hasn't come up since our boat ride on the Chobe River. I still sense her father has a potent pull over her—but I'm not sure how or why.

"When I was a kid, I was tasked to help him set the table for Thanksgiving. We used my grandmother's china. The process would take hours. My dad liked to make sure each spoon, each fork, each knife was exactly in the right spot. After we'd finished, he'd come around to check each setting. No matter what, I'd always mess something up. Like I'd put the wineglass to the left of the water. It probably doesn't sound fun… but he was always home for Thanksgiving, and it was such a great morning together." Her eyes spray with affection, talking about her dad.

"I can tell how much you love your dad," I say.

Tessa nods. "Yeah, he's my hero. I look up to him so much. He's the most important man in my life."

I smile but my heart nosedives like I've just stepped off an invisible ledge.

A thought smacks me in the face.

I want that title instead.

Sebastian reappears, delivering our first course: truffle mushroom soup with a scoop of cream alongside a crispy baguette and unsalted butter. "Enjoy," he says before retreating.

Tessa lifts her soupspoon, dipping it gingerly into the hot broth. She scrunches her nose, beaming with approval. "Wow, that's delicious. I can see why you ranked this place so highly."

"I'm glad you like it, and your dedication to good etiquette is pretty adorable, too," I enthuse.

And every other damn piece of you.

Instead of tasting my soup, I take another huge slug of wine, emptying my glass, wrestling against my temptation to be numb.

It's dreadful feeling an inebriating love for a woman on the verge of leaving me.

On cue, Sebastian returns, carrying our second wine. "This is our Cabernet Sauvignon. It's perfect when paired with a gamey meat, like the one you'll soon be served. It's quite special, as it was aged seven years in an unoaked barrel."

Tessa raises her eyebrows, listening to the history of the wine. "What's it aged in, then?" Interest piques her voice. I smile, imagining Tessa in a full lecture hall, the most attentive student in the class.

"A steel barrel," Sebastian answers, too enthusiastically, his red hair standing vertical. The wine appears purple under the sun's glare as Sebastian fills our glasses. "Sir, take a tiny taste. Please, let me know what you think."

I raise the wine to my lips, gulping half of it down.

Sebastian lets out a low gasp.

"It's good," I tell him dryly.

The wine is good.

But really, *all* fucking wine is good.

And right now, I would drink anything that would stop this ache from demolishing the pit of my stomach.

"Well… great," Sebastian chirps, forcibly closing his bottom lip before leaving.

Tessa shoots me a look.

I shrug sheepishly, the wine sloshing around my empty belly.

She stares at me, clearing her throat. "So, Corey, what's the craziest thing you've ever done?"

I take another long sip of wine. "What?"

"I was just wondering… what's the craziest thing you've ever done?"

I study her mouth as she speaks, noticing how her cheeks puff out when she says my name. *Cor-ee*.

I scoop three big bites of soup into my mouth, the hot liquid colliding with my stomach full of wine.

Tessa's russet eyes narrow. "So… what's your answer?"

The wine twirls through my brain, my head growing light, my thoughts becoming feathers. "Hmm… I would probably have to say, being with you."

The answer sounds horrifically stupid as soon as the words are out.

Tessa's eyebrows bunch together. "Being with me is the craziest thing you've ever done? How is that possible? I thought you'd say bungee jumping or tracking some wild animal!"

Fuck.

"Sorry, Tess," I say, scrambling to fix it. "Those would have been way better answers… but… I didn't mean it in a bad way."

"Help me understand, Corey, how is it a compliment?" Her eyebrows shoot upwards, forming her worried expression—I've learned to discern her emotions by the shape of her brow.

Fuck.

I take a deep breath. "Well… after Leona died, I sort of shut down… to survive. But somehow, around you, I started to feel my feelings again, even though I didn't want to. To be honest, feeling my feelings sucks, but since I can feel, I feel super crazy… and scared. Scared for caring about you so much because I know you have to go home soon, and it's going to hurt me… a lot." The words escape, but I'm no longer in control of my mouth.

The damn fucking wine.

The wine, which was supposed to numb me, has instead made me a truth-spewing pile of shit.

Fuck!

"Wow, okay, somehow you found a way to make that explanation really sweet, Corey… I care about you a lot, too. I don't want to go home, either."

I peer into her eyes—soft and inviting and enthralling. Eyes I could literally fucking drown in.

"You care about me?" I'm stunned.

"Yeah, of course. I'm really sad about going home." She reaches for my hand, vulnerability gushing through me.

"You are?" My voice is barely a grunt.

"Yes." Her gaze trails down my face. "Why do you seem so surprised?"

"I don't know. I guess I assumed… you'd be happy to get back to your fancy life in America."

Her cheeks turn white as she brushes a strand of hair from her face. "Corey, my life at home isn't fancy. It's a freaking mess."

"What are you talking about, Tess?" I've imagined a lot of scenarios about her world at home, but *none* like this.

"Well, in Philadelphia, Greg lives seven blocks away, and I'll be back around my dad all the time… and it's just… a lot of pressure…"

Greg.

Fucking Greg!

I'd blocked that bastard from my mind, but now, the thought of him being close to Tessa makes me frantic.

What if she goes back to him?

What if he tries to hurt her again?

Fuck!

"Tessa, I'm not just saying this selfishly, or maybe I am, but you *can't* go back to Greg. Please, I'm begging you. You deserve so much more—"

She waves her hand. "I won't, Corey. Don't worry. You helped me learn self-respect. I *never* want to see him again."

"Okay, thank god." Relief courses through me. "But what do you mean, it's a lot of pressure?"

Her forehead scrunches as her shoulders drop and suddenly, her deep inner layers are back. The ones I'd started to strip away.

But every time I think I understand her, there are more layers to discover.

To unwrap.

"You know what… can we please talk about Leona?" she asks. "I've told you a lot about my messiness, stuff I've never told anyone. But sometimes… I feel like I know *nothing* about you. It feels like I've been the only one to really open up."

She's right, of course, but her statement still punctures like a thousand daggers plunging into my heart.

Fuck.

Sebastian bounces over, merrily clearing our soup plates, entirely unaware of the moment he's interrupting. I drink some water, my body tensing against the wicker chair. I can't talk about Leona.

"Who's Leona?" Tessa asks again as Sebastian walks away. "Was she your girlfriend?"

At this notion, I snort.

Tessa studies me.

High-pitched squealing from the next table pulls my attention. I didn't notice them when we first sat. It's presumably two parents and their toddler daughter. The girl shrieks with glee, coloring a silly picture of a monkey as they sip on wine.

Leona loved coloring.

Leona loved living.

Leona is dead.

"Corey." Tessa's voice tethers me back to our table.

Sebastian returns, his hands full of two heaping plates of food. "This is Chef's special. Braised gazelle in a red wine sauce, with risotto and garlic-herb crusted potatoes." I shoot Sebastian a death glare. He hasn't done anything wrong—except be painfully annoying—and right now, I'm the frumpiest grump. Sebastian leaves, and Tessa drinks her wine, waiting for my answer.

Fuck.

Fuck.

Fuck.

I suck in a drag of humid air. "No, Leona wasn't my girlfriend. She was my little sister." My mouth fills with acid, speaking of her in the past tense.

"Oh, Corey. Wow... I'm so sorry." Tessa's eyes melt into a sea of compassion. She stands up, leaving her uneaten plate, dragging her chair beside mine. Wrapping her arms around my neck, she drops her head onto my shoulder. "Tell me about her." Her warm breath coats my sweaty skin.

Deep inside my chest, my shambolic scar starts to pulsate.

"She was a surprise addition to my family," I say, my words barely audible. "She died of leukemia when she was four. I was eighteen when we lost her. She was the happiest, silliest, smartest, cutest little girl in the world. I adored the hell out of her. Her death... well, basically, it destroyed me." The confession tears something open. A lump devours my throat, nearly choking me. Admitting it out loud, at last, I'm exposing my brokenness.

Tessa tightens her embrace. "I don't even know what to say. I can't imagine what you've been through. My heart breaks for you and your family." The empathy in her voice softens the blow of my grief, if only marginally. It doesn't erase the pain, but it dulls the sharp edges.

"She was the cutest damn toddler on the planet," I whisper, gulping. "She had curly blonde hair and these stunning violet eyes. She was so brave and compassionate." I pause, trying to get the words out. "At the playground, she would scale the equipment meant for the big kids. She didn't care about getting hurt. But if another kid got hurt, she'd cry hysterically. Once, we had to leave the park after this boy tumbled off the swings, and Leona was so upset, she couldn't stop crying."

"Wow," Tessa says, squeezing my hand. "That's painfully sweet."

"Leona loved the whole family, but I was *her* person. Out of nowhere, she'd say things to me like, 'Core, I love you. Does that make you happy?' And it did. So fucking much."

"Oh, Corey." Tessa's face crumples.

A string of tears threaten to spring loose.

My arm juts out to rub my eyes.

I accidentally knock my plate off the table.

It splatters to the ground.

"Fuck," I grumble.

"Corey, don't worry. I'll clean it up. I'll ask Sebastian for a new one. It's okay."

Her reassurance hangs in the air, but my mind isn't here anymore.

It jets back in time, to the kitchen of my childhood home.

I'm heating a bowl of spaghetti while Leona sits at the table, too sick to eat but keeping me company. Her legs dangle from the chair, impossibly tiny from chemotherapy, her eyes brighter than they should be given how frail the treatments have made her. As I take the steaming plate out of the microwave, I drop it, cursing and scowling, the white cabinets painted red from the sauce.

"Core, don't be sad," Leona chimes. "I'll help clean it up. You can make a new bowl. Give me a paper towel."

Her bony legs scurry off the stool. I hand her a wet paper towel, and she wipes the mess. But since she's only four, she creates an even larger one.

I smile.

"It's just dinner. It's okay," she reassures me.

My heart ruptures at how fiercely she cares for me.

How deeply good she is.

How hugely and irreplaceably I love her.

Three months later, she dies.

I blink, the memory evaporating.

Sebastian sweeps away the broken shards.

She's gone.

She's gone.

She's gone.

Fuck.

Fuck.

FUCK!

"Corey, are you okay?" Tessa whispers.

No.

No.

No!

She strokes my juddering jaw.

"Leona would have loved you," I manage. "In a lot of ways… you remind me of her."

As I say it, I realize it for the first time.

Maybe that's why I'm so drawn to Tessa—at their core, Leona and Tessa are both big-hearted empaths, believing the world to be kinder and fairer than it actually is.

Tessa keeps her arms draped around me, nuzzling my neck. "I wish

I could have met her. I'm so sad I can't. I know that probably sounds ridiculous, but I can tell how special she was."

After a tragic death, I learned people say the dumbest things to make you feel better. Or maybe, to make *themselves* feel better. But the words from Tessa oddly feel genuine and they do make me feel a little better.

"Yes, she was amazing, my Little Lion."

Tessa's fingernails scroll the lettering on my left arm. "Is your tattoo for Leona?"

My eyes drift shut.

I'm holding Leona's tiny, cold, just-lifeless hand in my fingers, whispering, "One day, we'll be together again, to live happily ever after, just like you deserve."

I open my eyes, a waterfall threatening to release.

Tessa gazes at me with concern.

"Yeah, the tattoo is of a lioness, for Leona, my warrior. She liked when I made up fairy tales about families living happily ever after. She never stopped believing in her own happy ending. Neither did I... pretty much right up until the day she died."

Tessa clutches my hand which now shakes wildly. "Oh... Corey... wow... I don't even know what to say."

"It's that way a lot with grief. Sometimes, there's nothing to fucking say." The words choke out, along with the crushing pain for Leona's beautiful life... truncated. A string of big, ugly tears rush down my cheeks.

I blink again, trying to contain the swell, but the pressure's built sky-high.

I'm Old Faithful, about to blow.

"Corey, it's good to let it out." Tessa pulls my head into her chest, wrapping her arms around me. I let my weight fall against her.

Then, for the first time in eleven years, I cry.

I cry for Leona.

And for myself.

I cry for the years of numbness.

And for the weeks of pain since I've been able to feel again.

I cry for everything lost along the way.

For all the milestones Leona has missed.

Every birthday.

Every school event.

All the joy she would have brought into the world.

I cry for all the time I've spent technically alive but not really living.

I cry at the truth I can no longer avoid.

That the world will remain inherently messy, whether I feel or not.

That nothing can stop bad things from happening.

Tessa runs her fingers through the back of my hair. "Shh, I'm here, Corey."

Sebastian returns, delivering a new entrée. "Enjoy Chef's delicious food," he singsongs before scampering away.

"That guy *really* needs to learn to read the fucking room," I mutter, shaking my head into Tessa's red shirt.

She laughs. "Poor Sebastian." She uses her napkin, still folded in her lap, to dab the leftover tears from my face. "It's okay, Corey."

It's not okay.

But that doesn't change it.

That was the truth I couldn't face eleven years ago.

In life, sometimes good things happen.

And sometimes bad things happen.

But no matter *which* things happen, the world keeps turning.

Life continues.

I squeeze Tessa's ribs, inhaling her lemony hair, the scent palliating me like a Xanax.

I love you, I want to say.

Instead, I clear my throat. "How about we finish our lunch? Let's lighten the mood a bit?"

"Okay, are you sure? Thanks for opening up to me about Leona."

"Yep." I force a smile. "Now, can we try to enjoy the rest of our weekend?"

"If that's what you want, absolutely."

She kisses me, and for a minute, I let myself get lost in her.

But in the back of my mind, I know that in two more weeks, another very bad thing's going to happen.

Yet, impossibly, but surely, there will be an *after*.

After Tessa.

Life will go on.

It always fucking does.

27

TESSA

"When's Marley coming?" I ask Liz, who's seated next to me in the maternal outpatient clinic.

"Friday! I can't wait," Liz beams.

It's Monday of our last week at the hospital. It's been a slow morning so far. We've only seen three patients, all needing routine prenatal care. I hope the trend continues for the rest of our shift. Selfishly, I want to escape our rotation without any more gaping emotional wounds.

In front of me, Dr. Sebopelo is discussing a patient with Jeremy, his long, solid fingers acting out his words. Some people communicate with their mouths, some with their eyes, but Dr. Sebopelo *definitely* speaks with his hands.

"So, what's going to happen with Mr. Safari Dreamboat when you leave?" Liz whispers.

My plane to Philly leaves in exactly one week. I came to Botswana determined to fall in love with medicine. But despite all I've seen and learned, my role as an actor feels more entrenched than ever. As much as I want to, I *still* don't love medicine.

But I have fallen for Corey.

And I have no idea what to do.

"I don't—"

The door to the clinic shoves open, the burst of air blowing a stack of papers off the nearby desk. "Please, I need help!" The voice is high-pitched and frantic.

And familiar.

Where do I know that voice from?

I glance up, realizing the rattled patient is Evah. Her large brown eyes blare with alarm, as she bows over, seizing her protruding belly, which has doubled in size in the five weeks since I last saw her.

When her baby was okay.

This fact has propelled me through my daunting days at the hospital. Through the dark moments of suffering and death, the promise of hope has continued to shine. In new life.

I leap up, rushing to her side. "Evah, what's wrong?" A spool of terror twists in my stomach, pushed up by a rolling pin into my lungs. I grasp Evah's clammy wrist, leading her to the exam area. Liz follows behind us.

Sinking against the exam table, Evah's words clot against her sobs, her speech indecipherable. "I'm... I... baby."

"Evah, take a deep breath. Everything's going to be okay. Just calm down so you can tell us what's happening." My voice is creamy and warm, but on the inside, I'm shaky and frozen.

I'm a pathetic, sham actor.

Evah's cheeks flush crimson as she struggles for words. "The bleeding is back... and my stomach hurts very much."

Shit.

The bleeding is back?

That's bad.

I know it instinctively, even though I wish it wasn't the truth. My hand shakes on top of Evah's wrist as words fail me.

"We'll help you. Tell us what happened, please." The sturdy voice belongs to Liz. I forgot she was even here. Liz's eyes are intent and focused, her hands coolly clasped, her posture steady but attentive.

I'm struck by our stark contrast. Composed Liz, who *wants* to be an ER doctor, who loves the thrill of the unknown, who's deeply passionate about interceding in human crisis. And me, terrified by the unpredictable, panicked by being the responsible provider in this situation.

I'm such a fucking joke.

Evah's words interrupt my self-loathing. "I've been taking it easy, like you said, and the bleeding stopped. But this morning, when I was at work, I felt a gush of blood, and it won't stop." Evah's face betrays her fear, even her ears seem to stand erect, every part of her braced for bad news.

"Please lie down so we can take a look," Liz instructs, her tone kind but firm. "We'll be right back." She hands Evah a gown and drape. Liz tugs me, paralyzed by fright, outside the exam room. "Are you okay, Tess?" Her hazel eyes squint, giving me a once-over.

"Yeah," I lie. "I saw Evah a few weeks ago when she had vaginal bleeding. I'm just really hoping her baby's okay."

Her baby has to be okay.

"Okay, let's check her out," Liz says, seemingly content to take charge as I falter. Liz knocks on the exam room.

"Come in," Evah cries. On the floor, Evah's white underwear lies in a pile, sopping red. She reclines on the exam table, her legs bent at the knee, a trail of red streaking down the exam paper. With gloved hands, Liz attempts to insert the speculum, but Evah's vagina is filled with too much blood. Liz shoots me a worried glance. I run for Dr. Sebopelo, who I find still talking to Jeremy, exactly as before, his hands moving in conjunction with his lips. Back in the exam area, Evah's world is falling apart. But here, in the front of the trailer, it's business as usual.

"Dr. Sebopelo!" I scream, my voice horror-struck. "This patient is hemorrhaging. We need your help right away!"

The words yank him into action, hands dropping mid-gesture, and he sprints behind me down the short hallway.

Please let her and the baby be okay.

Please let her and the baby be okay.

Vomit floods my mouth. I try to swallow it back down, gagging. I grasp the wall, wanting to collapse.

To disappear.

To be anywhere but here.

Liz is at the head of the exam table, comforting a shuddering Evah, who again clutches her abdomen, fingers white-knuckled. Within seconds, Dr. Sebopelo takes command. And minutes later, Evah's being prepped for emergency surgery.

***

Evah's rushed into one of the hospital's three operating rooms, quickly intubated and put under general anesthesia. Her surgery is performed by Dr. Doreen Morungu, a skilled Motswana obstetrician. Dr. Morungu makes a large vertical cut along Evah's abdomen. I watch in terror as she hurriedly separates layers of muscle and tissue. With one final cut, Evah's womb opens, blood spurting from the cavity. Dr. Morungu tears at her uterus, grabbing and pulling, trying to free the baby. Seconds stretch into what feels like hours as I forget to breathe.

Please let the baby be okay.

Please let the baby be okay.

Finally, the baby is out.

But it's blue, dangling limply in the air, suspended in Dr. Morungu's toned brown arms. Like when Simba is presented in *The Lion King*, only bone-chillingly silent.

"He's not breathing," Dr. Morungu calls out, cutting the umbilical cord and passing him to a nearby waiting nurse. She returns her attention to Evah, removing the placenta, hoisting the vascular organ high into the air. "A complete placental abruption," she states, without emotion. She might have said she wants potatoes with her eggs. But I know what her words mean. The lifeline between Evah and her baby severed, causing the bleeding and robbing the baby of precious oxygen.

A nurse places an oxygen mask over the miniature baby's cerulean face. He's a vibrant, almost beautiful shade of blue. If not for the fact that babies are *never* supposed to be blue.

Shit.

No!

Shit.

No!

Dr. Sebopelo's two fingers compress against the boy's unmoving chest. The very same ones that minutes before were gesturing merrily with Jeremy, now furiously work to save this baby's life. He pauses, allowing the nurse to give breaths in between compressions.

Please start breathing.

Please start breathing.

I'm not religious, but I frantically bargain with God—any God—to let this boy live. My desperation bubbles up, gushing out like a volcano furiously erupting after decades of dormancy.

Time stops.

I stand incapacitated, watching them perform CPR.

But the baby does not cry.

He does not move.

I flinch as my heart shatters.

In the end, he cannot be saved.

***

"Tessa, are you okay?" Dr. Sebopelo asks twenty minutes later. I'm slumped against the red brick building, sitting on the dewy concrete, tugging at my scrub top, trying to intake air.

"No, I'm not okay," I mumble in an anguished daze, for once admitting my truth.

I.

Am.

Not.

Okay.

Through all my training as a doctor, I've been hanging on by a single string. Like in the bungee jump, I constantly dangle over a perpetual cliff, held in place by one tiny rope. But that lone strand has now snapped, leaving me plummeting towards the cold, hard ground.

"That was very sad, Tessa," he says, sitting down beside me. "It's normal to feel upset." The tips of his fingers are red, the skin grated from his frantic compressions.

"I'm devastated," I whisper.

"Do you know what I've learned from working here?" he asks, his brown eyes wide.

"What?" I want to bawl, but instead, I forcefully dig my fingernails into my palms.

"Just like life, medicine has many hard parts and many good parts. It must always be a two-sided coin. Without rainy days, sunny days have no value. You can only appreciate the good in contrast with the bad. My work has shown me it's the same with pain. When someone dies, especially so young, it's terrible. There is no denying that. But pain has value, too, Tessa. Pain can teach us to appreciate the beauty in life."

***

An hour later, I crouch beside a sleeping Evah, unsure how my own body remains erect. Evah rests on a mattress on the floor near the entrance to the overcrowded women's surgical ward. Still sedated from the anesthesia, Evah looks bizarrely peaceful.

I wish she could stay like this forever.

Once she awakens, time for Evah will cleave. She will exist only in the *after.* After her son died. Next to Evah lies her stillborn boy, swaddled in a blue hospital blanket. His eyes are shut. His nose is stationary. His lungs are static. He doesn't cry.

He will never cry.

If I pretend, I can delude myself that he's merely sleeping. That, in the cruelest way imaginable, his little life hasn't ended before even being allowed to begin.

Evah stirs, her eyes flickering open, then closing, as the harsh hospital lights seep in. She rolls, wincing, her hands skimming her raw incision. "Shh, try not to move, Evah. You just had major surgery," I say, flattening her blanket, stroking her pallid cheek. Soon, Evah's physical discomfort will likely intensify, but the hospital has no pain medications to offer. She'll have to bear through it.

"Where's my baby?" Evah mumbles, her voice hoarse from intubation, her eyelids tugging down, heavy from the lingering anesthetic.

He's dead.

The world is an awful place, and your baby is dead.

Like the girl with rabies.

And the woman with pneumonia.

And little Leona.

My temples pound, my head on the verge of combustion.

Shit.

How can I tell her this?

It is the most tragic news I've ever personally delivered.

"Evah, I'm so sorry," I whisper, my hands quaking. "Your baby didn't survive. Your placenta broke away from your uterus. The baby had no oxygen. The team did everything they could to save him."

My explanation feels lamentably flat. It's technical but offers little in the way of how such a thing could *actually* happen. How could a world be so ruthless to take an unborn baby from his mother's womb?

Evah bellows a deep, guttural wail—the reverberation of a person in the throes of the most overpowering suffering life can deliver. A noise so excruciatingly pained, it instantly craters a permanent hole into my chest.

I pull Evah close, hugging her. It's probably inappropriate behavior from a medical student but I can't refuse my need to comfort Evah. Or myself.

"I'm so terribly sorry, Evah," I say, the sentiment feeling wholly inadequate.

Wordlessly, I pick up Evah's son, laying him face down against her chest, skin-to-skin. Evah wraps her arms around the hushed cerulean boy, plastering dozens of kisses against his soft head. She inhales his scent, sobbing wildly. "My boy, my boy, my boy."

I stay totally still, eviscerated by the unfairness of life.

Of the image of sweet Evah, cradling the son she'll never raise.

And then, with a bolt of clarity, I finally admit a long-brewing truth.

One which I've never been willing, or perhaps able, to acknowledge.

A career in medicine is going to destroy me.

28

COREY

I knock twice on Joe's office door, curling my fists from nerves.

What the hell am I doing?

I'm here to confess my relationship with Tessa to my boss, tired of the constant worries about losing my job. Plus, selfishly, I want to bring Tessa here to the lodge for her final weekend.

Fuck.

How is this her last weekend?

I fight off a wave of dread, the storm inside me churning towards a damn tsunami.

"Come in," Joe's deep voice gripes.

His office is located in the back of the main lodge, with floor-to-ceiling windows overlooking the watering hole. In my opinion, Joe has an undeservingly amazing view. He occupies the office which I dream of one day inhabiting myself.

I slink through the door.

I hope this doesn't end in total disaster.

Fuck.

In my five years at Impodimo Lodge, Joe's been a fair supervisor, although, mostly he keeps to himself. Joe's seated behind his mahogany desk, typing furiously. The glare of the sun reflects off his bald head, his round belly overhanging like a basketball beneath his too-tight Impodimo Lodge shirt. Although he works at a luxury lodge in the middle of nowhere, he always seems to be juggling a multitude of crises.

"Do you have a second?" I ask, my tone rickety. I take a seat in one of the open leather chairs. My eyes pull to the watering hole where several elephants are soaking, seeking a lull from the blistering sun.

Tessa.

My heart thwacks, wondering if I'll always associate these beautiful creatures with her from now on.

Fuck.

"Yeah, sure, Corey. What's up?" Joe keeps typing, not pausing to look up. He mutters to himself about one guest problem and then another.

It's now or never.

Fuck.

"Joe, I had a relationship with a guest. I know it's strictly against company policy, and I'm sorry. I wanted to tell you before word got back to you. I love my job and would never want to jeopardize it." Halfway through my statement, Joe stops typing and glowers at me, hard.

Fuck.

"You had a relationship with a guest?" he asks, flabbergasted. "I heard some rumblings, but I assumed they were gibberish. Jesus, Corey!"

"Yes, but it's not what you think." My chest stretches tighter than a rubber band. "She came here—Tessa's her name—eight weeks ago with her medical school classmates. Maybe you remember the group? But I've seen her outside of here several times. It wasn't just some stupid fling, Joe. I'm in love with her."

What the actual fuck?

I just admitted to Joe I'm in love with Tessa?

I haven't told her, or anyone, that.

This is a new low, even for me.

Joe's lips pucker in displeasure, eyeing me up and down, his eyebrows rumpling with fury. "What? You're in love with her?"

Fuck.

Have I gone insane?

"Yes." My voice is small. I'm entirely humbled by the ludicrous revelations spilling from my damn mouth. "I know, it sounds ridiculous. It is ridiculous, to be honest. So painfully stupid. I'm an idiot, Joe. She's going back to the U.S. on Monday, and I'm crushed." Despite myself, I just keep making it worse.

Shut the fuck up, man.

But my mind can barely concentrate. All I can think is that Tessa is leaving, in seven damn days. We've built a precarious tower of passion on the precipice of total collapse. I'm worried the rubble might swallow me whole—and I've just barely started to emerge from the ruins of life's last damning tragedy.

Fuck.

"Okay… wow, Corey… I'm, uh, sorry to hear about everything you are going through." Joe fidgets against his desk chair, rattling his pen. In our five years of working together, this is the longest we've ever spoken.

"Thanks, Joe. I'm sorry to make this so awkward, but I just… wanted you to know. I hope you can forgive my behavior. Again, I'm extremely sorry. It was deeply unprofessional, and I won't let it happen again. I promise." I peer into Joe's weary glare, begging for his mercy.

Joe's scowl eventually gives way to a more neutral expression, his eyes sprinkling with dabs of pity. So against all rationality, I continue. "Also, I was wondering… is there any way… Tessa could come stay here… with me… this weekend? I know I'm working, and I won't let her get in the way of that."

I really hope he doesn't fire me right this second.

Fuck.

Joe silently processes my brazen request as I wish I could slither out of my skin. Finally, he says, "Fine, but don't let her interfere with your work responsibilities this weekend or going forward."

I smile, grateful for his clemency. "She won't, I promise. Thank you for understanding, and again, I'm deeply sorry." I hold out my hand, which Joe inelegantly shakes.

As I'm halfway out the door, Joe calls out, "And Corey, please, and I mean this with complete professionalism. *Do not* fall in love with any more guests!"

"Yes, sir, I don't plan on it."

Never fucking again.

***

Hours later, sleep's just taken hold when my buzzing phone shakes me awake. I glance at the red lettering on my clock: 23:48. "Hello?"

"Corey, I had the worst day, and I don't know what to do." Tessa's voice is muffled by choking sobs.

I spring up in bed, a wild animal suddenly on high alert. "Tess, what happened? What's going on? Are you hurt?" She says more, but it's a jumbled mess of tears and hysteria.

"I'm coming now," I tell her without thinking twice.

I glance at the clock.

Six hours until I have to be at work.

But in seven days, she'll be gone for good.

***

"What's going on?" I ask Liz when she meets me outside of their flat, after I drove like a damn NASCAR driver, reaching Timali Court in fifty-four minutes.

"I'll let her tell you, but it was a pretty rough day in clinic," Liz says, pulling her robe tight against the cool breeze.

I hesitate, sighing out a gush of air. "Liz, will you take care of her… when you guys get home? I won't be there, but she can't go back to Greg. I'm worried… will you make sure she's okay?" I hadn't planned on saying this, but it just flies out of my mouth.

Fuck.

Liz looks at me, sympathy coloring her eyes—and suddenly, I'm immensely grateful for her presence in Tessa's life. "I will, Corey, I promise. I love Tessa."

"So do I," I whisper, stripped bare.

Another thing I hadn't planned on saying that just blurts out.

Fuck.

I'm really acting crazy today!

Liz's lips coil into a happy frown. "That's really sweet, Corey. Come, let me take you to our girl." She leads me to their shared bedroom, then quietly leaves.

I pause, slapping my cheeks, as if that will somehow steady my nerves.

God, love is fucking terrifying.

I open the door. Tessa's curled up in a ball on her bed, still wearing her hospital scrubs, her stethoscope thrown on the brown carpet. Her hair is a tangled web of knots. Pain blasts off her skin, spurting out and slicing my heart up like a filet. "Hey, *pragtige dame*, what's going on?" I sink down on her bed, scooping her weeping body into my arms. She softens into me, burrowing deeper, her lemony hair brushing my stubble.

How does she always smell so damn good?

How can I live without her smell?

Fear fills my brain as Tessa points to a crumpled paper lying beside her. "Open it," she whispers through tears.

Keeping my arms wrapped around her, I pick it up, unfolding it.

In messy handwriting is scrawled: *I don't want to be a doctor.*

"Tess? What's this? I don't understand?" I search her gutted, glassy eyes for meaning. Her pupils are distant, her lips still. "Tess? Talk to me. Explain." I hold her body, pressing my mouth against her pale cheek.

Her voice is granular. It sounds like sand slipping through an hourglass. "I wasn't sure I'd be able to say it, so I wrote it down, but it's true. I've never admitted it to anyone. But… I don't want to be a doctor. I never have." Her forehead scrunches into a tight ball, the weight of her confession throttling around my neck.

Wait… what!

My voice reveals my shock. "What are you talking about, Tess?" She doesn't answer. Down the hall, someone laughs at the TV.

"Tess, talk to me," I say, wiping her cheeks with a tissue, peering into her face. I silently plead for the same openness she asked of me at the Moreson Winery.

"Do you remember the patient I told you about a few weeks ago? Who was pregnant and bleeding? But her baby was okay and I was so happy?" She pauses, the golden specks in her eyes dim.

"Of course I do."

I hang on every damn word she speaks.

"Well, she came back today with heavy bleeding and we rushed her into emergency surgery, but her baby didn't survive. Afterwards, I had to tell her that her son was dead. It was just… awful. She cried this horrendous wail. I'll never forget the sound, Corey. I can't handle the pain. Medicine is going to break me." Her face emulates her words, even her cheekbones sinking with anguish.

I remember *that* horrendous wail—the visceral sounds my parents made the day Leona died.

"Holy fuck, Tess. That's horrific. I'm so sorry for you and your patient.

The world can be pretty shitty, sometimes." I stroke her back. "But you're amazing. Do you know that? Don't beat yourself up for feeling sad. It's a gift to your patients to feel so deeply for them. It's a gift to everyone. Somehow, you opened me back up, even though I was dead as a rock inside."

Tessa looks at me, her brow furrowed with skepticism. Like usual, she's unable to appreciate her strengths. The ones that are so glaringly obvious to me.

"So are you admitting you're no longer a dead rock inside?" she whispers, her lips creeping into a teeny smile. Her heart-stopping dimple briefly appears, making my heart thud like a freight train.

"Yeah. Now, I'm a messy bag of feelings and it sucks. I was a babbling fucking moron with Joe earlier today and a bit less so with Liz, now, too. It's all thanks to you, the magical powers you don't even know you possess."

"What'd you say to Liz?"

"Oh, nothing much…" *Just that I fucking love you.* "But, seriously, Tess, you don't have to be a doctor. Be whatever you want, do what makes you happy. You're incredibly smart and talented and will be good at anything you put your mind to."

She sighs loudly, her doubts gluing to the bottom of my chin. "Corey, that all sounds nice but we both know it's ridiculous. This is my life path. I can't just quit, even if I want to. *Everyone* expects me to be a doctor."

She searches my eyes, seeking validation—or maybe permission?—to believe something else.

"Who is *everyone*?" She seems to be referring to *someone*. Her layers are revealed again, but this time, I can tell I'm near her core.

"Just… people… back in Philadelphia." She cracks her knuckles, averting my gaze. Instead, she looks at her tuberculosis textbook, slopped on the carpet.

"Anyone in particular?" I ask, my fingers twisting around chunks of her honey-golden hair.

I'm determined to complete my excavation.

To unearth her nucleus.

To solve the mystery behind her aching.

"No, just… you know, people."

I arch my eyebrows. "Tess." My voice sinks to a hushed whisper. "*Who* expects you to be a doctor?"

Her breath hitches before the words leak out like the final drip from a closed faucet.

"My dad."

The drop splatters to the ground, her landmine uncovered.

I *finally* understand her.

My heart swells like a fucking balloon, filling with even more goddamn love for her. She buries her face into my chest, her hands shaking. I cup the back of her head.

"Why does your dad expect you to be a doctor?"

"It's just… always been his dream for me," she mumbles into my shirt. "He's my hero. I can't let him down. That would destroy me, Corey."

I tilt her chin upwards, gently forcing her broken russet eyes to look at me. "Tessa, what is *your* dream for *you*?"

Her pupils grow large, seemingly stunned by this question. Her fingertips press into my temples. "I'm not sure. I've never had a lot of space… to think about what I want… from my own life."

"Well, maybe you owe it to yourself to spend some time figuring it out? If I learned anything from losing Leona, it's that life is short. Too short to waste doing things you don't like."

Her lips spiral down and then she's lost inside her mind. Similar to the first night we met, I watch the wrestling match inside her brain. She's struggling with the inevitability of disappointing someone—her dad or herself or possibly, even me.

"Shit, Corey. I just… don't understand it. I'm so absurdly privileged but inside, I'm such a freaking mess."

"You're not a mess," I say. "The world's just really messy." Her lips sink further, her jaw stained with burdens.

A crazy idea springs from my mouth.

"Stay here. With me. While you figure things out?"

There's no damn wine to blame it on. Just my stupid fucking opened heart.

Her mouth plunges so low it practically reaches her belly button. "What?"

I gulp. "You could stay here, with me. While you figure things out… or even… after?"

Fuck.

What am I saying?

Being vulnerable is horrible.

Her fingers curl into my chest, gripping my shirt, probing my face with disbelief. "Are you serious, Corey?"

My stomach rolls into a ball of dread. "Yes." I feel painfully sheepish and one hundred percent exposed. "I don't want you to leave."

"Really?" Three vagrant tears whisk down her ruby cheeks.

"Yes," I say, more firmly this time. "Stay. I don't want to lose you."

Her fingers zip across her mouth. "Wow… Corey."

Fuck.

I'm an idiot.

Her silence is stifling, a black fog blocking my vision.

This is going to totally push her away.

Fuck.

Fuck.

Fuck.

"Don't feel pressured to say anything back," she says finally, her golden specks blazing once more. "I know we haven't known each other very long… but… you're the only person I've ever shown myself to… who's ever really accepted me… thank you so much for that… I love you, Corey."

She loves me?

She.

Loves.

Me!

The words unthaw my last frozen pieces, euphoria raining through me. "I love you, too, Tessa. So much, it terrifies the shit out of me."

"Oh, Corey," she mumbles, her smile swallowing her face.

Then, her lips sail onto mine, kissing me madly as she wraps her arms around my neck.

Our clothes rip off in a frenzied flurry.

My dick is ready to explode.

She

Loves

Me!

Ninety seconds later, I'm inside her, making furious love to her, melting against her warmth, consumed by raw emotion.

I have no idea if she's staying or leaving.

If she's becoming a doctor or not.

But she loves me.

And for one brief moment, it's enough.

NOW:

Eleven Years Later

October, 2018

29

TESSA

I ring the doorbell on the shiny black door to Liz's new townhouse. She just moved to Northern Liberties, a chic neighborhood in Philly. I'm holding a present I hastily wrapped in Christmas paper, even though it's barely October.

Camille, my (almost) four-year-old goddaughter, swings the door open. She's the spitting image of Liz's wife, Marley, with angular brown eyes, silky chestnut hair and the sweetest button nose.

"Auntie Tessa!" she cries.

The cheer in her young voice tugs at something deep inside me—Camille's pure enthusiasm for life, her sheer, perfect innocence. A stark contrast to the messier emotions I've been wading through lately.

I pull the little girl against me, her small frame melting into my arms. "I brought you an early birthday gift, Cami." Her lavender scent is soothing, briefly calming the nervous energy I carry everywhere since I learned of my dad's cancer.

"Camille, who is it?" Liz yells. "You aren't supposed to open the door! It can be dangerous, sweetie, remember?" Hurried footsteps thump from the kitchen. Liz appears in her hospital scrubs, her strawberry-blonde hair thrown into a messy bun, a spatula in her hands dripping with marina sauce. A large splotch falls onto the walnut floor. Liz bends over, wiping it onto her scrubs. "Tess, I didn't know you were coming. Sorry, it's chaos here. I just got home. I haven't had time to change yet. I'm throwing something together for dinner. Come in."

I step into the cluttered foyer, sidestepping a pile of matchbox cars, and make my way into the kitchen.

"Sorry." Liz frowns, gesturing around. Plates and cups are stacked by the sink, a cutting board with half-chopped carrots sits abandoned on the counter, and Camille's crayons are strewn across the table like tiny fireworks. It's not messy, really—just lived-in, the kind of home that tells a story of full lives and busy days. "My shifts at the ER have been crazy. I keep telling Marley we need a housekeeper. With both of us working so much, we just can't keep up around here. Camille, honey, I asked you to please clean up your toys!"

Camille makes a puppy-dog pout. "Sorry, Mommy, I forgetted." Her grammatical inaccuracy melts my heart. Camille bends down, plonking toys into a nearby basket. Liz kisses her daughter's forehead before returning the spatula to the stove and rummaging through the pantry.

I watch her with admiration. "You're such a good mom."

"Thanks, Tess. Honestly, most of the time, I have no idea what I'm doing." Liz produces a box of linguine. "Are you guys still thinking of trying soon?"

"I think so," I say, doubt muddying my insides like silt stirred in murky water. "I have to… for my dad. I want him to have a grandchild before"—a mass obstructs my throat—"you know…"

"Ugh, that's so hard," Liz says. "But I'm sure Jake's thrilled!"

I nod. For years, Jake's been begging for a baby, but I've put him off, with one excuse after the next.

The timing isn't right with my career.

We're still so young.

I want more time for just the two of us.

The truth is much messier.

It's felt too scary to bring a baby into our marriage. Once we have a child, I know I won't leave. And I've been too afraid to commit to that type of finality with Jake. Plus, years ago, I had a miscarriage—a shadow that still lingers. The idea of life growing inside me again is terrifying, so entirely out of my control. Similar to flying, I'll have to surrender, a helpless passenger. And deep down, I haven't wanted to trust that fate will be kinder to me than it was to Evah. I've never forgotten her guttural wails holding her stillborn son.

"Well, that's exciting!" Liz says with a genuine grin.

I nod again, but it doesn't feel exciting. Simply like another duty.

"All done, Mommy," Camille announces, throwing the last car into the container.

"Great job, Cami. I think you deserve your present now!" I say, handing her the package.

Camille's eyes spread wide as she rips into the wrapping, revealing a PAW Patrol vehicle. "Mommy, Auntie Tessie got me Marshall!" She jumps up and down, struggling to dislodge the toy from the box. I help her, and soon she takes off, pushing Marshall and his firetruck down the hall.

"Thanks, Tess," Liz says, dumping the pasta into the boiling water. "That was so nice. Do you want a glass of wine?"

I take a seat behind the island. "No, thanks. I can't stay long."

"Okay, but you're welcome to stay for dinner. Though I can't promise it'll be any good." Liz offers an apologetic shrug. "How's your dad?"

"He's doing okay… he's been on the immunotherapy for a few weeks… the side effects are pretty rough and he feels like shit. But he's still working every day. He has a scan soon to see if it's helping at all…" The unpleasant reality roars against my chest for the seven-hundredth time today.

My dad has incurable cancer.

Shit.

"Ugh. That sounds awful. How are you holding up?" Liz stops stirring the pasta and reaches across the countertop, putting her hand on my wrist. "Jesus, your pulse is racing."

"Yeah." I exhale. "I'm not doing so great…"

Really, I'm hanging on by a thread, teetering over that familiar cliff.

The one I've spent most of my life on.

Bracing for the inevitable fall.

Yet, somehow, I've never tumbled off.

And maybe that's the problem.

Sometimes, it feels like relief can only come from plummeting down.

From physically becoming as broken as I feel.

The energy it takes to pretend everything is okay all the time is exhausting.

"I'm so sorry, Tess. Has Jake been supportive?"

"Yeah, but it's hard. It's not his dad. He doesn't understand how much it hurts. Losing my dad is my biggest fear." My throat tightens. "He's *my* person, the one I can't live without. But things with Jake are *okay*… they're *fine*."

That's the truth.

Things in my marriage are *okay/fine*.

Nothing more, nothing less.

"When my mom died," Liz says, "I didn't think I'd be able to go on either. Especially since we never patched up our relationship… but you do. Things are different, obviously. But if you lose your dad… you'll find a way to continue. One minute at a time."

I shake my head, positive that's not true. Losing my dad will destroy me.

Down the hall, Camille crawls along the floor, loudly singing the *PAW Patrol* theme song. "I'm sorry you never got a chance to make peace with your mom," I say, unable to grasp the sorrow.

Liz rubs her temples. "Yeah… I mean, obviously… I wish things could've been different. But sometimes, things don't go how you want, and you can either fight against it constantly and let it ruin your entire life or just accept it and make the best of it."

My voice, when it comes, is packed with awe. "I wish I could be more like you, Liz. Your approach to life is so inspiring."

Liz gives me a half-smile. "You're so hard on yourself, Tess. Always! You're juggling so much." The water starts to boil out of the pot and Liz turns the heat down. "How are things at work?"

I sigh. "I'm just… burned out. It's hard to give to my patients when I'm so depleted." What I don't say is that I dread waking up for work each morning. Once there, I count the minutes until I can leave. It's been like this for years, but lately, it's getting worse.

"I wish I could do something to help," Liz murmurs.

"Primary care is just a lot harder than I thought it'd be," I admit. "Two weeks ago, I had a patient walk in with excruciating back pain. Her CT scan lit up everywhere—undiagnosed breast cancer that had already spread to basically every bone in her body."

"Wow, that's awful," Liz says.

"Yeah. She was hospitalized for intractable pain, and she died today in this morphine haze. She was never lucid enough to be told of her fate. I hate that she didn't get a dignified ending, that her life is just over… and that's it. She'll never come back." My shoulders slump.

Life always ends, and I still can't handle the pain.

Liz hands me a glass of water, patting my back. "That's a terrible story, Tess. That's the good part about the ER. I see people once and can't get attached."

"Do you ever feel… like being a doctor… sucks the life out of you?" I glimpse at Liz with hope, like, maybe just this once, she'll say yes, she experiences this feeling too.

But she shakes her head. "No. To be honest, I'm so grateful for the distraction of the ER. Being at work is so much easier than being at home, and it's always so exciting. I love how quickly the time passes."

Liz still loves the thrill, and I still hate it.

"Oh, okay." I force a smile, trying to conceal my disappointment. For a moment, I almost let the truth slip, the one I've dreamed of saying to Liz so many times.

I don't want to be a doctor.

I never have.

I freeze, my shame at being such a phony still too huge. "Anyway, I should go… my dad's waiting for me."

"Okay, thanks again for the present for Cami. Hang in there, Tess. You're a great doctor and daughter."

Her words feel like a spotlight I need to hide from.

"Thanks, Liz," I mumble.

She squeezes my hand.

I hug Cami goodbye, and then I'm out the door.

***

I've barely started my car when my mind transforms into a swirling cyclone. I have spent years—literally my entire adult life—trying to cultivate a passion for medicine. I have waited and waited and waited, wishing, begging and praying to love it.

But still, I don't love it.

I don't even like it.

On paper, I have an Instagram-perfect life—I'm a successful doctor with a great husband. A highlight reel that would make anyone envious.

I *should* be happy.

But inside?

I'm the same freaking broken mess I've always been.

For so long, I've coasted by on *okay-fineness*, drifting through a life of compromises.

My job?

Fine.

My marriage?

Fine.

Everything about my existence has been *fine*.

Not what I truly want.

But still *okay*.

Yet now?

Now, my dad has incurable cancer.

I'm going to lose him.

Beneath my seat belt, my core vacillates.

I seesaw between panic and despair.

My dad is my anchor.

My foundation.

He's the load-bearing beam that has supported my entire disastrous identity.

And my wobbly house of cards is readying to come tumbling down.

THEN:

Eleven Years Ago

October, 2007

30

TESSA

Modise's Toyota Camry bounces over a pothole, the suspension groaning as we near the village of Mochudi. Dust clouds swirl in our wake, coating the roadside shrubs with a fine, coppery layer. We're an hour outside of Gaborone, and with every mile, my chest fills with nerves.

"Thanks for driving me," I say, turning to Modise, whose eyes are focused on the road.

It's Friday afternoon, and I've just finished my last (thankfully uneventful) shift at Princess Victoria Hospital. Now I'm headed to see Evah. I don't know why I'm coming here, only that my heart compelled me to go.

"Of course," Modise says, turning up the volume on the radio. "I'm always happy for a reason to come home to Mochudi." His head bobs to the beat of the bass.

My phone buzzes.

    Corey: Be there at 16:00 to take you to the lodge.
    Did you decide what you're doing yet?

A bead of perspiration skims my neck.

Am I going home on Monday?

The question circles my brain. I don't know the answer. The notion of home feels more distant than ever.

What even makes a home?

Is it the place?

Or the people?

Or something else entirely I don't yet understand?

```
Me:  No...  not  yet  :-(  I'm  sorry.  Let's  talk
when you come.
```

The text feels heavy, an incomplete confession wrapped in pixels.

A war rages, two opposing, incompatible life paths tearing me apart.

Option 1: Return to Philadelphia. Be the medical student. Stay the girl I've dubbed *Phony Tessa*. That girl lives a life that looks good but feels wrong. Inside? That girl is a pretender, a liar, a fake. She seeks external validation at the price of inner happiness.

Option 2: Stay here. Stay with *True Tessa*—the untamed version of myself I've only recently discovered. *True Tessa* jumps off the Victoria Falls Bridge. *True Tessa* is brave enough to admit that being a doctor will make her unhappy. *True Tessa* wants to work towards respecting and loving herself. *True Tessa* is vulnerable and truthful with Corey. This girl is raw, imperfect and real.

But she's also terrifying.

```
Corey: OK. See you soon. Good luck at Evah's


Me: Thanks


Corey: Love you, pragtige dame
```

His words make me simultaneously smile and ache.

    Me: Love you too

"We're here, Tessa," Modise says, snapping my attention. He stops outside Evah's small plot of land, bordered by dry brush and uneven earth. "I'll wait for you in the car."

"Okay, thank you," I say, glancing at the back seat. It's piled high with bags from the local grocery store, where I filled two heaping carts with all the dry goods and toys that would fit.

The air is dusty as I step out. Evah's home is ahead, a single-story, tiny stone-walled structure with a thatched roof. Shirts and pants are draped on a nearby clothesline, strung between two crooked poles. An outdoor stove sits to the left, blackened with soot, and farther along, an outhouse leans slightly to one side. Down the way, a herd of cows moo in unison.

I take one deep breath, then knock twice on the tattered wooden door. A frail woman with greying hair and a cane comes, eyeing me curiously.

"*Dumela, mma*," I say. "I'm here to see Evah?"

A look of surprise crosses the matriarch's face. "This way, please." She uses her cane to wave me inside.

I step through the doorway, finding only two rooms: a bedroom and a living room. I'm surprised to see the house lacks overhead lighting or indoor plumbing. The windows are open, the sunlight gushing in along with the early October heat. I wave at two young children, running in circles, playing tag in the living room. Their screams echo off the walls. One pauses long enough to grin before diving back into the game. A pang of guilt spasms in my heart, comparing Evah's meager dwelling to my more luxurious flat at Timali Court.

How do some people end up with so much and others so little?

The disparity is almost unconscionable.

I find Evah resting on a mattress on the floor of the bedroom. My knees sink to the ground, my white jeans smudging brown from the mud floor. "Hi, Evah."

Evah's eyes open, a slow grin parting from her lips. "*Mma* Tessa? You are here? Thank you for coming."

My hand skims Evah's cheek. "Of course. I wanted to see you before I leave. I've been thinking about you and your son so much. How are you feeling?"

"I'm feeling all right," she says, rolling towards me, her forehead scrunching with pain. In the next room, the squeals of the children's laughter grow louder. Evah's eyes glimmer with love. "Don't mind them. The children are quite noisy. They just got home from school."

"Their laughter is beautiful," I murmur, awestruck by how miraculous it is for laughter to coexist with such grief. "That's your son and daughter?"

"Yes," Evah says, pointing to a taller girl and a smaller boy. "My mother helps with them during the week but she's aging, as you can see. It's hard on her, but their father is not around and I must work."

A wet spot drips through the roof, landing on my grey shirt. "How are you handling everything?" My voice is soft, trembling with the inadequacy of the question.

"It's very difficult, but I have survived many hard things. Somehow, I'll survive this, too. I am lucky to have wonderful support from my family."

"I'm in awe of your bravery," I whisper. It's the same type of bravery I naively wished to cultivate two months ago when I first arrived. But I realize now this isn't something you can create or aspire to—it's born out of necessity. And for me, it doesn't exist. The strength of Evah's being radiates off her. How is she so resilient? She's just experienced the most crushing loss, and yet, somehow… she'll go on.

Why do I lack this vital skill?

Why does life break me so easily?

It feels particularly shameful, given that Evah's clearly suffered so many more hardships than me.

"I brought some things for your family. I'll be right back," I say, needing a moment to collect myself.

I walk to the car, my inadequacy following me. Modise hops out and helps me shuttle bag after bag into the house. I feel ridiculous placing the overabundance of gifts on the mud floor, but besides my compassion, this feels like the most valuable thing I can tangibly offer.

"I'm sorry I can't do more. I wanted so much for your baby to be okay," I say, returning to Evah's bedside.

"Tessa, you have done so much. Thank you." Slowly, Evah sits up, navigating the pain from her abdomen. "You will make a wonderful doctor. I am lucky to have met you."

"I'm the lucky one, Evah." I reach into my jeans pocket, producing an envelope with my contact information. "Please, stay in touch. I'll never forget you or your little boy." I hug Evah tightly, relishing the strength of this phenomenal woman. Then, I stand, waving goodbye to her and her family.

I climb into the Toyota, my spirit heavy.

"Are you ready to go?" Modise asks.

I nod, watching in silence as Evah's home recedes from view.

31

COREY

"How do you distract me so much? I was supposed to be helping you pack," I mumble into Tessa's ear.

My arms encircle her waist. Her lemony hair nestles against my chin. I drink in her scent, wanting to stay wrapped around her, suspending time. Suspending reality.

Our clothes mingle together in a sloppy heap on Tessa's bedroom floor.

"I was so sad after Evah's, and then you got here and smiled at me, and somehow my worries flew out of my brain. Is this your plan to convince me to stay? Seducing me and turning my brain into mush?" she asks.

I smirk. "That depends. Is it working?"

"Yes," she utters, flinging her thigh around my hip, kissing me until my breath grows ragged and I start to get hard again.

I trace the beautiful imperfections of her body—starting at the red birthmark on her left shoulder, then, to the tiny brown freckles dotting her tummy, finally, reaching the jagged scar on her right knee. "You're so *fucking* perfect," I say, terrified of being vulnerable by loving her. Terrified at the prospect of losing her.

Tessa sighs, her stomach muscles quivering beneath my touch. "Shit, Corey. What am I going to do? How can I make this decision?"

My heart sputters, a train off the tracks. "I wish I could help, Tess. Of course I want you to stay, but most important is that you do what's best for *you*."

"I just don't know…" She shakes her head, looking like she needs the sun on a rainy day. "I think I want to stay, but it means changing my entire life course, and my dad will never understand."

"Why not?"

"He just… won't. I'm worried that—"

There's a loud pound on the door. I jolt, sitting up in bed.

Who's that?

We said goodbye to Liz and Marley barely an hour ago as they headed off to the Okavango Delta.

"Who's there?" Tessa calls, shrugging at me, yanking the sheets up to cover her breasts.

"It's us, Tess! Surprise! Your roommate Jeremy let us in," a female voice bubbles from behind the door. Seconds later, the door flings open.

An older white couple stands beside two suitcases. The man is average height and stocky, dressed in a plaid shirt and black dress pants. He has grey hair, silver-rimmed glasses and a dark mustache. The woman's features are soft. Her smile reveals a set of perfect teeth. Her blonde hair is blown into a neat bob. Her tiny frame is covered in jeans and a white T-shirt.

But it's her eyes that stand out.

Eyes that are wide and russet.

Eyes that I would recognize anywhere.

Because Tessa has the exact same ones.

A sense of doom floods my lungs, robbing me of all oxygen.

Oh fuck, no!

The man glares at Tessa.

In bed.

Naked.

With *me.*

The silence in the room becomes oppressive.

It's like a flannel blanket is being strapped over my head.

"Oh my god! Mom and Dad," Tessa finally chokes out. "What are you doing here?"

32

TESSA

Sheer mortification swallows my face. I feel my cheeks flaming cherry red. My throat burns from scandal. I instinctively pull the duvet up, leaving only my eyes exposed. It takes all my willpower not to disappear under the covers and never come out.

Not ever.

Oh my god.

My dad didn't just show up and find me naked, in bed, with Corey.

Shit.

Shit.

Shit.

No!

"We came to surprise you, honey," Mom says. "When we spoke a few weeks ago, you made us excited about the idea of a safari. I convinced your father to finally take some time off. In retrospect, we should've told you. Clearly... we're disturbing things... I'm sorry..." Her eyes toggle between me and Corey, an exultant grin plastering her face. Dad's eyes remain glued to my tuberculosis textbook, a deep grimace replacing his usually friendly demeanor.

"Can you give us a sec?" I plead.

"Then I will… somehow… explain… everything." My voice quakes like they've just busted me breaking curfew. I'm twenty-five freaking years old, but I feel like a teenager, in trouble again.

"Of course, Tess. Sorry for barging in like this. Come, Petey, let's give them privacy." Mom grabs a speechless Dad, tugging him out of the room, gently closing the door.

"Oh my god," I whisper. "I'm so sorry! I had no idea they were coming. I've never been so humiliated."

I often talk about sex with my mom.

But not my dad.

Absolutely *never* my dad.

I bury my face in my hands, trying unsuccessfully to block out the awfulness of Dad's expression, upon seeing a strange, naked man draped around me.

"Well, that was probably the worst first impression I could've made!" Corey mumbles, letting out a low laugh. He snatches his jeans and shirt from the floor, handing me my clothes. We dress in silence. I fumble with buttons, as if my hands belong to someone else.

What am I going to say?

Hi, Mom and Dad. This is Corey, my safari guide, who I fell in love with. And I'm thinking of staying here. And, oh yeah, I want to quit medical school. Because I'm very sensitive and I can't handle the pain of being a doctor. Or actually, the pain of being a human. But everything is great. Nothing to see here. Thanks for stopping by!

I open the door, my airway constricting into a tiny keyhole.

Maybe, they'll be gone.

Maybe, I imagined this.

Maybe, I've actually, finally lost my fucking mind.

But no.

My parents are still in the hallway, holding hands, looking like a united duo as usual. I step towards Mom, hugging her. Despite all the awkwardness, I immediately melt into her embrace.

"Sweetheart, it's so good to see you," she whispers, cloaked in her familiar Anais Anais L'Original perfume, the scent a momentary comfort. Then, I hug Dad, his posture stiffer than a metal rod. He meagerly pats my back twice, eerily silent.

Can he smell the sex on me?

Oh god!

"Mom, Dad. I'm deeply sorry you saw us like that. But this is… uh… my boyfriend… Corey." I point to Corey, who offers up his dashing, toothy grin, his eyes gleaming.

"It's an honor to meet you, Dr. and Mrs. Williams. You have a terrific daughter." Politely, he shakes both of their hands.

Shit!

Does his hand smell like my insides?

My airway shrinks smaller, my breath growing wheezy. Mom says something but I can't hear, my thoughts screaming so loudly as I look from Corey to Dad and back again.

How are they in the same room?

I need more time to figure everything out!

My dad isn't supposed to be here.

To see me.

Not like this!

During the past two months, I've transformed into a more genuine version of myself. But I never considered the possibility of my dad meeting this version of me. I'm terrified he won't accept the person I've become. That he will only love *Phony Tessa*, the girl molded in likeness to him, created from his own dreams. I need my dad's approval, and being without it will topple me, like the crucial Jenga piece that once removed, brings the whole structure down.

I glance at Dad, but his eyes are glaring at the brown carpet. His palpable displeasure is crushing, snatching back some of my new found agency.

Shit.

Shit.

Shit.

"Tess, are you okay? Do you need to sit for a second?" Corey furrows his brow, coming to my side, his hand resting on my hip, tethering me to gravity.

With clammy palms, I clutch my chest, trying to stop my heart from leaping out. I can't intake air. My pulse sprints like I'm running a freaking marathon. My vision starts to blacken, the room whirling in dangerously fast circles.

"I think I'm dying," I gasp.

"Sit. I'm going to get you some water," Corey instructs, leading me to my sex-tousled bed.

"Sweetheart, it's okay," Mom says, sitting next to me, rubbing my back. "Peter, check her out. You're the cardiologist after all!"

Dad kneels down, giving me the once-over, placing his cold palm on top of my wrist. "Tessa, your heart rate is very fast. Let's take some deep breaths."

He counts out a 4:4 breathing pattern. I breathe on his cue, trying to still my racing thoughts.

Corey.

My dad.

Together.

Here.

Oh.

My.

God.

No.

No.

No!

"I think you're having a panic attack, Tess," Dad says. "You're okay. Nothing is wrong."

Everything is wrong.

Everything is wrong!

EVERYTHING!

IS!

WRONG!

I have two divergent identities and I see now with absolute certainty that only one can survive.

But which one?

Dad looks into my eyes, his lips gradually softening into a smile as I silently plead with him.

In the eight weeks I've been here, Dad, I didn't mean to undo a lifetime of living up to your every expectation!

Suddenly, time vaults to one of my first memories, before Dad was promoted, back to when we spent tons of time together.

***

I'm five, learning to ride my bike without training wheels in the high school parking lot. Dad trails behind me as I complete my sixth loop, calling out, "Good job, sweetheart."

But then, I hit a bump, flying from my bike, slamming onto the ground. My knee collides with the pavement, blood spurting down my leg, tears bursting from my eyes. Dad's at my side, evaluating my gash, grabbing his medical kit from the car. Still sobbing, he carries me to the grass, which is littered with orange leaves. He cleans the wound, putting suture strips over it.

"You'll be good as new in no time, Tess," he whispers. "Falling off is no reason not to get back on your bike, but probably not today."

"Okay, Daddy," I mumble, tears running down my cheeks. "What's that?" I point to the white strips.

"Oh, these? They help hold the skin in place so your wound can heal."

"And what's this?" I point to my kneecap.

"That's your patella. You didn't break your bone, though, sweetheart, just a nasty gash. But the body is good at healing. You'll have a little scar when everything's said and done, but it'll be a good story. Scars are our body's way of remembering the things that happen in our life."

"How does the body heal, Daddy?"

He puts his finger to his lips. "Do you want the kid answer or the real one?"

"The real one," I say, Dad instantly grinning.

"Well, Tess, first the blood has to clot, forming a scab. Then, there's collagen, which forms granulation tissue. When the scab falls off, you're left with shiny, red tissue, and that becomes the scar."

"Wow. The body is amazing," I say, my voice filled with awe.

"Yes, very amazing," Dad replies, draping his coat around my arms. The October breeze causes a flood of leaves to rain down. "I love your interest in the body, Tess. I bet you'd make a great doctor one day. I used to ask questions like that when I was a kid. It's how I first realized I wanted to go into medicine." His eyes caramelize beneath the bouquet of light, as my chest twinkles from his glowing approval.

This is the first moment I hunger to make him proud.

At the time, it's only a small seed.

But once planted, through the years, nurtured by my perfectionistic tendencies and Dad's lofty expectations, it grows.

Until it becomes the tallest tree in the forest of my mind.

***

Corey returns, handing me a glass of ice water. "Feeling any better?"

"Yes, thank you all for helping." I paste on a weak smile. "I'm okay."

Apparently, I've defaulted back to lying, still feeling one hundred percent on the verge of death. I sip the icy water as Corey's eyes frantically analyze me.

Shit.

I look away.

"So, how'd you two meet?" Mom's cheery voice collides with the overwrought energy permeating the room.

Corey's tone is similarly perky. "I had the good fortune of meeting your wonderful daughter two months ago when she came to visit Impodimo Lodge, where I work as a guide. It's been great getting to know her. She's really special."

"That's so sweet. I wish Tessa had told us she'd met someone!" Mom smiles. "You work at Impodimo Lodge? We were planning to whisk Tessa there for the weekend. It was going to be our surprise."

At this revelation, I spit out my water, droplets flying all over the carpet.

Corey fidgets his hands in his pockets, shooting me a glance. "Yeah… um, actually, Tessa and I were just about to head that way ourselves…"

"Well, then, I guess we should wrap up here so the four of us can start our weekend at Impodimo Lodge!" Mom proclaims.

"Can we help you pack, Tess?" Dad asks, standing, not yet himself but closer than before.

But I just sit there, my mouth flung open, my brain pierced by a dozen arrows of shock.

It's bad enough that I have no idea what to do with my messy life.

If I'm going home on Monday or not.

But now, I have to spend what's potentially my last weekend with Corey, also with my parents?

Oh.

Shit.

No!

Reality is too much to bear.
My head spins.
The drapes around my eyes drop.
And then, everything goes black.

33

COREY

"I'd like to make a toast," Peter declares, raising his third glass of wine high into the air, the red liquid tinting silver beneath the moon. "To family, the most important thing in life, and to new friends, and to this beautiful setting. And to Tessa, the apple of my eye, for bringing us all together."

"Cheers," Claudia coos, her voice similarly loose, clinking her glass first with Peter, then Tessa, then me. "And to another great day of game viewing tomorrow!"

In my years at Impodimo Lodge, I've skillfully navigated every type of guest, endless awkward dining situations—but I never imagined a dinner quite like this: with my American girlfriend (who may or may not be leaving in thirty-six hours) and her increasingly drunken parents.

From the next table on the patio, Darian raises his brow as if to say: *You okay, bud?*

I give him a meek shrug, because truthfully, I'm a sagging roof, one damn shingle from collapse.

Despite the rocky start, things with Tessa's parents have actually been good. They're genuinely nice people, which isn't surprising, considering the daughter they've raised. But, since her father's arrival, Tessa's the one who's dramatically different. After her fainting episode, she snapped shut like a Venus flytrap, refusing to reopen—not even last night when we were alone in bed. Once again, her inner nucleus is hidden, her carefully swathed layers all tucked back in place. After feeling like I finally understood her, I now understand nothing, and it's fucking eating me up.

Under the starry night, new worry lines glisten off Tessa's forehead. She pushes her barely eaten steak around her plate, her first glass of wine unusually full. "So, Dad, what was your favorite animal today?" Her voice is put-on, like she's an actress donning a mask in front of her audience. I want to comfort her, to take her hand, to tell her things will be okay—but there's an impenetrable force field surrounding her that shocks me if I get too close.

"Definitely the birds!" Peter says. "Corey, which ones did we see again? Tomorrow, I have to remember to bring my bird book."

I plaster on my work face. *I'm a professional. Just get through this dinner.* "Well, Dr. Williams, we saw some kori bustards and superb starlings and the helmeted guinea fowl."

"Yes, the guinea fowl! Those were my favorite. They're incredible. I love the birds, but please, call me Peter," he says for the seventh time. But I'm struggling with such informality—Mum's big on proper titles— respect, first and foremost.

"Honey, you loved the birds more than the leopard climbing the tree? Or those lion cubs?" Claudia says. "The guinea fowl is your top choice?" She chuckles, slowly slicing a piece of her steak.

"Yes! The guinea fowl. Why is that so amusing?" Peter's gaze lands on his wife, spilling with affection. Tessa's told me about their solid marriage, about her shame for choosing Greg, despite the great example her parents set. I glance at Tessa, her eyes stony, our own bond feeling dangerously unsteady, a rope fraying thread by thread.

"Well," I say, swallowing the kneading knot at the base of my throat.

"I'll do my best to find some more birds for you tomorrow, Dr. Willi—err, Peter."

"You've been a terrific guide so far. Thank you," Claudia enthuses, her blonde hair dangling in front of her broad, russet eyes.

Tessa's russet eyes.

The eyes that dissolved my goddamn numbness.

Fuck!

I miss being numb.

"We're sad that tomorrow is our last day here," Peter says.

Is it your last day here, too, Tess?

I study Tessa, awaiting her reaction, but her mask clings to her face. The uncertainty starts to chew up pieces of my stomach, an ulcer seeming all but guaranteed.

As if reading my mind, Peter asks, "Tess, what time's your flight Monday? Do you need a ride to the airport?"

Her mask briefly falters, her cheeks turning pale, her heart-shaped jaw dropping. "Uh... my flight leaves Gaborone at one p.m."

Does that mean you plan on being on it?

"So you want to get there around eleven? Which means we should leave here by ten?" Peter calculates, counting off on his fingers. A purely logistical decision.

"Uh... yeah, Dad... that would be... great... thanks," Tessa says, avoiding my glare. My heart crashes onto the patio with a resounding thud.

"What's going to happen with you two when you leave?" Claudia says, using her fork to gesture between us.

"Mom!" Tessa admonishes, her white knuckles strangulating her water glass.

"Sorry, Tess," she says. "It just felt like the elephant in the room... or actually, on the patio, even though the elephants are actually down there, in the watering hole. Oh dear, I think I'm a little drunk..." She grins apologetically.

"We haven't really figured it out… but…" Tessa says, her golden specks starting to flicker. She sucks in a breath. "I was thinking… maybe… I'd apply to residency programs in South Africa?"

This is the first I'm hearing of such a plan, but it fills me with blossoming hope, my heart creeping back up towards my damn chest. Daring to believe there might be an *us* after all.

Peter's eyes nearly bulge out their sockets. "Tessa, what are you talking about? That's a huge decision. You already applied for Internal Medicine Residency programs back home. The training here isn't as strong. You want the best education possible! Plus, you're too late for this academic year. You'd be delaying your residency an entire year. Don't do anything rash."

My heart plunges back down. I'm riding the Tower of Terror, dropping at warp speed, leaving my stomach in free fall.

Fuck.

"Peter," Claudia says. "Tessa should make her own choices. Her priorities might not align with yours. I think you should let her figure it out?"

Yes!

Thank you, Claudia!

My heart undulates, riding this roller coaster. I'm in need of a vomit bag.

"Of course," Peter says, glancing at me. "Sorry… it's just… she's going to make one hell of a doctor. Do you know how talented she is? She absolutely blows me away. I'm so unbelievably proud of her."

"Yes, I'm in awe of her, too," I manage.

But she doesn't want to be a damn doctor.

I reach for Tessa's shaky hand, trying to channel strength into her. Her dad really is a nice guy, but I'm finding it tough to keep my cool, knowing Tessa's true feelings. Seeing how differently she behaves around him. She's pretending for him, for everyone, and I can see how it's destroying her piece by piece.

Why can't they?

Silence falls over the table, Tessa's eyes now blank.

"Well, I think you should take me back to the room, Petey, before I fall asleep here," Claudia announces, pushing her chair out. "Goodnight, you two. See you in the morning."

***

Thirty minutes later, I'm brushing my teeth, studying Tessa, who sits on my bed, wearing my raggedy T-shirt, which falls just above her knees. The sight of her in my clothes cracks me in two. From my nightstand, she picks up the old photograph of Leona, holding it like something sacred. The picture is from her fourth birthday, six weeks before she was diagnosed. In it, she's running through a field of red daisies, wearing a green pleated dress. Her white-blonde hair cascades in ringlets; her smile bursts with such innocence.

She had no idea what was coming.

None of us did.

"Wow. Leona is the absolute cutest. Those magical purple eyes. I love this photo," Tessa mumbles, gripping the picture close to her face, seemingly memorizing it.

Her tenderness towards a girl she's never met slices through me.

I consider correcting her: she *was* the cutest.

She's nothing anymore because she's *dead*.

I stop myself.

Tessa places the picture back, crawling under the covers. I turn off the light, climbing next to her, wrapping my limbs around her. Normally, I'd love the idea of her in my bed, but tonight her anxious energy seeps through the sheets, shrouding us both in a heavy cloud of uncertainty. "Tess, can we talk?" I mumble into the nape of her neck, hoping she'll soften.

Please soften.

"Yeah… I'm sorry, Corey… I just don't know what to do. It's a really big decision, and there's a lot to take into consideration…" Her body is taut like a cable. Her words feel restrained, like she's holding back the real ones. My fingers trace along her forearm, the motion more for me than her.

"I completely understand, Tess. You just seem different, closed off. I'm worried about you. The panic attack and the fainting… and since your parents got here, you're just so tense."

"I'm okay," she insists, tucking her chin down, her force field zapping pain straight into my goddamn heart.

Liar, liar.

"Tess, you don't have to pretend." I roll her torso to face me, tipping her jaw upwards. "Please, it's me."

"I'm okay," she says again, but her eyelids buck. Two droplets creep out.

"Tess, come on."

"Okay, you're right," she whispers. "I'm not okay. I'm panicking and I have no idea what to do."

Slivers of moonlight streak through the beige shutters, dispersing shadows. Half of Tessa's face is light, the other half dark. She exhales, her force field seemingly weakened, my body exhausted from absorbing its intense energy.

"Tess, granted, I barely know your dad, but I have a hunch he'll support you, no matter what. Maybe he won't be happy at first, but I think you should give him some credit. My parents didn't want me to work here, but they came around. Loving parents usually come around."

She shakes her head, her hands digging deep into my biceps. "You don't understand, Corey. It's just… really important that my dad's proud of me. Of the things I do."

"I didn't mean to imply it's simple. It's just—"

"I'll talk to him tomorrow. I'll tell him I'm thinking of quitting med school. I can't make this choice without his input." Her voice is firm. The forcefulness startles me. She seems unreachable again.

"Okay," I say, my lungs flat like two pancakes, the hope smushed out of me. Based off dinner, I'm one thousand percent certain how Peter will react. But I don't want to push Tessa into making a choice she's not ready to make.

"I love you, Corey. I'm sorry I'm a mess and that I'm putting you through this. Maybe a good night of sleep will help me sort everything out?" Her tone is foolishly optimistic as she offers a half-smile, the edges of her lips still furling down, her dimple noticeably absent.

"I love you, too, Tess. Just make the choice that's right for *you*. You should decide what matters in your own life. That's all I want."

She kisses me, wrapping her arms around my neck, her nipples poking my chest. I ache to make love to her, to feel close to her, to bridge the emotional distance between us with our physical connection—but Tessa's eyelids are heavy. Her breath slows.

"Good night, Corey," she mumbles, eighty percent asleep, rolling away from me. I scoop her into my arms. She whispers, "I like being the little spoon."

My brain sprints.

I'm back in Leona's bed, near the end of her life, when she'd said the same thing. "I like being the little spoon, Core."

I grasped to hold on then, to Leona's perfect, tiny voice, her battered, cancer-laden body—knowing she was slipping away.

Tessa quivers in the early stages of sleep. I tug her closer, like I can somehow keep from losing her, too.

I savor the memory of the magical girl I've already lost and the wonderful woman I'm about to lose.

Tessa's hair drapes against my pillow and I wish her lemony scent could plant roots there, to somehow grow in her absence.

Something to hold on to when she's gone.

Because I know.

She's going home on Monday.

Fuck.

Fuck.

Fuck!

A cavernous grief chisels into my chest—that awful feeling of someone still in your arms—but also already gone.

I lie awake all night.

Watching her sleep.

Trying to fathom how to let her go.

34

TESSA

I find my dad perusing *Birds of Southern Africa* on the wraparound deck, swathed in a pith helmet and binoculars, looking like the quintessential safari tourist. I walk slowly, my nerves making my feet lead weights.

Where to start?

Hi, Dad. Medicine is the wrong career and I want to quit?

Over coffee that morning, I talked to Mom about my relationship with Greg. It was a therapeutic conversation, Mom nurturing and supportive. "Tell Dad," she'd urged. "He'll understand. There's nothing to feel ashamed about."

But I can't.

I don't want to reveal how flawed and broken I am. How utterly poor my judgment is. Not now. Especially when I'm about to admit my other catastrophic truth.

"Hi, Dad." I take a seat, edging my chair closer to the railing. The view of the watering hole momentarily calms my anxiety. Below, a dazzle of zebras take ravenous gulps, their slurping sounds booming into my ears. Six impala bound in the grass, the glare of the sun illuminating their yellowy-brown fur. Through the acacia trees, I spot a herd of elephants, their thundering footsteps approaching.

"What a view," I murmur. No matter how many times I see it, I hope I never take it for granted.

"Spectacular," Dad agrees, his mustache blowing beneath the afternoon breeze.

The circle of life.

Remember what matters.

But what does matter?

How do I figure it out?

How does anyone?

A bird lands on the deck railing, its dusky eyes looking straight at us, its body streaked in patches of color. I remember this bird from my boat cruise with Corey. He'd said it brought good luck.

Great, I need all the luck I can get.

"Okay, Dad. Let's put your bird-watching skills to the test. What type of bird is that?"

Dad scrolls through his book, his finger tracing each picture. "A lilac-breasted roller," he says, pointing. "These birds are beyond imagination. I swear, in my next life, I'm coming back as a bird!" He gives me a radiating grin that briefly lifts my sagging spirits.

My reciprocal smile is automatic. No matter what, he is *my* person.

The bird chirps noisily, as if to say, *Get on with it, Tessa.*

I curl my fist into a tight ball.

Here goes.

Shit!

"Dad, I don't know what to do… I don't think medicine is the right choice for me… the sadness I felt at Princess Victoria was unbearable. I really don't cope well with serious illness and death. I can't separate from the pain. It consumes me. I'm thinking of… quitting med school." I stare straight ahead, terrified that my statement is a betrayal to the life he's imagined for me. The one he's guided me towards.

He stays agonizingly silent, causing the edges of my vision to blacken. I pull at the three top buttons of my shirt, trying to stuff oxygen into my lungs.

Breathe, Tess, breathe.

Don't have another panic attack.

Not now.

"Medical training is hard," he says, finally. "I had the same fears early on. It's hard to see people die, see sickness and not be able to stop it. It makes you think about your own mortality. When I was a fourth-year medical student, I was convinced I was dying of Lou Gehrig's disease. I never told anyone, but I went around thinking my days were numbered. Of course, it was just anxiety, but it was one hell of a terrible year." My fists slowly unclench. "It does get easier, over time. You learn to accept the things you cannot change, to focus on the things you can."

This is my first time hearing about Dad's hardships in his own training.

Is how I feel a normal part of the process?

Will it get better in time?

"What if… I never learn to love it, Dad? What if… I'm not like *you?*" My biggest fear spoken out loud.

"You are like me, so much, Tess. I see myself in you. You'll love it in time. Trust me."

I stare into his silver glasses, studying my reflection. I look like the same hot mess as when I landed two months ago.

I sigh, deeply disappointed in myself.

In my lack of progress.

Why can't I just figure myself out already?

Why is life so hard for me?

Like an old foe, that familiar sense of self-doubt settles back against my skin, wrapping me in ambiguity. "I'm just not sure that I'll ever learn to love medicine, Dad. And I feel at home, here, at Impodimo Lodge… I don't want to leave. I-I-I… want to stay."

Dad stares at the zebras splashing. "I can see why you find this place magical. Your hospital experience was very hard. It's natural to find relief in the stunning beauty here, but this place isn't real life, Tess. It's a magical fantasy, an escape. There's no future for you here. What would you do? Stare at animals every day while Corey works?"

Again, I'm holding that rope, engaged in a lifelong tug-of-war between my dad's vision and my own desires.

"I don't know," I admit.

My brain races, struggling to sort what I want. Minutes ago, it seemed clear. But now… it's all so muddled. My dad has more knowledge and life experience. What credentials do I possess to make life-altering decisions? Especially when I'm such a freaking mess?

"Tessa, don't lose sight of what you've worked so hard for. You're seven months from graduating. You're going to make an incredible doctor. Sad experiences won't ruin you, they'll cultivate your empathy as a provider." He rubs my back in light circular motions, the rope singeing my hands from the years of tugging back and forth.

Back and forth.

Back.

And.

Forth.

My body is so tired.

The lilac-breasted roller takes flight, soaring high into the cloud-splattered sky. I follow it until it's only a fuzzy dot.

Help!

Which direction should I fly in?

The choice feels excruciating.

"What about Corey? I love him, Dad." Fretfully, I tap my foot against the wooden deck, producing a *thump-thump-thump* sound. The same sound as Evah's son's beating heart. Back when he was alive. Before his placenta cruelly detached, killing him and a piece of me.

How many more pieces of me will die if I become a doctor?

Dad nods. "Tess, I'm sorry if I was cold when we first arrived. I was… shocked, and to be honest, Corey isn't the type of guy I imagined you with. But he seems like a very kind man. I get that you love him, but remember, you're young. You have your whole life ahead of you. Finish your training—don't get derailed by a guy. You're too independent. If it's meant to be, you can always come back once you finish your schooling, or he can come to the States. Love finds a way if it's meant to be."

The words hit like soft punches, each one landing, lingering. In my mind, the choice seemed binary: stay with Corey and quit medicine *or* go home and break up with Corey. But maybe our relationship can continue in some type of grey zone, a space in between all or nothing.

The circle of life.

Only a few things matter.

So, what matters to me?

My gut, which I'd started to hear more of in Botswana, is now eerily silent, my intuition a deserted street in the dead of night. Unable to find my inner compass, I turn towards Dad, my guiding light. "Dad, help. What should I do?" My newly grown confidence shrivels beneath the weight of his expectations, curling inwards like a dying leaf.

"Tess, trust me, you'll be a fantastic doctor. Don't give up." His tone is raw. It's not just advice—it's a plea wrapped in layers of hope and longing. In his eyes, I see the unfinished story of his dreams for me: med school graduation, finishing residency, becoming the second Dr. Williams. I imagine his brown eyes caramelizing with booming pride as he watches me cross each milestone. I desperately want to deliver him these pleasures.

Simultaneously, the past replays in a blur.

I'm sitting on the grass, five years old, my knee bleeding, Dad's face blooming with love over my budding interest in anatomy.

I'm eleven, resolving to be perfect.

For *him.*

I'm sixteen, shadowing him at the hospital, in complete awe of his career.

Of *him.*

I'm twenty, abandoning writing in favor of medicine.

The present comes into focus.

I'm twenty-five, standing on the deck of Impodimo Lodge, a scowl etched into Dad's face, born from my doubts. My insides mince under the jumble of his shattered dreams—dreams I am supposed to inherit and carry forward.

He pulls me into his arms, and immediately, the rope drops.

Again.

I can never manage to hold on to the goddamn rope.

My palms sting, chafed bare from our futile tussle—my will versus his love, my dreams versus his hopes.

Inside, there is only hallowing silence, my own voice wiped out.

Every choice feels wrong, but I have to make one.

I blink.

Dad's smile fissures, a tiny crack that deepens with each second of my hesitation.

"Okay, Dad. I'll finish med school… I'll go home."

35

COREY

Tessa shivers beneath the nippy evening air, the moon occluded by dark clouds. Earth is threatening to release a torrential downpour, not unlike the one building inside me. She sits beside me in the Jeep in front of the Tau Waterhole—the place I brought her on our "first" date. It feels like some type of terrible poetic justice to spend our last night together here, too.

"Are you cold, *pragtige dame*? Do you want my jacket or a blanket?" I gaze at her face, a twisted web of beauty and torment.

"I want you to warm me up," she murmurs, pressing her mouth to mine, but my lips shake too much to actually kiss her. Her fingers trace along my stubble. Her touch makes my skin purr, my heart splinter. Against my better judgment, like a complete idiot, I've let her inside—and now, I'm unprepared to lose her.

Fuck.

She sighs heavily, and it carries the weight of each path we leave behind at every fork in the road. "I'm sorry, Corey." Her voice shakes. "I can't explain how much I want to stay, but I have to finish med school. I have seven months left. Maybe I can come back after? I'm really thinking about doing my residency here. I don't want this to be the end..."

Somehow, despite all reasoning, until she says this, I've maintained the smallest hope that she might choose to stay.

With me.

For *me*.

Fuck.

"So, you decided you *want* to be a doctor, after all?" I thread our fingers together, trying to scrape my guts from the floor of the Jeep.

"No, I don't think I want to be a doctor… but my dad says I'll learn to love it in time. And maybe, he's right? It's just… I can't walk away from it… right now. I'm sorry… I am so incredibly sorry." Her eyes fill with tears, the agony of her choice evident.

"This is what *you* want, Tess? If it is, I'll accept it without question."

"I don't know, Corey," she sobs. "I'm so lost… I want to stay with you… but I just… can't."

Hearing this truth makes my body burn. My insides dissolve into a pile of ashes.

She wants to stay, but still, it's not enough.

I'm not enough.

I pull her head into my arms, letting her cry against my shirt.

My thoughts speed like bullets, but in the end, only one pierces. She'd told me: *My dad is the most important man in my life*, which, by default, means I'm not. I can love Tessa the most of anyone, but she's not going to choose me.

Not today.

Not in the future.

Fuck.

The sting is visceral, bile gushing into my mouth, making me gag.

"Can't we stay together? Do long distance? I still want to be with you. I love you," she says through wails, her fingers thrumming against my chest, as if trying to pound reason into me.

I want to scream yes.

Yes!

Yes!

A thousand times yes!

But I can't prolong this misery, knowing for certain it will only bring heartache. No matter what, I'll never be a part of her father's vision for her life. I gag again.

"I understand why you need to do this," I say. "But, I think it's better if we just end things now… our lives are too different. I'm a safari guide in the bush… you live in the U.S. I just don't see how we can be together long term. I love you… so much. The most I've ever loved a woman. You opened me back up… made me want to live again, and I'm so grateful for that. But I don't see a future for us… it crushes me to say that… because I wish it wasn't true. But… it… is." I stop talking, my voice jagged, the grief stabbing me everywhere. The golden specs in Tessa's eyes break into a hundred opaque shards.

In the silence, a few birds whine.

A meerkat rustles.

A lion roars.

It serves as a stark reminder that out here, life will continue. That unalterable, unyielding, horrible truth. Life always goes on. It doesn't stop for the loss of anyone or anything.

Not Leona.

Not Tessa.

No one.

After Tessa's gone, seconds will unfold into minutes, into hours, into days, into months, into years. Time will march on, regardless of the sadness inside me.

"Corey, you won't even entertain the idea that somehow we could make this work? You are willing to give up so easily?" Tessa's words harpoon my self-pitied thoughts. Her cheeks coat in red splotches.

Fuck.

"Please don't say it like that, Tess. Losing you is going to hurt so much. You've become my best friend." I stroke her silky skin, fighting all my urges to say whatever's needed to make her feel better. "I'm not sure I can even get over you once, but I can't handle the idea of losing you multiple times, of trying to hang on now, only for you to say in a few months, or years, it's not going to work. That's not fair to me."

A few drops of rain start to fall.

"But what about doing my residency here?" she asks, her frown so deep that her chin looks on the verge of collapse.

Your dad will talk you out of it.

But I can't say that, so instead, I say, "I… I… just don't think that's a very realistic idea."

"Wow, Corey," she mumbles, her voice a hollow seashell overshadowed by a loud clap of thunder. "I expected more from you. I thought we'd find a way to make this work."

I gag a third time, wanting to actually throw up.

To release this fucking turmoil whirling inside my stomach.

Why the fuck did I have to become un-numb?

Only to develop these horrible fucking feelings?

Only to have the woman I love leave?

"Tess, I'm sorry… I wish I was stronger." Rain lands on my hair, rolling down my face, blurring my vision.

Tessa's shoulders deflate until she's slouched motionless against me. "So what, then… this is the end?" Her words hang with thick finality, a knife slicing through the chilly air. I hold her, unable to speak.

A bolt of lightning crackles in the sky, illuminating the world with a flash of love and pain. The rain grows heavier until we are sitting beneath a punishing downpour. Our clothes drench.

Tessa lets out a laugh, gentle at first, but then it grows heartier.

Her honey-brown hair mattes against her ears. "Well, this is perfect *fucking* timing." She gives me a half-smile. "I'll find a way to make this right… somehow, I will, Corey. I promise. I don't know how… but I will."

"Okay," I mumble, unconvinced.

It's.

Fucking.

Over.

"When I get home, I'm going to email you every day, even if you don't want to hear from me." She cups her hands to my cheeks, pressing our noses together. "I'm not going to give up on us." Her warm breath collides with my wet skin, the sensation bitter and sweet.

"Okay," I mumble again, yearning to be numb—anything to block out this horrendous aching inside my damn chest.

"I'm sorry I'm hurting you," she whispers. "I'm such a mess. It's not fair to you. You deserve so much more. I love you."

"I love you too," I say, wishing I could change the part of her brain that sees herself as so broken. Maybe, then, she wouldn't leave.

But I can't change anything.

Instead, it's time to let her go.

"I'm going to miss you so much," she utters as the rain slows.

The moon reappears, beaming down on her face, which is raw and vulnerable and so damn perfect.

I clench my jaw to hold myself together. "You look so beautiful right now, Tess. I'm going to miss your stunning smile and your gorgeous heart and your all-around goodness."

"No, Corey," she says, shaking her head, crying again. "You're the good one. So kind and handsome and generous and sweet. You've taught me so much." Her lips sink on top of mine, her tongue moving in circles around the edge of my mouth.

Her taste.

How can I remember it?

I want to create a room in my brain with every sensation of her and wall it off for safekeeping.

She removes her soaked clothing, then mine, climbing into my lap, her teeth chattering. My arms wrap around her, holding her, transferring my body heat. Immediately, she relaxes—and it means everything that my touch is able to soothe her.

I kiss her harder, tugging strands of her lemony hair against my nose, sucking in her scent, bucking my hips to bring her closer. My heart is fucking eviscerated but my dick is still wildly needy for her. She nibbles on my neck as her hands scrape the water from my chest, and then, in one quick motion, she shoves me inside of her.

My brain tries to form words, but her insides wrap me in a deliciously snug embrace. "Tess, wait… condom?"

Her back arches against the steering wheel, her lips parting upwards, her dimple bursting through the rain. "I'm on the pill. I just want to be as close to you as possible for our last night."

Our last night.

Goddamn.

This sentence hits like a hammer striking my skull—but as she grinds against me, moaning, my thoughts melt, and for a beat, there is only her, claiming me.

"You make me so damn crazy," I mumble.

"I love you," she says, her russet eyes knotting like a string around my heart.

"I love you," I say, wanting her to know it. To never fucking forget it. I thrust deeper, needing to prove my damn love.

Then we're a mass of limbs and rain-soaked skin.

Moving as one.

Holding each other.

With the chirps of the crickets.

And the squawks of the guinea fowl.

And the hoots of the owls.

"Oh, Corey," Tessa whimpers as she comes.

I come, too, hard and fierce.

And then it's over.

Everything.

Is.

Over.

I crash down from my high, vast emptiness waiting on the sidelines, ready to guzzle me up.

I grasp Tessa's shoulders, securing her head against my chest, remaining limply inside her.

We stay like that.

Me just holding her.

Until dawn breaks.

36

COREY

I slump against the barstool in the main lodge, slurping my second whiskey. *Tessa's fucking gone.*

How is she gone? I keep telling myself it's true, but my brain won't believe it. I vaguely remember that after Leona's death, there were stages of grief—a lot of them.

But which came first?

The shock?

Or denial?

Or bargaining?

I don't know.

Now, I seem to be experiencing all of them simultaneously and it's only been a few damn hours.

***

Seven awful hours ago, Tessa climbed into her parents' rental car and drove away from Impodimo Lodge. From me.

For the last fucking time.

Beforehand, I stood outside the lodge, squeezing her so tightly, I worried her ribs could collapse. "Get home safe, *pragtige dame*," I said.

"Take care of yourself. Remember, don't be afraid of your own needs, no matter what. You're awesome." ·

She nodded, her lips twisting into a giant pout. "I'll email you when I get home. Don't give up on us, Corey. Somehow, I'm going to figure this out."

"Okay," I mumbled, sucking up the last drops of her hair, trying—but failing—to stop time. I handed her a wrapped gift—a photo I'd taken of her overlooking the watering hole with the elephants in the background. "Something to remember me by."

"I won't need anything to remember you," she said, her hand covering her heart, her gesture turning my lungs into two empty bags.

"I love you," I murmured into her neck, blowing the words with a puff of air to try to make them stick. She said the same and I knew it was true.

It was true, but yet, it wasn't enough.

I wasn't enough.

I kissed her one last time before helping her into the back seat. Through the window, she gazed at me, her eyes hazy and muted. I bit my lower lip, puncturing a hole in it to block the monsoon inside. Peter and Claudia walked out of the lodge, suitcases in tow. I loaded their bags into the trunk, hugging them goodbye, wishing them well and meaning it. Peter started the car, driving down the rocky path. Tessa waved miserably, her crestfallen face pressed against the glass until she was entirely gone from my sight.

I will never see her beautiful face again.

Fuck.

Fuck.

Fuck!

This thought made flaming knots explode in my stomach. I ran into the lodge, barely making it to the bathroom, before vomiting up all my breakfast—the last meal I'd ever eat in Tessa's company.

I felt that same crippling despair the night Leona was diagnosed, only this time, Mum wasn't there to comfort me.

I was all alone.

***

I squirm against the barstool.

Tessa is gone.

Fuck!

I clench my fist into a ball, pounding it against the granite countertop. I wish guests weren't mulling nearby, so I could beat the shit out of it—beat the shit out of anything, actually. To release some of this horrendous grief burrowing within me, settling into all its old crevices, taunting me. *I'm back, you fucking sucker. Here to crush your insides again.*

I'm so damn furious at myself. I knew from the start things with Tessa would end badly—but in spite of that, like a fucking moron, I fell in love with her, and now, I'm a broken mess of a man once more. Not a human, just a mass of ruins, unfrozen, to sit in this horrible grief.

"Hey. You okay, bud?" Darian's sturdy voice jolts me as he takes a seat at the next barstool.

"No," I say, averting his inquiring eyes. "Not right now." I take a long pull of my third whiskey. The burn doesn't help; it doesn't dull me the way it's supposed to. I guzzle it anyway. That familiar beckoning of my old, trusty friend Mr. Numbness is whispering sweet promises—escape, forget, disappear. I need to be anesthetized, if only for tonight.

"Well, how about I sit here and keep you company?" Darian says, motioning to Gus to bring him a beer. I nod. The buzzy chatter of guests feels like knives in my back. Outside the window, several elephants cluster near the watering hole, the sun slumped behind the horizon. I instantly regret looking. I'm unable to watch these beautiful animals without my damn heart fissuring.

Fuck!

Fuck!

Fuck!

Gus sets down Darian's drink, shooting me a pitied glance that makes my skin crawl. I'm disgusted with myself for being someone who requires looks of pity again. Life was so much simpler as a damn hardened rock.

Darian takes a swig of beer. "I'm sorry, bud. I know you care about Tessa."

"No, it's way worse than that, Dar," I say, my tongue sloppy from the booze. "I'm painfully, idiotically in love with her. She was this incredible light… but now, she's gone. It feels fucking terrible." The queasiness inches higher in my throat. I'm drowning in it, drowning in her absence.

"I'm really sorry, Core," Darian says. "It sucks, so much, she had to go."

She didn't have to go.

She *chose* to go.

This distinction is crucial, cutting worse than ninety-nine simultaneous knives, each one carving out a little more of me. I take another sip, determined to drink until the image of Tessa's face doesn't stomp my heart into a million goddamn pieces.

Come tomorrow, I'll face my new reality—life *after* Tessa.

Of course, I don't want an after.

I want a future *with* Tessa.

But life doesn't care what I fucking want.

It keeps rolling forward, grinding me beneath its wheels.

Yes, tomorrow, I'll wake up, start anew, find a way to push through.

But tonight?

I need this damn whiskey.

Just get through the evening.

I drink and drink and drink.

Until the darkness stops swallowing me.
Until once again.
The only thing I feel.
Is blissful nothingness.

37

TESSA

"Ladies and gentlemen, at this time, boarding is complete. The aircraft doors have been closed." The flight attendant's voice booms over the speaker, echoing through my ears, spiraling down into my broken heart. I'm in seat 22A on South African Airways Flight 6298, bound for New York City. To continue with med school. To chase a dream that was never mine. To go home.

Except it doesn't feel like home anymore—just a cage.

A cage I'm willingly stepping back into.

Hell, I'm practically locking the doors and throwing away the keys myself.

I'm clutching the present Corey gave me. The edges of the wrapping soften from my grip. I'm too scared to open it. It feels as if I'll be unwrapping the last piece of him, too. I'm not ready for that.

The flight attendants weave through the aisles, making final preparations. A squashing heaviness chokes around my neck. I stretch against my seat, trying to get it to release, but it won't.

My thoughts whiz like race cars around a track, each lap faster, more reckless.

If this is the right choice, why do I feel so awful?

I don't love medicine.

I do love Corey.

So why am I leaving?

How is it possible I'm more of a shitshow now than when I landed two months ago?

What the hell is wrong with me?

Why do I make the worst decisions?

I fumble for my purse, hands shaking as I retrieve my bottle of Ativan. I fish out three pills, triple my prescribed dose, letting them crumble onto my tongue. The bitterness spreads as I swallow.

Please work quickly.

I need to survive this sixteen-hour flight.

The idea of surviving beyond that feels impossible.

I glance at the seat beside me, fiercely wishing I could nuzzle into Corey's chest. That he'd cover my eyes, stroke my hair, and tell me everything's going to be okay. He reassured me so frequently, so seamlessly. And when he said it, I believed it.

But he isn't here.

And he won't be again.

Shit.

From the next seat over, an elderly woman watches me. Her concerned eyes loom, magnified behind red-rimmed bifocals. Her thin fingers hover near her lap, as if debating whether to reach out. "Are you okay, miss?" she asks, her voice angelic.

I want to bury my head on this stranger's shoulder and confess my ruinous flaws.

No, I'm not okay. I don't want to be a doctor, but I just chose a career in medicine to please my dad, again! And I'm leaving behind someone who I think could be the love of my life. I'm a total fucking mess.

"Yes, thank you. I'm fine," I say instead, forcing my tone to be even.

I arrived here a liar and evidently, I'm leaving here a liar, too.

The flight attendants review the safety briefing, movements mechanical and detached. The little yellow masks and life vests—they're supposed to save us if we crash, but I feel like I'm already plummeting.

For once, I don't worry about the plane crashing.

I'm about to fly seven thousand miles away from the man I love. The only person who's ever truly known me.

Oh god.

What am I doing?

My chest basins into a well of anguish, swallowing reason whole. The plane races down the runway, gathering speed. Normally, this is the part of flying I fear most. The acceleration, the inevitability of being flung into the sky. But instead of counting back from 214, squeezing the armrests until my knuckles turn white, I watch, eyes wide, unblinking, as the ground becomes achingly distant. With every second the plane climbs, it's taking me farther away from Corey. Farther away from the place where I found the most authentic version of myself.

Finally, we reach cruising altitude, a sinking despair caking to my intestines. I study the map of the plane's path, illuminated on the screen. JFK Airport is marked with a tantalizing white star. I stare at the star as the plane inches ever so slowly towards its final destination.

Towards the version of myself that chooses the safe route.

Phony Tessa.

Who doesn't jump off bridges or color outside the lines.

Who pursues a made-up ideal of perfection.

Who can't deviate from her life path, even at the expense of her own happiness.

Phony Tessa.

Who'll become a doctor because her father expects it.

Phony Tessa.

Who'll nag and pounce until *True Tessa*—the one who smiled, who lived, who loved—is all but dead.

The Ativan creeps into my bloodstream, its fog dulling the edges of my thoughts. Finally, it brings respite from the tortuous prison of my mind, pulling me into a dreamless, coma-like slumber.

***

A dozen hours later, I blink awake, my body jolted as the plane's wheels raucously thud against the hard pavement. For a moment, I don't know where I am. My head feels thick, my mouth parched, my limbs heavy.

Then it hits me.

We've touched down in New York.

I'm *home*.

All at once, a horrendous emptiness unfurls. It's not just my heart—it's my entire soul, sliced in two. One half is here, in this world I've known my whole life. The other half is still seven thousand miles away.

With Corey.

With *True Tessa*.

Grief slams against my center, clarity barreling through me with shocking precision. Tears sting my eyes like needles.

Holy shit!

I just made the biggest mistake of my life!

PART TWO

NOW:

Eleven Years Later

October, 2018

38

TESSA

The warmth of Jake's body radiates through the blanket, the wont scent of his charcoal bodywash oozing into my nostrils. "Tess, wake up. I know it's late," he murmurs.

I open an eye and peek at the clock: 11:48 p.m. A haze of sleep still bathes me.

He gives me an apologetic kiss. "Sorry, babe, I got stuck at the office." Jake works as a forensic accountant, his hours long during investigations. "You said you're ovulating today, right?" He sits on the edge of the bed.

I nod.

Two weeks ago, I stopped my birth control pills and started using urine test strips to check for ovulation. And this morning, before I rushed out the door towards my packed schedule of patients, the test turned positive.

I've reluctantly committed to the idea of having a baby—for my dad. I need to make him a grandfather before it's too late.

"Can we still try? I'm dying to have a mini-Tessa running around here." He gives me a smirk, threading his hands through his thick hair.

"Yeah… okay."

"Great."

He stands, peels off his boxers and T-shirt then removes my pajamas, throwing them all into a pile on the navy carpet. He climbs on top of me, kissing my neck, reminding me this is something we're supposed to share.

But I don't feel it.

After a minute of halfhearted foreplay, he enters me. The moment he does, I'm acutely aware of how still I am. My body responds—automatically—but my mind feels disconnected, hovering above.

Jake's desire for me is never an insatiable hunger. To him, I'm a dessert he enjoys after dinner. I'm not a delectable chocolate cake that needs devouring. He appreciates my body, my taste, but he doesn't crave it. Doesn't require it. He never has.

A few minutes later, he moans. "I'm about to come," he whispers.

I imagine his semen seeping deep inside me, racing to fertilize my ovum.

To make *our* baby.

A flash of fear swallows me into a dark, black vortex.

In a swoop, Corey's face appears, his toothy grin I loved—*love?*—jutting out, piercing holes of panic into my body.

"Do you want to go on top?" Jake asks, his smile loose from release.

"Not tonight, I'm okay. Thanks," I say, barely able to breathe.

He climbs off me, dresses and snuggles against my still-naked body. His warmth should comfort me, should feel like home. Instead, it prickles against my skin like a scratchy sweater I can't take off. Within minutes, his breathing slows, evening out into steady snores.

But I can't sleep.

I'm fixated on the idea of our fates permanently entwined by the addition of a baby.

Together, forever.

Isn't that what I want?

It's true I want my dad to have a grandchild.

But the idea of being sealed to Jake forever petrifies the shit out of me.

***

An hour later, I slip out of bed, my insomnia roaring, my therapist's advice drumming in my mind: *When you can't sleep, get out of bed and do something boring.* I stumble into my home office, plopping into my leather chair, turning on the lamp, illuminating the three pictures decorating my desk.

There's me and Jake on our wedding day. Jake beams in his tuxedo but my smile is drawn on, like I'm a marionette with strings and my lips are being forcefully yanked up. A lie in plain sight, immortalized in print.

Then, there's me and my parents at my med school graduation. I'm sandwiched between them, their pride radiant. My smile is present but achingly fake. That day, I didn't feel pleasure. Only crushing heaviness. The weight of pretending.

And then, the third. Me on the wraparound deck of Impodimo Lodge. *Paradise.*

My eyes close and for a second, I'm back there, mockingly posing against the deck railing, as Corey aimed his camera.

"Smile, *pragtige dame*," he'd said.

I touch my cheek, which is hot and flushed. Eleven years later and Corey's smoldering cobalt eyes still make my body burn.

Like usual, I try to shove the past away.

But tonight, my hands reach for the photograph, gripping it. The wooden frame is frayed, on the verge of collapse, just like my life.

For years, I've told myself I keep this picture because of my love for the elephants. Their grace, their wisdom, their enduring strength. But really, it's another convenient lie in an innumerable list.

I keep it because it's from *him*.

The only thing that remains.

The only proof I was ever once *True Tessa*.

My fingers trace longingly over my twenty-five-year-old smile, so genuine and relaxed. My eyes so happy, sparkling with those golden specs that Corey loved. They haven't twinkled like that since I left.

A tremor runs through me, sadness bleeding into my hands. The photo drops, splattering onto the floor, the frame cracking open. I pick up the fallen picture, noticing something I've missed all these years—an inscription written on the back.

Tess, don't forget, your needs matter. I love you, -C.

Corey's clunky handwriting sears into me. Regret shoves up through my lungs, a gasp bursting from my mouth.

He wanted me to remember my needs matter?

Holy shit.

I've spent a lifetime focused on making my dad proud.

And I have made him proud.

But at what cost?

My fingers clutch my chest. At the base of my thorax, buried beneath layers of fascia and muscle, is the scar formed from losing Corey. For the past decade, the fibrous tissue has been feebly held together by my lies and delusions.

I'm fine.

My career is fine.

My marriage is okay.

Life is okay/fine.

The lies were brittle stitches holding together a wound that never truly closed.

But now, my dad is terminally ill. My foundation is gutting and this gaping scar is re-exposed. The pain I've hankered to forget barrels through my body until grief literally drowns me.

With teary eyes, I jostle my computer awake, clicking on my email.

It springs open, revealing the towering number that mocks me: 10,985 unread messages. My inbox is notoriously a disaster, one of the few pieces of my identity that's not hyper-polished. I search for the folder entitled "Elephants." It's beneath dozens of more important folders, effectively hiding it from myself.

And Jake.

It contains the four hundred and twenty-three unsent messages I've written to Corey over the years. I haven't opened this folder since my wedding day, when I swore off Corey's memory forever.

So why am I opening this now?

But I know the answer.

As my worst fears are being realized, I still yearn for *his* comfort. The only person who's ever really known me.

My fingers singe against the trackpad.

Four hundred and twenty-three unsent messages.

Perfectly preserved artifacts of my broken heart.

And then, unable to stop myself, I start to re-read them all…

THEN:

Ten Years Ago
October, 2008

39

TESSA

From: Tessa.Williams2@bmail.com
To: Coreytheranger@ImpodimoLodge.net

Subject: One Year

Date: Sunday, October 5, 2008

Dear Corey,

One year ago, you emailed me these words:

Hallo pragtige dame,

I'm glad you're home safe. I miss you, so damn much. A fucking horrendous amount. After you drove away, I vomited and then drank myself into a stupor while Darian looked at me like I'd lost my damn mind. Maybe, I have lost my damn mind. I can't see the elephants without wanting to cry.

During the game ride today, I've been thinking… and Tess, I don't think it's a good idea to talk to you right now. I'm too weak. It's killing me that you're there and I'm here. I need a little time to accept this new reality. I'll contact you when I'm feeling better.

I love you, Tess. Please don't forget, I just want you to be happy. That's all I care about.

Yours,
Corey

I read your note and fell apart. Inside, I was already an empty shell, devoid of the life force that had coursed through me in Botswana. When we said goodbye, perhaps I was naïve, but I really believed we'd remain in each other's lives. Just because I left, I didn't stop wanting to be with you.

For the past 365 days, I've emailed you every day like I said I would, hoping you'd come around. That you'd realize that the pain of *not* talking was even worse than the pain of talking. But there's been zero response.

What's going on? Did you stop loving me? Have you moved on to someone new? Or do you still hurt as much as me? It eats me up not knowing.

This morning, I promised myself I'm not going to send these emails anymore. I might not be able to stop myself from writing them, but I can prohibit myself from sending them. From continuing to make myself vulnerable to you when obviously, you want nothing to do with me. Not anymore.

Corey, this makes me so freaking sad.

You have no idea how horrendous this past year has been. How many times I've stopped myself from buying a plane ticket back to South Africa. How many nights I've lain awake, desperately regretting my decision to leave.

It was the wrong choice. The worst choice. I made the freaking worst, wrong choice.

I miss your adorable little tummy, the way you made me feel so safe and protected.

I'm home but this place is empty. I keep waiting for it to get better but it hasn't. I graduated from medical school in June. I'm officially a "doctor." I should be happy (spoiler alert: I'm not). I still don't want to be a doctor. I've never admitted that to anyone except you.

I researched residency programs in South Africa. I almost applied to two, thinking if I was there, maybe you'd talk to me again. But when you wouldn't respond to any of my messages, I got too scared. So instead, I started my residency in Internal Medicine here in Philly. Every day, I go to the hospital, hoping to fall in love with medicine. And every night, I come home further from that feeling.

You asked me what I wanted from my life, and the truth is, I have no idea how to figure that out. But I've learned two important things this year:

1) The power of resilience. I still communicate with Evah, and her hardiness has sustained me. She recently mailed me some photographs of her family. And you know what? She continues. She's endured a terrible loss, but she's still standing. What a freaking inspiration!

2) Self-respect. I haven't seen Greg since I returned. Being with you, I saw how I deserved to be treated. I will never tolerate that type of abusive behavior again. Thank you for that gift.

After I got home, I got back into running. It helps with my constant worries a little. When I get home from the hospital, I run. I put on my headphones and just go. Running is the only thing that makes me feel free. That makes me feel a sliver of how I did when I was with you. Sometimes, I pretend I'm running in the bush. But in my fantasy, there are no lions to eat me. And since you're the only one I'm honest with, I'll even admit this. I run 90% for stress relief, 10% to stay thin.

Okay, actually, the real balance is 80%, 20%.

Or maybe, 70%, 30%.

You get the point.

Corey, I miss Impodimo Lodge so much. It's still the most amazing place I've ever been. Having to be around humans all day is terrible. Animals are so much better. I'm still insanely jealous of your job.

I miss the elephants, Corey. And you.

I can't stop thinking about you, no matter how hard I try.

Please, reach out to me. Say anything.

I love you,

Tessa

NOW:

January, 2019

40

PETER

I sway against the plastic chair in Dr. Burkland's office. I pat my thigh to ease the hiss in my brain. I stare at the empty seats beside me. Claudia and Tessa begged to come today—but I asked to go alone, to hear the news about my latest scans, first by myself. Yet now, the silence feels cavernous and I desperately crave their comfort.

A small mirror hangs behind the door. I stand, glaring at my reflection. The man looking back at me is a stranger. The four months of cancer treatments have weathered me. My grey hair is gone, replaced by a shiny bald head marked with brown age spots. Behind my silver-rimmed glasses, my once lively eyes appear desolate and weary. My dress shirt droops like it belongs to someone larger, the fabric hanging off my diminished frame. Nearly twenty-five pounds gone. Despite Claudia's gentle nudging, I've yet to update my wardrobe.

Dr. Burkland pushes against the door, forcing me to shuffle backwards. "Peter, I'm sorry. I didn't expect you to be there," she says, hugging me tightly, exuding that unique compassion of a doctor who's both my provider and friend.

"That's okay, Kelly. I was taking a quick glance in the mirror. Probably best to avoid doing that from now on," I joke, my fingers grazing the area above my lip where my mustache used to be.

"You look great, Peter."

It's a blatant lie, but I appreciate her sentiment. I walk towards my chair, pausing as a stabbing ache shoots into my hip. My pain is worsening. I bear through it at work, but it's getting harder. In the evening, I've started to find release in oxycodone, but it makes my mind fuzzy. I hate the feeling as the medication clouds my thoughts, but I also hate the nonstop pain. I oscillate between which I hate more.

Dr. Burkland takes a seat. Behind her, rain falls from the sky, a few wandering drops sluicing against the window. "So, Peter, how've you been feeling?"

My throat tightens. "Fine, pretty good."

"Really?" She studies me, eyebrows arched.

My jaw tightens now, too. "Yes."

The truth is no, but my father raised me to be stoic. Despite my treatments, I've missed only a handful of days at work. My job remains my *raison d'être*. Usually, I wake up consumed by pain, but I hoist myself out of bed anyway. Outside my office, I vomit into a paper bag. Then I walk through the door, plastering on a smile. Each morning, my longtime receptionist Elaine greets me with the same cheery wave, just as she has for the past twenty-seven years. I match it—because routine is survival. The busyness of my job is my lifeline.

"How's your mood, Peter? Are you feeling anxious or depressed?"

I fumble for an answer that sounds strong. "Maybe, a little, but I expect that's normal, given the circumstances?"

Really, my worry is held at bay only while working. Some people use pills or alcohol, but my drug of choice has always been my career. It's at home, in the quiet, when my mind races. It's then that the fear of what's to come slowly devours me.

"Yes, it's normal," she says. "But there are medications to try if the worry is getting to be too much. You're dealing with a lot, and you don't have to do it alone. Medication can provide a much-needed break from the overwhelming reality of living with cancer."

I was raised in a family that didn't acknowledge mental health. Troubles were glossed over, smoked, or drank away. It's unconscionable to take medication to manage my mood.

My cancer?

Yes.

My feelings?

Never.

"Thanks, Kelly, but I'm really okay." I grow restless, my fate dangling above me like a rope, waiting to knot around my neck. "Anyway, can we please discuss my scans? The anticipation is *killing* me." It's a miserable attempt at humor.

She chuckles obligingly. "Yes, of course, Peter." Her eyes grow dark and stormy. A sense of dread overflows my stomach. "I'm sorry, but the scans don't show good news. I really wish I could say something different, but your cancer's progressing. The spot in your liver is bigger. There are two other spots in your ribs and a new questionable mass in your left lung."

Her words stall, a stunning silence saturating the room.

I'm dying.

Outside the door, someone cackles, perhaps a patient who's received better news.

On the street, a train whistles, speeding through University City.

My world was just delivered a crushing blow, but everywhere else, life persists.

I'm dying.

The treatment isn't working. My cancer can't be stopped. I had feared this—had felt it deep inside—but now, with certainty, I know it. Within my chest, my hopes for the future fracture apart, my heart thundering with damning sorrow.

As a cardiologist, I've spent a lifetime studying the inner workings of the human heart, but there's still so much about it I don't understand—like how such raw pain can flow through it, completely paralyzing you at times.

I'm dying?

How can I be dying?

Claudia and Tessa need me.

I'm not ready to die.

I stare at the artwork on the wall, taking note of a boater on the ocean. The text reads, *You can't stop the waves, but you can learn to surf.* I struggle to make sense of it.

I can't stop my cancer, but I can learn to what?

To live?

To die?

How the heck do I do that?

"Peter, say something." Dr. Burkland's benevolent smile pulls me from the black pit of my thoughts.

What about my grandchild?

Just last week, Tessa told me she's pregnant. It's still very early; she's only six weeks along, but I'm going to be a grandfather. A grandfather! I've waited for this for so long—but now I wonder if I'll even live long enough to meet the baby.

Dr. Burkland reclines against her chair, gazing at me with compassion. I know how hard it is to deliver bad news to a patient—any patient, really, but especially the ones you feel a deep kinship for.

"Wow, Kelly," I utter, sighing. "That's devastating."

"I know. I'm so sorry, Peter. Do you want to see the images?"

Against all rationality, the perpetual doctor's brain inside of me says "yes." So, she pulls up the images from my CT scan. I stare at the cancer masses entangled within my organs—overtaking me, killing me.

The enemy is within.

How is this possible?

I'm at life's apex. I have everything I want—a successful career, a terrific daughter, a happy marriage. I planned to slow down soon, to travel, like Claudia's always wanted. We were going to eat *spaghetti al cacio e pepe* in Rome, sip *Cabernet Franc* at a vineyard in Bordeaux, ride the *Tramway du Mont Blanc* through the French Alps. I put these joys off for so long—too long—because I thought there'd be time later.

But I'm dying.

Time isn't promised.

I knew this conceptually but forgot it practically.

"Is there anything left we can try?" My voice is pleading, desperate, needy.

"Yes. There's a clinical trial for a new immune therapy agent with promise. I think you'll qualify. I'll try to get you enrolled as soon as possible."

"Good, let's do that."

"Of course, Peter." She reaches across the desk, squeezing my hand.

Hope.

The antidote to fear, to death.

Hope.

As long as it remains, I'll cling to it.

For my sake.

For my family's sake.

Hope.

It is everything.

It is now the only thing.

41

TESSA

I'm running along Market Street, weaving through the throngs of tourists crowding Independence Mall. It's a clear Wednesday morning in early January. The sun is out but the air is frigid. The cold constricts my huffing lungs.

To keep my mental health (and weight) in check, I run every day. A creature of routine, I always run the same route. From my apartment on Rittenhouse Square, I run along Walnut Street to the Schuylkill River pathway. The path leads past Boathouse Row to the Philadelphia Art Museum, where I veer off down the parkway. I snake through Chinatown, to the Liberty Bell, before running back up Walnut Street. It's just shy of five miles, and I run an 8:24 pace, so I'm usually gone forty-two minutes.

I shove my headphones deeper into my ears, turning up the volume on my Spotify playlist. Calum Scott's "You Are the Reason" blares.

I zigzag through Old City, my arms shuffling at my sides, the lyrics blizzarding into my brain.

It's almost as if the song was written about my feelings for Corey.

Years ago, I told him, "I'll find a way to fix this."

But I never did.

And now I'm married to Jake.

Shit.

I run faster, passing through Washington Square Park, clicking onto the next song, trying to thrust Corey from my mind. Bruce Springsteen's "No Surrender" croons. My dad's face pops up instead.

"My treatment isn't working," he told me three days ago, his voice glum at admitting there were few options left to stop his cancer.

Corey.

My dad.

Shit!

I gallop rapidly, focusing on the hordes of people—babies being pushed in UPPAbaby strollers, couples sipping La Colombe coffee, dogs running, dogs walking, dogs being toted in designer bags. An older woman plays Pachelbel's "Canon in D" on her violin. It's the song I, flanked by my parents, walked down the aisle to.

At my wedding to Jake.

Shit.

Jake.

I yearn to trade places with any of these people.

Please, let them live my life instead!

I run even faster, my thumb grazing my belly.

Where a *baby* is growing.

Shit.

Fear hovers like a dense cloud. I all-out sprint, but the cloud chases me.

I'm seven weeks pregnant but something is off.

And it's not just that I'm a wreck about having a baby with Jake.

Although, I am.

The pregnancy itself feels *wrong*.

Years ago, during the six weeks I was pregnant, I experienced every symptom—nausea, food aversions, fatigue, sore breasts, back pain. The line on my pregnancy test was dark pink.

But now?

I feel zilch, nada. Disconcertingly normal. And my home pregnancy test lines are barely pale pink.

Jake and Liz both think I'm being my usual, overly cautious self.

"Try to relax," Liz advised yesterday over coffee. "Enjoy your pregnancy. I know it's scary. Marley felt that way too, but it'll be fine. If you worry so much, you can't enjoy the experience."

Eleven years later and Liz is still doling out the same advice as at Impodimo Lodge. She was right then, and maybe she's right now. But I can't relax. My gut keeps whispering: *Something's wrong.*

I pick up my speed, violently shaking my head, my ponytail ricocheting. I pass a red-haired child wearing a hat that reads: *Do what you love.* I nearly laugh out loud at the absurdity of this idea. Given the chance, I wouldn't have a clue where to start.

Now, I'm racing madly, mimicking the feeling of my workday, which soon awaits. The happiest moment of my day will be when I get home tonight and can collapse into bed, tugging the covers over my head, hiding from the world. When sleep finally whisks me into a brief respite.

A sudden wrenching in my belly causes me to screech to a halt.

I rub my stomach.

Everything will be okay.

I'm back in the outdoor shower at Impodimo Lodge, my first day there, holding all the broken pieces of my life, optimistic I could glue them together.

I didn't then.

But I will now.

Somehow.

The throbbing in my stomach stops.

I take a deep breath.

I have to deliver this grandchild for my dad.

He's dying.

Besides, what does my gut know?

Absolutely nothing.

With the pain gone, I shoot off, sprinting again, desperate to outpace my thoughts.

Wishing, if I only run fast enough,

Just this once,

I can finally outrun my brain.

THEN:

Five Years Ago

June, 2013

42

TESSA

From: Tessa.Williams2@bmail.com
To: Coreytheranger@ImpodimoLodge.net

Subject: My Wedding Day

Date: June 22, 2013

Dear Corey,

Today is my wedding day. I can't even believe I'm typing that. It doesn't feel real. I'm supposed to be downstairs starting my updo with Kacey, the 5-star Knot-rated stylist my mom booked. And then, my makeup with Claire, who promised to smoke my eye. Not so much that I look scary, but enough that the pictures are "enchanting."

But I can't bring myself to walk down the steps. Instead, I'm sitting here, on my childhood bed, writing to you one final time. I know I'm really writing to myself. For the past five years, I've only been writing to myself. Hundreds upon hundreds of unsent emails. But it's kept the idea of you alive. But today, when I get up from this bed, I'm letting go of you. Of my dream for our happy ever after.

It's been almost six years since we saw each other. Sometimes, it feels like six hundred years. Other times, like six minutes, because my life has become so repetitively stale. I still can't believe in all this time you never reached out to me. Not once. How can that be? It hurts so freaking much, Corey. I expected more—you said you loved me, the most ever. You said you'd contact me when you were ready.

What happened? How did you let me go so easily?

I waited for you for so fucking long. For three years, I didn't get close to another partner. I wasn't a total prude but my heart belonged to *you*. But then, I saw your Facebook page and realized all hope was already lost. That I was delusional in thinking you still felt the same. I promised myself I wouldn't stalk you, and most of the time, I was well-behaved. But occasionally, I'd give in and look at your pictures on the Impodimo Lodge website. They were so beautiful and I always sobbed seeing them. Nostalgic for that place, for that person I was with you.

But that day, I made the *huge* mistake of checking your Facebook. We weren't friends, but I could still see your profile picture. It was you, with your arms wrapped around Alice! She was looking straight at the camera, her red curls bouncing with joy, her green eyes sparkling with love. You were turned towards her, your impeccable lips curled into a broad smile as you planted a kiss on her cheek. In the background was the clear blue of water. Were you together at the Chobe River Lodge?

You looked freaking smitten, Corey. And it made me horrendously, fucking sick.

I closed the page, deleted my browsing history, considered deactivating Facebook. But before I could do anything, I threw up.

It hurt so much to see you with *her.* I felt like the biggest fucking idiot. I'd been pining over you for years when clearly you'd more than moved on. With Alice. Alice, who you once told me you'd never even had *any* feelings for!

I cried to Liz for hours. She begged and pleaded with me that it was time to *finally* move on.

A few months later, I met Jake at Liz and Marley's wedding. That day, I should have been so happy. It was my best friend's wedding, and she was marrying the love of her life. But I was without you. And now I knew you were with Alice.

Fucking Alice.

Jake found me near the bar, drinking my third vodka soda, drowning in self-pity. He asked me to dance. There were no crazy sparks, not like with you. Not then and not now. But he was nice, and it felt good to be wanted. From the dance floor, Liz gave me a big thumbs-up. She already loved Jake because he was Marley's close friend from Emory. And Jake really wanted to be with me. So, I let him.

Things with him are good. I say good because that's the best word to describe it. They aren't magical or awful. Everything is okay. It's fine. He's generous and smart and treats me well. He loves me and I love him. We get along and enjoy each other's company.

When I turned thirty, my dad started hinting that it was time to get engaged. By then, I'd finished residency and was working at a busy family practice in Philadelphia. According to my dad, I'd conquered my "professional goals" but not my "personal life." So, Jake asked me to marry him. And I said yes. Because I still do what's expected. *Phony Tessa's* habits die hard.

So now, I'm going to go downstairs to get made up into something I'm not. To keep being someone I'm not.

To say my vows to Jake.

At the Four Seasons Hotel.

In front of two hundred and fifty of my family's nearest and dearest friends.

And I'll try my hardest to live a happy life with Jake.

And when I'm standing at the altar beside Jake, I'll try not to imagine your breathtaking smile.

Or your electric blue eyes.

To not wish I was marrying you instead.

Because I still love you, Corey.

And I don't know how to stop.

Tessa

NOW:

January, 2019

43

TESSA

I bolt awake, a sharp knife-like sensation twisting in my belly, yanking my organs apart. I squeeze my eyes shut, the darkness behind my lids offering no escape.

Please let this be a dream.

The stabbing pain ascends from my perineum, racing through my intestines, stealing my breath. "Shit!"

My scream pierces the quiet, rousing a sleeping Jake. He jerks upright, squinting at me in the dim light. "Tess? What's wrong?" He glances at the clock. "It's four in the morning, babe."

I clutch my abdomen, gasping as another wave of agony grips me. "I'm not sure," I squeak between breaths. "I just woke up in the worst pain of my life."

Jake's hand hovers uncertainly over my back. "Tess. Is it…" He hesitates. "The baby?"

According to my period tracker, I'm seven weeks, four days pregnant. Long enough for hope to start to sprout, short enough for it still to be so fragile.

"I don't know," I gasp, rolling onto my side, curling into the fetal position. Jake runs his fingers along my back, panic tightening his features.

His helplessness only deepens my own.

Count back from 214.

Maybe, by then, the pain will be gone.

By 209, I'm drowning in another round of searing pain. It doesn't just hurt, it commands every molecule of my being.

"Jake," I gasp, scrunching the sheet between my fingers. "I need to go to the ER. Now!"

***

Two hours later, I sag motionless in the hospital bed, my body drained. Jake's beside me, clutching my hand, his leg jerking up and down one hundred cycles per minute. The door shoves open. The attending physician enters, wearing jade-green scrubs. A worried look overtakes her initially cheery expression.

"Shit! Tess? What's going on?" Liz demands.

"Thank god you're working right now," I utter, relief briefly deluging my pain-addled body. "I should've texted you but I'm in such agony, I'm not thinking straight."

Liz is at my bedside in two strides, grabbing my free hand. "Why are you here? The resident was just telling me about this case, but I didn't realize it was *you!*" The automatic blood pressure cuff goes off, inflating around my left arm. A dull squeeze compared to the pain everywhere else. The machine beeps every few seconds until displaying its verdict. "Ninety-six over sixty," Liz mutters, crinkling her brow. "It's low."

"I'm not sure what's going on," I say. "I woke up from a dead sleep with this horrendous pain. I'm seven and a half weeks pregnant. I haven't had an ultrasound yet. My first OB appointment isn't until next week… but, you know, I've been worried something is off…"

Liz listens intently, her fingers tracing down my clammy cheek.

"It's okay, Tess. We'll figure everything out. I'm going to ask the ultrasound tech to come right in and I'll page the OB on call to see you after."

"Thanks, Liz. I love you."

"I love you too." Liz kisses my forehead before rushing out.

Jake's thumb strokes slow circles over my knuckles. I wish he would stop. His tension bleeds through. "Everything'll be okay, Tess," he whispers.

His words are earnest, but they fall flat on my ears.

He doesn't know how to comfort me.

He never has.

A few minutes later, the young ultrasound tech enters the room, pushing a cart of equipment. "I'm Jamie," she says, dimming the room lights. She washes her hands and grabs gloves. "Scoot to the edge of the bed, please," she instructs as she applies petroleum jelly to the ultrasound probe. "This may feel cold and a little uncomfortable."

Evah.

In a flash, I'm back at Princess Victoria Hospital, performing a pelvic exam on a terrified, bleeding Evah. With ultrasound equipment like this, maybe Evah's son would have lived.

Or maybe not.

I've come to understand that some things—like my dad's cancer—can't be fixed, even with all the resources in the world. Sometimes, the natural order of life cannot be stopped.

I wince as the cold probe slides deep inside me. Jamie moves the wand around, scanning for my pregnancy. On the screen, I study the pictures of my uterus. I've performed enough ultrasounds to know immediately that something is wrong. My uterus is empty. There's no fetus, not even a gestational sac. It's as void as my soul the day my plane landed back at JFK.

My heart plunges down to my stomach, which still wallops with pain.

The tech remains expressionless as she takes several measurements of my uterus, then she moves the probe to the left, evaluating my ovary. She travels further down, scanning my fallopian tube.

And then, I see it.

There, in my right fallopian tube, is a protruding mass. The pregnancy isn't in my uterus but *wrongly* inside my tube. It's an ectopic pregnancy. My gut was correct, but like usual, I didn't listen.

Shit.

Shit.

Shit.

My lower lip quivers.

This can't be happening!

Shit.

I'm not going to give my dad the grandchild he wanted.

The tech takes some measurements of my left ovary and tube before withdrawing the probe. "The doctor will be in soon. Good luck." Despite her neutral words, her face splays with excruciating pity. I look at Jake, whose brown eyes teem with distress. I already know what the OB will say, but I don't have the heart to tell him.

It feels like an eternity before Dr. Clarke enters, brisk and straight to the point. "Tessa, I'm very sorry to tell you this, but based on your bloodwork and ultrasound, your pregnancy is ectopic. Your right fallopian tube is rupturing. We need to take you to surgery right away, to remove the pregnancy and save your life."

To save my life?

Holy shit.

The severity of the situation dawns on me. I have so many questions, but I find myself entirely speechless, my mind a frozen pond in the dead of winter.

Jake starts sobbing loudly.

Liz rushes in, grasping my shoulder, steadying me. Amazing Liz, that solid anchor through so many hard moments in my life. Another powerful swell of pain erupts, and I scream, clutching my belly.

"Now that we know your pregnancy isn't viable, I'll have the nurse give you some morphine," Liz says.

A minute later, my left arm tingles as the medication gushes through my vein. Within seconds, the relief floods over me in one enormous wave.

All my pain melts.

Not only the physical agony but the years of emotional baggage I tow.

It's all miraculously, instantaneously, *gone*.

My eyes drift shut as every muscle in my body unclenches.

I become weightless, floating outside myself.

Away.

It's euphoric.

Blissful.

Perfect.

In this space, my dad isn't dying, and I haven't married the wrong partner. I haven't spent my entire adult life pursuing a career I don't want, nor am I losing a second pregnancy.

None of it is tangible here.

I soar to the only place I've ever been truly happy, completely whole.

To Impodimo Lodge.

Suddenly, Corey's brawny arm scoops around my waist, his sapphire eyes gleaming beneath the fading glow of sunlight. His skin smells of salt and sunscreen and *hope*. He quietly whispers, "I love you," a trail of goosebumps springing from my neck, encircling my chest, filling the deep wounds in my heart.

We gaze together at the watering hole, where the elephants splatter in the mud. I feel an overwhelming sense of peace, of belonging.

In the distance, a young girl runs in a field of scarlet daisies, holding a yellow balloon. I recognize those violet eyes, those white-blonde curls.

Leona.

Leona's tiny hand waves, beckoning me.

I untangle from Corey, rushing down the steps into the sprawling meadow of flowers. Leona runs to me with that exuberant joy of childhood, leaping into my arms.

The yellow balloon floats high into the sky.

I clutch Leona, inhaling deeply as if, somehow, my soul missed her.

It makes no sense because we've never met.

But in this space, we *have.*

The floral aroma intoxicates my senses, quieting my mind. The perpetual clamping around my neck dissolves.

I'm released.

From my dad's expectations.

From the societal pressures.

Mostly from myself.

Corey's here now, too, hugging us both. And as a trio, everything is right. My cheeks burn rosy with joy.

Corey pulls me close, his breath tickling my earlobe.

"Tess," he whispers. "I finally figured out my third lesson for you."

My heart screeches to a halt. "Oh yeah? What is it?"

And then, he utters the words that will change everything.

"Stop fighting yourself. Just trust your damn gut, already. Use your pain. It's your greatest teacher. The knowledge can finally set you *free.*"

44

TESSA

Dr. Clarke enters my hospital room. I wince as the harsh lights from the hallway collide with the blackened room. It's after ten p.m. Shavings of moonlight sneak between the blinds, making her chin-length hair shimmer silver. In the corner, Jake is sleeping on a lounge chair, a blanket draped over him.

"Tessa, how are you feeling? I'm heading home, but I wanted to check on you," Dr. Clarke says, peeling back my hospital gown. She examines the covered incisions through which my right fallopian tube and pregnancy were removed twelve hours ago.

"Sore," I mumble. "But all things considered... I guess I'm okay."

"You're very lucky you came in when you did. A little while later, and you would've gone into septic shock."

"Wow." I shake my head, still unable to process anything that's happened.

My pregnancy is over.

There's no grandchild coming.

I didn't listen to my gut, and I could have died.

"Get some rest," Dr. Clarke says, stroking my arm. "I'll be by to check on you tomorrow."

"Thank you"—I gulp—"for everything. For saving my life."

Dr. Clarke smiles. "Of course. It's my job."

Mine too.

But I wish it wasn't.

The door shuts, the room shadowy again, tinged by the reddish glow of medical equipment. I shut my eyes, desperate to return to Impodimo Lodge.

It felt like a fairy tale, being back there again.

Corey's words coat my insides like viscous honey, sticking to everything.

Stop running from yourself.

Pain is your greatest teacher.

Trust your damn gut.

Trust your damn gut.

Trust your damn gut.

The pain medication takes hold as I drift off, leaving reality, chasing after only Leona and Corey.

45

TESSA

I creep in through the back of the hushed hospital auditorium. The room lights are dim, the crowd of faces blurred silhouettes, illuminated by the scattered shine from cellphone screens.

It's four weeks after my surgery and today is my first day back to work. Typically, every Monday morning, I start my week by attending the hospital-wide grand rounds. The topics of the lectures are random but informative. Usually, I half-listen, half-doom scroll on Twitter before rushing out to my full morning of patients.

I take a seat in the last row, hoping to avoid pitied looks from concerned colleagues who've heard about my ordeal. As my belly folds unto itself, I flinch. At a follow-up appointment last week, Dr. Clarke said my wounds are healing nicely, but "nicely" doesn't cover the raw ache that radiates beneath my skin.

My phone vibrates with a text.

Jake: Have a good first day back, babe. Love you.

I sigh, muting his message without replying.

Since I got home from the hospital, things between us are strained.

Every touch feels like a question. Every look, a reminder. Jake's crushed about losing the pregnancy, his eyes widening with hope whenever he mentions trying again.

But I can't match his enthusiasm.

Not anymore.

Not even for my dad.

Lying in the hospital bed, I saw the truth: I don't want a baby.

Not with Jake.

Not for anyone else.

Not to hold something together that's meant to fall apart.

My own brush with mortality showed me how lost I am from myself.

For years, I've been treading in a choppy sea of *okay-fine*ness, looking for land, barely keeping my head above water.

This isn't the life I want.

I deserve more.

I need to trust my damn gut.

"Ladies and gentlemen, thanks for being here. I'm absolutely thrilled to have a terrific speaker with us…" I look up as my boss, Dr. Rachel Jones, introduces the lecturer. "I'm not sure how we convinced him to come from South Africa because he's quite open about the fact he doesn't enjoy public speaking." A few stray chuckles ripple from the crowd. "But his work as a radiologist has been published in the prestigious medical journal, *JAMA*. I'm so glad he'll have a chance to share it with us. Without further ado, I'd like to extend our warmest welcome to Dr. Carl Diallo!"

Dr. Carl Diallo?

A generous round of applause follows as Carl's PowerPoint slides spring onto the projector. With shaking hands, I read his title slide: "The Use of Telemedicine Radiographic Interpretation to Improve Health Care Outcomes in Rural South African Villages."

The words blur as my fingers tighten around my phone. The room feels at once too large and impossibly small.

Carl ambles to the stage. He's tall, dressed in a sleek grey suit with a crisp red tie. His build is lanky, his eyes aquatic green, his nose slender. But none of these details matter. It's his fleshy lips that draw me in. They're the same as Corey's.

I sit frozen, body locked as he approaches the microphone, his golden wedding band reflecting under the stage lighting.

"Hi, mates," he says. "Thank you for having me this morning. I'm a bit jetlagged and terribly shy, so I hope you'll bear with me." I gape as he feebly offers up an analogous toothy grin to his brother. His South African accent enchants me, catapulting me straight into the past. My heart sputters, then briefly stops beating.

How is it possible that Carl is here?

Haunting me with echoes of the man I left behind?

It's the closest I've come to Corey in eleven years—aside from my four hundred and twenty-three drafted emails and my morphine-induced voyage to Impodimo Lodge. In all that time we've had *zero* contact. Not a single text, no accidental calls. I don't even permit social media snooping.

What's the point?

Corey long ago moved on with Alice.

Fucking Alice.

Carl's voice draws me back to the present as he shuffles nervously against the podium and clicks onto his second slide. "I'm thrilled today to talk about my work as a radiologist in South Africa. One of the major barriers to care in many of our remote villages is a lack of access to basic imaging, such as a chest X-ray. And even when these services can be performed, often no one's available to interpret the results in a timely manner.

"My team at the University of Pretoria has been working on a pilot study where radiographic images from local centers are sent to us via text message. We remain remote, often hundreds of kilometers away. But we read the images and provide an interpretation, via text message, usually within the hour. This has had broad consequences at improving diagnosis and management of many treatable conditions…"

I sit paralyzed as Carl speaks about his inspiring work, about how the use of simple technology is transforming care in underserved areas.

An hour later, Carl reaches his last slide. "Thanks so much for having me today, but I'd be remiss if I didn't thank the two most important women in my life. My wife, Bess, and our four-year-old daughter, Leona-Anne."

On the screen bursts an image of the pair hugging in front of a sparkling white Christmas tree. Leona-Anne has oversized chestnut eyes and Leona's white curly locks. Her smile radiates off the screen, zipping electricity into my worn body.

There's a thunderous round of applause as the room lights flicker on. The crowd begins to disperse.

I check my watch, stressed to see I'm already late for my first patient.

I stand slowly, bracing my stomach.

Maybe I should just walk out the door. Leave the past behind. Maybe that's where it belongs.

But I can't.

I haven't been able to in eleven years.

And now, by some crazy chance, Carl is here, in this very room.

An invisible magnet yanks me towards him, towards that life, that person I long ago left.

A line has formed to talk to him. I impatiently wait at the end, my pulse gathering velocity with each passing second. I've never met him, yet I feel profoundly connected to him.

Finally, we are face-to-face.

"Dr. Diallo, I'm Tessa Williams. Your lecture was incredibly motivating. Years ago, in medical school, I trained at Princess Victoria Hospital in

Gaborone. Your talk evoked a lot of very powerful memories for me."

Like how I loved your brother, the most ever.

And have never moved on.

Carl's vibrant green eyes ignite in surprise. "Did you say your name is Tessa Williams?"

I feel my face flush. "Yes."

Time seems to halt.

He raises his eyebrows. "This may sound weird, but did you know my brother, Corey?"

My voice is barely audible as a swarm of memories stings my chest. "Yes."

"Oh, wow. I can't believe it," he muses. "What are the odds?"

That's the crazy thing about life. Most people worry endlessly about the things that never happen. But the things that actually change your life course are usually the ones you never see coming.

I clear my throat, struggling to speak, a mouse chewing up my tongue. "I knew Corey… very well, actually." For a moment, I can feel his lips trailing up my neck. I gulp. "But I haven't heard from him in years. How is he?"

I hold my breath, terrified to know.

Great.

Married to Alice.

Loving life.

"He's good."

The room sways.

Oh.

Carl elaborates. "He's still working at Impodimo Lodge. He's the manager, completely adores the place."

That deep scar in my chest, the one formed from losing him, suddenly bursts apart.

I'm happy, he's happy.

But also…

I'm sad, he's happy.

Without me.

It was a huge mistake to talk to Carl. I need air, light, an escape. "I'm glad he's doing well. Please send him my regards. Anyway, it was an honor to meet you. Have a good rest of your stay and keep up your amazing work."

Despite my throbbing incision, I'm ready to break into a sprint.

"Tessa, wait." Carl's hand grazes my shoulder, and I reluctantly spin around.

"Yes?"

"Corey might kill me for saying this… but…" The pause is eternal, time now seeming to operate in an alternative universe. "He never… got over… *you*. I'm not sure if you have any interest in talking to him? I'd certainly understand if your life circumstances don't permit it, but I know he'd love to hear from you."

My mouth plunges open, my bottom lip practically falling off my face. I try to close it, but my brain won't cooperate, so it hangs strikingly agape.

What?

Shit.

What!

"Are… are… are you sure?" I stammer. "I reached out to him, so many times, years ago, but he never responded. He didn't seem interested in talking to me at all."

"Yeah…" Carl says, tone shifting. "He had a pretty rough year or two after you left, drinking way too much. He was really depressed and pretty self-destructive. But thankfully… he got help and he's doing great now."

My jaw judders, imagining Corey suffering.

Without me.

"Wow, I'm so sorry to hear that," I say. Carl offers up another toothy smile, turning the deepest layers of my core into Jell-O. "And your daughter is beautiful. I love her name. What an honor to your sister. And how special to have a new little girl in the family."

His expression softens. "Wow. Corey told you about Leona?" Shock swivels through his eyes. "Back then, he never talked about her. You really must have been special to him. But yes, Leona-Anne's amazing and being a grandmother has brought our mum back to life. It's been magical to watch it happen."

I force a smile—I wanted to give this same gift to my dad.

But it's not going to happen.

Let your pain teach you, Tess.

Stop running from life.

My phone buzzes. It's Taylor, my longtime medical assistant.

Taylor: Hi. Hope you're feeling better! Are you almost here? Your first patient is getting antsy.

"I'm so sorry, Carl, but I have to run. I have patients waiting. Maybe we can talk more later? And, if you don't mind, could you hold off on mentioning our encounter to Corey? As long as you think it's a good idea, I'd like to tell him myself."

Carl's face lights up like the Rockefeller Christmas tree. "Of course! Corey would love that."

I turn again to leave but I stop myself. "Just one more question, Carl. Is he married? What happened to Alice?"

Carl scoffs, infinity passing before his words finally reach my ears.

"Married? No. He's single. And Alice? She's been out of the picture for years."

46

TESSA

"Welcome back, Dr. Williams. We missed you! Mr. Dorn is ready in Exam Room 8," Taylor calls as I stagger through the door like a lost doe twenty minutes later.

My thoughts are a jumbled dumpster fire.

Corey never got over me.

I'm not happy in my marriage or my career.

My dad is dying.

It's all too much to process.

I swallow hard, that familiar tightness strangulating my neck. In my office, I stow my briefcase and grab my white coat. As the coat hits my shoulders, a fresh sense of dread settles into my stomach. One month away from this place but I didn't miss a single damn thing.

My watch displays the time: 9:35 a.m.

Shit.

Now, I'll run behind the rest of the day. Mr. Dorn is the first of twelve patients booked every fifteen minutes in my three-hour morning session. I hate running late, but also, I hate rushing. Over the years, it's been a constant source of frustration that my schedule never allows adequate time to deliver good care.

Lacking time to digest my feelings, I rush towards Exam Room 8. I knock quickly, entering without a response. "Mr. Dorn. I'm sorry I'm so late."

This is the sentence that most often leads my patient encounters. I've found the practice of medicine to be a fraught balance between customer service and skilled care.

Cal Dorn sits on the exam table, wearing a blue-and-white checkered gown, his sock-clad feet crossed at his ankles. He's an up-and-coming environmental law attorney with a husband and three-year-old twins. I know him well, having been his primary care provider for the past seven years. I also served as a strong advocate during his adoption process.

"Don't worry, Dr. Williams," he says. "I heard you were out on medical leave. It's great to have you back."

"Thanks. It's great to be back," I lie, the falsehoods slipping off my tongue as seamlessly as ever. He gives me a warmhearted grin, causing a flurry of emotions to churn within me.

It's an odd paradox I experience as a doctor. On the one hand, I sincerely like him and (almost all) my patients. But the cumulative emotional toll of caring for him, and the others, costs me heftily. The burden I carry is what makes me hate the job.

I pump the hand sanitizer, then take a seat by the computer. "So, how are things?" I open the electronic medical record, half-listening, half-trying to skim his last office note.

"I'm great." Cal beams. "I actually need to thank you, Dr. Williams. You may not know it, but you saved my life!"

I stop reading, looking at him, caught off guard. "Huh? I did?"

"Yep. Last time I was here, you noticed a new murmur in my heart." He stares at me as if I'll remember.

I nod yes, but it's another lie. I see upwards of one hundred patients a week. Eventually, the stories and faces all blend together. I recall nothing of our last exchange.

"I went to the cardiologist, like you suggested, and they ran some tests. Turns out, I had three arteries that were ninety-five percent blocked, even though I'm only forty-one and have no history of family heart disease. I had three stents placed two weeks ago. The cardiologist said I was a heart attack waiting to happen, but you stopped it. I can never thank you enough. Just thinking about the years I would've missed with my sons, I can't believe it."

"Wow. That's really incredible news," I say. "Tell me the entire story."

Cal keeps talking, and I keep trying to listen, but my brain blasts off, lost in the galaxy of my mind.

I saved his life.

It's not the first life I've saved. In my years as a doctor, there've been many. But most times, it accompanies a vast sense of accomplishment. It's a reminder of the power of my profession. *I can save a life.* Those rare, rewarding moments have given me the courage to persevere through the innumerable times I've wanted to quit.

But now, I feel neither happiness, nor pride, nor joy.

I'm so emotionally depleted that for Mr. Dorn, there's nothing left to feel.

There's only that hollow space.

The one that's waited for years,

To be filled by a passion,

I finally understand is *never* coming.

"How are you feeling since the stents?" I ask, straining to focus. "Did the cardiologist start you on Plavix?"

"Yes, he did, and to answer your question, I'm feeling great. I woke up this morning, crept into my sons' room and just watched them sleep. Why is it we only appreciate the tiny, beautiful, everyday miracles in front of us after a terrible wake-up call?" A tear escapes from his left eye, traveling down his freshly shaven cheek. "I'm going to scale back my work hours, be there for my kids more. This experience just made me realize that time is so precious."

His words are the truth. Time isn't guaranteed, never promised—but everyone lives like it is.

I, too, have made the mistake of assuming time was plentiful. That I'd have many more years with my dad. That, someday, in the far-off future, I'd have time to finally figure myself out.

But now, my dad is dying, and I can't stop it.

His time is running out.

And so is mine.

The clock continually ticks, but when we rush around at a nonstop feverish pace, we don't hear the minutes passing by.

"Well, Mr. Dorn, it sounds like you've taken a scary health experience and are making the most out of it. Sometimes, that's all we can do. Let our pain teach us, use it to make our lives more meaningful." I feel like a fraud, proclaiming this since I've only just learned it myself.

But when am I going to listen to my own advice?

Give myself permission to live a life that feels good?

For me?

The rational side of my brain, *Phony Tessa*, furiously claws for control. *Not now! This isn't the right time. Your dad needs you! Your patients need you! Jake needs you!*

Phony Tessa, my trusty leader, called by duty, concerned with how things look but never how they feel.

From a faraway distance, left behind a lifetime ago, *True Tessa* roars back to life. *You deserve more! Do what makes you happy. It's not too late! All you have is now.*

Shivers of nostalgia blaze through me upon hearing the voice of my long-lost inner warrior, dormant for years.

"Dr. Williams? Are you okay?"

I sputter, realizing it's been over a minute since I last spoke. "Yes. Sorry. Some of the things you said got me thinking… about my own life, actually."

Hoping to avoid explaining, I stand to examine him. While he breathes quietly, I press my stethoscope to his chest. *Thump, thump, thump.* The beautiful sound of his miraculous heart, pulsing life into him, beat after beat. There's no murmur; whatever I heard before is gone.

"Your physical exam is perfect," I say. "Hopefully, you'll have many more years of wonderful life with your amazing family."

"Thanks again, Doc. Is it okay if I hug you?"

"Of course." His arms wrap around me, and for a moment, I'm content in our exchange. It's always nice to help a patient.

But it isn't worth the personal cost. Not anymore. My time on Earth is too fleeting. This notion stings, but it's also the realest thing I've admitted to myself in years.

I say goodbye to Mr. Dorn, rushing on to my next patient. I'm too far behind to ponder things further now.

At the door, I knock quickly before entering. "Ms. Buzby, I'm terribly sorry to keep you waiting…"

***

For the rest of the day, despite my best efforts, my mind continually strays, that tiny spark becoming an explosion.

My needs matter.

I need to trust my gut.

It's not too late to stop pretending and start living.

Twenty-two visits later, I limp back to my office, totally spent. The day is blessedly over, my bed beckons.

I have one foot out the door when I turn, heading for my boss's office instead.

My knuckles tap the wood.

"Yes?" Rachel calls. "Come in."

Scared I'll lose the nerve, I expunge the words in one breath.

"Rachel, it's been an honor to work with you, but I *quit*."

47

TESSA

I sigh, staring at the tiny closet Jake and I share.

It's been four days since I gave notice at my job. Four days of living with the secret. And aside from one very surprised but supportive Liz, no one else yet knows I'm quitting. Not even Jake.

His dress shoes shove against my sneakers. His ties dangle between my cocktail dresses. His pants brush beneath my handbags. Our closet is tangible proof of the way two lives intertwine in five years of marriage, thread by thread, until they are a single, woven tapestry.

But there are countless intangible ways we're connected too. I know his habits as intimately as I know my own. The way he leaves little dabs of toothpaste on the sink every night. How he snoozes his alarm, thirteen minutes each morning, before reluctantly crawling out of bed. How he shuffles his hand through his hair when he's nervous.

Jake is good.

And kind.

And wonderful.

And yet.

Despite it all, it's not enough.

That truth has been growing like a splinter, small at first, now impossible to ignore.

He's the wrong partner for me.

We both deserve a marriage with *that* spark.

For years, I've yearned to be fulfilled by a relationship that lacks organic chemistry. The kind you can't fake or create but simply must exist.

The front door opens, startling me. A sweaty Jake enters, his gym clothes molded to his athletic frame.

He removes his earbuds. "Hi, babe, how are you? I went for a run. You were still asleep." His grin is sincere and familiar and fully breaks me.

"I'm fine," I say as he heads for the bathroom.

I watch him go, the ache in my chest spreading.

Shit.

I have to stop lying.

Right now.

Timidly, I follow. "Actually, I'm not okay. Can we talk?"

He pauses, hand on the shower knob. Steam curls faintly around his shoulders. His shirtless frame turns and looks at me, first with curiosity, then with alarm. "Is this about losing the pregnancy? We can try again, Tess, as soon as you get the all-clear. I really want that. I'm sorry for everything you've been through."

I slump onto the marbled floor, my legs folding like wilting stems. A tidal wave of guilt rises inside me, for all the ways I'm about to hurt him. This good, kind man.

"No, it's not about the baby. Or maybe, it is. But really, it's about everything… it's about *me*."

"Oh, okay. What's going on?" He shuts off the water, sitting beside me, his bare back resting against the cold toilet. He reaches for my hand.

The bathroom fan blows noisily as I search for the words.

Leaving him is the right choice.

Sometimes, the hardest choice is the right one.

Tessa, trust your damn gut, and if you can't, at least get out of your own fucking way.

"I want a divorce, Jake."

The words slop out, messy and ugly and terrible and true.

Jake flinches as if I've struck him. "Shit! What?" The pink departs from his cheeks as his hand grips mine so tightly that my palm vibrates.

"I'm so sorry, Jake. I don't want to hurt you. I love you, very much. But… I want a divorce." My voice cracks, tears flooding from my eyes for my poor unsuspecting husband—another victim of my tragically horrendous decision-making.

"Tess, what are you talking about? I know things have been hard since your surgery, but not divorce-level bad. Give us some credit. I know you're grieving. I know there's a lot going on with your dad, but we'll figure it out. I love you."

This is the moment you're supposed to cling to someone.

To fight for what you've built together.

Instead, I'm about to tear it all down.

"I know you think you love me," I say. "But the truth is, you don't even know me. And it's not your fault. It's mine. I've never let you in. I've spent our entire relationship pretending to be someone I'm not. Actually, I've spent most of my life pretending to be someone I'm not."

His brown eyes burst with confusion, disbelief and pain flashing across his face. "Tess, you're really worrying me—"

"Jake. I never wanted to be a doctor. My dad wanted me to be a doctor, so I became one. And he wanted me to get married, so I got married. And he wanted a grandchild, so I tried to give him one. I've been living the life he wants for me but not the one I actually want for myself. And the ectopic pregnancy and his cancer… it all made me realize life is short. His life is short but so is *mine*. Everyone's time here is short. I'm sorry, Jake. I never should have let it get this far… but I don't want to pretend anymore."

Jake recoils his hand, his fingers forming a fist against his thigh. "You *never* wanted to marry me?" His words ooze with a stinging blend of fury and sorrow. A grief I can't unhear.

The hurt in his eyes is unbearable, a mirror to every wrong choice I've made, every truth I've avoided. I wish I could undo it all.

"I… I… I…"

Stop lying.

"No."

"Jake, you're wonderful," I whisper, "but you should be married to someone who really wants to be with you. I know you'll find that person, but it's not me. It devastates me to say that. I've tried, so hard, to make these feelings go away. But they're not going to change. I'm sorry. Please know, above everything, I'm deeply sorry."

His hand rumbles through his shaggy auburn hair, his lips bowing into an exhaustive frown. A paralytic silence echoes off the tiled walls. My tears pick up, the pain I'm causing him becoming unbearable.

His eyes glare into my soul, making me feel naked. "Is there someone else? Are you having an affair?"

"No, I've never been unfaithful to you. There was someone I loved before we met, but I haven't talked to him in eleven years." I gulp. "Our marriage has just always felt wrong, even on our wedding day. Jake, I gave notice on Monday. I'm quitting my job. I don't want to live a life that *looks* good anymore. I want to live a life that actually *feels* good."

"Well, shit, Tess, that really fucking sucks, for me." His words are punctuated by the upstairs neighbor who stomps against the floor.

"I know, Jake. It sucks horribly for you. I never meant to hurt you. I'm a lost fool and you deserve so much more. I hope one day, you'll forgive me."

"Fuck, Tess." His bare belly quakes as his face oscillates between resentment and sadness.

In every marriage, there's a beginning, middle and end.

"So… this is the end? How is this possible?" he whispers.

"I don't know, Jake," I heave. "But yes, this is the end."

He stares at me for a long, agonizing moment. "I can't believe this," he mutters.

And despite what I'm doing to him, to us, he wraps his arms around me, pulling me close, holding me as I wail.

Above, the neighbor stomps louder, the sound of laughter agonizingly spilling through the ceiling.

We sit, crying on the bathroom floor, wrapped together.

And as the world around us continues to spin, our marriage quietly, but completely, splinters apart.

48

TESSA

"Hi, Tess. What's going on?" Mom asks me three hours later. I'm standing outside my childhood home, two huge suitcases in tow.

On the walkway, despite the winter, the daffodils in Mom's garden have started to bloom, subtle proof that life can flourish after bitter darkness.

Mom's face overflows with kindness, making me crumple. "Mom, can I live here for a while?"

"Of course, love. This is always your home, but what's going on?"

The truth bubbles out of me like an uncorked bottle of champagne. "I just told Jake I want a divorce. And a few days ago, I gave notice at my job… I'm quitting… I don't even know what I'm doing, only that I can't do *this* anymore. Help me, Mom."

Help me, Mom.

These words have softly whined inside my brain for years, never spoken aloud, until now.

Mom hugs me. "Sweetheart, come inside, we'll talk it through."

I savor that one-of-a-kind comfort only possible from your mom. Mom goes to make me tea as I collapse onto the couch, recalling Jake's heartbroken expression as I packed my bags.

My perpetual self-doubt still clings. What if I'm making a huge mistake?

Trust your damn gut.

The hardest choice can still be the right one.

As Mom returns with a steaming cup of peppermint tea, her movements slower than I remember, I can't help but notice the toll Dad's illness has taken on her, too. Mom's always been so put together, but today, her face is raw, bare of all makeup. New wrinkles crease along the edges of her mouth. Grey roots glisten from her scalp, abruptly colliding with her blonde highlights. A reminder that when your partner suffers, you do, too.

Mom sits, handing me the teacup. "Tell me, my girl, what's going on?"

So I tell her everything. About not wanting to be a doctor. About marrying Jake because I thought I should. About running into Carl. About still loving Corey. About wanting more from my life but being too gutless to admit it.

Mom's eyes plug with tears. She takes my hand in hers—her swollen, arthritic knuckles a glaring reminder of time slipping through my fingers. "Oh, sweetie, I'm sorry you're going through this. I wish I could take your pain away, but the most important thing is to live your life for *you*. That's all Dad or I have ever wanted."

I'm overwhelmed by her love.

Unconditional.

Unrelenting.

Unending.

I remember the mother elephant nudging her baby into the watering hole at Impodimo Lodge. Motherhood, in all languages, somehow looks the same.

Kernels of regret pop in my heart for treating Mom unkindly growing up. I spent my formative years idolizing Dad without acknowledging the pivotal role Mom played.

"Mom, I'm sorry I was so hard on you as a teen." A confession long overdue. "I didn't appreciate how much you did for me. You gave up your career to raise me since Dad was always working. You're the glue that held us together."

Mom tucks a strand of half-grey, half-blonde hair behind her ear. And as she does, I study her hands again—a lifetime of sacrifice embedded in their curves.

One day, I'll lose her too.

Shit.

"Thanks, sweetie, that means more than I can tell you."

"I love you, Mom, so much. And I respect you. You're an amazing woman. If I can be half as amazing as you, I'll consider myself so lucky."

Mom smiles, flecks of color splashing her cheeks, lightening her demeanor. "Tess, you've already accomplished that. You just need to see it in yourself." She pauses for a moment. "But you have to share all of this with Dad. He'll love you too, no matter what."

I scowl, unsure that's true.

But it's time to take the risk, anyway.

***

Dad's napping, so I head to my childhood bedroom and unpack my bags. The room hasn't changed much. Same lavender walls. Same white bedspread dotted with yellow daisies. Same corkboard above my desk, plastered with decade-old pictures of friends I no longer talk to.

I push my suitcases against the foot of my bed, gaze landing on my closet. I slide the door open and find my mermaid-cut wedding dress, preserved by Mom, in plastic wrap. The sight of it causes my face to warp like I've just bitten into a sour lemon. I shove it aside. Beneath the dress are boxes of documents.

I bend down, riffling through, finding my old Kodak photos, high school term papers, algebra exams. And then, at the bottom of the first box, my breath catches. A stack of papers, crinkled at the edges but otherwise intact. My stories.

I pick up the top one, *Twin Hearts*, and sink down on the carpet to read it.

I wrote it in ninth grade. It's about identical twins, Olivia and Claire, who attend separate colleges and unknowingly fall in love with twin brothers. The plot is juvenile, predictable, but as I read, I'm stunned by the writing itself.

It's good.

Really good.

I quickly devour another piece, *Final Musical Notes*, a sixty-page novella about a violinist named Ursula, who's murdered following a performance at Carnegie Hall. I can almost hear the music Ursula plays before her untimely end.

Beneath that story, I discover ten more. I flip through, briefly transported back into the brain of *The Girl Who Wanted to Be a Writer*. My fingers tremble as I trace my name written in the corner of one page.

I remember sitting my parents down—sophomore year of college—with the intention of declaring a major in creative writing. I'd rehearsed my pitch: writing was my passion, my calling. But Dad had smiled that convincing smile, the one that made me feel silly for ever questioning him. *You can write anytime! You can't always be a doctor.*

And just like that, I majored in biology.

Never writing a single creative word again.

***

I find Dad asleep in bed, his CPAP mask resting inside his nostrils. From his bedside, the machine hums rhythmically. His rail-thin arms rest atop the blanket, his cheekbones eerily prominent. He looks more like the skeleton Mom used to hang outside our house at Halloween than my hero.

I inhale, grief seeping into the deepest tissue of my lungs.

Somehow, he's *not* Superman but a mere mortal.

And he's dying.

"Daddy?" My voice is young, more like a child's than a grown woman's. I rustle him awake.

I've been dreading this moment for the past thirty-seven years. I'm about to admit to a lifetime of wrong choices. Of constant acting. All with the goal of making *my* person happy and proud.

His eyes flutter open, bleary at first, then sharpening with recognition. His grin breaks through the greyness like a beam of light. He removes his CPAP mask. "Tess, what a pleasant surprise."

I worry my truth will devastate him. Why am I doing this now, near the end of his life? It seems unfair, selfish even.

Suddenly, *True Tessa* speaks, loud and insistent. *Because he deserves to know the real you! You owe that to him. And yourself.*

"Dad, I have to tell you something." I sit down beside him.

"You can tell me anything, Tess. You know that." His hand reaches for mine, squeezing it three times.

Dad's always been an advocate of extremely firm handshakes. As a child, he would make me practice on him until my palms throbbed. *A handshake says a lot about you*, he'd proclaim. But now, his grip is weak.

It's another thing, in an endless list, that cancer's taken from him.

From me.

I suck in a big breath, my head woozy like I'm about to summit Mount Everest without an oxygen tank.

Shit.

Here goes.

"Dad, I never wanted to be a doctor, so on Monday, I gave notice.

In six weeks, I'm quitting."

The words drape a chasm between us, the truth disbanding my long-worn façade.

Dad gapes, a response seeming to fizz at the tip of his tongue, but he remains quiet.

"You wanted me to be a doctor, and I wanted to make you happy, so, I became a doctor. And sometimes, I like it. But a lot of the time… I wish I could be doing *literally* anything else. I'm a good doctor, but medicine is hard for me. I care about people and it hurts me when my patients suffer. I can't separate from their grief. I tried to get better at it, but I just suffer, too. I dread going to work, every day. I'm so burned out and I'm only thirty-seven."

His eyes darken with thunder, my confession evidently downpouring inside him. I feel so ashamed, revealing my brokenness. Heaviness squashes on my shoulders, making me feel like the size of an ant.

"Dad, I'm sorry. I never wanted to hurt you. I've always wanted to please you, to make you proud." My stomach twists, heaving high into my throat, my pulse sloshing inside my ears. "Please, say something. Say anything."

Dad turns in bed, facing me, his fragility more pronounced than ever. Through the partially drawn shades, the afternoon sunlight streams in fashioning a rainbow on the wall.

"It's okay, Tess. I'm glad you're telling me. I just wish you would've told me sooner."

I swallow, my throat like sandpaper. "I tried, a few times, like that day at Impodimo Lodge. I really wanted to quit med school. And to be honest, I should have. But you talked me out of it because your voice was more persuasive than my own. I *wanted* what *you* wanted for *me*. But I have to listen to my own gut, finally."

Dad's expression is soft, curious, understanding. Not at all like the angry demon I've long since feared.

"So if not medicine… what do you want to do?" he asks.

"I have no idea. I just know I don't *want* to be a doctor."

"That's okay, sweetheart," he says. "If cancer's taught me anything, it's not to waste time doing things you don't love. Honestly, I've adored my career as a doctor. Not every single moment, but pretty darn close. But if you don't, you owe it to yourself to try something else, find what you love." My entire body trembles with profound relief. "You know, Tess, Grandpa Sam didn't want me to go to medical school. He was so disappointed I did."

"Really?" My eyebrows arch with surprise. "Why?"

"He wanted me to take over the family business, to become an accountant. I applied to medical school and didn't tell him, or anyone, for seven months. The day I finally told him, he was furious. He didn't speak to me for two years. It felt terrible not having his approval. Over time, outwardly, he became more tolerant, but deep down, I know he always thought I made the wrong choice. But it wasn't his life, it was *mine*."

My eyes grow wide. "Wow, Dad, I never knew that."

"I just… I can't believe… somehow, I unknowingly put you in that same position." His withered cheeks collapse. "What a terrible mistake."

I think about the bad patterns inadvertently passed down, generations of mistakes, looping needlessly, time and again, like *Groundhog Day*.

Maybe the spell doesn't break until someone finally gets it right.

"I should've known better," Dad says. "You were just so interested in my medical stories, so smart and driven. I knew you'd make a great doctor… I guess I got lost in my own dreams for you. I'm sorry."

Tears gather at the edges of my eyes, a bittersweet mix of understanding and heartbreak. "I forgive you, Dad. I love you, so much. Maybe, too much. I wanted to give you what you wanted, even at the expense of myself… but I don't want to keep living like that."

"I'm so sorry," he mumbles again, his eyes filling with a depth of sorrow I've never seen.

I lean over, holding him, his bony thorax pressing into my chest. I smell the coffee on his breath, the Pert Plus on his fuzzy head, the Dial soap on his tattered skin. All the small features that form his irreplaceable person. I try to memorize them all, to stuff them into a box deep within my heart. I sit up.

"There's more, Dad."

He groans, clutching his chest. "I'm not sure I can take much more." His tone is joking, his expression is serious.

"At Impodimo Lodge that day, you told me to focus on my career, to leave Corey. But he was the love of my life. I should've chosen him, Dad. And I've regretted that decision, in some form or another, every day since." My lips tingle, speaking Corey's name to my dad again after years of vexing to forget. A chill sprints through me, from the sparkling fiber of *hope*.

"Wow, Tess. I'm sorry I led you down the wrong path. I was only trying to help. My wants and yours got so confused." Dad starts to cry, the dark circles under his eyes bulging as they stain wet with tears. "But what about Jake? What does this mean for your marriage?"

Jake.

Shit.

The image of his crushed face helixes through my mind, mincing my heart into hamburger meat. "This morning, I told Jake I want a divorce." Each syllable is sticky in my throat. "I love him but I'm not *in love* with him. I feel awful, Dad. He's a terrific guy, but I don't feel tingly all over when he walks into the room. It probably sounds silly but I want that feeling."

Heat swamps my cheeks, admitting such personal feelings to my dad. After a lifetime of lying, somehow, now I'm oversharing.

"It's not silly, Tess. That tingly feeling? I still feel it with your mom.

She's the love of my life, and that feeling hasn't stopped in all the years we've been married."

A smile whooshes across my face. "I know, Dad. I see it when you look at each other. And I felt that, too, around Corey."

"So, why were you going to have a baby with Jake?"

I sigh, louder this time. "Because… I wanted to make you a grandfather. I knew you'd be incredible at it."

It sounds dolefully ridiculous.

But it's also the truth.

"Tessa, that's the nicest and stupidest thing you've ever said to me." He grasps my hand, wrapping it around his emaciated fingers. His skin feels paper-thin. "Please, live your life for *you*. I'm sorry you felt obligated to live your life for me. When I held you the day you were born, I looked into your eyes and I was utterly blown away. You owned me. You were perfect. You still are. You're compassionate, intelligent, funny, loving. I hit the jackpot with you. I've always felt that way. I only want you to be happy, I promise. I love you, more than anything."

His words decisively sever that crushing baggage. Those heavy expectations that, for years, have wrenched around my neck, suffocating me. That clamping weight lifts, and suddenly, I am free.

At last, I've admitted my core truths to my dad, and he still loves me.

He *sees* me.

In my hands, that rope we've yanked back and forth vanishes, my palms still marked by dark red grooves, scars of our decades-long battle.

But now, the war is over.

Maybe it never even needed to happen.

Perhaps I've spent years living a total lie without reason.

But I can't go back.

Time only moves forward.

"I thought I was doing the right thing by hiding parts of myself, being who you wanted. But I was lost," I mutter. "I've been lost for so long, but I want to find myself, Dad… I hope it's not too late."

"It's never too late, Tess. The perfect time to start is *now*."

49

TESSA

"Petey, hold still, sweetheart. We'll be as quick as we can. I'm sorry if this is painful." Mom's voice is tender as she grips Dad's frail body, digging her feet into the carpet, bracing him on his side. Dad lies helpless, confined to his hospital bed inside their bedroom, unable to support his weight.

For the past four months, since I've been unemployed, I've spent lots of quality time with him. We've lounged, doing all types of normal father-daughter activities that we rarely did because Dad was usually too busy at the hospital. We played cards (Gin rummy, his choice), watched movies (*Father of the Bride*, my choice and *Happy Gilmore*, his choice), and listened to old records (the Beatles and Simon & Garfunkel, which we both agreed on). Using my phone, I recorded hours of footage of him talking about his childhood, career, marriage, greatest lessons and hardest challenges. We were both stripped of our usual coping mechanisms (work for Dad, lying and *okay/fine*ness for me), allowing us to just *be* with one another.

And it was entirely magical.

But three weeks ago, Dad's scans showed a continual progression in his cancer. Lacking further treatment options, he entered home hospice, with Mom and me assuming the role of his caretakers.

And within the past thirty-six hours, his health has rapidly deteriorated. He's now unable to eat or get out of bed and is sleeping most of the time. And this morning, much to his utter humiliation, he also started to lose control of his bowels.

"Dad, I'm going to clean you up," I say, breathing through my mouth to avoid gagging on the putrid smell permeating the air.

"Oh god, this is so mortifying." Dad cries. "I can't believe you have to do this."

He howls as Mom buries her face into his chest. "Sweetheart, it's our pleasure to take care of you. Please don't apologize."

With gloved hands, I remove his diaper, lifting his shriveled leg. I use a soapy washcloth to wipe his perineum, swiftly rolling away the stained bedsheet. In a second smooth roll, I place a fresh sheet below, fastening a new diaper around him. With Mom's help, we hoist him upward, back onto his pillow.

"All finished, Dad," I say, throwing my gloves into the trash.

"Thank you, sweetheart. You're unbelievable," he murmurs, bleary-eyed and sniffling.

In the bathroom, I scrub my hands vigorously, already desperate to wash the memory away. I bite my cheek to stifle my tears. As a doctor, I know dying is unavoidably messy. But it's horrendously different watching it happen to my beloved dad. Seeing his body shut down in such agonizing detail.

Needing air, I wander into the kitchen, grabbing scissors and a vase. I step outside into the August heat, which drips with humidity. From Mom's garden, I trim a selection of red roses, blue hydrangeas, orange dahlias, purple lilacs, and yellow daylilies, plopping on the grass, fashioning the flowers within the vase.

Next door, my parents' neighbor, Jamil, is mowing his lawn. The shrill buzz of his machinery storms my ears, briefly blocking my booming anxiety over Dad's failing body.

Jamil's son dribbles baskets into the hoop, waving hello.

Meekly, I wave back.

In my house, the world is collapsing.

But, for Jamil and his son, life is impossibly normal.

It's a terrible pill to swallow.

I allow the sun to pound against my weary forehead before dragging myself back up to face reality.

Inside, Mom tucks a cotton blanket on top of Dad. Despite the scorching temperatures, he's always cold now. Mom retrieves a second maroon fleece, placing it over him, checking her watch. "In thirty minutes, it's time for your next morphine dose, darling."

To keep Dad comfortable and ease his transition, per the hospice team, we've started dosing his pain medication around the clock.

Dad wearily nods.

Mom bends down, kissing his lips before retrieving the laundry basket, heading to start her third load of the morning.

I set the flowers on the nightstand. "I made you a rainbow, Dad, from Mom's garden. I know you love to be outside and since you can't go out right now, I thought I'd bring a piece inside to you."

He gives me a wholesome grin.

And of all the things I've done in my life to make him smile, this feels like the most genuine.

I sit on the edge of his bed, grasping his wasted hand. My once all-powerful superhero is now a collection of drooping skin and cancer-ravaged bones. I've watched it happen—over the course of months—but the reality is still so staggering, acid floods my mouth.

"Tess—" he starts to say.

"Dad, please, please, please, don't feel embarrassed. It's not your fault what your body's doing. I *want* to take care of you. My career as a doctor was almost worth it just to train for this. Honestly, it's the most important job I've ever had."

It's true.

More than anything, I want to usher him out of this world with the same love and grace he brought me into it.

"I'm not sure how I deserve a daughter as wonderful as you." His voice is hoarse, his ribs visible with each ragged breath. "It's just… so humbling… that as you're dying, you return to the physical neediness of infancy… nobody warned me how hard this dying shit is." With that proclamation, he lets out a teeny laugh.

Dad *never* curses, but some situations warrant an exception.

"Dying is hard, Daddy, just like living. It's all so fucking hard." I remember Corey, on the Victoria Falls Bridge, telling me life was a fucking shitshow. He was *so* right.

So many times over these past few months, I've drafted an email to him. But… somehow, after all these years, that gesture feels wholly inadequate.

Dad's eyelids droop from exhaustion.

How is our time almost up?

How can I survive in a world without him?

That known lump blocks my throat as my fear spikes.

This can't be real.

I'm going to wake up from this nightmare soon, right?

It was moments ago I was sitting at my desk. Reviewing his CT scan. Calling to tell him the news. First meeting with Dr. Burkland. And now, less than a year later, the end is upon us.

How can my dad be dying?

I'm not ready to lose him.

The circle of life.

The lions and the impala.

Everyone dies.

Even my treasured dad.

Even, someday, me.

Again, I want to run.

To hide.

To be someone, literally *anyone*, else.

To change things.

To switch places.

To stop this.

But I can't.

There's nothing I can do except sit with him and help him leave.

I don't know how to let go.

My voice slivers, a destabilizing sadness engulfing me. "Dad, I just want you to know how special these past few months have been, spending all this time with you. It's been such a gift. I'm so grateful."

"For me too, sweetheart," he says. "But remember, I'll always be with you. I'm not sure what it will be like… wherever I'm going. But I'll find ways to talk to you. Listen, look for the signs. When you need me, I'll be there."

This idea brings me a small amount of comfort, although I don't know how such things are possibly possible. But in this moment, I urgently need to believe.

He reaches for me, my cheek landing against his pointy sternum. Through his delicate skin, his heart gurgles loudly. *Thump… thump… thump.* A sign of continued life, however fleeting. I inhale, smelling his Pert Plus shampoo, yearning to hold him.

To never stop.

Why does life have to end?

It's so insanely, horrendously, fucking cruel.

"Tess," he mumbles, "do you know what I've learned from dying? Well, actually, from living?"

"What, Daddy?" My head nestles into his chest, hanging on his every word.

"Of all the things you do, nothing lasts except love. Do what you love, be with who you love. If you do that, you won't go wrong. Do I wish I had more time? Yes. But I loved my career, adored the hell out of you and Mom. I have no regrets. I had an amazing life filled with love, and you know what? *Love lasts.*" His voice trails off, his body spent.

"I love you," I say, clutching him as the minutes pass.

He sinks to sleep.

My eyes shut, too, and I imagine Corey's hands stroking my back, frenziedly craving his comfort. But he's continents away, not even aware of what's going on.

"I love you, Dad," I murmur into his neck, a waterfall of grief spilling out.

My tears are met by the irregular rise and fall of his chest.

"I love you," I whisper again. "You're my hero, for always."

Against my face, his nostrils flare out with each snore.

Time rewinds and fast-forwards—at once.

I'm five, falling off my bike as my dad tends to my knee.

I'm sixteen, shadowing him at the hospital, swept up in his awe.

I'm twenty-six, hugging him at my med school graduation.

I'm thirty-one, gripping his arm as we stroll down the aisle towards Jake.

So many mistakes, and yet, all made in the name of love.

I'm thirty-seven, crying on his chest, as he slowly slips away.

"I love you," I mumble, "and that will never end."

His arm hair coils against my ear as he moans in his sleep.

In my dad's final months of life, we were given a miraculous gift—the opportunity to be completely authentic with one another.

And our love only flourished.

For so long, I feared my dad's love was conditional.

But I understand now it's boundless.

Yes, his life is ending.

But not our love.

Some types of love—the magical ones, the uprooting ones, the ones that spark us to life, that cake to the very core of our beings—those types never end.

You can leave.

You can flee.

You can even die.

But that feeling, that connection, somehow, *someway*, endures.

In the end, almost nothing remains.

But love does.

Love lasts.

50

PETER

"Petey, wake up. It's time for your next morphine dose."

My eyes flicker open. I'm weak and disoriented, floating between this world and the next.

Claudia stands above me, her hair a ragged mess, her clothes unchanged for the past three days.

"You're stunning," I whisper, meaning it.

She smiles, lifting the syringe, squirting the medicine into my cheek. The sour taste makes me wince. "Do you need anything?" Her familiar voice momentarily tethers me to this world. I shake my head no, too tired to open my mouth, grasping her hand, savoring the energy that's emitted as our fingers lock. She nuzzles beside me, burrowing into my arms.

Home.

Whenever I hold her, I'm home. It's not a place, only a feeling—one that's never wavered in our thirty-seven years together.

I know my time here is slipping away. Largely, I've made peace with dying. I've lived an extraordinary life, loving my work and family. In the end, what more can a guy ask for? In retrospect, should I have spent some of my time differently? Should I have worked less and lived more?

Maybe.

But regret is a waste of time, and time is a precious luxury, of which I have none to spare.

"My love," Claudia says into the nape of my neck, "you can go whenever you're ready. I'll be okay. You don't have to stay for me. I'll miss you terribly, but I'll find my way. So will Tessa. We'll both be okay. Go, find your peace. I love you."

A lone tear escapes from my eye, and Claudia quickly dabs it away. I muster all my remaining energy to talk. "I love you, Claudia… you were everything I wanted and all that I needed. Thank you for being the love and light of my life."

She speaks again, but the morphine takes hold.

I find myself tumbling… to the other world. My mother's there, and my father too. And other meaningful people, like my cousin, Cindy, my best friend, David, and my grandfather, Poppy. They've all passed, some long ago. But they are waving and joyful, clustered together at the tail end of a rainbow.

I step towards them, a sense of tranquility twirling through me.

"Not yet, Petey," my mother says, her blue eyes gleaming. "Soon, honey."

"You did good, sonny. You did real good," my father purrs, a cigarette shoved between his lips.

I smile at the cigarette.

Maybe some things never change.

I tumble again… to the past. I'm heading off to Yale Medical School, my father's arms crisscrossed. My mother says, "I'm proud of you. You'll make an amazing doctor."

Seconds later, I'm moving into my new apartment to start my cardiology fellowship in Boston. In the lobby of my building, overloaded with three heavy boxes, I collide with Claudia. As my fingers graze her arm, an electric shock zips through me, awakening my entire body.

"Can I help you with those?" she asks, her smile siphoning my breath.

Instantly, I know—life will never be the same.

Moments later, I'm in the delivery room, following Claudia's emergency C-section, cradling Tessa in the nook of my arm. Her tiny hand folds into mine, and it's love at first sight.

Tessa gently shakes me. "Dad, it's time for your next morphine dose."

I can't open my eyes, lack all strength. I have no idea how much time's passed.

Tessa squeezes my hand, and I squeeze back with the little force I can muster.

I'm here, Tess.

I'll always be here.

The syringe pierces my cheek.

The sour taste.

Then… blackness.

I tumble again, back to my wedding, kissing Claudia for the first time as my wife.

The luckiest guy on Earth.

Next, I'm at the hospital, using a defibrillator to save a young mother's life. I wander into the waiting room to tell her partner she's alive. The husband's eyes gush with relief, reaffirming my passion for my work.

Then, I'm on the deck of Impodimo Lodge beside Tessa, watching the lilac-breasted roller soar off into the horizon.

Time to fly away.

In the distance, Claudia and Tessa are discussing the latest episode of *The Bachelor*, arguing over which contestant will get the rose—a show they love and I hate.

In my mind, I smile.

They'll be okay.

Sheer blackness, again.

Sometime later, "Dad, do you want water?"

I can't nod, can't move, but I'm so parched. A wet toothbrush glides over my lips and tongue, the precious substance trickling down the back of my throat.

Relief.

Tender care.

Tessa's breathtaking love.

Time slips away once more.

Claudia's voice pulls me. "Petey, my love, here's your medication."

The syringe.

The acerbic taste.

The tight grip of her hand.

Her warm breath.

Her interminable strength.

My beautiful home.

The darkness envelops me.

Then, again. "Dad, it's time for your morphine."

The syringe.

The sour taste.

Total blackness.

Later, minutes, hours, days—I have no idea—Tessa lays her head on my chest. I savor the rise and fall of her trunk, the lemony smell of her hair—that comforting, citrusy aroma of my empathic, perfectly imperfect daughter.

"I love you, no matter what, Tess. For eternity."

I speak the words only in my head, but she exhales against me, and I hope she hears.

I want her to live for herself. I never meant to put so much on her, never meant for my vision to eclipse her own.

Time passes.

Tessa quivers, serenely asleep on me.

She'll be okay.

From another place, my mother waves again. I'm ready to collapse into her nurturing arms, the comfort of which I've never stopped needing.

Above, the lilac-breasted roller flies in circles.

Time to let go, Peter.

The rainbow ahead is vivid and sparkling, urging me forward.

A young girl awaits with outstretched fingers.

She has iridescent violet eyes and white-blonde ringlets.

I don't know her, but her childlike enthusiasm puts my nerves to rest.

I take her hand, my large fingers encircling her tiny ones.

A smile bursts from my lips.

We walk together through a kaleidoscope of color.

The prism shrouds us, bringing a sensation of total peace.

I feel whole again, dissolving into nothingness and everything all at once.

And then...

I go.

51

TESSA

I sit up with a start. "Dad?" His mouth hangs open, his head tilted to the left. His eyes are wide, his pupils glassy and fixed. His skin is a deep greyish hue, like the sky just before rain. I grab his icy wrist, crying out for him, more desperately this time. "Dad! Daddy!"

I *knew* this was coming, but still, I'm not ready.

The sight of him—like *this*—whips me back in time.

It's twelve years earlier and I'm in Princess Victoria Hospital, a terrified med student, standing above the first woman I ever saw die. The space between then and now falls away, fusing both moments into a single instant. Everything about the situation is different, but my dad's face looks exactly the same as that woman's.

Death is life's only ending.

I shriek for Mom, releasing a bellowing wail.

My watch displays the date: August 30.

It's the end of life as I know it.

My dad, my hero, my *raison d'être*, the bolt anchoring my life for its entirety, is *gone*.

52

TESSA

"Tess, open up or I'm coming in!" Liz calls, pounding on my bedroom door.

After a long silence, the door swings open, cascading the tomb-like space with flakes of light. I'm curled up in bed, the blanket shoved over my face. Liz pulls the blanket down and juts the window shades apart, letting the tepid September sun fleck in.

"Liz, what're you doing?" I grunt, blinking rapidly, clutching a photograph of my dad beneath the covers.

I can only tolerate darkness.

A world without him should be dark all the time.

There's no space for light.

"Your mom told me you haven't gotten out of bed in two weeks, not since the funeral. I know you're grieving, but get up, get dressed. We're taking you to the zoo." Liz rifles through my drawers, grabbing a pair of blue jeans and a grey shirt, tossing them on top of the blanket.

"I'm in no state to go to the zoo," I protest. "Look at me, I'm a mess." I gesture to my unwashed hair, my oily skin, my unshaven legs, my red eyes. My outsides finally match my insides: utterly broken.

Liz scrunches her nose with compassion. "That's exactly why you need to come. Camille is downstairs with your mom. I promised her Aunt Tessa's coming to the zoo. If you don't, she'll be crushed."

"It's low, even for you, to use your child as a weapon against me," I drone. But the faintest smile slinks out from beneath my frown.

"Tess, I want to help. You can't stay in bed, shutting the world out. Your dad would hate to see you like this. He'd want you to keep living. Please, come with us. If not for him or yourself, then Camille."

My dad is gone.

How can he be gone?

It's been three weeks, but I still can't grasp it.

How is the world still turning?

How is my own heart still beating?

It's so horribly wrong.

My grief is like a five-ton mass strapped to my chest, making everything impossible.

Even breathing.

Especially breathing.

"Liz, I'm so grateful to you, but I'm not going." My voice is quiet, hollow, the sound of someone unraveled. I give her a pleading glare.

"Okay, I didn't want to have to do this." Liz walks to the door and calls for Camille. Moments later, the girl's footsteps bound up the stairs. She bursts into the room, wearing a frilly pink dress with ruby red slip-ons and a yellow bow clipped in her hair.

"Aunt Tessa!" Camille screams, seemingly unfazed by my pitiable state. Instead, she jumps onto the bed, burrowing her head into my chest, swiftly unhardening my heart.

Love.

I continue to feel it in spite of myself.

"Hi, Cami," I whisper, pulling her close, inhaling her lavender scent, my lungs exhaling fully for the first time in weeks.

"Come to the zoo!" Camille pleads. "Puh-lease. Pretty please." She offers me her trademark puppy-dog pout, instantly crumbling my resolve.

I can't say no to her. I never could.

"Okay, I will."

***

Outside the Philadelphia Zoo, fall's in full swing. The air is cooler, the leaves tinge yellowy-orange and the pumpkins are out.

I stare at a browned hydrangea bush near the entrance. In the peak of summer, its color was undoubtedly a vibrant fuchsia. But now, its beauty has dissipated. Beauty, like all things in life, has a season.

The trees are emitting the telltale signs that soon, they, too, will drop their leaves to start anew. I admire the way foliage just lets go. Trusts in the cycle of life.

Why can't I do that too?

"What should we see first?" Liz asks, staring at the map by the entrance.

"Lions! Then tigers! Then elephants!" Camille yelps, jumping up and down, her yellow bow dislodging.

Liz laughs, tucking the bow into her messenger bag. "Okay, sweetie, sounds like a plan."

Camille grabs Liz's hand with one arm and mine with the other, pulling us hurriedly towards the first exhibit. She doesn't walk—she literally bounces with exultation, humming to herself.

Despite my grief, a grin sneaks across my face, too. Camille's excitement for the zoo—for life, actually—is infectious.

As we pass under an archway, I take in my surroundings. It's the small, fleeting beauty that grabs me—the shimmer of dew on grass, the fall sun glinting through branches. I'm grateful to be here. To be alive. After such dark pain, mundane things like these can become extraordinarily stunning.

The words of my patient Cal Dorn float into my brain: *Why do we only appreciate the tiny, beautiful, everyday miracles in front of us, after a terrible wake-up call?*

Beauty is everywhere.

Woven into every moment.

Waiting to be seen.

You just have to remember to keep your eyes open.

To move slowly enough to actually see.

This afternoon, I *see* the world.

Gorgeous and harsh.

Filled with so much pain.

And just as much promise.

***

We visit the lions, then tigers, before Camille takes off towards the elephant exhibit. There, I spot two young elephants enclosed by a stone wall. They stand restless in a dirt patch, brushing their ears together. By a tiny watering hole, the matriarch towers, her trunk swaying listlessly in the breeze, her eyes heavy with a quiet aching dejection.

I remember standing on the Impodimo Lodge deck, awestruck by the elephants' zest for life, by their very freeness. But these creatures are nothing like the African elephants. They appear bored and depressed, traipsing around their meager space. They're supposed to be roaming in the wild.

They don't belong here.

I start crying, a quiet drizzle that quickly becomes an uncontrollable downpour. Liz sends Camille to the front of the viewing area, turning to me, her eyebrows fused with worry. "Hey, what's going on?"

I shake my head, unable to form words. These elephants—they're me. I intimately recognize the suffering in their eyes because it silently screamed within me, too, unanswered for years. And no matter how hard I tried to accept being enclosed, I couldn't. I never stopped wanting to be *free*.

A caged animal is never at peace.

"It just makes me so sad, seeing the elephants like this," I weep. "They should be roaming in the wild, like at Impodimo Lodge. This isn't enough space for them. They're miserable."

Miserable, like me, for years, pretending to be okay.

Before I tore down my cage.

By quitting my job.

By leaving Jake.

By admitting the truth to my dad.

Liz places a hand on my shoulder. "I know, I get it," she says. "But this way, kids like Camille can see the elephants. Otherwise, they might never see these amazing creatures in real life. But you're right. It comes at a major cost to the animals."

I swipe the tears from my face. "One day, we'll take Cami to see the real thing?"

She squeezes my hand. "Yes! When she's older. That's a great idea."

Overhead, two cardinals swoop low in the sky and all at once, I crave the beauty and freedom of the bush.

To be standing on the deck of Impodimo Lodge.

To stare into Corey's glimmering eyes.

To stroke his face.

To finally fix what I long ago broke.

For weeks, grief has blackened my mind, but now, the sun shines unencumbered.

Light overtakes the dark.

"Liz, that was the happiest time of my life, at Impodimo Lodge, when I was with Corey. It's the only time I ever felt like myself."

Her eyes grow wide and green. "So, what are you saying, Tess?"

A weight lifts from my chest as I exhale. "I have to go back. To find him. To see if those feelings are still there. It's time to trust my own damn gut."

Liz delivers an expansive grin. "Oh, thank god! I was wondering when you were going to go!"

I squint, surprised. "Wait! What?"

She laughs, pulling me into a hug. "Yeah, since you ran into Carl six months ago, I've been waiting for you to go back."

"You were?"

"Of course," she says, matter-of-factly, arms crossed. "But I didn't want to push you, especially with everything happening with your dad… but now, the timing makes sense."

I suck in a breath, my arms tingling. "So… you think I should go?"

"Is that a trick question?" Liz asks, voice tinged with exasperated affection. "Of course you should go! He's *your* person. It's painfully obvious. You have to go!"

My heart blooms like a hydrangea in the summer.

Liz knows me.

The real me.

"You don't think it's crazy? Given that we haven't talked in twelve years?" Doubt still pastes to my skin, trusting my gut a formidable challenge.

"Who cares how it looks?" Liz says. "Just worry about how it *feels*, to *you*."

"It feels right to me," I whisper.

"Then go!" Liz says. She pauses. "A few days before we left Gaborone, Corey told me he loved you and he asked me to take care of you, since he wouldn't be there."

"Wow, he did?" This revelation snakes a wide crack straight down my chest.

"Yeah. I don't know what happened to him in all the years since… but he did really love you. Of that, I'm sure."

My eyes dampen again. "You took care of me beautifully, Liz. Med school was almost worth it just to find you."

I hug Liz—so hard—until the air drains from both our lungs and we're two empty balloons, holding onto each other.

For the first time in—well, *ever*—the idea of chasing my happiness doesn't feel so terrifying.

"I'm going to miss the hell out of you if you stay in South Africa," Liz mutters, her face buried in my hair.

"You might be getting a little ahead of yourself there, champ…"

But fireworks explode inside my chest at the idea of returning to my happy place.

"I don't think so," Liz says with a laugh. "But it's okay. Marley's been begging to go visit again."

"I love you," I murmur. "Thank you, for everything."

"I love you." Liz smiles. "And you're welcome."

All this time, I thought if my dad died, I would too.

But somehow, he's gone and I continue.

And I owe it to myself to live.

To *really* live.

The breeze blows an orange leaf with red spots into my hand.

I clutch it between my fingers, staring at it.

It's entirely impermanent yet stunningly perfect.

True Tessa's voice hums in my head. *Time to let go. Time to begin again.*

"Okay, so… wow," I say, the ground unsteady, trying to get my bearings. "Does this mean I'm really going back?"

"Yes!" Liz shouts. "You're really going back!"

53

COREY

It's almost dawn; the morning air drags a tremor down my back. In the far-off distance, a purple hue streaks the blackened sky. I shut the Jeep door and stop to zipper up my fleece, tugging my hat against my frosty forehead.

It's been a horrendously slow two days for game viewing. Up since four a.m., I've already driven thirty minutes deep into the Madikwe Game Reserve. Today, I need to make sure my guests are satisfied.

Striding away from the Jeep, I use my flashlight to follow the lion footprints caked into the soil. Beneath my left arm, I clutch my gun, not expecting to need it—it's just in case.

I tiptoe slowly, following the paw prints. I hear rustling and stop to get my bearings. Beneath the light from the moon, I spot a lone impala.

No danger there.

I trudge along, taking care with each step, studying every print before continuing.

From my pocket, my walkie-talkie buzzes.

"Found anything yet?" It's Janet, one of my guides.

"Not yet," I radio back.

"Be careful, boss."

"Will do, thanks." I twist the receiver volume to silent and shove it back into my pocket. A gentle gust blows my hat off my head. I pull it back, my mud-streaked hands skimming my unshaven face. I'm not exactly growing a beard, but I don't care about my appearance—not anymore.

The night's stillness rings through my ears. There's nothing but the sound of my boots shuffling along the frozen ground.

The paw prints continue. I keep my light trained on them. Alongside the lion prints, I recognize the distinct larger print of a white rhino. I sidestep to avoid a heaping pile of rhino dung.

Fucking hazards of the job.

A smile parcels from my lips. I stop walking, pausing to listen. Out here, you never know what's waiting to hunt you, to make you prey. I've learned you can never be too careful—but for the moment, I'm alone.

The prints continue. I follow them with painstaking precision, nearing a thick grassy patch. I stop again, my ears curling up, my heart pounding. I listen harder, detecting the gentle snoring of an animal. I study the sound—it's coming from my left.

I trek slowly, following, as it grows noisier. Behind the horizon, the sun is readying to spring up. Under the glare of purple light, I spot them. Thirty meters ahead, in the long bronzed grass, lies a sleeping mama lion, her two cubs nestled on either side.

Fucking incredible.

This damn work never gets old. The thrill flings goosebumps down my arms.

I love being out here, in the wild.

I reach for my camera, slung around my neck, snapping a few photos. With my eyes still fixed to the sleeping lions, I focus on my breath.

Inhale, exhale.

One.

Inhale, exhale.

Two.

Inhale, exhale.

Three.

With one final breath, I turn around, cautious again, to ensure I'm not being tracked. I get to the Jeep and climb in, heading towards the lodge, ready to start my day.

54

TESSA

"**L**adies and gentlemen, at this time, boarding is complete. The aircraft doors have been closed in preparation for takeoff." My stomach fills with butterflies as I shift against seat 37F aboard South African Airways Flight 2242, soon-to-be departing for Johannesburg.

I glance up at the ceiling.

Dad, I hope this is the right choice.

I yearn for a sign.

You said you'd be there when I need you.

I need you now.

But there's no sign, only chatter from nearby passengers.

I reach for my purse, fish out an Ativan, let it dissolve on my tongue. I feel immense gratitude for the medications that have been instrumental in helping manage my anxiety. That have made flying—and living— bearable.

The flight attendants come through the aisles, closing the overhead bins. I pull out my phone, texting Mom.

> Me: We're about to take off. I miss you already.
> I still feel guilty about leaving. Thanks for

encouraging me to go. I'll text when I land.
Thinking about you and Dad. You're my hero.

Mom: Safe flight, sweetie. Love you! Good luck.
And be your own hero.

I grin.
Be my own hero.
What a freaking concept.
Then, I text Jake.

Me: Thanks for coming to my dad's funeral. It
meant a lot. I hope you're doing okay.

Not expecting a response, I text Liz.

Me: About to take off. Thanks for your endless
support. Give Cami a kiss from me.

Liz: Go get Mr. Safari Dreamboat and never
let him go :-)

My grin creeps larger.
Mr. Safari Dreamboat.
It's been years since Liz has called him that.
The flight attendant's voice booms again. "At this time, all electronic devices must be placed in airplane mode or powered down for takeoff."
Shit.
Time to do this.
With unsteady fingers, I open my email app, finding the "Elephants"

folder. I click Select All on my four hundred and twenty-three drafted messages to Corey.

What if he wants nothing to do with me?

I shake my head.

I need to trust my own damn gut.

Even when it's excruciating.

I press Send, my head flopping back against my seat.

No turning back now.

THEN:

Nine Years Ago

November, 2010

55

TESSA

From: Tessa.Williams2@bmail.com
To: Coreytheranger@ImpodimoLodge.net

Subject: My secret

Date: November 3, 2010

Dear Corey,

I've never talked about this before, with you or anyone, but three years ago, I lost our baby. I'm not sure why I'm writing about this now, but the anniversary of the loss still cuts me up. What hurts the most is you don't know about it. That we don't share our grief. Because we don't share anything at all anymore.

Two weeks after getting home, after that last night together in the rain, I started to feel weird. I was nauseous a lot, and my boobs kept tingling. But I hadn't missed any of my birth control pills, so it didn't occur to me I could be pregnant. But a few days later, I had some weird cramping and my period was late. I decided to take a test just to be sure. It was instantly positive—a dark pink line.

I was shocked. How could I be pregnant? We only had unprotected sex once. The odds were so small. But somehow it was true. It almost felt like a sign that we were meant to be together. I was pregnant with *our* baby.

I sat on my bathroom floor, staring at the positive pregnancy test. I didn't feel scared or panicked, just so happy. Because it meant I had a piece of you with me. *In* me. That I had a reason to go back. I wanted to tell you right away, but I was too nervous because you still weren't responding to my emails. So I decided to wait until I knew more. Until I could make a plan.

I knew we loved each other, so much, and this would give us a reason to be together. It felt like fate.

I called my OB right away, but the office didn't want to see me until I was eight weeks along. I went to the pharmacy and bought prenatal vitamins. I started imagining the future we'd have—you, me and our baby, together, in the bush, living at Impodimo Lodge. It felt so right.

But one night, ten days later, I woke up with terrible cramping. The pain was intense. I wanted you to be there so badly. I needed you so much. But you were a continent away, unaware I was pregnant. Not even speaking to me.

I ran to the bathroom and found blood all over my underwear. I thought of Evah and how she'd lost her son. I didn't want to wake Liz or my other roommates. So I stayed up all night, alone, my knees tucked to my chest, rocking back and forth on the bathroom floor. The blood kept coming. I couldn't make it stop.

In the morning, I called the OB, and they told me to come right in. They did some bloodwork and an ultrasound. By then, there should have been a heartbeat, but there wasn't. There was no baby, just an empty sac. The pregnancy had stopped developing at around five weeks and was slowly being expelled from me. Our baby would never be.

I hadn't wanted a baby, wasn't ready at all to be pregnant or become a mother. But it was beyond devastating. It wasn't just the pregnancy but also my future with you, all wrapped up in one gigantic loss. And the worst part was you didn't know. I went through it alone.

I stayed home sick from clinical that day and the next. The cramping was so awful. Finally, I expelled a huge clot into the toilet. I remember staring at it for so long. It was the remnants of our baby, the remnants of our life together. *Gone.* I looked at it in horror before finally flushing it down.

I don't know why I didn't just tell you then. I wish I had. I don't know why I never told anyone. I guess it felt like the last piece of *us*, and for some reason, I wanted to keep it just for myself.

I still think about our baby, Corey.

It makes me so sad you don't even know what we lost.

What could have been.

What should have been.

If only life had turned out differently.

Tessa

PART

THREE

NOW:

September, 2019

56

COREY

I lean against my desk chair, soaking in the view from the floor-to-ceiling windows. The midday heat has chased off most of the animals, but a few zebras are in the watering hole, swallowing eagerly. The sky is riddled with bulky clouds hanging low in the air.

Sometimes, it's still hard to believe this is *my* office. I've been the manager of Impodimo Lodge for nine years—ever since Joe retired—but for me, the magic of this place has never dulled.

I sip my coffee, taking stock of my messy desk, overflowing with photographs and too much damn paperwork. Safari brochures peek out from under a stack of invoices.

At the edge of my desk, I study the picture of Darian, his partner Lynn, and their three sons, on top of the Empire State Building. Their arms stretch high into the air, ecstatic about their long-awaited trip to New York City. The boys' grins radiate joy and for a moment, I picture Darian yelling something goofy that made them laugh.

Miss you, bud.

Darian left seven years ago to become the manager of the competing Tiou resort. We're still best buds, but things are understandably different now that he has a family.

Next, is a photo of me kneeling beside Leona-Anne—my incredible five-year-old niece—at the Cape of Good Hope. Behind us, the rough sea slams into the rocky cliff.

Watching Leona-Anne grow has been amazing—a little bit like getting a second peek at Leona.

Beside that, is the photograph of Leona, running in the field of red daisies, the same one I used to keep on my nightstand. But now, it's here in my office, so her glory can be appreciated by others, too.

I look into Leona's violet eyes and smile.

There's something eternal in her expression, like she'll never truly leave.

Miss you, Little Lion.

Over the years, the hole of her loss has slowly been supplanted by an enormous gratitude, for the privilege of once being her brother.

I take another sip of coffee.

Time to focus, man.

This paperwork isn't going to do itself.

Searching for the lodge expense reports, I open my desk drawer, fumbling through documents. I stop when I uncover *that* photograph, buried facedown.

As I turn it over, my jaw trembles, a small earthquake juddering inside. *Fuck.*

I study—too carefully—the sight of Tessa's stunning face. She's seated on the boat, on our cruise to the Chobe River. The golden-hour light bathes her, highlighting the waves of her honey-golden hair, perfectly matched by the ripples on the water's surface.

So damn beautiful.

I keep this picture tucked away, hidden from myself. Even after all these years, it's like a loaded weapon, one look capable of firing pain straight into my chest. It's one of the most striking photographs I've ever taken.

Every now and then, withstanding all damn reason, I look. I remember.

***

I tuck the photo of Tessa away, clearing my throat.

Seriously, pull yourself together, man.

Unable to find the expense reports, I browse the sticky notes my assistant, Julia, has draped over my desk with various guest issues:

Mr. Mickey wants a partial refund. He's very upset he didn't see any wild dogs. Please call ASAP.

Ms. Golding wants a private walking tour of the bush with you, Thursday morning.

Mr. Fitzpatrick says there are too many insects in his cabin (#5).

Ms. Wildy feels the lodge should be more gender-neutral. She says: "We're painfully behind the times."

I grunt, then smile. Sometimes, the utter bullshit I'm expected to manage is laughable.

The next ninety-minutes float by, as I use a slew of well-honed managerial skills to keep my guests happy. I check my watch. Two hours until the game ride—the happiest part of my day, when I can just *be* with the animals.

I open my computer, clicking the Outlook application. I still dread email—it brings me too close to that rush paced of society, the one I eagerly left, to come to this remote sanctuary. But once daily, I check it, only because it's a requirement for my job.

My inbox loads, displaying four hundred and thirty unread emails.

What the fuck?

Was my email hacked?

But then, I see *her* name. Email, upon email, from Tessa.

Seriously, what the fuck?

I grip my chest, wincing as it's yanked apart by that invisible string continually knotting me to her.

My head wobbles.

Am I imagining things?

I slap my cheeks, blinking rapidly, scrolling down, finding her first email, entitled *One Year.*

Why is she contacting me now?

I forget to breathe, forget everything, as I open her messages, frenzied to discover what she has to say after a decade of total fucking silence.

57

COREY

I slump against my desk, my head collapsing in my hands. I've been reading Tessa's emails for the past two hours, but I have more questions than answers. Yet, I've pieced together a few notable facts:

1) Tessa was pregnant—with my baby.

Holy fucking shit.

Reading this twists my guts into a tight ball, while simultaneously kicking me deep in the fucking nuts. How could I have missed that? The pain is visceral. I'm nauseous, even gag a few times. The thought of Tessa going through that alone destroys me.

2) It's also clear Tessa missed me deeply for years, which gives me renewed hope—until I get to point three...

3) Tessa is now *married*. The last email seems to be written on her wedding day. Six years ago. To *Jake*. At the Four Seasons Hotel. In Philadelphia. A horrendous blow.

Married?

Holy Shit.

Why is she emailing me if she's married?

My entire body shakes with dread. That scar from losing her is barely stitched closed, held shut by the puniest of threads. It constantly threatens to burst open from even the most mild tussle. What does she expect from me after all these years?

When she's married!

Fuck!

I glance at my watch. Time for the afternoon game ride. I need to push Tessa far from my mind. I stand to stretch my legs, inhaling a slow, cleansing breath.

Inhale, exhale.

In a daze, I wander past the check-in desk, where my trusty assistant, Julia, waves hello. Her grin is bright and unburdened, the kind only youth can conjure. I find myself wildly envious of all the ways she remains blissfully naïve to life's harsher truths. I wave hello back and then I'm outside the lodge, where the bright sun temporarily blinds me.

As my eyes slowly adjust, the warmth already prickling my skin, time abruptly stops.

Because leaning against the front of my Jeep, with her hands crossed at her sides, fidgeting a gold bangle around her wrist, stands Tessa.

Tessa.

My Tessa.

Holy fucking shit.

She's here?

How is she here?

Am I dreaming?

Yes, this must be a dream, a cruel mirage.

I've willed this moment for so long, never believing it could happen.

Holy shit.

Has the sun driven my eyes mad?

I blink once, then twice, then three times.

But when I open my eyes, Tessa is still standing there, her figure solid against the earth.

I haven't seen her in twelve years, but as our gazes lock, time collapses into tiny grains of sand. It feels like only minutes have passed since she was in my arms beneath that punishing rain on our last night.

The sight of her is soul-crushing. Her chestnut locks are longer but still infused with those same honey-golden streaks, cascading in gentle waves down her back. She wears a sleeveless navy dress with a black belt cinched at her waist. Her skin looks soft but pale, as though life's brightness hasn't quite reached her lately. And my attention pulls to a sagging heaviness drooping against her shoulders.

She's carrying a hefty burden again—or *still?*

I try to find her brown eyes—those deep, golden-specked pools that used to be my refuge—but they're hidden behind oversized black sunglasses.

At the sight of me, she offers up a teeny half-smile, which is just enough to make her dimple pop out, instantly zipping my heart through a shredder.

She's still so damn beautiful.

I try to walk, but my feet are rooted in place, my brain too shocked to respond to commands.

Fuck.

Tessa stares at me, shifting her feet, hugging her arms around herself. It tugs at something deep inside me, buried but not forgotten. I instinctively want to run to her, to close the chasm, but my mind screams at me.

Stop it, you idiot!

What are you doing?

She's married!

She'll crush you again.

The breeze blows, moving a few wisps of Tessa's long hair around. She tucks it behind her ear while I watch, transfixed, as if this is the most miraculous feat any human has ever achieved.

A hand pats my back. "Corey, mate. We're ready for another great ride this afternoon!" It's two of my guests, a retired couple—Sal and Laura—making their way out of the lodge.

I smile at them without managing one single word. My brain has short-circuited.

Get it together, man.

You have a job to do!

I will my feet to move, although walking now feels like trekking through thick sludge. Time moves in slow motion as I get to the Jeep, my guests waiting. Tessa's eyes glower, but I don't dare return her stare for fear of losing my composure completely. "Um… hi, guys! Are you ready for a great game ride? Everybody, please get settled into the Jeep. I will… I will be right with you in just a second. I… um, just have to talk to this guest here… quickly… about an issue… we're experiencing."

Wow, I'm babbling like a complete fucking idiot.

I reach in Tessa's direction, motioning her to follow me to the side of the building. My fingers skim her elbow, grazing her skin. Even this minimal contact sends tremors quaking down my back, into my legs.

That electrical spark—still one hundred percent there.

Fuck.

It remains a magnet, sucking me towards her. I want to resist it, but its force is overpowering.

We walk together, in a silence both awkward and familiar, rounding the corner of the lodge.

Tessa leans against the stone wall, looking like she requires it to prevent her from crumbling down.

What happened to her?

"Tessa, what are you doing here?" My tone is pointed, maybe even accusatory. I instantly regret my intonation—but she's married to someone that isn't *me*.

I'm terrified of being this close to her, can already feel my self-control tumbling away.

Fuck.

"Wow, that's not really the greeting I was hoping to get." Tessa's disappointment is palpable. Her half-smile sinks into a pouty frown that tugs at my years-broken heart. The thought of hurting her makes my stomach jump up through my throat, past my eyeballs, into my throbbing temples.

She brings her hands to her face, shaking her head. "I'm sorry, I feel like an idiot for coming here. I have no idea what I was thinking."

She starts to turn, to walk away, but despite myself, I reach out, spinning her back around, taking ahold of her shoulder. My knees grow weak from touching her. It feels like I'm sitting on the electric chair, about to be zapped into a fatal arrhythmia.

Tessa's hands remain over her stunning, melancholy face.

I look at her left hand.

No ring.

A slight hope winds around my chest, softening me. "I'm sorry, that really didn't come out right… I just… I can't believe you're here. I never thought I'd see you again. I was just in my office, reading all your emails, and I have to admit, I'm pretty confused."

"I know, I'm sorry," Tessa says. "I shouldn't have sent them without explaining. I was just afraid I'd chicken out, so I emailed them before my plane left to make sure I'd follow through with coming here."

Being this close to her again is like ingesting the most intoxicating drug on the planet—I can't think, can barely function.

I force myself backwards, dropping my hand from her shoulder, turning to look at the Jeep. Some of the guests look impatient.

Fuck.

I want to stay, talk to Tessa for as long as it takes, but I can't. "How long are you here for? It seems we have a lot to talk about, but we need to head out on the game ride in a minute."

Tessa hesitates, looking like she's about to reveal all her cards, even though we've just sat down at the poker table. "I'm not sure? I don't have anything to get back to, not anymore. I can stay… if you want me to?" Her voice drops to a hushed whisper.

She wants to stay?

My brain is a shitstorm of questions, but only one feels urgent. "In one of your emails, you said you were getting married. Don't you have a husband?"

Jake.

The words blurt out, but I'm terrified to hear the answer.

Unless, the answer is no.

Please, let the answer be no.

Tessa furrows her brow. "Well… it's complicated. I do have a husband."

Fuck.

She pauses, her words dangling in mid-air, a searing pain radiating back and forth between my ears.

"But I left him. Partly, because of you, actually. It's a long story. I want to tell you the whole thing, but bottom line, we're getting a divorce."

She left him?

For me?

This news has my heart on the verge of exploding out of my goddamn chest. "So, that means you're available, then?"

The words squeak out, a large bead of sweat dripping from my forehead.

God, it's hot out here.

Or maybe it's just the extreme heat generated being this close to her again.

Tessa crinkles her nose. "That depends, *Corey.* Do you want me to be available?"

A flood of nostalgia washes over me, hearing my name roll off her lips. It's like hearing your favorite song come on the radio after years—

suddenly, no matter where you are, time morphs you back into the person you were when you loved that song.

And I still love that song.

"I-I-I… yes. Of course, I want that… I *never* stopped wanting that." I'm stammering like a fucking moron again, revealing my deepest feelings within five minutes of seeing her after twelve years apart.

How does she always bring it out of me like this?

Fuck.

Fuck.

Fuck.

Tessa's lips twist up into her breathtaking smile and I abandon my doubts, my fears, my hold-ups.

The gold bangle on her arm jingles. "What about you, Corey? Are *you* available?"

My response is but a whimper. "Yes."

After a pause, I add, "It was always you, Tess."

Our eyes lock again but this time I don't force my gaze away.

Tessa drops her sunglasses, and I can finally peer into her sparkling brown eyes. Beneath the sun's orange flame, the golden specs within them glisten wildly, melting what little remains of my insides into a pile of fucking slush.

The rest of the world fades to black.

My hand finds the small of her back, pulling her towards me.

She stumbles, her citrusy hair brushing my chin.

The lemons.

The goddamn fucking miraculous lemons.

I let out an unintentional cry of joy.

The smell is like coming home after a horrendously painful trip— back to a place my body continuously ached for, in spite of itself.

"I can't believe you're really here," I mumble, nuzzling her close.

In our embrace, the tension in her body dissolves. She squeezes my waist.

This still feels so damn right.

"I know, Corey. I'm sorry it took me so long, but I'm here *now*." Her enunciation rocks me to my core. She leans closer, her lips grazing mine. Even that teeny kiss leaves me breathless, wanting more.

Needing more.

But we can't.

Not now.

"Good," I mumble, overwhelmed. "Come, let me take you to see some of your favorites—the elephants. We'll talk more tonight, Tess." I glance down, her smile dripping off her cheeks. A few stray tears sail along her chin, and I wipe them onto my shirt.

Slowly, I unseal our bodies.

Reaching for her hand.

Leading her back towards the Jeep.

Back towards an unexpectedly new chance.

Improbably,

Impossibly,

Together.

58

TESSA

Corey's fingers remain laced with mine as we arrive at the Jeep. From the safari vehicle, five confused faces peer at us with raging curiosity.

Why'd I think it was a good idea to corner him right before the game ride?

Embarrassment crawls up my neck at sharing such an intimate moment with complete strangers. I fumble to unhook our hands, trying to untangle from *that* overpowering spark. That unexplainable, organic feeling that made me want to give up everything twelve years ago.

If only I'd listened.

That spark—literal fireworks set off by my soul—letting me know I'd found *my* person. But for so long, I was too afraid to trust it. Yet now it's clear, that feeling is the only thing worth trusting in.

Corey resists my attempts to separate us, keeping a solid grasp on my hand as if to say: *I'm never letting go again.*

"Sorry about the delay, guys." His voice is breezy, bearing no hint of the discomfort I feel. "You'll have to forgive me. I was a bit surprised, just now, to see the love of my life, waiting for me. I haven't seen her flawless face in twelve years."

Did he just say I'm the love of his life?

His blue eyes lock with mine, heaving me momentarily into outer space. We are the only two people in the atmosphere.

Is this what swooning feels like?

I press my feet firmly into the ground. I'm about to topple over.

His hand brushes my hip bone, steadying me, as his face radiates joy. From the Jeep, someone shouts, "Congratulations, mate!" There are a few awkward claps. I feel my cheeks blush seven shades darker.

"Thanks, Sal… everyone, this is Tessa." He lifts our hands together, high into the air, like I'm his most valued treasure. I manage a smile, with a slight wave of my free hand. "Now, let's get going on our game ride!"

He opens the passenger door, closing it behind me. I nod appreciatively, pleased to see he hasn't lost his manners.

Before starting the engine, he squeezes my thigh affectionately, splaying goosebumps down my legs.

Being seated next to him again, in the wilderness, feels like an actual freaking dream.

I pinch my forearm to make sure it's real.

It is.

The Jeep rumbles forward and I turn to him, speaking in a muffled voice. "Oh my god, that was seriously so embarrassing! I should've waited to approach you after dinner instead." I let out a hearty laugh, shaking my head.

"Stop. I know you *fucking* loved my public display of affection." He offers up his toothy grin, my chest promptly dissolving like a marshmallow dipped in fire.

"Well, I did enjoy hearing I'm the love of your *fucking* life."

"Good, because you *fucking* are, Tess."

I bask in the glow of his words, the first sunbeam after a storm. "I feel the same, Corey." My hand grasps his elbow. I'm finally touching him, after years of longing for this very pleasure.

We drive deeper into the bush. I'm vaguely aware of the striking scenery outside, of how breathtaking the Madikwe Game Reserve remains.

But mostly, my eyes are glued to Corey.

The years have weathered him some. He's rougher around the edges, transformed from a boy into a man. One who's lived through significant loss, but still stands tall.

His hair is longer, shaggier, less blond and more caramel.

His face is covered in stubble, mostly brown, but with grey specs sprinkled in—a sign of all the days in his life I've missed.

His forehead is scattered with new creases. Proof of the price he paid to love me.

To lose me.

His blue eyes bear the same stunning ferocity, but something dark still lingers below.

The pain of grief.

A pain I now know intimately.

As he upshifts gears, his biceps flex, coming into generous view, and I notice his lioness tattoo. But the lettering is different. It no longer says *Happily Ever After*, but instead, *Happily Ever Now*.

I make a mental note to ask him about this later, letting my eyes settle onto his stomach. Where he still has the same little tummy pudge, maybe even slightly more. And the sight of it still cracks my heart into a thousand fragments.

The car accelerates down the dirt road.

I close my eyes, letting the fiery sun beat against my tired body. I take several deep breaths, relishing being back here.

Everything is just as I remembered.

But somehow, better.

Corey's South African drawl drags me from my sunbaked reverie. "We're here, mates." I open my eyes to find the Jeep parked outside the Tau Waterhole.

Without warning, a flurry of memories blizzard through me.

Our first date here, when he rejected my advances.

Our last night here, making love under the rain, creating our baby.

Everything we were out here, together and all that we lost.

For an instant, I hold it in my heart.

But then, from within, *True Tessa* whispers: *Just be here, now.*

And so, I release the memories, to flow through me, away from me.

It's the past.

We can begin again.

Now.

Corey helps the guests get out. Then, he comes to my door, offering me his hand. I start to step down but pause, looking around the bush, my pulse picking up.

Corey smiles, leaning close. "I guess some things never change. Don't worry, Tess. I'll protect you. *Always.*" His raspy breath causes desire to ooze from me, his promise weaving a chill down my spine.

He breaks away, going to the back of the Jeep, unloading supplies for Happy Hour. I stare at him as he bustles around, still doing what he loves, something I've never figured out for myself. He returns, handing me a glass of Chenin Blanc. I sip it, letting the cold wine melt on my lips. With the other guests enjoying cocktails, he threads his arm around my waist.

The buttery sun is starting to drop, giving way to pinches of tangerine orange and ruby red. On the opposite end of the watering hole, I see a herd of elephants slurping and soaking. These majestic creatures still stun me. The biggest one lingers by the edge, her grey ears swaying, her huge eyes sad. She raises her trunk and lets out a long cry. The rest of the herd wanders to her side, surrounding her, using their trunks to comfort her, speaking a language all their own.

"Remember the matriarch?" Corey asks.

"No, should I?"

Corey reaches for his camera, taking a few shots before saying, "That's Betty."

Who's Betty?

But before I can ask, I remember. Betty the elephant, who comes here to grieve her son. Corey pointed her out on our first night at this watering hole, a lifetime ago. But here Betty is, some sixteen years after her loss, apparently still grieving.

The truth charges through me then, like the frantic stampede of wild animals.

Grief never ends.

That all-too-familiar lump seizes the back of my throat, as an ache gnaws in the pit of my belly. The longing for my dad is suddenly so acute, I can't breathe. I was momentarily swept away by the happiness of reuniting with Corey. But now, I feel my loss again.

My dad is still gone.

Corey seems to sense the abrupt change in me. "Hey, *pragtige dame,* what's wrong?" His voice is tender and loving, as he pulls me into a tight embrace.

I inhale his musky, grassy familiarity. "I'll tell you tonight."

And I will.

I want him to know everything.

I'm done stowing away parts of myself from those I love most.

He holds me, while we take in the beauty and pain of our surroundings. Then he goes to talk to the other guests. I stand alone, gulping the last of my wine, staring at Betty and the other elephants.

In the distance, I see a rainbow-colored bird flying towards me. Its vibrant wings flutter in the fading light. I saw a similar bird, years ago, first with Corey and then with my dad—the lilac-breasted roller. A supposed sign of good luck. But it hadn't brought me good luck on the day I'd decided to leave.

I watch in awe as it swoops closer, landing on the hood of the Jeep. Carefully, I tiptoe towards the car, not wanting to scare it. But peculiarly, it seems unperturbed by my presence.

I crouch near the hood, mesmerized by the bird's brown eyes, its solid black beak, its fluffy green-and-white hair, its lilac neck. It stretches out, revealing its wings, marked by stripes of vibrant azure and cobalt blue. It dances, back and forth, beneath the golden hue of the sun.

And then, in a flash, my dad's face appears.

I hear his words.

Clear and certain.

I'll find ways to talk to you. Just listen.

"Dad?" I whisper, acknowledging that the idea of him being there is crazy.

The bird tilts its head, as if answering me.

A quiet warmth blooms within me.

Somehow, it feels real.

A sense of peace sweeps through me.

Not a loud, overwhelming flood, but a soft steady tide.

He's okay.

Wherever he is, he's okay.

I don't understand.

But I do.

Tears blur my vision, rolling down my cheeks, onto the Jeep. The wet spots mix with the mud encrusted on the hood, forming dark brown splotches. Visible imprints of my grief.

These are the types of marks others can see.

There are internal scars too, ones only I know about, buried deep inside.

Both types hurt, so badly.

The bird inches closer, chirping happily, almost conversational, like it wants to speak to me.

I grin. "Dad, I love and miss you so much."

It squawks louder, flapping its wings.

Behind me, I feel Corey's eyes tunneling into my back. Heat seeps up my neck. I must look insane, talking to a bird and crying.

I watch it take flight.

I watch as the pigments of its body—the reds, purples, browns, greens, blues, pinks, whites, and yellows—meet the colors of the horizon.

I watch with bated breath until the bird is entirely absorbed into the sunset-streaked sky.

Until the two become one.

"Bye, Daddy," I say to no one but myself.

The wind rustles and without my dad to guide me, I feel impossibly alone. I desperately want to share this moment with Mom. When we get back to the lodge, I'll call her right away.

Seconds, or maybe minutes later, Corey burrows his stubbly face into my neck, his strong arms wrapping around my waist. I let the weight of my grief collapse against him.

He's my safety rope, offering to tether me from the freefall of my pain.

I just have to trust enough, to let go.

To jump.

"Hey, are you okay? What's going on?" His tone is worried and protective.

I manage a half-smile. "Yeah. I'll be okay. Here. Now. With you."

I'm surprised to discover I believe it.

He kisses my cheek as I clutch my chest, stroking that raw, messy wound, sculpted from my dad's death.

Likely, the scar from losing him will remain forever.

Over time, it may shift.

Mold.

Fade.

Open.

Close.

Reopen again.

No matter what, it will persist.

"I'm so glad you're here," Corey whispers. The coarse skin of his fingertips trace along my wrist, causing me to shudder.

My dad's parting words dance above.

Love lasts.

And how wildly miraculous that it does.

59

COREY

"I can't believe I'm sitting in this lodge again," Tessa says, taking a sip of her vodka soda. "I forgot how even the air here is magical. And the animals. And you. Most of all, *you*. Seriously, how are you real?"

"I'm still in shock, too," I admit, looking down at my hand, which is somehow touching Tessa's leg.

Tessa's sexy damn leg.

Dinner is over and the last guest is gone. We're now the only two people in the main lodge, seated on a leather couch, not unlike how we spent our first night together, twelve years ago.

Tessa rubs her eyes, tucking a pillow beneath her head, keeping her legs draped in my lap. "So… should we start talking? We have a lot to discuss."

I massage her calf. "Aren't you tired from your trip? We can go to sleep and catch up tomorrow? We have time, because, after all, you're staying." I beam.

"Yeah," she says. "I'm exhausted. But I've waited so long to talk to you. I can't wait, not even one more night."

"Okay, that's fair," I concede with a small laugh, but really, I'm terrified to hear about everything I've missed in her life.

To hear about *Jake.*

To rip open old wounds—barely closed, never healed, when we've hardly had any time to adjust to our new reality.

Tessa slips deep in thought, silent for minutes, leading me to conclude that her list of items to discuss is long.

Very, very, very long.

Fuck.

My stomach sinks, beads of perspiration streaking down my back. I lift my Coke, the cool glass sweating in my hand, and take a sip. Tessa seemed a little surprised when I passed on a drink at dinner, but I've got rules now—ones my therapist and I hammered out:

1) I never have more than two drinks on any occasion.

2) I only drink when I'm feeling emotionally stable.

Tonight, considering Tessa's unexpected return, I'm anything *but* stable.

Tessa shifts against the couch, finally speaking. "Okay, so… six months ago, I ran into Carl."

I spit out my Coke. "Carl? Like, my brother, Carl?"

"Yeah. He was a guest lecturer at my hospital. Afterwards, we talked and he said you never got over me. Obviously, I hadn't gotten over you either, but I'd assumed the feeling was one-sided. But Carl made me have hope again, in us."

Us.

The word crystallizes in my ears.

"Wow, that's wild. Carl never said anything to me?"

"I know," she says. "I asked him not to. I wanted to tell you myself… I was hoping to come back sooner, but a lot happened since then…" Her voice grows small, her head slinking down on the pillow, a potent gloom invading the air.

What happened?

She starts to say more, but stops.

Her fingers move towards her mouth.

My gaze lands on her lips.

I shouldn't, but I can't help but stare.

Her top lip is broad and plump, two mountain ridges fused seamlessly in the center. Her bottom lip is rose-pink and curvy. Both are literally begging for my immediate, undivided attention.

I want to forget the past, exploring only her lips—the only lips I want to kiss for the rest of my life.

Tessa glares at me, starkly serious. I clear my throat. "Well, I'm thankful Carl told you that, especially if it led you to come back to me."

"But, Corey… why didn't you tell me yourself? Why did you cut off contact? You told me you loved me, the most ever and that you'd reach out when you were ready. But you never did. You broke my heart."

Under the lodge lights, her eyes pool with sadness. The pain I caused her is so tangible, my chest tears straight down the middle.

Fuck.

I'm a monster.

"Shit… I'm sorry, Tess, I didn't mean to hurt you. I hope you believe me. When you left… I was honestly… a mess. Not that that's an excuse. It's not." I sigh. "Do you want to know why I didn't reach out?"

"I don't know. Do I?" Her pupils constrict as her forehead rumples.

She looks as scared as I feel.

My stomach drops lower, now barely contained within my body. "When you left, I was positive it was over."

"But why, Corey? From my side, that wasn't true."

"Because… I just… didn't think I was enough. I didn't think you'd ever choose me… over your"—I suck in a huge breath—"*dad.*"

I wince, terrified of how she'll react.

Even though it's the truth.

Especially because it's the truth.

"Oh." Her cheeks crater as her chin dips.

Fuck.

I shouldn't have said that.

She starts to open her mouth but stops, looking completely gutted.

What if this conversation makes her leave?

This thought makes me panicky, my back drenching with sweat.

"Tess, obviously, I made a mistake, but it was too painful to stay in contact with you. That doesn't mean I wasn't thinking about you, a lot, because I was. But I drank too much, trying to be numb, to shut out my feelings, to stop…" I glance down. "To stop loving you."

She swallows audibly, her jaw trembling. "Carl mentioned your drinking. That makes me really sad. I'm sorry if I was responsible for that."

I shake my head, needing her to believe me. "No, you weren't. No one's responsible for my actions but me." My hand finds hers, warm and soft against my clammy palm.

The words tumble out, uneven, messy, but honest—about agreeing to see a counselor, about being diagnosed with depression and unresolved grief, about the relief of learning *something* was actually wrong with me and that it could be helped, about the painstaking work of learning coping skills to process Leona's death. I tell her about my meditation practice, the yoga, the endless hours of clawing my way towards my new self.

"I'm really impressed with all the steps you took to get better," Tessa whispers. "I'm just crushed I wasn't there to support you, that I didn't know about any of it."

"Me too." Regret cakes to me like thick molasses. "I'm sorry. I should've reached out."

She tucks her hair behind her ear, and I have to physically restrain myself from burrowing my head into her lap and never leaving. Not ever.

"After I got home, my anxiety was really bad, too," she says. "I started this medication called Lexapro. That and exercise helps, but some days are still tough. Managing mental health is so hard."

"Yeah." I nod, squeezing her fingers tighter. "In retrospect, I definitely needed to sort myself out... before I could really be in any kind of healthy relationship."

She gulps, her russet eyes thoughtful. And piercing. And so damn striking. "So... are you sorted out now?"

"Pretty sorted out. As much as anyone can be in this shitshow of life."

Tessa lets out a wholesome laugh that causes my own breath to release.

"I'm really proud of you," she says.

"I'm proud of me, too, and I'm so happy you're here." I cup her heart-shaped jaw, pulling her into my lap, wrapping my arms around her neck. My tongue probes her mouth.

Her taste is old and familiar, new and exciting.

A nibble of my past and the flavor of my future.

My fingers comb her hair.

The electricity flying between us zaps my nerve endings, making my dick practically explode.

Fuck.

Just kissing her is enough to set me off.

I'm so screwed.

"God, I want you so bad," I mutter.

But Tessa pulls away. "Corey, I really think we should finish talking first."

A splash of cold water. "Oh, okay, of course." I try to stow my disappointment.

"So... how did *Alice* fit into the picture?" Tessa asks, her lips puckering into a spicy pout.

The shift in her tone is sharp, and it takes a second for my brain to catch up. The look on her face is half-curious, half-annoyed.

She's *jealous.*

And this turns me on even more.

The ache in my pants throbs harder. I squirm, trying to shift subtly, to hide what's increasingly obvious. My desire to be inside her this very second—insane. I pinch my wrist.

Pull it together, man.

This is serious. I'm supposed to be concentrating on this very important conversation. But, fuck, everything about her—her scent, her touch, the way her lips move—still drives me absolutely wild. It always has.

I sit up straighter, to tell her about Alice—an instant mood killer. My pants quickly retake their normal shape.

"Alice came back to work at the lodge, and slowly, with a lot of hesitation, at least on my part, we started dating again. Please know, Tess, there were never any fireworks between us. But, I was starved for human contact. A lot of the time, as strange as it sounds, I felt like I was cheating on you. Even though you lived on another continent and were living what I thought was a happy life, without me. Alice was a loyal partner, and I tried to fall in love with her. But, Tess, I couldn't. At some point, being with her became lonelier than being alone. So years ago, I ended it, and she left, and I've been by myself since. Alone but doing well."

"Why couldn't you fall in love with her?" Tessa asks, her voice low, her eyebrows high.

I think she already knows the answer but needs to hear it anyway.

"Because I was still in love with you." My eyes hold hers, channeling my devotion. "My brain… my body… my heart… it just always wanted *you*."

"Oh, Corey," she mumbles, collapsing into my chest.

My thumb trails her cheek, landing in her dimple. "Do you know how insanely beautiful you are? The years only made you better."

She grins wider. "You still give killer compliments… and I feel the same. You're ridiculously handsome, like a finely aged wine, left for twelve years to mature in an unoaked barrel."

The laughter spills out of us, recalling Sebastian.

Fucking Sebastian.

But then I think about *Jake.*

What type of compliments did Tessa give *him?*

Jake's existence is a puncture wound delivered from twenty-seven equally jagged knives. "So… now that we've covered my romantic history, let's talk about *Jake.*" I hope my tone conceals the four-alarm fire blazing inside my body.

Tessa crinkles her nose. "Ugh… well… Jake's a really good guy. In another world, maybe you'd even be friends."

Friends with Jake?

Friends with Tessa's husband, Jake?

"He treated me really well," she continues. "I feel so bad about how much I hurt him. But our marriage never had *that* spark. We went on our honeymoon to Tanzania, and I tried to convince myself it was the magic of Africa and the animals, not you, that I'd fallen in love with. But the whole time, I missed you and was so cranky. Jake was upset, kept asking me what was wrong. But how could I tell him I'd married the wrong person?"

Thoughts of Tessa honeymooning with *Jake* swarm my mind, coating me in insecurity.

"So, who is the *right* person for you?" I desperately need her to say it.

"This yoga-loving dude who lives in South Africa. He's my other half, even though he didn't talk to me for twelve years." Her tone is teasing but her grimace is real. My emotions yo-yo, from extreme jealousy to horrible guilt.

I failed her even though I didn't mean to.

Fuck.

"A guy who didn't talk to you for twelve years sounds like the biggest fucking idiot on the planet," I finally mumble, trying—*but* failing—to smile.

"Maybe." Tessa nods, her hands solid against my chest. "But I love him an impossible amount, the kind of love I couldn't forget, no matter what I tried." She looks straight into my eyes. "Corey, you're *my* person. Always were, still are."

Her words slam into me.

She loves me.

Despite everything.

"Holy shit, I'm so lucky," I whisper, a mass of gratitude clogging my throat.

"We're both lucky," Tessa murmurs.

My stomach unclenches.

Maybe we've survived the worst of this conversation… but there's still something left unsaid. I don't know what, but it's responsible for the heaviness on Tessa's shoulders.

"So," I ask carefully, bracing myself. "Anything else I should know about your life?"

I hope she'll say no.

But her face darkens as the pressure in the room builds like a flash summer thunderstorm.

Fuck.

"Tess? What is it?" My stomach scrunches back into a web of knots as Tessa's chest looks almost concave.

Then, the words seep out.

"My dad died."

Terror explodes from her eyes, the shrapnel flying off and slicing me up, too.

What?

No!

"Oh my god, Tess. I'm so sorry. I don't even know what to say… I know how much you loved your dad. That's terrible."

Tessa's body shakes as she tells me about her father's last year of life— and even though I can't, I want to scoop all her pain up and carry it myself.

I clasp her hands, allowing space between us for her inner nucleus, once again unearthed.

"From the time he was diagnosed until he died, was less than a year," Tessa says. "Nothing could stop it."

"I'm so sorry," I whisper, knowing that type of unstoppable, soul-crushing loss.

"It's been a really, really shitty month. He died on August thirtieth."

"August thirtieth? You're fucking joking." The words fly out of my mouth before I can make them pretty.

Tessa's eyes narrow. "What's that supposed to mean?"

"That's the day Leona died. August 30, 1996."

In the years since, I've had plenty of hard days—but that one still holds the title as the single worst of my life.

"They died on the same day?" Tessa mutters, her lower lip stuck open.

"I guess so?"

We both fall quiet, lost in this impossible coincidence.

Finally, Tessa says, "I saw Leona in this morphine-induced hallucination I had. In the midst of my dad dying, I decided to give him a grandchild. It was ridiculous. I didn't even want a baby with Jake. Anyway, I got pregnant and—"

"Wait," I wheeze. "You were pregnant? With *Jake's* baby?" Another enormous bomb has just detonated. Vomit floods my mouth.

"Yes. It was a terrible decision. Literally, this is TMI, but the night we conceived, I saw your face."

I cringe, then blush, then cringe again.

She thought of me.

While Jake *was inside her.*

But I've been there, too.

With Alice.

I close my eyes, struggling to control my heart rate. "Corey, are you okay?"

"Honestly, no. The thought of you and Jake having a baby is pretty awful for me." I take three slow breaths. "But… what happened with your pregnancy?"

Tessa frowns. "I'm sorry, Corey. If it makes you feel better, I was really conflicted about having a baby with Jake, too. But it wasn't meant to be. The pregnancy was ectopic. I had to have emergency surgery."

Fuck.

Poor Tessa.

"Oh gosh, Tess. You've been through so much… you're so strong."

She starts to shake her head as if she's once again going to deny the strengths I perceive, but she stops herself. "Thank you, Corey. It's been a lot… and I'm surprised I'm still here. But I guess I'm tougher than I gave myself credit for… anyway, while I was having surgery, I dreamed I was here. I saw you and Leona. When she hugged me, it felt like I'd been missing her my entire life."

Upon hearing this, my breath slams against my throat, leaving me speechless.

"You told me you had your next lesson for me," Tessa whispers, clutching my face. "To stop running from myself, to let my pain teach me, to trust my damn gut. That notion changed everything. After that, I quit my job, I left Jake, I spent priceless time with my dad. Those words shifted my whole path."

My brain is unable to process it all.

Tessa's dream about Leona.

Her marriage to *Jake*.

Her ectopic pregnancy.

Peter dying.

How somehow, despite everything, she found a way back to me.

Gasping sobs seep from my mouth. Tessa hugs me. "Shh, it's okay, let it out. We both need to." Her chest presses against me, her body ebbing up and down, weeping too.

We stay like that.

Wrapped together.

Crying.

Mourning.

"I saw my dad today," she says. "That bird you saw me staring at. I had this weird flash. Maybe it sounds crazy, but for a second, it felt like him."

"It doesn't sound crazy. I have those moments with Leona, too. I live for them."

We're both silent for a long beat.

"But Tess, I can't explain how sorry I am for missing so much in your life. For not being there to support you… I really fucked up. I don't expect you to forgive me."

Tessa wipes my cheeks. "It's okay, Corey, I fucked up a lot, too. The truth is, you were right. When I left here, I was more concerned with making my dad proud than living my own life. I was so lost."

I look at her again, finally noticing the ease with which she now occupies her own skin. There's a cool confidence resting in place of that old self-doubt. "Well, you look remarkably found to me—brave as a lion, strong as a buffalo and beautiful. Did I mention insanely fucking beautiful?"

Tessa's lips curl up, her dimple resprouting. "Thank you, Corey, for always seeing the best in me. Basically, I have no life plan anymore except to trust my damn gut."

I grin. "That's a pretty solid plan. I guess I give good advice in your dreams?"

"The best."

"So… what's your gut telling you now?"

"To be here, with *you*." Her voice drops to a shallow rasp. "This is the only place I've ever felt free, ever felt at home, ever felt like myself."

She tugs my shirt collar, wrapping her legs around my back. Despite all the heaviness, my need for her is back, even more frantic than before.

"I'm not sure how I can ever be worthy of you," I say. "But I want to spend every day trying to prove I am."

"It's okay, Corey." She brushes my hair from my forehead. "I forgive you. We both made mistakes. Let's let it go. Start again. *Now.*"

"That sounds insanely *fucking* perfect."

She kisses me hard. Wiping out my breath. Wiping out everything except my unending love for her.

"Okay," I mumble, talking into her neck. "I feel like we've covered every topic except one."

"What's that?" Her brownish-gold eyes grow serious.

"Jennifer Aniston. What's her latest hairstyle? I'm so out of touch."

She laughs, swatting my arm. "I *fucking* love you."

"I *fucking* love you more. Honestly, the most ever. I really did mean that. Thank you for coming back. You made my dreams come true today." A warm, buzzy feeling swims through me, washing some of my old scars out to sea. "So, can I please take you home now?"

Her mouth climbs my neck. "Hmm... where's *home?*"

"Well, as manager, I have the nicest lodge in the staff quarters. It even has a king bed."

"Corey, I don't know... I paid for a room tonight, here." She uses her pointer finger to motion to the cabins just outside the lodge.

"I think management can be flexible in giving you a refund. Plus, what kind of guide would I be if I didn't try to seduce you in the staff quarters?" I give her a devilish wink, recalling my terrible pickup line from another lifetime—one that changed both of our lives forever.

Her lips rearrange into a menacing smirk. "Should I be worried, Corey? Do you *always* try to take guests home?"

My expression grows somber. "No, Tess, only ever you."

It's true.

In my seventeen years at the lodge, despite interacting with thousands and thousands of guests, she's the only one who's ever tempted me to cross that line.

She kisses me, biting my lower lip, driving me mad. "Good. I have one more question, too." She reaches down into my pants. I'm about to lose all control, to rip off her damn clothes, when she asks, "Are you HIV positive?"

We both dissolve into a delirious fit of laughter.

"Yes, Tess," I deadpan. Her eyes get wide. "Sorry, bad joke. No STDs, I promise."

"Okay." Her smile relaxes, ingesting her cheeks. "Take me *home*."

She stands up, untangles herself from me, helping to pull me up, too.

I wrap my arms around her, not moving, just holding her.

We are both upright now.

Pain tried to swallow us both.

But it didn't.

It won't.

We've both learned to stand on our own.

But together, we are something stronger.

Something better.

Something unbreakable.

60

TESSA

My eyes blink open. I squint from the bright sunlight gushing in. The ancient-looking clock displays the time in clunky red numbers: 11:42.

Oh god, I slept so long.

The details of last night drift back—Corey's bed, his arms swathed around me like the most protective blanket. It feels like I'm waking from a coma, the literal deepest sleep I've had in years. Turning my head, I spot a note on the nightstand.

Tess, I didn't want to wake you—you looked so peaceful. Out for the morning game ride, back around lunch. Coffee's warm, in the kitchen. Help yourself to anything. Love you -C.

Smiling absurdly wide, I clutch the note to my chest, savoring every loop and line of his handwriting. Then, with a sigh that feels impossibly light, I wander into the bathroom. There, I swallow my Lexapro and strip my clothes off, stepping into the piping-hot shower.

The rushing water is therapeutic, cleansing the physical muck plastering my skin.

The emotional muck plastering my soul.

I stand for minutes, letting it pound on top of me.

Letting it rinse away all that I don't need to carry.

Not anymore.

True Tessa whispers: *Just keep letting go.*

The bathroom door creaks open, and suddenly Corey is beside me, naked, his nearness making my legs wobble.

"Good morning, beautiful, or actually, I should say, good afternoon." He pulls me against him, tipping my chin upwards, until his lips are just a breath away.

"Wait! I have morning breath," I warn, blocking my mouth.

"I don't care if you have venom on your breath. After twelve years, nothing is going to stop me from kissing you anytime I can." His lips crash into mine—hungry, fervent—as the water pelts down on top of us, surrounding us with heat.

His hardness presses into my leg, and lust flames through me.

"Fuck, I always wanted to shower with you. It was a fantasy of mine," he murmurs, taking some shampoo, lathering it into my hair.

"Hmm, that feels good," I mumble, barely able to stand. My eyes trace along his left bicep. Corey continues rubbing soap into every inch of my body, my curiosity clashing with an overwhelming need for him to keep touching me. For him to never stop. "I wanted to ask… what happened to your tattoo?"

His hands pause for a beat, and his voice comes out low and gruff. "I had it changed a few years ago."

"What does it mean: *Happily ever now?*" The words barely squeak out, my head woozy from his wholly enchanting touch.

"After you left, it felt dumb to have a tattoo that said *Happily Ever After.* Waiting for some ideal future. When I got into meditation, I wanted my tattoo to reflect something more mindful." He pauses, looking at me, his blue beacons vaporizing my insides. "So I changed it to *Happily Ever Now*. It's my reminder to take life one minute at a time. To stay present with whatever's going on—the good, the bad. Now is all we have." His voice softens. "To be in the moment, even if the moment sucks. Not to spend all my moments waiting for a future that may never happen. To just... be okay with whatever is. To enjoy my life, as much as possible, right this second."

I study his irises, littered with dark specs from grief. But now, I appreciate something new. A glitter to his eyes: the wisdom borne from suffering.

"You learned from your pain, and the lesson is beautiful," I whisper, profoundly touched. "To be happy in the now, because that's all we ever have?"

"Something like that," he says, smiling, guiding me under the showerhead, using his hands to rinse away every last morsel of soap.

I let my eyes close, letting the moment consume me.

Just this.

Just now.

"Mmm... I can get used to showers like this."

"Me too."

He gently pushes me onto the small bench in the corner, the water cascading over us like a protective curtain. His lips find my neck, snaking their way down my body with a reverence that feels almost sacred. Every kiss is a soft explosion, every touch a balm to the pieces of myself I thought too broken to repair. He finally reaches the still-healing wound on my belly. His thick fingers run over its jagged edges, his lips delivering delicate little pecks.

"I love every piece of you," he whispers. "Especially your scars."

Despite the hot water, a shiver blasts through me.

I have plenty of external scars.

But also, many deep internal ones.

Yet, here is Corey, seeing them all—accepting them, cherishing them, and promising without words to stand by me as I work through the healing.

The learning.

"I love you, Corey Diallo. The most, ever."

He grows shockingly hard, hearing me say his full name.

"God, I love you," he growls, reaching my thighs.

He sinks down onto his knees, his hands encircling my waist, licking me like a famished man who hasn't eaten a nourishing meal in years. I moan from the sensation of his tongue against me again. His mouth moves in rough circles, blackening my mind, my fingers meagerly gripping his wet hair.

"Damn, you still taste amazing," he whimpers between hearty sucks. His tongue parses me apart, shredding my thoughts. The shower water gushes over us as I wiggle beneath the pressure of his mouth, surrendering myself. His tongue moves in forceful swells, pushing me close to the edge.

"I missed this so much. *You* so much," I mutter, my voice husky from a blizzard of need.

Everything about sex with Corey is the polar opposite of *okay/fine*.

He stops and smiles, his hands moving up to cradle my breasts. "I have a lot of catching up to do, Tess."

I smirk. "So… are there any lessons in self-respect today?"

He gives me a sinful grin. "No, you've mastered all my lessons. Today's just about orgasms. Tons of them." His tongue twirls in every possible motion. It doesn't take long until I'm tumbling fast over that cliff. Until I come, so hard, gripping his hair for dear life. The waves are a tsunami, crashing against the shore, releasing years of pent-up need in one violent, magnificent fury.

"Shit, Corey," I scream.

He grunts devilishly but keeps licking me, new waves smacking into the old ones. I dig my fingernails into his scalp, arching my back, shaking from pleasure, trying to push him away. He's going to undo me. His licking grows lighter, but my pelvic muscles continue to contract uncontrollably beneath his tongue. Finally, the waves recede.

Breathe, Tess, breathe.

I've entirely forgotten to breathe.

"Corey, seriously, you're going to ruin me." I try to collect myself.

But it's futile as he pushes two fingers inside me, mumbling with delight about my warm crevices. His lips and fingers move together, while I squirm furiously, not sure I'll survive it.

Survive *him.*

Another wave shakes me, lifting me high into the sky. I'm flying, shivering from pleasure, crying out and pulling him into me.

"I don't think my body's going to survive this," I gasp.

"Oh, it will, Tess. Trust me." His voice is hushed and brutally sexy.

"I want to feel you inside me," I whisper, hoping he'll stop. Not wanting him to stop.

But it's too late. The waves are impossibly rippling again, releasing around his fingers, squeezing. Helplessly, I surf towards the shore, struggling to crash onto land.

Looking deliriously pleased with himself, he removes his fingers, trying to pull me up.

"You have to give me a minute here, champ," I manage, struggling to come down from my high.

He bends down to kiss me, the shower water intermingling with our saliva. I reach for him again, finally standing.

"Wow," I mumble.

Wordlessly, he spins me around to face the wall, entering me. Being this close to him again, feeling *him*, is so insanely delicious, my mind practically implodes.

"Damn, Tess, you feel like paradise," he rasps. "I just want to spend the rest of my days inside you."

"Hmm, that sounds *perfect* to me."

And it does.

I need to pinch myself again.

He steadies himself, his hands on my hip bones, thrusting gently, his lips trailing along the small of my back.

"I missed you, so damn much." His voice is a mix of happy and sad.

I wish I could see his face, but instead, I rock my hips, moving against him, squeezing my pelvic muscles to clench him tightly.

"Shit." The sensation causes him to thrust hard.

His need seems primal, almost animalistic.

I'm the object of his desire, and he needs me.

Now.

He plunges into me so ferociously, it feels like I'll break apart.

I shake, pushing back against him harder, tempting him, hoping to drive him over the edge.

"No, I'm not ready yet. I don't want this to end. Please." His voice is begging, dripping with desire, trying to resist.

"I want you to come. Right now," I command, squeezing hard.

He screams, his hands grasping at my breasts, his teeth biting into my shoulder, muttering about how beautiful I am, how much he loves me. I can feel him giving into his need, about to rupture apart, inside me.

To release his pain and joy.

Sorrow and hope.

Into me.

He slams against me one final time, quivering, yelling out as he's swept away. "Fuck. Oh my god, Tess."

His pleasure drives me out of my mind.

He limply collapses, his face drooping against my back.

Spent, he sinks onto the shower floor, pulling me down into his arms.

We let the water cascade on top of us, kissing.

Suspended in bliss.

61

TESSA

I'm perched on the deck, my laptop nestled in my lap, the midday breeze tugging gently at my hair. I tip my sunglasses, spotting Corey through his office window, chatting with Julia. His jaw is rigid, his eyes focused.

I grin, gripped by a love that feels as vast and unending as the horizon stretching beyond the watering hole.

I close my email, having sent a flurry of messages, first to Evah to arrange a visit next week and then to my mom and Liz. I miss them so much, but for now, Skype visits across the ocean will have to do.

Below me, two elephants flop their trunks against the blueish-brown water, creating a wide-spraying mist that reaches the deck. I blink away the water droplets, trying to envision the life I'll have here.

It's been two weeks—two wondrous, disorienting weeks—but the unknowns still feel plentiful.

My chest twinges with a familiar pang of anxiety, *Phony Tessa*, stirring within, the consummate planner who demands life be all mapped out. She reminds me of all the questions I haven't answered yet.

But I've already jumped off a metaphorical bridge.

There's no roadmap here.

No color-coded life plan.

Not anymore.

True Tessa whispers her increasingly familiar advice: *Just be here, now. Let go of all your ideas of what you should be doing. Get out of your head and just live.*

I shake off my long-groomed impulse to have everything figured out, to plan, and re-plan. Despite its discomfort, I try to embrace the sensation of the free fall.

To not worry about where I'm going to land.

Maybe, the final destination isn't important.

Maybe, what matters, is the minute-to-minute process of getting there.

But what do I want to do?

The question still floats, lingering like a thread I'm afraid to tug. I've spent my career as a doctor—and a darn good one. But even at my best, medicine was always a rigid script I was trying to memorize rather than a story I was born to tell. I tried to force it to be my passion, over and over, when it never was.

The truth sits quietly now, waiting for me to finally look it in the eye.

So what is my passion?

My mind drifts back to that afternoon at my parents' house, discovering my writings. Those forgotten pieces of myself, buried beneath years of striving to be someone else.

Phony Tessa instantly reacts, sharp and biting: *You're a doctor, Tessa, not a writer. What are you going to write about? You're going to sound like the biggest fraud.*

True Tessa counter-argues: *Write whatever comes to mind! It doesn't matter. Open the page and go.*

In that moment, I realize these conflicting personas will continue to cohabit my brain, yanking me in opposing directions. It'll remain a lifelong challenge to trust *True Tessa's* guidance. *Phony Tessa*, always skeptical, always critical, isn't going to shut up. But I don't have to listen to her. By rejecting her advice, I can diminish her power.

I click on Microsoft Word, my eyes gaping at the empty screen.

It's frighteningly blank.

But also brimming with possibility.

My fingers find the keys.

They hover just for a second.

And then the words begin pouring out, flowing like a long-dammed river, wrestling impatiently for release.

[Untitled Draft]

By Tessa Williams

Years ago, a wise mentor, Dr. Masego Sebopelo, told me: *Pain can teach us to appreciate the beauty in life.*

At the time, I was a medical student training at Princess Victoria Hospital in Gaborone, Botswana. I'd just witnessed the tragic death of a stillborn baby boy.

Back then, I was too naïve to understand the power of his words. In fact, for most of my life, I believed pain was something bad to avoid at all costs.

Which, of course, proved fruitless, as pain is as essential to life as oxygen or water.

It took me twelve years—including the death of my father and losing and re-finding the love of my life, to understand what Dr. Sebopelo really meant.

The purpose of life isn't to avoid pain.

Or avoid scars.

It's to collect them humbly.

To understand them.

To let them litter your body as proof of a life well lived.

Well loved.

To realize that the things that break us—that tear us open, that rip us in two—are actually the things that make us.

That teach us the most.

That force us to grow.

Life universally breaks everyone.

But when we're receptive, the knowledge gained from our breaking and rebuilding can be our most valued teacher.

Life is a continual loop.

We break.

We learn.

We grow.

We break again.

We learn some more.

Pain unfurls profoundly beautiful lessons, if we're willing to listen.

I listened, and what I discovered is a way back home.

A way back to *me*.

***

"Hey, *pragtige dame*. I missed you. What are you doing?" Corey's delicious South African accent startles me. I look up to see him carrying a bottle of wine, two glasses and a cheese platter, his cheekbones shining beneath the fading daylight.

I click Save on my document, closing my computer. Writing is a spark, alive again, a bit like that electrical force field generated with Corey. But different because it's just *mine*.

"I was writing," I say, taking the wineglass from Corey's outstretched hand. "I used to love it, but I got pulled away by medicine. But, I think… I'm going to pick it up again."

His cobalt eyes gleam. "That's amazing, Tess. I'm so proud of you." He leans over, his kiss a blistering flame that warms my entire body.

"Hmm, how do you smell so good?" I mumble, swept away by his raw scent. My hand settles against his tummy. "I love you."

"I love you more." He pulls up a seat beside me. "I thought we could watch the sunset out here?"

"That sounds perfect."

And it does.

How is this my real life?

Above, the cottony clouds stain pink.

Soaring high in the dimming sky, I notice a lilac-breasted roller.

I smile.

Hi, Dad.

I blink.

The bird flies on.

My grief is still coiled deep inside my chest.

Corey's exuberant voice tugs me back. "Fuck, Tess, check that out!" He points below, fumbling for his camera.

My eyes follow to just outside the watering hole, where a gazelle limps, its eyes muddy with fear, its antlers perched high, fiery blood trickling from its hind leg. A trail of rouge dots behind, tarnishing the spots where it's been.

From the left, three lions stalk, their whiskers erect, their nostrils flaring, their tongues pulsating. The gazelle tries to sprint, but the lions easily tackle it onto the blood-stained earth. One lion swiftly bites its neck while the others gnaw its abdomen. The gazelle flails before its head slumps in defeat, succumbing.

My heart thumps for the poor gazelle. So alive one moment, gone the next.

Not unlike the first woman I saw die at Princess Victoria Hospital.

Or my precious dad.

It's the circle of life.

The march of time.

Nothing stops it.

I saw a similar scene on my first day at Impodimo Lodge. In that moment, I perceived so much clarity about life. About what truly mattered.

But that singular flash of knowing was tempered by years of forgetting.

Years of living for the future.

For the *someday* when I'd finally give myself permission to follow my gut, to live the life I *actually* wanted.

But, really, I never had any time to waste.

Life's greatest truth is once again achingly displayed for me.

Time is our most fleeting, precious, finite resource.

This knowledge makes living difficult and painful.

But also magical and meaningful.

Each singular moment is a gift if only we remember this fact.

The trick is to resist being swept away by memories.

By worries.

By what-ifs.

To stop planning for years down the road.

For what might be.

What *could* be.

It doesn't matter.

In the end, the past and future are mere concepts that detract from a fulfilling now.

Today, this moment, is all we ever have.

Beside me, Corey snaps photos for the lodge's Instagram account, awe mortaring his handsome face. "Wow, you don't see a scene like that too often. Fucking incredible."

"I know," I whisper, my gaze glued to his beaming smile. I trace my hand along his back, relishing the moment for what it is.

Utterly ephemeral.

Impossibly perfect.

It took me so long to find a way back here.

To him.

To myself.

Home.

And I don't know what the future will bring.

But for now, Corey's beside me.

And it's enough.

It's everything.

Three Years Later...

62

COREY

I smile at Tessa and Claudia, my mother-in-law, as they fuss over a wailing Leo.

Leo.

My baby boy, Leo.

My beautiful, sweet, amazing four-month-old son.

Leo.

Leo.

Leo.

Leo.

Leo.

My lips will never tire of the name.

Leo Peter Diallo.

Leo, the lion, my warrior.

Leo, whose creation just happened, without planning or intention.

Leo, our missing puzzle piece.

Leo, who made everything harsh about the world, somehow *soften*.

Leo, whose existence finally convinced me to (at least try to) stop cussing.

Leo, with his plump lips and heart-shaped face that are pure Tessa.

Leo, with his violet eyes, like Leona.

Leo, with his stubborn, determined personality, like Peter.

Leo, a perfect tribute to both.

Leo, through which Leona and Peter live on.

***

Tessa cradles Leo, mumbling softly in a language all their own. Her love for our son radiates through the living room, encasing it with a warm yellow glow. From her pocket, she pulls out her phone, playing a video of an ailing Peter. At the sound of his grandfather's voice, Leo stops crying and sinks to sleep.

Claudia scoops him up, whispering about things she'll one day teach him, her lips dotting kisses along every spot of his fluffy head.

Tessa appears, grinning. "Hey, you," she mumbles.

Her arms circle my waist, and I feel alive beneath the spark of my wife's touch.

***

Eight months ago, just before sunset, we got married on the deck of Impodimo Lodge in front of our most cherished people: Leona-Anne, Carl, Bess, Mum and Pa, Darian and Lynn, Claudia, Liz, Marley and Camille.

With pictures of Leona and Peter as the primary decorations.

Calum Scott's "You Are the Reason" played in the background.

Our vows: "I promise to love you for all my nows."

The only promise we could truthfully make.

***

On our kitchen table is the manuscript of Tessa's memoir, *Totally Broken and Completely Whole*. She hasn't decided what to do with it now that it's finished, but writing it, she says, brought her back to herself.

Besides writing, she volunteers her time at Princess Victoria Hospital and helps Carl with his telemedicine work. She says she enjoys being a doctor more, doing it only in little bits.

But, for the time being, she's focusing her energy on Leo.

And on Claudia, who, because of the pandemic, has rented a place down the road with no immediate plans to leave.

***

I gaze at Tessa, amazed by the changes motherhood has spawned.

Her fuller hips.

Her softer belly.

The sags beneath her sparkling, worn eyes from countless sleepless nights.

That radiant glow only possible from pure, inner contentedness.

Her flawless beauty has only magnified.

Sure, we have our moments, our fights—like just yesterday, Tessa was mad when I tracked two lions on foot after dark. She's worried something bad will happen to me now that we have Leo.

"You need to take your safety more seriously," she said, her lips sloping as she hunched on the couch, trying to nurse a cranky Leo.

At the sight of her anxious eyes, I immediately relented. "Okay… you're right. I'm sorry. I won't do that again."

Our relationship will continue to have its ups and downs.

Life will continue to have its ups and downs.

But for now, things are good.

"I love you, *pragtige dame*," I whisper into her ear. She nuzzles against my neck, allowing me to inhale her lemony hair. The sweet smell of *home*.

***

Claudia enters the kitchen, grinning, clutching a slumbering Leo.

Leo.

Leo.

Leo.

My heart explodes with love for Leo.

Perfectly imperfect Leo.

Leo, who's taught me…

That in spite of sadness, endings can unfurl into wild new beginnings.

That pain is necessary for knowledge to sprout.

That despite death, the scars of love blossom eternally.

That for all its agony, sometimes, when we least expect it…

Life finds astonishingly beautiful ways to begin again.

The End

AUTHOR'S NOTE

JANUARY, 2023

This is a work of fiction, but like many novels, parts are rooted in true experiences and feelings. In 2001, my dad, an infectious disease physician at the University of Pennsylvania, founded the Botswana-UPenn Partnership (BUP). The mission of the program was to help deliver free HIV/AIDS care within Botswana.

At the peak of the HIV crisis, twenty-five percent of Botswana's population was infected with the disease. But in the past twenty years, partly due to BUP, Botswana's annual AIDS-related death rate has fallen to under 5,000.

Because of my dad's work, in my early twenties, I was extremely fortunate to travel to Botswana four times. I fell in love with the culture and developed a lasting affection for the people I met. On one visit, I spent several weeks as a nursing student working on the wards of Princess Marina Hospital.

Tessa's scenes and the hospital itself are fictionalized, but the grief she experiences is real. Like Tessa, Princess Marina Hospital was the first place I saw anyone die. During my first week, I witnessed four deaths. The suffering of the patients was immense, the resources limited, the line between life and death so unbelievably thin.

The revelations Tessa has on safari are also based on my true feelings (although the character of Corey—is perhaps, sadly—fictionalized). I was mesmerized by the elephants and the freedom of the animals living in the bush. Being in the wilderness, combined with seeing death in such dramatic form, revealed what truly mattered in life.

Back in America, I went on to complete a master's degree, got married and had two kids. Swept up by my hectic life, the crucial lessons I'd learned in Botswana sadly fell by the wayside.

During the pandemic, I found myself burned out, both professionally and as a parent. I was sprinting on a treadmill, unable to keep the pace my life demanded. I was working as a nurse practitioner, caring for patients who were struggling, but inside, I, too, was struggling. Like Tessa, I was living a life that *looked* good, but it didn't *feel* good. I lacked passion and an outlet for my pain.

Since my teens, I've loved writing but was never brave enough to share my work. It always felt too vulnerable, a piece of myself I hid away. But one day in April 2022, I sat down at my computer, and this story began pouring out of me.

In writing it, I found a way back home.

Ultimately, this is a love story. But really, it's a story about coming into yourself. About accepting that life is too short to worry about how things look. That you should never be afraid to follow your gut. That the only explanations you ever owe are to yourself.

I have come to understand three important facts about life:

1. Inside, each of us is a broken mess. It's not a sign something is wrong with you. It's a part of the human condition, and it's universal.

2. Pain and grief, which are things I was always terrified of, actually provide huge opportunities for growth and development. When we're open to them, they're amazing teachers. The philosopher Rumi sums it up best: *The wound is the place where the light enters you.* Wow!

3. Most of the bullshit of modern life is not important. It's hard to hold onto your core values in our rushed society. But in the end, very few things actually matter. Try to live your life every day for the things that matter.

ADDENDUM

APRIL, 2024

Two months after I wrote this note, my mom was tragically diagnosed with esophageal cancer. She had just finished reading an early draft of this novel when she got the results that changed everything. Like Tessa, her illness was my worst fear come true. My mom was my rock, my foundation, my friend and my support system. Her disease stole the rug out from under me. It unfortunately played out much like Peter's story—she tragically died just six months after she was diagnosed, at age sixty-eight.

My mom didn't have the serene passing that Peter did. But now, when I re-read his final scenes, it gives me comfort. I fiercely hope my mom was able to find a similar peace on the other side.

My grief is physical and mental and emotional. It is exhausting and at times, unrelenting. But when I feel the lowest, I try to remember the thesis of this book.

Yes, my mom's death broke me.

But it can also teach me.

Make me better.

Would I give anything in the world to have her back?

Yes.

A trillion percent, *yes.*

But since I can't do that, the next best thing is to use her loss to make my life more meaningful.

To use my time on Earth purposefully.

My mom was an incredible quilt artist, and her final gift to me was to help me rediscover that I am an artist, too.

A writer.

So, this one's for you, Mom.

I love you fiercely.

In life and death and everything in between.

Till we meet again.

Xo,

Lisa